THE BONE FIRE

BOOKS BY GYÖRGY DRAGOMÁN

The White King

The Bone Fire

THE BONE FIRE

GYÖRGY DRAGOMÁN

Translated from the Hungarian by Ottilie Mulzet

Mariner Books
Houghton Mifflin Harcourt
Boston   New York
2021

First US edition 2021

For information about permission to reproduce selections from this book,
write to trade.permissions@hmhco.com or to Permissions,
Houghton Mifflin Harcourt Publishing Company,
3 Park Avenue, 19th Floor, New York, New York 10016.

hmhbooks.com

Library of Congress Cataloging-in-Publication Data
Names: Dragomán, György, 1973– author. | Mulzet, Ottilie, translator.
Title: The bone fire / György Dragomán ; translated from the Hungarian
by Ottilie Mulzet.
Other titles: Máglya. English
Description: First US edition. | Boston : Mariner Books,
Houghton Mifflin Harcourt, 2021.
Identifiers: LCCN 2020009424 (print) | LCCN 2020009425 (ebook) |
ISBN 9780544527201 (trade paperback) | ISBN 9780544527218 (ebook)
Subjects: GSAFD: Occult fiction.
Classification: LCC PH3382.14.R34 M3413 2021 (print) |
LCC PH3382.14.R34 (ebook) | DDC 894/.51134—dc23
LC record available at https://lccn.loc.gov/2020009424
LC ebook record available at https://lccn.loc.gov/2020009425

Book design by Margaret Rosewitz

Printed in the United States of America
DOC 10 9 8 7 6 5 4 3 2 1

The translator would like to acknowledge the kind support of the
Hungarian Translators' House, in Balatonfüred, Hungary,
where a large portion of the translation was completed.

To Anna

THE BONE FIRE

1

I'M WAITING IN THE CORRIDOR in front of the headmistress's office. I look at the photograph of the graduating students, all wearing white blouses. In only five years, I'll be graduating too. I look at their hairdos; most of them have their hair in a ponytail. I grab my own ponytail and I decide that when it's time, I will ask permission to wear my hair loose for the group photograph of graduating students. I pull the hairband out from my ponytail, I loosen my hair, I run my fingers through it. It's pretty long now. I've been growing it out for quite some time.

I'm waiting. I look out through the windows at the park. On both sides of the path, on the top of the black poplar trees, sit black birds. They are waiting.

I look at the crows. I wait.

I'm thinking about what the headmistress could possibly want from me.

I've been in the institute for almost six months. Everyone is nice to me — the other students, the teachers, the caretakers. They feel sorry for me because of what happened to Mother and Father.

I look at the trees; I don't want to think about my parents. I wait.

At last the door opens. The headmistress tells me to come in.

I enter.

There are two armchairs in front of the headmistress's desk. One of them is empty—the headmistress nods for me to sit down.

Someone is sitting in the other chair. An old lady. She leans forward, hunching. I see only her black sweater and her bony shoulders and, over her shoulders, a large black scarf. She holds a small coffee cup between her two palms, warming it, turning it around, shaking it slightly. The saucer, turned over, sits atop the coffee cup, and with her bony fingers, the old lady holds it down, as if she were afraid something might escape.

I sit down, say hello to her. The leather cushion of the armchair is uncomfortable and rigid.

The old lady looks at me; she greets me, calls me by my name. She has cold gray eyes; her face is stern, and her voice is cold too.

The headmistress says that the old lady has come to fetch me.

The old lady says that she's my grandmother, and she has come to take me home with her.

I say that I don't have a grandmother. Or grandfather. I don't have anyone at all.

No, that's wrong, says the old lady. She is my grandmother. She is my mother's mother.

I say that's not true. My mother was an orphan.

The old lady says no. She wasn't an orphan, of course she wasn't an orphan. She only had a very bad falling-out with her own parents. She went away; she left them after a huge argument, saying that she never wanted to see them ever again. That's what she wished, and lo and behold, that's what happened, although it really wasn't what she wanted. They never heard from her ever again, didn't even know if she was alive or dead, didn't even know if they had any grandchildren. Now my poor grandfather would never know. He never would have believed that my mother could have been so coldhearted.

That's not true, I say. I'm not her grandchild.

The old lady says, But it is true. It's certainly true. It's as true as her sitting right here.

The headmistress says something to the old lady — it might be better to try being a little gentler, a little more tactful, with me.

The old lady motions at her with her coffee cup, tells her to be quiet and not get involved, it's much better to be clear about this from the very beginning. This makes the saucer on top of the coffee cup move; it makes a squeaking sound as it turns, but it doesn't fall off, as the old lady's fingers are holding it in place.

The headmistress says nothing. The old lady asks her to kindly leave the office; she'd like to speak to me alone.

I want to ask the headmistress to stay, but then I don't say anything.

The headmistress slowly gets up. It's clear she's not too happy about leaving the office, and at the door she turns back, saying that she'll be right outside in the hallway.

I nod in reply.

The door closes. I don't look at the old lady. I look at my shoes, at the buttons gleaming black on the straps of my shoes, down there by my ankles.

I sense the old lady taking my hand; her palm is warm and damp. I hear her wheezing. I look up and I see that there are tears in her eyes.

For a while she just looks at me, not speaking. I watch the tears slowly falling down her face.

She runs her tongue over her lips; it's a pale rosy-pink color. She speaks. Her voice has changed. It's softer — warmer.

She tells me not to be angry with her. She didn't mean to say anything bad about my mother. How could she say anything bad about her own daughter? Her own dear sweet daughter. She hadn't seen her in over thirteen years — and now she will never see her ever again. If she was ever angry at her, she has long since forgiven her. And she knows that my mother has forgiven her as well. Yes. She feels it in her heart.

She pulls her chair closer to mine; her hand caresses my hair.

She says that I am a great gift to her from fate. Now that my poor grandfather has died, she has remained alone; she has no one. Only I am left to her. I need to realize that I am her granddaughter, that we belong together, and she will love me just as she loved her own dear daughter — even more than she loved her own daughter. I should go with her now. She's asking me nicely — I should go with her.

I don't answer. I don't say anything.

She says I have to go with her. I must go with her, I can't do anything else — it's my fate, she says.

I speak to her. I say no.

There appears to be a gleam of anger in her eyes, but her face and her mouth are smiling. She says she can prove it's my fate.

She takes my hand, pulls it over to her coffee cup; we're holding it together, with two hands. The porcelain is warm.

She tells me to look at the coffee cup.

I feel my hand moving, and we turn the cup over once; the saucer is now below, with the upturned coffee cup resting on top of it. Dark brown coffee grounds ooze out from the cup, flowing around the saucer, growing tentacles. I watch the tentacles as they get thicker, knitting together.

The old lady turns the cup over, places it on the saucer. She tells me to look inside.

I look.

The intricate pattern of grounds has formed an image on the inside of the cup, something like a labyrinth of sand.

The old lady slowly turns the cup around, telling me to watch.

I watch.

In the pattern, I suddenly see my own face. It is depicted in fine contours, as if it had just been drawn in tints of brown wash —I recognize my eyes, my nose, the outline of my mouth, my chin. It's me, and I'm smiling.

The old lady puts her finger on the rim of the coffee cup and draws it all around, and as her nail touches it, the porcelain makes a ringing sound, and on the inside of the coffee cup my face changes; the contours flow, grow thicker, as if I were becoming an adult and then growing old. I see my mother's face. I recognize her as she looks at me and smiles, sweetly yet sadly, then she too grows old; her face becomes more wrinkled, her chin becomes sharper, and now I see the old lady's face, now it is she who looks out at me from the coffee grounds; she looks out at me and smiles.

I feel in my palm that the coffee cup has grown cold. I let the old lady take it from my hands; I let her place it on the table.

I look up with tears in my eyes; I listen as the old lady is saying something to me.

She's telling me to call her Grandmother.

GRANDMOTHER SAYS THAT IT WOULD be better for us to set off as quickly as possible. We can be home by midnight if we catch the afternoon train. I should collect my things, pack everything up, and say my goodbyes. It would be good, she says, if I could be ready within half an hour.

She asks if I have a watch, and before I can tell her that I don't, but that there is a large wall clock in the dormitory upstairs, she's already unbuckled her own watch. She places it in my hand, saying that she had always meant to give it to my mother. It's a family heirloom.

The watch feels warm in my palm; Grandmother says to look at it.

I open my palm. The face of the watch is rectangular, and on the thin dial there are no numbers; instead, there are tiny stones like the heads of straight pins, glimmering like drops of water. The tiny stone that marks one o'clock is nearly transparent, and the stones grow darker up to the one that marks twelve, which is nearly black.

I've never seen a watch like this. The second hand doesn't jump around like the big wall clock but goes round and round in a circle without stopping, thin as a strand of hair; it glides round and round in a circle. I watch it, I can't take my eyes off it; it swirls around like water in a sink when the plug is pulled out, as if a strand of hair had been pulled into an eddying vortex in a sink, as if that eddy were pulling the strand of hair into itself, ever lower and lower.

I look at it; I can't take my eyes off it; it really is like water swirling in the sink. I watch it as it spins round and round, the basin full of water, ice-cold water. I let it fill up so I can wash my face, so I won't cry so much; Comrade Police Commissioner told me to go wash my face when she finally let go of me. She was nice; she patted my arm even though I wanted to hit her again, and I wanted to kick her again, and I wanted to bite her again; I wanted her to go away, to disappear, to go back to where she had come from, so it would be as if she had never come up the steps, as if she had never stood in front of our door, as if she had never rung the bell, as if she had never come in, as if she had never sat me down and said what she said about Mother and Father and the coal-delivery truck, as if she had never said that she was sorry, that she was truly sorry from the bottom of her heart, as if she had never said that I would have to be strong now. I want her to take back what she said, I want it not to be true, I want her to make everything the way it was before she came and ruined everything; I want Mother and Father to come home.

I plug the sink, and I turn off the water; I don't want to see the swirling water anymore. Enough.

I lean forward, thrusting my face under the water; it's very cold. I thrust both of my hands into the water and press them to my face, press them over my eyes; I hold my breath, I don't want to breathe, I don't want to think about Mother and Father, don't want to think about anything; the water is ice-cold, my face is ice-cold, the palms of my hands are ice-cold, but in my lungs the air is burning. I pull my hands away from my face. I grab the sides of the sink; I open my eyes and I blow out the air. I see the bubbles my breath has made in the water; they break off as they touch the sink, they separate; they become smaller bubbles, they swim up before my eyes, swirling. I think about how I must not move, all I need to do now is not move; I must inhale the cold water so as to fill my nose, my mouth, my windpipe, and my lungs, I must absorb this cold water as deeply as I can — wherever there is air in my body, I must fill it with water. I look at the sink's white porcelain; it's very close to my face. I see the fine cracks in its surface. I want to inhale the water into myself, and I can't.

I wrench my head up from the sink wildly, as if it were not even me, nearly smashing the back of my neck against the faucet. My hand moves as if it were not even me moving it; it reaches down, grabs the metal ring of the black plug, grabs it and pulls out the plug; a gurgling sound comes from the drain as it swallows up the water. I'm not crying; once again I'm watching the eddying water; the eddy turns and turns and turns around, and I see that within it there is a long black strand of hair, and I know that it's a strand of Mother's hair swirling down into the sink, the hair she was brushing out before she left. I reach down

into the water. I want to grab it, I want to grasp the strand of
hair with two fingers, and I can't—the vortex whirls it around
and around, wrenches it down the drainpipe. I look at the empty
sink. My face is cold; I can't cry anymore. I want to turn on
the tap again, I want to see the vortex again. From far away,
from outside, I hear the voice of Comrade Police Commissioner,
she's asking if everything is all right. I look at the sink, I want
to scream that no—nothing, nothing, nothing, nothing is all
right—then I say that yes, I'll be there in a minute. My voice
is cold and calm; it sounds foreign to me, and yet I know that it
is mine, and I reach out to a tiny shelf beneath the mirror and
take Mother's comb, and as I comb my hair with it, it scrapes
against my skull.

Somebody is saying my name, a strange voice; it is Grandmother's voice, she's asking me for the exact time. The watch
is there in my palm; I'm staring at the second hand as it goes
around and around in a circle, without stopping, above the watch
dial. I answer her, I say that it is a quarter to four. Grandmother
says fine, I should be downstairs in front of the large entrance
gate with my baggage at four fifteen.

Fine, I say, I'll be there. I'm still looking at the watch.

Grandmother says she will help me put the watch on. She
reaches over, takes it out of my palm, and only then do I notice
that it has a metal strap. Grandmother pulls it between her fingers and then places it on my wrist, but in such a way that the
dial is facing inward, the inner side of my wrist. She says that
this watch must be worn like that. As she buckles it, the cold
metal watchband circling my wrist, I get goose bumps on my
lower arm. Grandmother says I have nice slender wrists, this
watch fits me perfectly, the strap doesn't even need to be adjusted. Look at how well it fits, she says.

The silver watchband gleams white against my skin as if
it had been woven from three silver wires; you can't even see

where the strands intertwine. I feel its weight on my wrist, and I say thank you.

Grandmother nods and tells me to wear the watch in good health.

THE DORMITORY IS EMPTY. THE others are in class—that's where I was too before I was called to the headmistress's office. I go over to my bed, lean down, and pull out the round suitcase underneath. It's burgundy, and the zipper doesn't work properly; it broke almost as soon as we bought it. Mother was very angry because we couldn't get it fixed, and we couldn't return it either. I put the suitcase on the bed.

I go over to my cupboard and open it. My clothes are there on hangers: my worn-out, quilted red winter coat, my three blouses, my two skirts, my one pair of jeans, which now extend only to the middle of my shins. I take out the clothes and place them on my bed.

I go back to the cupboard. On the middle shelves there are three pairs of underwear, socks, stockings; on the upper shelf are my gym clothes and my gym bag, as well as Mother's old competition tracksuit; on the lower shelf are my two Norwegian-patterned knit sweaters.

I take everything over to the bed.

I take my shoes out of the cupboard; apart from my Mary Janes, which I'm wearing, I have one pair of black patent-leather shoes, and one pair of white tennis shoes with green rubber soles.

Now only my old school uniform and my Pioneer uniform are left in the cupboard. Ever since New Year's we have not been permitted to wear them; since then, we don't need uniforms, and the Communist Party and its youth branch, the Young Pioneers, no longer exist. But I still take these items out of the cupboard. The woven yellow insignia is falling off the button of my Pioneer shirt; the threads of the tassels are tangled together.

The cupboard is almost empty now; there is just one more thing left in it. It is a photograph pasted on the inside of the cupboard door. It's a color photograph, but the hues are fairly pale, Father said because he wasn't able to develop the film properly. The picture shows the three of us, Mother, Father, and me. It was taken up in the mountains by the shore of a lake; it's the only picture of all three of us together. Father took it with a self-timer. We were all laughing at him because after Father placed the camera on the stump of a tree and pulled the timing mechanism, he ran over to us so quickly that he wasn't paying attention and he tripped over a tree branch but then just as quickly he jumped up and kept on running to make sure he would get into the picture on time, and he did. He even had enough time to put his arms around me and Mother too, and there he stood—and it was only then that we noticed that a pine branch had gotten stuck in his sweater, and that made us laugh even more.

I look at the picture, at Mother's loosened hair; I place my index finger on it, and I caress her hair. I don't feel anything, only the smoothness of the photograph's surface. I dig my fingernails underneath the picture and carefully pry it away from the cupboard door. It comes off nicely, not tearing anywhere, only a tiny piece of chipboard from the cupboard door sticks to a corner in the back.

I walk over to the bed, and as I pick up my red, blue, and black Norwegian sweater, the plastic bag stuffed into one of the sleeves makes a crackling sound. I pull a small yellow bag from the sleeve. Mother's French silk scarf is folded up nicely inside; tucked in one corner of the scarf are Mother's and Father's wedding rings. I haven't touched these since the funeral, and even now I hold them only through the plastic bag, thinking about the jasmine scent of Mother's perfume, thinking that it should still be there in her scarf. I slip the photograph between the layers of the silk scarf, and I pick up the bag, feeling the rigidity of the photograph between the layers of plastic and silk.

I am about to stuff the bag back into the sleeve of the sweater when suddenly I think of Grandmother's fingers and how she fastened the watch onto my wrist. I place the bag on the bed, and I don't stuff it back into the sweater. I open the suitcase. Father's two old belts are rolled up together in it next to my old pencil case. I take out the pencil case, remove my old pencil sharpener from it—the blade is getting dull—and with my little finger, I unscrew the screw that holds it in place. I take out the blade, cut the inner lining at the bottom of the suitcase, and put the bag with the scarf and the wedding rings between the lining of the suitcase and its fake leather exterior, then smooth it out from the inside and the outside. The fake leather is nice and thick, and there's no way to tell that there's anything in the lining.

I take out Father's two belts, hook the buckle of the black one into the last hole of the brown one, pull on the buckle, and push the end of the belt underneath the steel-riveted leather strap. Now it's long enough to use as a strap around the suitcase.

After I pack my clothes and my shoes, I take my nightgown out from beneath my pillow and place it on the top. I close the suitcase, lift it up, shove the belt underneath the handle of the suitcase, tug on it strongly, then buckle it up.

I'm ready; I've packed my things.

I take my quilted winter coat, pull my scarf out from the sleeve, and wind it around my neck, but I don't put my knit cap on my head.

I look around the dormitory. I'm leaving nothing here.

I go over to the window one last time, and I look out at the park. I see that someone is standing motionlessly in the middle of the path, the wind making her scarf flutter in the breeze, and I know that it's Grandmother, I know that she's looking at the crows.

I WALK ALONG THE CORRIDOR, my shoes clattering on the concrete. With every second step, the belts strapped around my suitcase make a creaking sound.

I reach the classroom, and I stop. I don't have to go in, and as a matter of fact there's no one I want to say goodbye to.

I wait for a moment, then I raise my arm, knock on the door, go in.

The red-haired teacher jumps up from behind her teacher's desk, smiling at me; she's not surprised to see me with my coat on and my suitcase in my hand. The headmistress must have spoken to her already.

She motions for me to come closer. As I walk in front of the blackboard, the teacher gestures to the class, and the girls stand up all at once.

I know I have to say goodbye to them somehow, but I don't want to say anything at all. I look down at my shoes and at the black floor that smells like kerosene. Then I raise my head. I know what people usually say at times like this, but still, I can't speak.

The red-haired teacher comes very close to me, stands beside me, and places her hand on my shoulder. She says, Dear girls, it has happened that our sister Emma will be leaving us today; she thanks you for all the goodness you have shown her, and she asks you all to keep her in your memories. Although she was with you for a very short time, she will never forget you. The voice of the red-haired teacher here falters, as if she were very moved; she sighs, takes a deep breath, brushes a curly strand of hair away from her face, smiles at me again, and speaks.

She says that goodbyes are hard for everyone, so she would ask the girls to make these difficult moments a little easier with a beautiful song, because while the girls are singing, I can gather my things and pack them up.

She raises her arms above her head, ready to conduct them.

The girls at once begin to sing, and the red-haired teacher sings with them. I know this song; I too have sung it many times. It is beautiful and sad; it speaks of long journeys and the dust of long journeys. For a few moments I stand still, listening to them and looking at them, then I walk over to my desk, where my math textbook lies open. I close it and my exercise book, take the rest of my textbooks and exercise books out of my desk, and place the suitcase on top of it. I don't loosen the strap but merely tug on the faulty zipper by one of the corners, then shove the textbooks and the exercise books into the suitcase; the yellow metal teeth of the zipper scratch my skin as I push the books and the exercise books in deep among my clothes.

The face of the red-haired teacher has also grown red; she sings while conducting the girls with wide gestures as if she were standing in front of an entire choir, not just the girls who are boarders at the school.

She stands right in front of the middle of the blackboard; on the wall above it there are three rectangular blotches, one perpendicular and the other two horizontal, all lighter in color than the wall. Where the perpendicular blotch is, there used to be a photograph of the Comrade General; on the two horizontal ones there used to be inscriptions, written in red, about the nation, the people, the party, and peace. They aren't there anymore; since New Year's there are no inscriptions like that anywhere, and the photograph of the Comrade General is nowhere to be seen.

I shove my pencil case into the suitcase, looking into the face of the teacher. I can hear her voice amid the girls' voices, and her screams come to mind, those loud piercing screams with which she ripped away the blue insignia of the leader from her Pioneer shirt and began stamping on it. I think of how, in the assembly hall, she kicked a chair over to the wall, jumped up on it, grabbed the enormous photograph of the Comrade General, three times life-size, ripped it from the wall, and threw it onto the floor. The glass shattered, and the teacher spat on the photograph of the Comrade General and ripped it out of the frame, and all the while she was screaming, *It's the end, no more, no more, it's the end,* and we all stood up, and we all pushed back our chairs, the chairs in which we had just sat down so we could watch the Comrade General's ceremonial New Year's greeting together, but then, jostling, we all ran forward to get closer to the TV so we could see better, and we all began to yell, *No more, it's the end, the end,* and we ripped the flags off the walls, and the inscriptions written in red, and I saw the face of the Comrade General on the television set, wax yellow and bloody, as his body lay in the gray slush, and somebody picked up a large bronze goblet from the Corner of Glory — the pupils of the institution had won it in the Peace Competition — and sent the goblet, spinning, at the television; the face of the Comrade General, covered in blood, gave out sparks and shattered into fragments on the screen, and then we all began to run. We ran through the classrooms of the institute, and we tore all the pictures and all the inscriptions from the walls, and in my ears now there is the sound of frames cracking, the clatter of glass breaking, the hissing of thick cardboard sheets being ripped apart, and then the bonfire was ready. It was hard to get it to catch on fire, so we doused the books with their thick red covers with diesel oil — every Saturday, the seventh-formers used it to polish the floor — and when the fire finally began to burn, amid the sizzling flames, the face of the Comrade General looked out and smiled at us one hundred times and one thousand times, and we all stood around the fire and we sang: *No more, it's the end, hooray,*

hooray, and where the bonfire had been, there remained nothing but soot-covered shards of glass, like black teeth that had been burned apart. Two days later I took one of those shards and put it into my pencil case—it's still there, among my pencils and pens.

I look at the red-haired teacher, then I turn my head and I look at the girls. I watch as they sing; they're singing another song now, not about the long journey, but about the nation, about how our nation is our home, about how we will be faithful to it unto death. I'm not singing with them, but I'm imagining what they see, I'm imagining that they see me as I straighten my battered coat, pick up my suitcase, head out of the classroom, then stand on the threshold one last time and wave to them.

I open my mouth; I want to say, *Goodbye, God be with you*, but I don't say that. Instead, I whisper very faintly, *It's the end, it's over, hooray, hooray*, then I turn and leave, closing the classroom door behind me.

I go down the steps, and I hear how they are still singing, ever more loudly.

AS I WALK OUT THE door, I see that Grandmother is still standing in the same place, in the middle of the path, though now she is not looking at the crows but at the institute.

I walk down the steps, the wind snatching at my coat. I put on my hat, pull it down over my ears, but even so I feel the wind against them.

I walk over to Grandmother; she looks at me, says that I'm late.

I tell her it was because I had to say goodbye.

Grandmother says that's all right, we still have time. She's turning a small rosary between her fingers; the black stones

keep knocking against her ring. She tells me to give her my suitcase, says that she'll carry it, and she reaches over to my hand.

I don't give it to her. It's not heavy, I say.

Grandmother nods, says I can carry it if I want to. Let's go,
she says, and she turns and starts walking.

I nod and walk beside her.

As we set off, suddenly the wind dies down.

We walk in silence, the only sound is the gravel crunching beneath our shoes. Then we walk on a wide strip of black
gravel; there it sounds different, louder, making even more of
a crunching sound. Grandmother suddenly bends down and
picks up something from the ground. I look and see that it's a
charred piece of wood, one part of it glimmering where the gilt
isn't fully burned off. Grandmother clasps it, rubs the burned
section of wood between her fingers.

When we reach the gates of the institute Grandmother asks
me if I have any memories of Father and Mother, or at least a
photograph of them.

There's nothing, I say, I wasn't able to keep anything. The
words are cold as I utter them; I turn back and look at the institute.

It is a large gray building; in many places, the plaster has
fallen off the façade, and where the plaster is missing, the bricks
and the mortar are visible. I know which window is which, and
it looks like somebody is standing in the dormitory watching
us—but I glimpse this for only a moment, then the figure disappears.

Grandmother asks how long I've been here.

I don't want to answer, but I say: One hundred and fifty-two
days.

Grandmother says, Well, that's long enough—more than
five months.

She reaches out and takes my left hand; she draws four
black lines on my palm with the charred fragment of frame,

then draws a fifth line through the others. She puts the piece of frame into my hands, telling me that when we walk out the gates, I should throw it behind me, over my back.

As we step across the two gleaming tracks of the institute's sliding gates, I swing my arm and throw the piece of wood behind me.

I don't look back, but I hear as it falls to the ground.

2

BY THE TIME GRANDMOTHER AND I arrive at the station, both of my arms are aching. No matter how often I keep switching hands, the suitcase grows heavier and heavier with every step. The sidewalks are rough and uneven, so I don't even try to pull the suitcase on its wheels, they always keep getting caught on everything anyway.

We climb the steps. Inside, the concrete floor looks fairly smooth, so I put my suitcase down and pull it. The clatter of the wheels fills the entrance hall of the station; everyone looks at us.

A boy in a flat cap is selling snowdrops; they're lying on an old newspaper folded into a square. He holds them out toward us, and he says, Spring is here. Beneath the small green bouquets, his mouth smiles, only half visible, but even so, I recognize him. The boy holds the bouquets out to us and repeats: Spring is here. Then he adds, Only one twenty-five for a bouquet. Grandmother says, Thank you, but we won't take any.

The boy says that spring will come anyway; he turns away, but I see that he's still watching us from the corner of his eye.

The wheels of the suitcase roll along a metal grid, making a sound like a rusty ratchet. I can feel the bumping of the wheels in my elbows. I look down; beneath the metal grid is dark water, cigarette butts floating in it.

There's only one ticket desk open, a long line in front of it.

Grandmother says that we have to get tickets, so we should get in line. We do.

Grandmother takes out her wallet, puts it in my hand, and tells me to buy the tickets.

I tell her that I don't know where we're going.

Grandmother says that we are going to her house — where else would we be going? Then she laughs to herself, tells me the name of the city. She tells me to get tickets for second class.

The line moves slowly. I look at my watch; the second hand revolves without stopping, but very slowly.

Grandmother says she'll be back right back; she steps away to look at the schedule nailed up on the tiled wall.

I look at the wallet. It is heavy and full; I can feel the metal coins and the crumpled banknotes through the thin gray leather.

The wallet is round, almost spherical. It has an interesting clasp — two long serrated metal straps hook on to each other, and in the middle of the serrated metal, a small round face with a pointy chin juts forward, and a curved nose forms the clasp itself; on each side of the nose there is a tiny blue eye with a black pupil formed with enamel paint.

I dig my fingers between the nose and the chin of the face and pull them apart; the wallet opens with a loud snap. There's a lot of money in it, tens, one hundreds, and twenty-fives all crumpled together, with many coins between them. I don't know how much money I'm supposed to take out, so I close the wallet again.

I get to the ticket counter. Behind the bars and the murky glass sits a woman with a scarf over her hair; she tilts her head to one side, asks me where I want to go.

I tell her the name of the city, and I say, Two tickets, then I add, Second class; the woman punches something into the cash register, and she pushes two tiny, rectangular cardboard tickets through the slit in the window.

I open the wallet, asking how much it will be, and the woman says, Sixteen fifty.

I'm about to reach into the wallet, but suddenly, it's hidden behind the folded newspaper with the snowdrops. The boy selling the snowdrops is standing there on the other side of the iron railing in front of the ticket counter, and he is saying that he wants to give me a bouquet as a present because I'm beautiful. Pick one, he says.

No, thank you, I tell him, and at the same time I feel something pressing into the wallet. I want to reach over with my other hand, but the newspaper, with the bouquets on top, is covering the wallet. The boy says: Well, pick one, the middle one is the most beautiful, and he smiles widely, I see the silver gleaming between his teeth. No, thank you, I say, please leave me alone. I know what he's doing, I want to cry out, *Help, thief!* but Grandmother is already standing next to me. She grabs the corner of the newspaper, says, Thank you, we'll take one, then rips the newspaper with the bouquet out of the boy's hand and reaches underneath the newspaper with her other hand. Her fingers wrap around the clasp of the wallet; the boy draws his breath sharply and in pain, and I see that his hand has been swallowed by the wallet up to his wrist. Grandmother is tightening the saw-toothed clasp of the wallet right around his wrist. Through the leather I can feel the boy's fingers squeezed around the banknotes; I see the teeth of the clasp sinking into his skin; I sense his fingers releasing the banknotes. Grandmother smiles, looks at the boy, and says that he can take as much money from the wallet as he wishes, as long as he doesn't mind his hand withering away. She says nothing else and then suddenly releases the clasp. The boy jerks his hand away from the wallet —there's not even one metal coin between his fingers—and he says, Please forgive me, my dear lady, in the name of the saints, please forgive me. He wraps his other hand around his wrist, rubs it and massages it as if it had grown numb. Grandmother says that she forgives him this time, then she tells him to get lost.

The boy turns his back on us, and he runs away, through the station hall, out the door.

Grandmother tells me to hold out my hat.

I take off my knit cap and hold it out in front of Grandmother, and she spills the bouquets of snowdrops into it, then throws the folded newspaper onto the floor.

She takes the wallet out of my hand, looks at the woman at the ticket desk, pushes the tickets back through the opening in the window, and says that we've thought it over, and we'd prefer to travel in first class.

THE FIRST-CLASS CARRIAGE IS NEARLY empty. We find an unoccupied compartment and go in.

We sit down on the battered red leather seats. Both Grandmother and I sit by the window. I want to put my suitcase up on the luggage rack, but Grandmother says to leave it there and not bother lifting it up, it's fine to keep it on the seat.

I lean back, looking at Grandmother. Between the seat and the hat rack, there is a large mirror along the entire wall of the compartment, above Grandmother's head and above my head too; it's something like an infinite gallery of mirrors. I see Grandmother and myself in it many times over, growing ever and ever smaller, the mirrors mixing up our faces, forming a long face-snake, and when the compartment jolts, the snake convulses; it makes me dizzy to watch it.

I see in the mirror that my hair is disheveled. I reach into the suitcase—the zipper scratches my skin—feel for the handle of the comb, pull it out, and begin to comb my hair.

Grandmother looks at me and smiles. She says that ever since she knew that I was in the world, she has wanted nothing else than to bring me to her. She says that she thanks me for coming with her; she thanks me for trusting her.

I say nothing, slowly combing my hair. I notice the sign that Grandmother drew on my hand is still there.

I look at my hair in the mirror as it slowly emerges from between the teeth of the comb, and I feel how sleepy I am; both of my eyes will start to close any moment.

Grandmother says I should try to sleep, that she will watch over me: Go to sleep, she says, and don't be afraid, there won't be any bad dreams.

I put the comb next to myself on the seat, next to my knit cap full of snowdrops, and I close my eyes.

I DREAM OF FIRE. I don't know what's burning. I see huge red flames, sooty smoke rising from their tips; the fire crackles, sputters, and hisses; the flames roar like the wind. It's dark; only the fire gives off light. I don't want to look at it, but I can't turn my head away; I must look at the flames. In the depths of them I see planks and beams, charred sheets of paper, and within the crimson embers something dark moves —I don't see what it is, I don't know what it is, I don't want to know what it is.

I WAKE UP VERY HUNGRY. Outside it's dark. On the ceiling of the train compartment a pale fluorescent light burns, and in this light Grandmother's skin looks bone-white; in the mirror above her seat, I see that my face is also completely white.

Grandmother asks me if I had any dreams. None, I say. I'm

quiet, but my stomach rumbles loudly, persistently, and I sense my face turning red.

Grandmother looks at me, then laughs out loud. I watch her face as she laughs; her nose wrinkles. She's quiet for a moment, then she says, Take note: Never begin a journey without food, because you can't know in advance how long the trip will be. One time, she says, when my mother was still a little baby, Grandmother didn't bother packing anything for a trip because she planned to travel only to a neighboring city, a mere forty kilometers away, so she didn't take any food, only water. Then the trip took two days because of the floods, and if a kind old auntie had not given them a little bread, cheese, and milk, she says, she doesn't know what would have happened to them. Grandmother looks into my eyes, and she says, Take note: If a person sets off on a journey, the most important thing to bring is food.

Grandmother says this the way Mother would have said it; not in exactly the same way, but I know that I heard this sentence from Mother. I don't remember when, but I do remember the emphasis as she uttered the words.

My throat tightens; I feel a teardrop in the corner of my eye. I turn away, wiping it with the back of my hand.

The darkened window reflects my face back to me; behind it are the pylons in the darkness.

I try to smile. I look at Grandmother, and I ask, So where is the food?

Grandmother laughs to herself, and she says that she didn't bring anything. Then she says, Let's go and see what they have in the dining car.

We get up. I take my suitcase with me; no one can get by us in the corridor.

We walk through two carriages, then reach the dining car.

It looks like a bar, with counters on each side, and leaning on the counters are miners and men in work clothes. They're drinking beer and plum brandy. I can smell it.

I go over to the counter. A man stands behind it; under his gray apron I can see his green sweater. On the counter is a waxed canvas chessboard with a few figures on it; the man is staring at the chessboard and chewing on a matchstick.

Grandmother asks what there is to eat.

There's nothing, says the man. Nothing to eat.

Grandmother says that's impossible. There has to be something. In this new free world, there has to be at least something to eat.

There's nothing, says the man. There's beer, you can eat that.

Grandmother looks at the chessboard, reaches over, and pushes one of the figures forward.

The man says that black has to win in three moves.

That's child's play, says Grandmother. Her ring shines in the fluorescent light as she moves the figures. There, she says, there you have it.

The man looks at the chessboard, shaking his head. He takes one of the figures Grandmother moved, puts it back in its original place, looks at it, repeats Grandmother's moves, puts the figure back again, looks at it, then repeats Grandmother's moves once more. That's it, he says. He takes a plastic box from behind the counter and sweeps the figures into it.

He looks at Grandmother and says, There are fish patties with pickled cucumbers and black bread.

Grandmother nods; she doesn't even ask if I like this. She says, That'll be fine.

The man turns away, then places two paper plates of food on the counter.

Grandmother looks around the compartment, points to a counter next to one of the windows, and tells me to take the food over there.

I pick up the two paper plates. As I walk, the liquid from the cucumbers drips onto my fingers.

I hear Grandmother asking for a large vodka for her and a raspberry soda for me.

I put the plates on the counter, inspecting the brown and oily crust of the fish patties, and I wait for Grandmother to bring the drinks.

The patties taste only a little bit like fish; they're as dry as sawdust, and they fall apart in my mouth as soon as I bite into them. I'm so hungry, though, that I don't mind. Never in my life have I been this hungry.

Grandmother is eating too, and she looks at me. She says it's a joy to see how well I eat. My mother used to eat like that, she tells me. When she was little, she was very picky, but as she began to grow she ate everything, just like me. Eating is very important for growing up.

I don't say anything in reply but I put down the last fish patty; I just bit into it, and I can see my own teeth marks. I'm still hungry, but I don't want to eat it. I'd rather have a bite of the bread.

Grandmother sniffs the vodka, then throws it back in one shot.

I eat my cucumber; the liquid is good and vinegary. My hand is moist from it. I have no handkerchief, so I wipe my fingers on the edge of the paper plate.

Grandmother gives me some money, tells me to get her another vodka and another raspberry soda for myself. She says she shouldn't, but today is a special day.

Behind the counter, the man stares at the empty chessboard. I push the money toward him; he nods and puts the drinks on the counter. The train suddenly jolts, and the vodka sloshes around, gleaming greasily on the side of the glass.

As I grab it from the counter to take it over to Grandmother, I hear music—an accordion, a violin, and a drum, playing a long mournful ballad, one I've never heard before.

Grandmother takes the glass out of my hand, pours a bit

of the vodka into my raspberry soda, and says, Just a little lick won't hurt. She clinks her glass against mine. May you grow to be big, she says.

She puts the glass into my hands, and I take a sip. The raspberry syrup has suddenly become acrid; as I swallow it, it scratches warmly against my throat.

Grandmother says that my face will get a bit of color from vodka, and I won't be so horribly pale.

I hear the music again, and now it's much louder. The door to the dining car is flung open, and three men enter, each with a different instrument; the first one has an accordion, the second a violin, and the third a drum, and they're playing that same sad song, slowly, so slowly, like that suppressed, gasping crying. I think of the dormitory and how the girls, every night, their faces plunged into their pillows, hid crying beneath the blankets.

The last time I cried was the night before my parents' funeral. I cried almost until morning, but at the funeral, not one tear dropped from my eyes; I wept only inside. I shake my head; I don't want to think of the funeral, so instead I look at the musicians standing in the middle of the dining car playing that same sad song. Everyone's looking at them, and no one speaks. The accordion player begins to sing; his voice is high, cracked, and raspy, and all I can understand from the words is that a dove, a white dove, has flown away and isn't coming back, never will it come back. I don't want to look at them, I don't want to hear the song, but I have to, I must listen to it. The drummer strikes down on the drum, and I think of the black surface of the earth shining greasily, the cold touch of the clump of earth; I think of how I raise my hand, swing it, and throw the dirt into the ditch and how, as it slides out from between my fingers, I immediately regret that movement. I want the clump of earth to stop in midair, to remain there forever, to remain suspended there above the open grave, but it doesn't; I hear it as it falls down onto the lacquered wood with a loud resounding thump, and I know that I will never forget that sound. The gravediggers swing their shovels; the clumps of earth fly onto the coffins. I don't want to hear this. I turn away; I begin to run; I run away from the open grave. I slip on a clump of frozen mud, almost fall down, and grab onto a gravestone, catch myself, and I keep on running. I run away among the graves, away among the wooden crosses; I hear my name being yelled out; I don't look back, I know they're coming after me, I don't look back, I don't even slow down, I run. Beyond the rows of graves the meadow is empty, and beyond the meadow is the forest; that is where I have to go, I know that in the forest there will be silence, among the trees there will be silence. My kerchief becomes undone, and I don't even bother to fix it; the wind tears it away from my hair. I don't bother with it.

I shake my head—enough. I don't want to think about the funeral anymore. I look at the drumhead; the skin is worn in the middle. The drumstick is raised and then thumps down on the surface. I look at it and I think about how it's just the beat of the drum, it doesn't resemble anything else. I look at the drummer's hand, the signet ring on his little finger, the green-blue dove tattooed on the back of his hand, and as the drumstick moves, it's as if the dove is waddling, stepping along and nodding. The accordion player is still singing about the black shroud, the cold earth, then suddenly he falls silent. He squeezes the accordion together very slowly, and the violinist lowers his bow.

The accordion player wipes his eyes, clears his throat, then says: Well, now they have buried poor Milán, may the earth lie lightly upon him, and everyone keep him well in their memory—whoever heard him play the zither even once will never forget it. The drum player goes over to the counter, and as he passes me, I see the zither hanging crosswise on his back. As he reaches the counter, he takes it off his shoulder, swings it, and thumps it down on the counter; the zither makes a resounding noise. Banknotes folded in half are stuffed beneath its strings — tens, twenty-fives, fifties, and even one hundreds — and in the middle there is a picture, an old man wearing a black hat playing the zither. The drummer snatches two one-hundred notes from beneath the strings and yells out: Vodka for everyone!

THE MUSICIANS CIRCLE AROUND THE dining car; each one of them has a liter bottle of vodka, and they're pouring it out for everyone. I look at Grandmother, and I say to her quietly: Let's go back to the compartment. Grandmother says that we can't go back now because we'll offend the musicians and the memory of the dead, but I shouldn't worry, because she'll be watching over me — there will be no problems.

The violinist gets to us first. If I do not offend you, my dear lady, he says, filling Grandmother's glass to the brim, then he looks at me, and he says: Aren't you lovely, my little flower, and he pours me vodka as well; I want to say that I don't want any, but Grandmother indicates with her eyes for me to be quiet, so I hold my glass without a word.

The musicians are standing in the middle of the dining car; the drum player raises his glass and says: Now we have wept enough, now there has been enough of sorrow, let us drink! He throws his head back, pours vodka into his mouth from his arm held up high. Everyone raises their glasses, everyone drinks. I just raise my glass to my mouth and pretend to drink, but even so, the vodka's biting smell floods my nose.

The drummer throws his glass to the ground, and then the drumstick is in his hand again; he's beating the drum, and the others also begin to play, the rhythm now quick and cracking. The drummer sings in a high voice; he's singing about silver, about diamonds, about the golden hair of girls, and the accordion player keeps yelling out, Jump! The music gets faster and faster; I feel the rhythm in my legs, and I can hardly bear not to move.

The music gets even faster, and all the people in the car are tapping their feet, the musicians too; the steel-toe boots of the violin player clap on the floor like cymbals. Even the train seems to be going faster now, the rattling of the wheels mixing into the rhythm of the music; the drummer is singing about deceitful girls who are deceitful even in hell, even there they just dance with their beautiful hair, their beautiful necks, their fine slender waists. I see the violinist looking at me; he's moving closer to us, leaning forward a little, as if he were pointing at me with the tip of his bow, and he motions with his head. I know what he wants; he wants me to dance. The floor is vibrating to the rhythm of the music, and I feel the soles of my feet itching through my shoes. I don't move, and now the accordion player is also looking at me, then the drummer too, and he's singing that coldhearted girls are the worst, those who just play with men's hearts, those who laugh out loud at men's sorrow, their voices ringing out, acting as if they never even noticed any man. Now everyone is looking at us, at Grandmother and me, and the violinist speaks, he says: Dance, little girl, don't put on airs.

Grandmother takes my arm, looks at the violinist, and says: Fine, my boys, that'll be enough for now, we have our own things to mourn, our own sorrows.

It's as if the violinist didn't even hear her; he's looking straight at me. He plays ever more vehemently, tapping his hobnailed boots on the floor ever more wildly.

Grandmother speaks again, and again she says, Boys, that's enough now, but by then all three musicians are standing in front of us, playing very quickly; the drummer is singing that the beautiful girl raises her ankle, she pulls her skirt up higher, she raises her ankle, she pulls her skirt up higher, she raises her ankle, she pulls her skirt up higher. The violinist speaks to me again, and he says: Start dancing already, what are you waiting for? Dance for poor Milán, and he motions toward the zither with the neck of his violin.

I feel chills running up and down my back. I lower my head and look at the floor; I want them to go away and leave me in peace, but I don't say anything, I can't even speak. I turn away, back toward the window of the dining car, and as I move I knock the glass of vodka off the counter with my elbow. I watch as it spins in the air, the drink splashing out from it. The glass falls onto the ground and doesn't break; it rolls over to the front of the violinist's boots.

The violinist looks down at the glass, then once again he yells out: Dance, little girl, don't you hear? Start dancing. He steps across the glass, and now he's very close to me.

Grandmother lets go of my arm, steps away from the counter, stands between me and the musicians, and says: That's fine, boys, if you ask very nicely, then I don't mind.

The violinist shouts at Grandmother, I wasn't talking to you, you old cro—

But he doesn't finish his sentence, because Grandmother raises both of her arms, she raises them up high, up above her head, then for a moment she stands motionless, and suddenly there is silence. Even the musicians don't move; they stand as if they have been frozen into statues. The music stops, or not completely, because the last sound still reverberates in the accordion, and the last beat of the drum still echoes back, and one of the strings of the violin still resounds, deeply and out of tune.

Grandmother looks at me, licks her mouth, smiles, then lowers her arms and begins to dance. As the heels of her shoes strike the floor, the musicians start to play; at first they play slowly, because Grandmother is dancing slowly, then, as Grandmother begins to dance more quickly, they play more quickly.

As Grandmother dances she bends down, picks up the glass that had rolled away on the floor, holds it with both hands, then holds it up in front of herself as if it were her dance partner, and I see that there is still a drop of vodka in it. Grandmother spins around, and the drop of vodka also spins around inside the glass. At first it's at the bottom of the glass, then it climbs up the side, and there it runs around and around like a rosy-hued drop of quicksilver; I see it between Grandmother's fingers.

The musicians are now playing at full speed. I know this song, it's a wedding song, and it speaks of how the devil wants to make the little bride dance, but it comes to naught, because the little bride is unrulier than he, and she makes the devil dance until his hooves are worn away.

Grandmother turns around and around; she doesn't sing, but murmurs, not the words to the song, but its melody. As she turns, she ambles too; while dancing, she moves away from my side out to the middle of the dining car, then over to the counter where the zither is, the musicians following her. Grandmother dances in front of the counter; she turns around and around as she reaches the counter, then she snatches the photograph out from beneath the strings of the zither, places it on the counter, strikes the glass down on top of it, and stops.

I see, on the inside of the glass, the rosy-hued drop of vodka is still circling around; the musicians are watching the glass, they're playing very quickly. Grandmother steps in front of them, but they do not turn to follow her; they're still looking at the glass. I see how the banknotes flutter beneath the strings of the zither; the strings themselves are also moving. They ring out; the zither speaks as if somebody were still playing it, and Grandmother says it's time for us to go back to our seats, let us not disturb the men in their reminiscences.

I pick up the suitcase and follow Grandmother, and as I reach the carriage door, I turn around and look back. The musicians are staring at the zither, still playing to a very quick beat.

WE GET BACK TO OUR compartment, and we sit down.

Grandmother says that during this great dance, her hair, gathered into a bun, became loosened. She pulls out her hairpins, places them on the small foldout table next to the window, and begins to comb her fingers through her hair.

She has long gray hair. I hear it scraping between her fingers, and I think that any moment now she's going to ask to borrow my hairbrush, but she doesn't; she reaches into her bag, takes out a curved ivory comb, and combs her hair with that.

I look at her hairpins, which roll back and forth on the small compartment shelf in rhythm with the jolting of the train. They are long and pointy with heavy rounded tips, and on these rounded tips are flies formed by pearl insets; their wings, surrounding them, are made of mother-of-pearl and copper wire; they're all the same, but the eyes of each fly are formed by different colored pearls. I don't like flies, but these hairpins are beautiful.

I reach over and touch one, a fly with red eyes.

I think of the musicians, the violinist's smirk, the fluttering banknotes, the ringing sounds of the zither's strings. I look at Grandmother, and I ask her how she did it.

Grandmother finishes combing her hair, then she plaits it, licks her lips, and smiles. How did I do what? she asks.

I say: All those things that happened today — how did you do those?

Grandmother takes the end of her plaited hair, pulls out a hairband with black pearls on it, twists it around the braid, and says that it's a secret — she can't tell anyone.

She winds her plaited hair into a bun; she holds it with one hand, then extends the palm of her other hand out to me, saying that I am her granddaughter. She gestures at the hairpins with her thumb, and I reach over and place one in her hand; she sticks it into her hair, and she says that for me, she can make an exception. Once again she extends her hand, and again I place a hairpin on her palm; she sticks the hairpin into her hair, and she says she can make an exception, and she can teach me a thing or two, but only if I really want her to. Yet again she extends her hand to me; again I place a hairpin in her hand, and I say: Yes.

Grandmother inserts the pin into her bun, and she says: Fine, we're agreed. She holds her hand out to me; now only one hairpin remains, the fly with red eyes. As I place it in her palm, Grandmother grabs my hand. She takes the hairpin from my fingers, and she says that the promise must be sealed. I know what she's going to do; I also know that I can pull my hand away, but I don't. Grandmother turns the pin over and stabs the point of it into the tip of my right ring finger. It doesn't even hurt, I hardly feel it, just a little prick, and a tiny drop of blood emerges on that spot.

Grandmother lets go of my hand; she doesn't wipe the pin, but sticks it into her bun. She sees that I'm looking at the drop of blood on the tip of my finger, and she tells me to lick it, what am I waiting for?

The drop of blood is dark crimson, like a tiny pearl, and as I raise my hand, I see my face reflected in its surface, and suddenly I feel intense pain, as if a burning needle had been thrust into the tip of my finger, as if it had been stabbed all the way through. I wince in pain, feel one of my eyes beginning to tear up, and I quickly stick my finger in my mouth.

It was just a moment—now it's not hurting at all, it's not even bleeding; there is only a tiny crimson spot where the needle pricked my finger.

I look at Grandmother. She's putting on lipstick in the reflection of the window, and she says I shouldn't fall asleep now because we'll be home in a moment.

The train is passing by a large factory; on a hill behind it, a series of housing blocks are being built. The tower cranes stand between the buildings, but it's as if there were large fires blazing behind the windows. I look at Grandmother, and she says that's the new housing being built for the ironworkers and that we'll be there in a moment, so we should gather our coats and our things, we'll be at the station in half a minute.

GRANDMOTHER GETS OFF THE TRAIN first; she stands in front of the steps and tells me to hand her my suitcase. She takes it and places it by her feet while I get off the train.

No one else gets off the train; it leaves the station.

It's cold on the platform, and there is only one light, where the overpass leads across the tracks.

It's hard to drag the suitcase up the slippery iron steps; Grandmother helps me. As we reach the overpass, I look down through the grid. The station is very big, with freight cars standing on fifteen or even more tracks. As we're coming down from the overpass, the suitcase slips out of our hands; the sound reverberates as it slides down the steps, I'm afraid that the strap will loosen and my things will spill out onto the trampled gray snow, but it doesn't.

Across the station, the huge clock above the exit has no clock hands, and before we step out of the building, I look at my new watch and see that in six minutes it will be midnight.

Outside there is a white taxi, looking as if it were waiting for us; it rolls over to where we are standing. The driver doesn't say hello; he just tips his cap and takes my suitcase. He puts it on the passenger seat in front instead of the luggage compartment in the back.

The driver opens the door for us, waits for us to get in, then closes the door.

We set off. The city is dark; I try to look out the window, but I don't see anything. Grandmother says not to bother, we'll have a good look at the city in the daytime. This is my new home, she says, I'll see it often enough. It's better for me to rest; with the long, difficult day behind me, it's no wonder I'm sleepy.

As she says this, she puts her arm around my shoulders. I want to say that I'm not sleepy, but before I can, I feel that, yes, my eyes are closing. I lean my head against Grandmother's nutria-fur collar, and my nose is filled with the scent of the bristles. I think of Mother's old fur coat, the one that she never wore, and the word *mothball* comes into my mind. With that word on my tongue I fall asleep.

3

IT'S EARLY MORNING WHEN I wake up, gray dawn. For a moment I don't know where I am; my nose is full of strange scents. I sit up on the creaky divan.

I'm alone in the room. I hear noise coming from outside, soft creaking, dull knocking sounds. I climb down from the divan; the white nightgown that I'm wearing is not my own. I run my hands along its fabric and then I remember the trip, Grandmother, everything.

I go out the door into a long vestibule. At the end of the hallway is a partly open door; a light shines through it, drawing strips of light on the rag carpet. As I step into the light, I see how pale my feet look.

The door opens into the kitchen; that's where the noise is coming from. It's Grandmother. I stand in the strip of light, and I watch from there; I can't bring myself to go in.

Grandmother is standing next to a round table, a kneading board in front of her, and on the kneading board there is flour. She leans above it; with her right hand, she draws something in the flour and looks at it for a moment, then with her left hand she wipes it away. I can't see what she drew, only that with the palm of her hand she has made the flour smooth again. She looks at it, then once again she draws something in the flour. For a short while she looks at the new drawing, then she wipes it away. Once again she draws something, and then she wipes it away. She does it again and again. She draws something, and she wipes it away, she draws something and wipes it away. I stand in the door, opened just a crack, and no matter how much I crane my neck, I can't see what she's drawing, only her swift movements. I hear as the tips of her fingers tap on the kneading board, as her fingers, gliding, plow lines through the flour; I hear the table creak as she leans on it with both hands and looks at the drawing. I hear as she sighs, as she smooths out and wipes away the drawing. I stand, and I watch, and I don't dare step into the kitchen; I don't dare ask what she's doing.

The clock on the wall strikes half past the hour, and Grandmother looks up, straight at me. Good morning, she says. With the palms of her hands, she quickly brushes the flour over to the edge of the kneading board into a small mound. It's not very much, at the very most half a handful of flour. Grandmother holds a mug next to the kneading board, sweeps the flour into it with her hand, and pours it back into the flour tin. She motions for me to come into the kitchen, puts the cover back on the flour tin, and says that she hopes I slept well and that I like hot chocolate, because she's already warmed up the milk.

GRANDMOTHER PLACES A STEAMING PORCELAIN cup in front of me. I lean above it, and my nose is filled with the heavy, sweet scent of cocoa. Grandmother says it's good and hot, I should drink it up, it will give me strength.

The cocoa is very thick but not that sweet; it flows down my throat smoothly and warmly. I hold the cup with both hands, and as I drink it, I look out above the cup at Grandmother, and she looks at me, smiling.

She says that this was my mother's favorite cup, and she was the last one who drank from it. She says it looks nice in my hands.

As I put down the cup, the kitchen light shines on it, and a pattern appears between my fingers. I turn it around; on the white porcelain of the cup, a dancer in a black dress stands on tiptoe, her arms held above her head. Her back is arched, her face in profile, her eye a dot of paint, her mouth a thin line, and yet it seems as if she's looking at something in anger.

I want to see what she's looking at. I turn the cup all around, but apart from the dancing woman, there's nothing else there.

I GET DRESSED, AND GRANDMOTHER shows me around the house. It's not big. There are two rooms, then there's the vestibule, the bathroom, the kitchen, and the larder. Grandmother shows me everything.

The house is clean; the fringes of the Persian carpets are neatly arranged; the inlaid patterns gleam on the old pieces of furniture.

Everything is tidy and yet not tidy at all; everywhere there are objects strewn about. On the arm of one chair there's a jacket that's about to slide off; on the small table an open vocabulary notebook with a pocketknife and a sharpened pencil on top of it. Next to the divan there's a pair of shoes, a green knee sock hanging out of one of them. A polished leather belt hangs from the window latch. It has no holes.

Grandmother sees that I'm looking at the belt. She says that it's a razor strop. It was Grandfather's, she says. I'm not allowed to touch any of Grandfather's things; they must remain

untouched, just as he left them. Everything in the same spot
and in the same way. His Sunday-best trousers, nicely ironed
and folded on the divan; his reading glasses on the little table; his French dictionary, left open, on the bureau next to the
little lamp; his Doxa watch with the black strap on the floor
by the divan; his small radio and the headphones, coiled up, on
the credenza in the kitchen; his toothbrush with the toothpaste
squeezed onto the bristles sitting on the edge of the sink in the
bathroom; his razor placed on the shelf beneath the mirror; his
telescope in the shoebox beneath the bed; and so on—in time I
would get to know it all.

I ask when Grandfather died.

Grandmother says: On New Year's Eve. It hasn't even been
two months.

To this, I say nothing. I look at the vocabulary notebook,
the French words written out in pencil. Grandfather's writing
is thin and fibrous, slanting heavily to the right; it's hard to
read.

We go out to the kitchen, and now I see that on the arm
of one of the chairs there is a thin-rimmed black hat with a
jay's feather in its ribbon. I look at the blue-black pattern of the
feather; it shines as if lacquered. I don't ask, for I know even
without asking that this is Grandfather's hat.

A photograph of Grandfather is hanging next to the wall
clock in a golden frame formed by thick tendrils and leaves. It's
a black-and-white photograph, and in it, an old man looks at
himself in the mirror; a camera on a thick black strap hangs
around his neck; a thin cigarette dangles from the corner of his
mouth; his index finger is on the camera's shutter release. You
can see that, although he is standing in front of the mirror, he's
not looking at himself but off to the side, somewhere far away.

I see a great sadness on his face, a thick black sorrow that
sits behind his eyes.

As I look at him, I suddenly realize that the surface of the picture is full of lines, as if it had been torn into tiny pieces and then put back together like a puzzle. The picture is hanging a little crookedly on the wall. I reach over to straighten it; the frame is dusty, and the trace of my finger remains on it. In the picture, the leather strap of the camera looks like it's been varnished; it's very shiny and black.

I blow the dust off the frame; it flies up in the air, swirls around, then settles on the glass that covers the picture, obscuring Grandfather's face.

I know I should wipe it off, but I don't move. I look at the specks of dust.

Grandmother comes over to me, and she says this is the last photograph of Grandfather; he might have taken this picture of himself about one week before his death.

She's silent; she reaches for the wall clock, she pulls on its weights, and the clock begins to murmur and click.

THE KITCHEN DOOR OPENS UP onto the courtyard, then you have to go down three stone steps. The courtyard is empty; there are only four pine trees standing in it, across from an unplastered firewall. The courtyard is separated from the garden by a large walnut tree and a small building; beyond the walnut tree there is proper grass growing; Grandmother calls this the lawn. In the middle of the garden, there is a round flower bed surrounded by boxwood, and in it are the bases of rosebushes, covered with newspaper and tied up with string. Grandmother says that Grandfather planted this flower bed, and he grew all the roses in it himself.

The garden isn't too big, but still it has many fruit trees: two sour cherry trees, one regular cherry tree, three plum trees, and a greengage tree.

Grandmother says that all these trees are hers; Grandfather

planted the cherry tree, but she planted all the rest, and there's only one tree in the garden that is older than she is — the large walnut tree. It's one hundred and fifty years old, maybe even older than that.

A swing hangs down from the walnut tree, a gray board attached to a fraying rope. We stand next to the walnut tree; its trunk is almost completely black, with coarse finger-size indentations winding all around it. I place my hand on the trunk, and I look up at the crown of the tree. Above my head, the trunk branches into two; both of the main branches are as wide as a person's waist. There are no leaves on the branches; they move slightly, showing me that above the roofs of the houses, the wind is blowing. I spread my fingers apart wide, imagine the wind blowing through them. The branches of the walnut tree cut the gray sky into shards; I watch the wind changing the pattern of the branches and it makes me dizzy.

Grandmother steps over to me; she too places her palm on the trunk of the tree, and she too looks up.

Something black moves on the branches of the walnut tree. At the top of the tree there are crows; I hadn't noticed them before. They sit perched on the thinnest of the limbs, swaying back and forth in the wind. They lean forward, stretching out their necks, at times fluttering their wings, then stepping forward on the branches.

We watch them, then Grandmother says: Shoo! She strikes the palm of her hand on the trunk, and I move suddenly; the crows fly up, cawing and circling above the walnut tree.

Grandmother says that she really loves this tree. She can tell that I'll love it too.

NEXT TO THE WALNUT TREE there is a small wooden house; its blue double doors are bolted shut, and from the bolt hangs a large black lock. It looks something like a garage or an old stable; the back of the house is supported by the firewall. There's one window on the side, but you can't see in because it's covered over with tarpaper.

Grandmother says that this is the old woodshed and that I must never, never go anywhere near it. I can play in the garden and in the courtyard, I'm allowed to climb up all the trees, but I must stay away from the woodshed. She looks at me and asks if I understand.

I nod, say, Yes, I understand. I look at the two blue doors and at the lock, and I want to ask, Why, what's inside? But Grandmother looks at me and I don't ask anything.

She says that now I've seen everything and we can go back in; it's time for me to unpack my suitcase. I should go and bring it out from the larder. Then she'll show me which wardrobe will be mine.

THE LARDER IS VERY BIG, almost as big as the kitchen, and on the floor is a battered Persian rug. Facing the door is a low, silver refrigerator, and next to it, on the ground, is my suitcase. The belt is still tied around it. As I pick it up, I think I hear footsteps.

The noise is coming from above, and I look over; the wooden stairs leading up to the attic are making a creaking sound, but there's nothing there. I look at the green linoleum on the steps, held in place by thumbtacks, and I hear the creaking once again. Now it's the middle steps that are creaking, and I see that on one of the steps, the linoleum is moving; a thumbtack pops out of the edge of the step and falls onto the rug two hand-widths from my foot.

The thumbtack is pointy and shiny, the kind where the head

and the pointy end are all one piece. I lean down and pick it up from the carpet.

As I straighten up, somebody grabs my shoulder. I turn around; it's Grandmother. She takes the thumbtack from my hand and puts it back into the front of the step, pushing it completely down with her thumb. She motions toward the trapdoor and tells me that the stairs are falling apart; I'm not allowed to go up to the attic.

We go back to the inner room. I take my suitcase with me.

The room is large and filled with light. It has two divans, one with a thick white woolen blanket, one with a red and black blanket. Grandmother points to the white blanket and says that since I slept on that, it will be my bed.

She opens up one of the wardrobes, takes out the tea cloths and linens from the top three shelves and places them on the bottom three shelves. She says that the top three shelves are for me, and I should put my clothes there.

I begin to unpack. The shelf at the very top is empty, as is the one right below it, but in the middle of the third shelf there is a blue cardboard box, with the image of a sailor printed in white on its lid; he has bulging muscles. In his mouth there's a pipe; as he flexes his biceps, he smiles.

I take the lid off the box. In it there are two shining wooden handles and between them three long and thick metal springs. I know what this is: it's a chest expander.

As I touch the box, the springs make a ringing sound, and the echoing drones as if it were coming from the depths of a well. I take one of the wooden handles. It fits in my palm perfectly.

I lift it up and the springs graze against one another; the sound sends chills down my spine. The springs make a jingling, clanking sound, and the second handle of the chest expander slowly begins to lift as if somebody is picking it up—but nobody is picking it up.

The handle of the expander is cold in my palm; I can't catch my breath. I squeeze my fingers around it; the springs straighten and stretch out, and the expander tightens as if somebody is trying to yank it out of my hands.

I don't know what to do.

Suddenly Grandmother is standing beside me; I didn't even notice her walking over. She looks at the expander; the expression on her face is slightly angry. That's enough now, she says. The expander immediately falls down, dangling heavily in my hand.

Grandmother takes it from me, folds it up, and puts it back in the box.

She closes the box and she says that Grandpa doesn't like anyone rummaging around in his things. There's no reason for me to be afraid of him; if we get to know each other he won't do any harm, and I'll see that he's really very nice. Later on, if I want, I can watch him as he trains. I should watch the tassels on the Persian carpet; that's how I can tell when he's about to begin. If I really want to see him, I should squint and then hold my breath.

THE SUN IS SHINING INTO the living room; the tassels on the Persian carpet are like two long white combs. I stop and look at the carpet, at the white lines woven into its meandering pattern. I hear the floor creaking. It's as if the creaking sound is running along the strip of light.

As the sound reaches the edge of the carpet, I see that the tassels are moving. They open up and close again, open and close, as if somebody is marching all along them, stamping his feet back and forth, and then I hear the stamping on the floor, *stomp-stomp-stomp-stomp-stomp*.

The light has grown sharper, making me squint. The dust swirls in the strips of light.

I look down at the Persian carpet; the tassels on it are still moving.

I still hear the knocking sound; somebody is walking back and forth on the tassels, stamping on them.

I suddenly think that I'd like to see him. I take a deep breath of the air, which tastes like dust, and I hold it. I close my eyes, squeeze them shut so tightly that the colors swirl together behind my eyelids. I wait a moment, and then I slowly open my eyes. Squinting, I look through my eyelashes into the light.

At first I don't see anything, but then the specks of dust swirling in the light begin to trace out a figure—I recognize Grandfather from the photograph. He looks as if he's made of glass. He's stamping on the tassels of the Persian rug, quickly, going back and forth, and in the meantime with both hands he's massaging his scalp.

It looks funny; I have to smile. I'd like to know what he's doing.

I blow out the air. Grandfather disappears, but when I hold my breath again, I see him.

Grandmother is standing beside me, and she whispers: Gymnastics, hair-strengthening gymnastics. Grandfather always said that it stimulates circulation in the scalp, and it strengthens the roots of the hair; he always told me to try it, it's very good for one's hair.

I look at Grandfather's stamping feet, and I ask Grandmother very softly if she ever tried it.

Grandmother says no, unfortunately she never tried it.

Well, I say, the time has come. I blow out my breath, stand at the other end of the carpet on top of the tassels. I begin to walk, stamping my feet; I plunge my fingers into my hair and massage my scalp.

When I reach the end of the carpet I turn around and start again, and I see that Grandmother is standing on the other edge of the carpet; she too is raising her hands to her hair. I close my eyes, massage my scalp more intensely; it slowly grows warmer, and I imagine the warmth creeping along the strands of my hair.

4

ON MONDAY MORNING, GRANDMOTHER SAYS she will accompany me to the school gates and that I should take note of
the route: we will go out to the tree-lined path, then along the
Castle Barracks and past the Great Linden Tree to the end of
the road paved with yellow bricks, where we will turn off next
to the church, cross the main square, go up to the third small
street, and we'll be there. Later on, I will have to get home by
myself.

As we walk, Grandmother suddenly says that my mother
also went this way to school every day. There's another, shorter
route, which she'll show me later, but this one is prettier.

When she stops speaking, I realize that I don't have my
schoolbag with my notebooks and my pencil case. I say to
Grandmother that we should go back for them, but she says no,
one must never turn back on the first trip, it brings bad luck. I
want to tell her that this isn't true, but I stay silent.

We reach the main square. Grandmother tells me to
wait, she'll be back in a moment; she just has to run into the
pharmacy to pick up some medicine, it won't be so crowded
right now.

. . .

IN THE MIDDLE OF THE square, between the benches and the flower beds, there is a small house. It's something like a tent but made from concrete, and around it on the asphalt are dried-out flowers and pine branches.

I go over to have a look.

Amid the bunches of flowers on the asphalt are candle stubs and many small puddles of spilled wax; two beeswax candles are still burning.

I look up. The back wall is completely covered with photographs, color ones and black-and-white ones, identity-card photographs, images cut out of family pictures, women, men, and children too; from the wires sticking out of the concrete, dried flowers hang, and above the photographs there is a ribbon in the national colors attached to the wall with the inscription *We will never forget them*, and above the inscription is a flag with a hole cut out of the middle.

I look at the faces, all unknown to me, and my eyes come to rest on the picture of one girl; she could be my age. She stares out stubbornly, her mouth pressed together; the picture is black-and-white, her face cut out with scissors. I look at her eyes, and she looks straight through me, out onto the main square.

One of the candles flares up, then begins to flicker, as if blown by the wind. I crouch down, and I place my two palms around it, one on either side. The flame grows longer and straightens out; I feel the warmth of it on my skin.

Behind me I hear somebody speaking, saying that after the first round of fire there were nineteen that remained on the ground. It's a hunched-over old woman with a black headscarf; her hands are filled with wax candles.

I tell her that I'll help her. The old lady holds the candles out to me; I take half a handful. We both crouch down; the old lady lights a candle, and she says: There were only four places in the country where they fired straight into the crowds, but here, there were the most dead. She holds the candle so that the flame touches the clumps of wax on the asphalt; the candle hisses, its smoke black and sooty, the wax melting into small puddles. The old lady begins to set down the candles in these pools of wax, and I light a candle too, and I set it down in the pool of wax. All the while, the old woman is talking. She says that elsewhere, the soldiers fired their shots above the people's heads first, but not here—here, there were no warning shots, they shot directly into the crowd. They fired once, then they fired again, and then they fired a third time.

Now that every candle is burning, the old woman falls silent; she looks up at the photographs, stands up, reaches over, straightens a dried flower beneath one of the photographs.

She looks at me again, and she says I should know, the ones who did this are still among us. They're as free as birds, the ones who pulled the triggers as well as the ones who gave the orders. She says that every single day she prays for her poor precious dead, and she prays for the evil ones to suffer for their crimes. She knows she should forgive them, but she doesn't. She can't, and she doesn't even want to. Not until the dead have been given proper burials—no, not until then.

I see that there are tears on her face. I take out my handkerchief and give it to her.

The old lady wipes her face and gives me back the handkerchief.

As I take it, she grabs my hand, caresses it, and says that I'm a good little girl, and I should pray for the innocent. For the souls of the innocent.

She looks at me, squinting, and says she recognizes me from somewhere. I tell her that's not possible, I've only just moved here.

The old lady says even so, she recognizes me. She looks up next to me, and suddenly her face goes dark; she grabs her hand away from mine as if it has been scorched. Grandmother is standing next to one of the flower beds; the old lady looks at her. Grandmother speaks, says, Let's go or we'll be late, then she turns her back to me, to the monument, and to the old woman; she gestures with her large black umbrella for me to leave.

The old woman screams that I'm one of the guilty ones, that I should be ashamed to even step foot in this sacred place, I should get out of here.

I tell her that I didn't do anything. I feel the tears beginning to scratch at my throat.

The old lady yells at me again: Get out of here, I can't hear you, get lost!

I tell her I don't understand what she's saying, I didn't do anything, I'm just a child.

The old lady hisses at me, says that the ones who died were also children. I should get lost, understand? By now she's screeching at me, but her gaze is fixed on Grandmother.

I feel my eyes filling with tears; I don't want this old woman to see me crying, so I slowly turn away and start walking toward Grandmother, all the while saying that I still don't understand.

I look back, and I see her crouching on the ground among the candles; one after the other, with her fingers, she's putting out the flames that I lit.

I turn away, take a deep breath; I don't want to burst into tears. I lower my head, and I walk, following Grandmother.

When I catch up with her, my throat is scratching so much that I can't speak. Grandmother doesn't say anything either; without a word she takes my arm. I feel that she is caressing it with the exact same movement that Mother used to; it's making the chills run down my back. I know what's going to follow, she's about to tell me that everything's fine, that I should calm down, there are no problems.

I ask her if she heard what that old lady was saying to me.

Grandmother says that she heard, but I shouldn't be bothered by it. All of the losses the old lady had suffered made her confused, and in the end one can understand it.

I ask Grandmother: Why did the old lady say that they haven't been buried properly?

Grandmother clears her throat and then speaks. It's because after the shooting, the Interior Ministry people took over the hospital where the dead and the wounded had been taken, and they disappeared all the corpses, and they've never been found to this day. Instead of the corpses, empty coffins were laid in the earth.

The muscles on her face tighten; she shakes her head, and I know it's better if I don't ask anything else.

We walk up the third side street and arrive at the school, now we are standing in front of the school gates. Grandmother says that she has accompanied me this far, but she won't come in with me, they don't like her there, but I shouldn't be afraid, she has already discussed everything with the headmistress. I should go in and knock at the teachers' room, tell them my name and that I'm looking for the headmistress, and there will be no problems.

Fine, I say. I look at the school. A long road leads up to the entrance; the school is bigger than my old one. The walls have been plastered gray, and the whole thing looks like a castle; it also has a high tower. I begin to feel cold.

I grab the iron fence with one hand; it's ice-cold, but I don't let go. I remember how when I was little, I didn't want to go to nursery school; Mother took me there for the first time, but I cried and I screamed so much, screamed for her not to take me there, that Mother was ashamed to bring me in, and at the gates of the nursery school we turned back, and on the way home I was so happy that I jumped across one puddle after the other. When we got home, I wanted to go inside, but Mother said no, I should wait outside a little bit in front of the door. I didn't know why she was saying this, but then Father came out; he didn't say anything, just grabbed my hand, and as we headed off down the steps, I already knew that he was going to take me back to the nursery school, and I also knew that there was no point in crying and no point in yelling, he would take me there anyway. Then we went by a different route than I had gone with Mother, by a route that followed the banks of the brook and was next to a row of black poplars, and I was thinking that we weren't going back to the nursery, but then I saw we were on the street where the nursery was, and once again I began to cry, but then Father crouched down next to me; he embraced me, and he picked me up, and he said, Don't be afraid, nothing bad was going to happen to me, and he reached into his pocket and he took out a yellow ribbon, and he tied it into my hair, and he said that the ribbon would watch over me, now let's be off.

I'm thinking about the ribbon, wondering what happened to it. When I started going to primary school, I still had it. Father took me to that school for the first time as well.

I'm still holding on to the gate; it's so cold that I can't even feel my palm anymore, or even my fingers, but still I keep on squeezing it as hard as I can; I don't want to go into this new school, I don't want to let go of the bar of the gate.

Grandmother puts her hand on mine.

Her fingers are bony, but a mild warmth radiates from the palm of her hand. She says I should go in. Better to get it over with.

I let go of the gate, turn away; I know that I really have to go in now.

One more thing, Grandmother says. She takes out her wallet, opens it, pulls out three banknotes, all of them tens, presses them into my hand, and says that this is my pocket money, I should be careful with it. I should go, be good, and if I hear anything bad about her or Grandfather, don't believe it, she says. It's all lies. The wagging of envious tongues.

I nod in response, stuff the money into my pocket, and start walking toward the school.

THE HEADMISTRESS'S SHOES CLATTER ON the concrete floor in the hallway. Her shoes are green, open in front, you can see her toes; her toenails aren't painted. She tells me that my class is at the end of the hall. I've come just in time because the homeroom teacher is giving a class right now, and it would be very good if she could introduce me to the other students.

I ask her what class it is, and she says math. She asks me what my favorite subject is. Geography, I tell her. The headmistress says of course, she could have guessed, it's because of my grandfather, right? I say I don't know, maybe. The headmistress puts her hands on my shoulders, and she turns me around to face her. She looks me up and down; her expression is stern. She says that my grandfather taught her geography and French, and she got a few slaps in the face and on the wrist from him as well. Apart from that, the old man was a wonderful teacher. But this isn't what she wants to say. She wants me to know that there will be no exceptions for me here because of my grandfather, neither in the positive or negative sense. No matter what he did, I'm starting here with a completely blank slate. For her and for all the other teachers too. She wants to really emphasize this. Do I understand?

I don't know what to say. I look down again at her shoes; there are scale-shaped, black indentations on the green leather, an imitation of either snake or crocodile leather. I look at the headmistress's toes, and I see that they actually are painted with transparent white nail polish. I look up, and I say, Yes.

The headmistress nods, and she says it would be good for me to understand that if any of the teachers tries to take advantage of the situation in any way whatsoever, then I should come to her, and she in turn will do everything she can to make sure that nothing like that occurs again.

We get to the end of the hallway; we stop in front of the last door. The headmistress knocks, then she opens the door right away. I hear the benches clattering inside as they're being pushed back; the pupils call out *Good day* together, and in the meantime, the headmistress has put her hand on my shoulders again and she's pushing me into the classroom.

I'M STANDING ON THE PLATFORM next to the teacher's desk; the homeroom teacher is talking about me, saying that I am the new classmate that she was telling everyone about last week, and that from now on I'll be going to school here, so they should all make me feel welcome.

I'm listening, but I'm not looking at her; I look at the class. There are two rows of desks, the boys and the girls sitting separately, the girls on the right-hand side of the classroom, the boys on the left. There's only one empty spot; in the second row of the girls' section, on the inside, there is a desk with no one sitting there.

I don't want to listen to what the homeroom teacher is saying, and yet I still hear her words as she says, She lost both of her parents; I hear her as she says, Car accident; I know that in a moment my face will be red and burning, I don't like this, so instead I look down at the floor and follow, with my gaze, the black gaps between the obliquely laid floorboards. They form long zigzagging lines, branching off, breaking up everywhere into paths; I follow one single line, my gaze sliding over it slowly as it turns, depicting jagged spirals, and then goes back to where it began.

The homeroom teacher pronounces my name loudly and clearly; I can't avoid hearing it. I look up—she's holding a piece

of chalk out to me, it's my turn now to introduce myself nicely
to the class and, if I want to, say something about my old school.

I take the piece of chalk. I look at the class, and for a moment I think that I won't be able to say anything, and yet I do,
I hear how my voice is sharper and deeper than usual; I greet
them, I say my name, then I fall silent. I know I should say
something more, I should say that I'm happy to be here, say the
name of the city I came from or, at the very least, the name of
the institution where I had been living for the past few months,
but I don't say anything; they look at me and I look at them,
nobody even moves, everyone stares at me fixedly—only one
pupil doesn't. In the first row, next to the window, there sits
a boy with black hair, he's not looking at me but out through
the window; he yawns, not even placing his hand in front of his
mouth. Still, I say something, I say that what's past is past, and
at the same time I know that this isn't true, it's an immeasur-
ably enormous lie, it isn't past, and it won't pass; I turn my back
to the classroom and step over to the blackboard, which might
have been wiped down quite recently because it still hasn't completely dried, the edges of the streaks left by the sponge are
blacker and lighter than the freshly poured tar.

I press the chalk onto the blackboard, and in large block
letters I write my last name; the chalk makes creaking noises. I
turn the chalk around, and I write my first name as well, then
I put the chalk next to the sponge on the ledge next to the
blackboard.

Very good, says the homeroom teacher, I can now go to my
seat. She says that I'll be sitting next to Krisztina and that it's
high time for that empty desk to be filled.

KRISZTINA DOESN'T LOOK AT ME as I sit down next to her.
She has wavy brown hair and a long face; I see her from the side.

I say hello, but she doesn't say anything to me, she just begins writing something down in her exercise book.

This desk is different from my old desk at the other school; I look at the scribbles on the desk, the inscriptions scratched into it with the point of a compass.

I didn't bring anything; I don't have any books, exercise books, or even a pencil.

The homeroom teacher tells me to ask for a piece of paper and a pencil from my desk mate.

Krisztina doesn't wait for me to speak; she rips out a page from her exercise book and pushes it toward me.

She keeps her pencils in a black wooden box; as she opens it, I see something brown and crimson between the colored pencils and the ballpoint pens. Krisztina pushes the pencil case in my direction for me to pick one out, and I see a fox paw—it still has its claws. As I reach in and take a black lead pencil, I'm careful not to touch the paw, and yet the fur touches my wrist, and goose bumps run all up and down my arm.

I think about the institute and the fox that I saw there once in the garden, sleeping curled up on the snow.

THE HOMEROOM TEACHER IS TALKING about the smallest common multipliers and the largest common dividers; I learned this already in the institute, but still I write down everything on the sheet of paper so I can copy it into my exercise book later on.

The same light-colored blotches as the institute has on its walls are on the wall here too: in the middle the big perpendicular rectangular one, on either side the two horizontal rectangles. On both sides of the large brick-shaped one there are pale blue splash marks; before the pictures were ripped away from the wall, someone must have splashed blue ink on them while standing on the teacher's desk. I look at the ink blotches, then at the blackboard again.

The homeroom teacher explains everything quickly; the chalk creaks in her hand. I copy it all down; the front of the piece of paper fills up fast.

When I turn the piece of paper over, I see something written in the middle of the page in pencil; it says that this is not my seat, this is Réka's seat.

I look at Krisztina, and I ask her in a whisper who Réka was.

She doesn't answer, just continues looking at the homeroom teacher, and as the homeroom teacher turns toward the blackboard, I feel a sudden sharp pain cleaving through my ankle. I look down, and I see that Krisztina is pulling back her foot; she's wearing shiny black patent leather Mary Janes, she just kicked me with the tip of her shoe, and it really hurts. I reach down with my hand to touch it, my eyes fill with tears, but even so I don't cry out.

I continue to copy the lesson from the blackboard; the homeroom teacher is now explaining prime numbers.

I get to the middle of the page, to where Krisztina wrote the inscription. I can go around it and keep on writing down the lesson, but I don't. I press my pencil hard on the paper; I draw a line through the sentence. Once, twice, three times, with thick black lines, so that it's not even visible.

I hear Krisztina as she exhales loudly in rage, then she kicks me again, more strongly this time, and yet it doesn't hurt so much.

Softly — so that my mouth hardly even moves — I whisper in front of myself: If you kick me one more time, you're going to really regret it.

The desk gives a creak; I know it's because Krisztina has leaned to one side so she can kick my ankle even harder, just as hard as she possibly can. I could pull my ankle away, but I don't.

I look down at the floor and at my shoe. Krisztina kicks me, and I think it's not going to hurt, that I won't feel the pain, but I feel it, I feel it very much; it reaches up to my waist, it feels as if my bones have turned to glass. Enough — I don't say it aloud, I only think it, clearly and sharply: Enough; the chalk is squeaking in the homeroom teacher's hand, it creaks, and it breaks in two; the larger piece flies behind the teacher's desk; she makes a wry face, throws the stump of chalk remaining in her hand down onto the edge of the blackboard, steps behind her desk, and crouches down while she looks for the other half of the piece of chalk; our desk squeaks loudly again, and I know that Krisztina is getting ready to kick me, and she's already kicking me, and I lean forward onto the top of the desk, and at the same time I pull my legs up — Krisztina misses the target, and the momentum of the kick pushes her over to the side and to the back; she nearly falls out of her chair, but at the very last moment she clutches the edge of the desk; the freckles jump on the back of her hand as the skin is stretched from the effort. I reach for her pencil case, pull off the cover, quickly pull out the fox paw, and as I clutch it in my hand, I feel the bristles brushing up against my palm; goose bumps run all the way up and down my arm, but I don't bother with that. I bring the fox paw down hard on Krisztina's hand; the claws dig deep, dragging all along her skin; I see four scarlet streaks, from the middle two streaks the blood is already seeping out in needlepoint drops; Krisztina cries out, flings her hand up to her mouth, and licks it.

In the meantime, the homeroom teacher has found the piece of chalk; she stands up and goes back to the blackboard.

I still have the fox paw in my hand; the bristles on the bottom part of it are completely black. I throw it into Krisztina's lap. Krisztina grabs it and looks at me, the back of her hand still pressed up against her mouth, her eyes gleaming and moist.

She looks somewhere next to me; her face changes — she's not looking at me but at someone else. I know I should think that's what she deserved, but still, I feel sorry for her, and suddenly I realize: she is the girl who I saw in the photograph, the photograph of the girl pasted onto the concrete memorial among all the other photographs. It's her—and yet it's not her—it really looks like her, so it might have been her sister.

I think of what the old lady said about how the soldiers fired into the crowd. I don't want to speak, but I must, so I softly whisper, I'm sorry.

Krisztina slowly puts the fox paw back into her pencil case; for a while she doesn't answer, then she whispers that I should go back to where I came from and take all of my lies with me.

I don't say anything to that; I turn my piece of paper over once again, and I continue copying the lesson as the homeroom teacher writes it on the blackboard. As I place my feet on the lower crossbar of the desk, I feel how much my ankle hurts. I lick my mouth and try not to think about it.

5

THE BELL RINGS, AND EVERYONE runs out of the classroom. I fold up the piece of paper from the exercise book and put it in my skirt pocket. I pull up my leg; through my stockings a great big blotch is already visible on my ankle. I press down on it with the palm of my hand. I think about Father, about how when I was little and I bumped into something, he would always make it better. He always asked me where it hurt, waited for me to show him, and then said, Don't be sad, it will go away now; he put his hand on the spot that hurt, and all the while he sang softly: There once was a little girl, and her leg was hurting, but then a little bird sat on it. Then he blew onto his hand and said: Fly away, little bird, and suddenly he raised his hand, making a fluttering noise with his fingers, as if they were bird's wings, and he would whistle softly or make chirping sounds, and he did it until I began laughing. I suddenly thought of his hand; I thought of his fingers, how they were almost always covered in paint and smelled like turpentine; sometimes he even did this when I was older; there was no use in telling him that I was too big for this, he always answered that of course, he knew that too, but the little bird didn't know, and that little bird just laughed at everyone — I shake my head, I don't want to think about Father, and yet I still see clearly in my mind's eye his hand, his fingers, how there were small black dots of paint on his wedding ring; the memory is making my eyes moist, just one teardrop in the corner of my eye. I wipe it away, I don't want to cry.

Somebody touches my shoulder. I look around; a fat girl is standing next to my desk, she's holding out a handkerchief to me, and she says, Don't cry, it'll stop hurting, it always does in the end. I shake my head, and I say that's not why I'm crying. I take the handkerchief and wipe my eyes; it smells like eau de cologne and menthol. I wipe my face with it.

The girl tells me her name, she's called Olgi. She says I shouldn't worry about Krisztina; ever since her twin sister died, she acts like that with everyone. I nod. I want to give her back the handkerchief, but I see that I've smudged it. I tell her that I'll bring it back tomorrow washed and ironed. Olgi says I don't have to, she doesn't mind a few tears. In the end it's just salty water. I shake my head, saying, No, no, I won't hear a word of it, the right thing to do is for me to wash it out.

Olgi shrugs her shoulders and says it's all the same to her; if I want to, then go ahead.

She's a very fat girl with black hair cut boyishly short, which makes her face look even rounder. She tells me that she too is new here in the class, she's been here since the beginning of the year, when she moved here with her parents.

As she smiles, rings form under her chin, and I notice a thin golden chain around her neck. I ask her how she likes it here.

She says, In the end you can get used to it. Before, her family lived in a village high in the mountains; the air is different down here. But at least you can go to the movies. She asks if I've been to the movies yet. I shake my head; she says we should go one day, these days there are really good films. I nod. I'm still looking at her neck; on the chain there dangles a tiny pearl, black and shiny.

Olgi notices that I'm looking at her chain; she touches it with her index finger, and she says that it's a real pearl, she got it for her confirmation. I can touch it if I want to, she says, and she holds her head to the side slightly while bending above me.

This makes the muscles of her neck stretch as the chain cuts into her skin a bit. I don't want to reach over there, and yet my hand moves anyway; the pearl feels lukewarm beneath my index finger.

Olgi says that you can tell it's a real pearl, not plastic or glass, by how it gets nice and warm. As she speaks, her voice causes the pearl to gently tremble beneath the touch of my finger.

I quickly lower my arm, press the tip of my finger onto the cold iron of the desk, and say it's very beautiful, and it looks really nice on her.

As I speak, I feel that my head is beginning to ache terribly.

I'M WALKING TOWARD THE BATHROOM. Olgi told me that it's at the end of the hallway. I'm almost there and then suddenly a boy steps in front of me. I recognize him; he was the one who, yawning, was looking out the window from the first row of desks. He says, Stop, stop, orphan girl, do you hear me, stop, I want to ask you something. I shake my head; I want to say, I don't have time for that now, but he grabs my hand.

His fingers are damp; his grip is warm. I've never had a boy take my hand before. I keep on walking, I don't stop, and at the same time I feel the blood draining from my face; he walks along beside me, his hand still holding on to my hand. We take two or three steps holding hands like this before I manage to speak, and I tell him to let go right away. I know that I should have slapped him, I should have turned to him and I should have slapped him in the face, and I don't know why I didn't; maybe it's because I've never hit a boy before, I've never had anything to do with any boy before. I pull my hand away from his, and, angrily, I tell him to leave me alone, and at that he smiles, says: Don't be afraid, orphan girl, and then he says something else, but whatever it is, I don't hear, because by that time I've gotten as far as the door of the girls' bathroom; I go in and shut the door behind me.

I stand in the bathroom, the pain seething white in my head.

IN THE GIRLS' BATHROOM, THERE'S no mirror above the faucets, only the boreholes from the screws and the battered white tiles reflecting the fluorescent lights, cutting coldly into my eyes.

That's exactly how my head is aching, just as cold and white and vibrating as these tiles. I turn on the cold water, bend forward and splash the water onto my face; it smells heavily of chlorine, it suits the lights perfectly. I know it won't make my head stop aching but I keep washing my face. Then I stand in front of the sink, holding my two hands below the faucet, waiting for the chill of the water to reach as deep as my bones.

I hear people coming along the corridor, girls; they've stopped in front of the bathroom and I can tell they're going to come in. I don't want them to see me like this, my face is wet; I don't want them to think I've been crying.

I look for somewhere to hide. There are two bathroom stalls, but the door doesn't extend all the way to the ground in either of them. Still, I almost go into one when I notice that to the back, next to the radiator, in one of the corners, there are large wooden panels propped up against the wall. I get closer and stand behind them; I can just fit. I have to press my back against the wall; beneath the soles of my shoes there are glass shards and wood shavings, and if I don't want to make scraping sounds, I can't move.

The girls come in sniggering about something; one of them says that she really has to pee. I hear as she goes into one of the stalls, while the other one opens the tap and the water begins to gurgle out.

I don't want to listen, but still I hear as they mention some boy who told everyone that he had been kissing someone, and it was real grown-up kissing, not only her cheek, but her mouth too; they say some names, the boy's name and the girl's name —I really don't want to hear this. I look at the wooden panels. Facing me are the front sides of plywood panels where some-one had clearly tried to tear off the red crepe paper along with the photographs and the inscriptions; in many places, however, the glue was stronger, and thick strips remain on the surface. Even in the semidarkness I recognize the curly hair of the Com-rade General, a piece of his earlobe, a piece remaining from his mouth as well, the exact middle of his lips, the part that was al-ways shiny; enough of the gold lettering remains for all the slo-gans and mottoes to complete themselves in my head. I think of Father's voice as he told me that these were just empty words, meaningless lies, that nobody believed even one of them, not the people who wrote them out, nor those who made them up, nor those who uttered them; everyone was just pretending to believe, everyone just lied, and I too would have to learn how to lie, but I shouldn't be afraid, because it's easy. Father's voice is scratchy and smells of vodka; he holds my hand, he's taking me to school.

I feel Father's hand holding mine, but I must not think of this, because if I think about it, I will start crying again, and I've had enough of this rotten crying. I reach over to the wooden panel, and with the nails of my thumbs I begin to scratch off pieces of the Comrade General's lips; I feel the repulsion in my throat, but even so I can't stop. The girls are no longer talking about kissing but about the new girl — about me.

I don't want to hear this. I slowly pry the pieces of paper from the surface of the panel; the glue is hard and rough like glass; the girls are saying that I'm stuck-up and ridiculous; they can tell by how I continually play with my hair that I think that I'm a beautiful girl, although in reality I'm as ugly as a dog, and it's obvious I'm going to get even uglier, that's for sure, you just have to look at my grandmother, well, she's so hideous, they weep just thinking of her.

The tip of my finger is really hurting — something pricked it — it's bleeding a bit too; I stick my finger in my mouth, and I lick the wound. I feel with my tongue that a fragment of sizing got stuck underneath my nail, I bite it with my teeth, pull it out, and spit it onto the wood panel. My finger starts bleeding even more; I suck the blood up some more; I hear how they are still talking about Grandmother, and one of them says that she's crazy, she went crazy after her husband passed away.

Krisztina is speaking, her voice hissing with rage; she says that he didn't pass away, but he croaked, he strung himself up, and that's what he deserved, because he was a filthy informer, and he was even lucky, because he deserved much worse, a thousand times, a million times worse than what he got. He deserved to be dragged out of his bed naked in the middle of the night and torn apart by the crowd, because everyone had trusted him, everyone thought he was a nice old teacher, and all the while he was nothing but the most vile and despicable filthy monster. Who knows how many lives he ruined, who knows how many people got sent to jail or to the forced labor camps at the Danube–Black Sea canal because of him; he was the ultimate shitty coward, a filthy member of the Securitate who didn't even have enough spine to ask his victims for forgiveness, at the very least he could have said he was sorry for what he did — he hanged himself out of pure cowardice, that was certain.

I press my hands over my ears; I don't want to hear any-more, but I can still hear as Krisztina says that my parents must have been filthy informers as well, just like my grandfather, and for sure they weren't dead, they just escaped somewhere abroad, and I'm one too, I'm also a rotten informer, she's one hundred percent sure I'm down there already with the home-room teacher, that I went in there to tell on her because she kicked me in the ankle, even though I was only getting what I deserved.

I don't want to hear any more of this; I want to push the wooden panels away so they'll come crashing down on top of the girls, I want to scream into their faces that what they're saying isn't true, none of it is true, they should be ashamed, I'm not a spy, they should be ashamed of themselves. My hands are already beginning to move, and then, as the tips of my fin-gers touch the panels, it flashes through my mind that, yes, I am a spy, I'm standing here listening to them, and suddenly all the anger and all the strength drain out of me. It's as if my legs don't want to hold me up anymore; my head is spinning, and then suddenly with a clang the bell starts to ring with its rattling tinny sound, as sharp as if it were boring right into my skull.

I hear the girls leaving the bathroom. I have to leave as well, the next class is beginning, I have to go back to the classroom. I can't move.

Everything that they said about Grandfather echoes in my head, and what they said about my parents too. Slowly I move my hand, once again I reach for the panel; my nails scrape across the surface as I scratch what's left of the Comrade Gen-eral's face off the wood.

I think of Grandfather's notebook, his sharpened pencil, the French words written down one beneath the other, the slant of the thin sinewy letters, the idiotic gymnastics as I stamped all along the tassels of the Persian carpet while massaging my scalp.

I clench my hands into fists, feel the pieces of the picture crumpling up. I open my palm, and I let them fall to the floor.

I push the wooden panels aside; they fall over, over onto the sinks, bounce back with a huge clattering sound.

I can't stay here anymore. Not here in the bathroom, not here in the school, not here in this city. I run out of the bathroom, along the corridor, past my new classroom, down the steps, out the doors, along the walkway, and out through the iron entrance gates.

I LEFT MY COAT IN the classroom; let it stay there, I don't need it anymore, I don't need anything. If I run quickly enough, I won't get cold, I won't catch a chill, I won't have any problems whatsoever.

I'm lying on the air, I'm leaning forward, I don't want to know where I am, I don't want to know where I'm going, I don't look ahead, I don't look up, I just look down at my shoes and at the asphalt, at my shoes and the cobblestones, at my shoes and the paving bricks, at my shoes and the steps; my shoes clatter, they clatter *informer-informer*, *Securitate-Securitate*, I don't want to hear it, I'm running even faster, it doesn't matter where, just upward; my thighs and my back strain and they hurt, and I remember what Mother always said about taking breaths while running, but I don't do what she said; I feel a stabbing pain in my side, let it stab me, let it stab me all the way to my heart.

I run on gravel, then I'm running on asphalt again; I'm running on icy, slippery ground; I'm running on a road paved with wide, round stones, I'm running on concrete tiles placed next to each other, I'm running on asphalt made bumpy by tree roots,

I'm running on cobblestones, on yellow bricks, again on asphalt, again on the ground, again I'm running on stones.

I don't know where I am, I don't know how long I've been running. I hear someone coming up from behind; for a while now there has been someone running behind me, someone who's getting closer and closer, running right after me, and now that person is very close, perhaps only a couple of meters away. I recognize the rhythm of the footfall, and I recognize that intake of breath; it's Mother—I know I'm just imagining it, but still I can hear her running after me, just as when she used to teach me how to run: she always let me go first, then she ran after me, she called out to me to run, run, because in a minute she was going to catch up with me, she was going to catch up with me in a minute and leave me behind, I needed to run quickly, faster, faster, as fast as I possibly could, and when she caught up to me, she always put her hand on my back, and she said, Run, run, now you're it, then she ran off away from me, and it was my turn to overtake her, I know I'm just imagining it, I know she's not going to overtake me, but still I run faster, as fast as I possibly can.

In vain, because she's right behind me, and at times like that she would always call out to me: Let's go, let's go, you're almost there, but now she's not yelling, although she's right beside me, I hear her running beside me; I don't look at her, I look down at my shoes and at the asphalt, she's faster than me, she's going to leave me behind, she's going to run away from my side, and there she is already. *Mother, don't leave me*—that's what I'm thinking, but I don't say it out loud, I know that she's gone, but I also know that she's right here beside me, she's running here beside me, it's just that I can't look at her right now, I can't look at her, because then she will disappear, she will leave me forever; I turn my head in the other direction, but even so I hear her running next to me. I want to see her,

I want to see her one last time, even if I'll never be able to see her ever again, she's there—no, no, it isn't Mother, it's something else, a dark shadow. I want to yell at it to get lost, then I see that it's Grandmother, she's running alongside me in her long fluttering black coat; she looks at me, panting, she yells at me: Enough of this hysteria! Didn't she tell me not to believe what I heard in school? Now we are going home. Then she reaches out to me, claps my back, and says that I'm it, and there she is already in front of me, the black wings of her coat flapping behind her, as if her feet weren't even touching the ground, as if she were gliding above the asphalt; she's already at the corner, she's already vanished at the end of the street. I run after her, I feel the skin between my shoulder blades tingling where she clapped me on the back.

I run; my legs carry me, I feel that even if I wanted to, I wouldn't be able to stop. I run in the direction Grandmother went; her trace is in front of me, an invisible black path from which I must not diverge.

I'm standing in front of Grandmother's house; the black gate is open. I enter, I close the door behind me. I can hardly catch my breath, every part of my body aches.

When I go into the kitchen, Grandmother is already there. She's not wearing a coat, and she's just placed the kneading board on the table; as she sees me, she smiles at me.

My hair is disheveled; I'm panting and sweating, there are stabbing pains in my sides. Grandmother goes to the credenza, opens it, and takes out a brown blanket; she says that it's camel-hair, it's the warmest blanket in the entire house. She steps over to me, drapes it over my shoulders, and says that she uses it for ironing and that all the warmth from fifty years of ironing is in this blanket, and if I wrap myself up in it well, not only will I not get pneumonia, I won't even get a cold. She can't even imagine what I was thinking, running off into the great wide world without a coat, I could have been a little smarter than that, then she gestures and says that my mother was just the same.

The blanket is warm and soft; I wrap it around myself. I feel the warmth seeping out of it, making me shudder; my teeth clatter so much I can't even speak, I can't even grab the edge of the blanket to pull it around myself more tightly. Grandmother pushes a chair behind me, and she tells me to sit down. Everything will be better in a moment; the shivering will stop in a moment.

I look at Grandmother, and I ask: Is it true what they say about Grandfather? That he was an informer, and that's why he killed himself?

Grandmother's eyes flash for a moment; she claps her hand down on the kneading board, and she says, very angrily: Their father's cock, how the hell could he have been an informer when his whole life he detested the Communists, he was sent to a reeducation camp for five years by the Danube Canal—well, there he really did want to kill himself, but they didn't let him die, even though he tried to cut his own veins with the edge of a shovel.

She falls silent, leaning with her two arms onto the kneading board as if she is focusing on the vortex-like pattern of the veins in the wood; the sleeves of her black sweater are rolled up to her elbows, and as I look at her, I see that starting from her left wrist, her skin is crisscrossed with white scars.

She shakes her head, takes the cover off the flour tin, grabs a fistful of flour, sprinkles it onto the board, smooths it out, and covers the board with flour. She looks at it for a long time and then she speaks; she says: No. Grandfather was not an informer, and it's not even true that he killed himself, no. The truth is that they killed him. They hung him with the leather strap of his camera at the very end of everything, when it was finally over, at the very last moment, so they could desecrate his memory and his life, so they could smear their own filth on him. No, my grandfather did not kill himself. Ever since he came back from the internment camp, all he wanted to do was to survive what had happened to him.

Her hand moves; she's drawing a line in the flour. She looks at it for a little bit, then wipes it away. She speaks; she says: He did not survive. She draws a line in the flour, then she wipes that away too. He did not survive, she says again.

6

IT'S NIGHTTIME, I'M LYING IN my bed and I can't fall asleep. Grandmother is also lying down, perhaps she's asleep; I heard her turn off her reading lamp and shift over to one side. I think of Mother and Father, I think of the day I saw them for the last time. I can't recall their faces, neither Mother's nor Father's— I try to envision them, but in vain. I can't see them in my mind's eye, I see only blurred, murky blotches, as if I were looking at them through fogged glass; this isn't possible, I can't allow myself to forget them. I close my eyes, I think of them as hard as I can, and it doesn't help.

I recall the photograph that I hid away. I want to see it.

I get up very slowly; the moon is shining through the window, providing enough light. I feel my way out of the bedroom to the hall, open the door to the bathroom, turn on the light, but I don't go in; I press down loudly on the handle, making sure that the door remains open just a crack. A strip of light is cast into the kitchen, right up to the larder door. It's something like a bridge. I quickly walk along it, the door to the larder doesn't creak as I open it, and I go inside. I take the suitcase from underneath the shelf, pull the small bag out of it, and stuff it underneath my nightgown. I return to the bathroom, sit down on the toilet with my nightgown on, and press the small bag to myself. I reach in and I take out the photograph, pull it out, look at the date written on the back in Mother's handwriting. I turn the photograph over—there they are. I look at their faces for a long time. I close my eyes, and I think of their faces—now I can see them—and open my eyes; I look at the photograph, and once again I make sure I can see them with my eyes closed. This is how I learned the words when Mother was trying to teach me French.

I'm not going to put the picture back in the suitcase. I slide it back into the bag. I go back into the room, and I place it underneath my pillow. As I move my head, I can feel it there, below my head, even through the pillow I hear it rustling softly.

I dream that Mother and Father never died. I know I'm just dreaming, that it isn't true, but at the same time I know that they're alive. They didn't die, there was no car accident at all, and they didn't flee abroad either; they're at home, everything is just as it used to be, they're at home and they're working; Father is in the living room and he's painting, Mother is in the bedroom sewing together colorful leather patches that will become ladies' handbags. Everything is just like it used to be, only I'm not there; all that's missing from my childhood bedroom, from my writing desk, from my textbooks and my exercise books, from my lesson, is me.

I'm not at home, I'm somewhere else, with this strange old lady who stole me and who lied about being my grandmother. I never should have believed her, this whole thing is my fault; if I hadn't believed her, then everything would be fine, everything would be like it used to be, and it's all up to me—if I can somehow get home, if I can somehow find our home in our old city, our old neighborhood, our old block, our old apartment, then everything will be just like it used to be.

I'm going already, I'm in the hallway, I'm walking along the

striped carpet, I'm going and going and going, but the carpet
never ends, the hallway never ends; the faster I go, the longer
it gets, I know that I'm never going to get up to the front door.
Father waits for me in vain, and Mother waits for me in vain,
never again will all three of us be together. I think of the photograph, I think of the photograph and Mother's silk scarf with
the wedding rings, I think of the jasmine scent of the scarf, and
there it is in my hands. I press it to my nose, I breathe in the
scent, I hold it before my face, and with it there I run all the way
down the hall, and I'm finally at the front door, finally I can go
outside.

It's dark outside in the courtyard; the wind is shaking the
branches of the walnut tree. I don't head for the doors leading
out of the courtyard; instead I go to the walnut tree. I stand in
front of its trunk, I look up, across its black branches, up at the
black sky; I touch the trunk of the tree, and I already know what
I must do. I take the two wedding rings out of the corner of the
scarf, pull Father's ring onto my right thumb and Mother's onto
my left, and in that way I climb up the walnut tree. I climb all
the way up the trunk, I climb up the thick branches to the very
highest point of the crown of the tree. And now I'm standing
on the slender branches, they sway and bend beneath my feet; I
won't fall down, I know what I need to do. With my two hands
I take the two opposite corners of the scarf, hold it to the wind;
the scarf is suddenly pulled up, whoosh, it carries me up to the
sky, it flings me across the darkness, below everything is black.
I fly above water and I fly above forests, I fly above mountains,
then I'm flying above our old city, everything below me is dark
like when the power is cut, but still I know I'm there, I sense it
from the smell of the wind.

I'll be home in a moment now. I'm going to land on the balcony, just as I believed, when I was a little girl, that the angel
alighted there with the Christmas tree and all the presents in
its hands. I fly above the blocks of apartment buildings; this is

our street, Independence Boulevard, it's as if no one lived here, every window is black, and I think that I won't be able to find our balcony, then suddenly in one of the windows I see a light, blinking yellow. I recognize it, it's the light from our kerosene lamp, it always stood on the kitchen table right between the clock with the phosphorescent dial and the box of matches so that even in the greatest darkness, it could be lit quickly; the light vibrates, then nearly goes out, and I know why, it's because the wick on the lamp isn't good, it gets sooty. If the electricity was out, I did my homework sitting next to the kerosene lamp, and neither Father nor Mother would be working; they would both sit down at the table and chat, as they will be doing now, they'll be sitting there, and once again I'll be sitting there with them, I'll finish my homework, then we'll drink tea and eat potatoes roasted in the oven, then we'll play rummy and I'll win.

The scarf carries me along, flings me above the balcony; I only have to wish it, and there I am, and already I am lowering myself down. I balance on the iron banister; yes, it's our balcony, I recognize it, there in the corner are Father's old plaster molds for his statues, covered with plastic.

The door to the balcony is cracked open; in a second I'll go in, and then I'll be in the living room, which in fact is Father's studio. I want everything to be exactly as it used to be, for there to be the same smells of paint, oil, turpentine, for the floor to be covered with newspapers and brushes placed in empty mason jars and tin cans, rags covered in paint, and empty wine and beer and brandy bottles, and there should be Father's canvases nailed up on the walls, every single one of his black pictures, even the ones that scared me, and the ones that I loved — everything should be exactly as it was before.

I step across the threshold. Yes, there is the smell of paints, of varnish, but it isn't the same, it's not the same at all. Suddenly there's light, a sharp, painful white light is blazing. I know what happened, the electricity just came on again, and the old light fixture isn't there on the ceiling, just a bare light bulb hangs down; the walls are white, and the floor has been freshly sanded, freshly varnished.

There's no one here, and there won't be anyone here; I want to wake up, I don't want to see the empty apartment, I don't want to see how not even the slightest trace of our old life remains.

I hear sounds coming from the kitchen; something is rattling. I don't know what it could be, it's like bird's wings fluttering; my legs are already carrying me there, I want to see what it is. The kitchen isn't empty; our credenza is there, the table is there, I recognize the tablecloth, and Grandmother is sitting at the table playing solitaire; the cards slap against the waxy oilcloth. As I walk into the room, she looks up at me, puts the cards back in the pack, and says, Time to wake up.

I wake up to an aching back; my shoulders, my arms, my wrists, and my fingers are aching too. Mother's scarf is really there in my hands, I squeeze it tightly. As I raise it to my face, I can faintly smell Mother's jasmine perfume. The rings are still there, knotted into the corners; I grab the knot and I don't undo it. I fold the scarf together and quickly place it back in the bag, then beneath my pillow.

WHEN GRANDMOTHER ASKS ME WHAT I dreamed about, I say, Nothing. Grandmother says she heard as I was talking in my sleep. I said that I wanted to go home.

I bow my head. Softly, I say that I did not wish to hurt her feelings. Grandmother says there's no problem, she knows it's not easy for me.

She asks me to go over to her. She's sprinkling flour on the kneading board; she smooths it over; the flour covers the entire board. She tells me to watch her, to note what she's doing, and she draws a line with her index finger into the flour. She waits a minute, then she wipes it away. She says it's my turn now, I have to draw it.

I reach into the flour, and I trace my index finger over the board. The line looks like the one that Grandmother drew, but not exactly. Grandmother says it's not good; she wipes it away. Try again, she says. I look at the flour, and I imagine the imprint of Grandmother's finger beneath the flour; I allow my own finger to find it, let it run all along it. Grandmother nods, draws another line in the flour, and the lines cross over each other to create a gnarled lightning bolt that I see for only a moment. Grandmother wipes it away immediately. Now it's my turn, I have to draw it again. My fingers can't find the trace. Grandmother asks me what the problem is, am I blind, didn't I see what she did? I answer that I'm not blind. I saw it, but I forgot it. Grandmother says it was a moment ago, I couldn't have forgotten it. She says I should think—I should remember. I look at the flour; I think of her movements, how her arm moved, her wrist, her hand, her finger. I reach into the flour in the same way, and I move my arm in the same way, and then the lightning bolt emerges from beneath my finger. Well, you see, says Grandmother. You did remember after all. She wipes it away, and now she's drawing not just straight lines but circles, spirals, patterns weaving into each other, birds, fish, cats, flowers, a large tree, flames. She wipes all of them away, and then I copy all of them.

She says I'm doing well. But now comes the hard part. She draws a face in the flour; I recognize it. It's the face of Grandfather. Grandmother wipes it away, tells me to draw it. I try, but I can't get it; the nose isn't in the right place, the mouth isn't in the right place, the eyes are too far apart. Grandmother wipes it away, and she says try again, she's not going to draw it again. Once again I try, once again it doesn't work out.

Grandmother says, Try again. I try, but already while moving my hand, I know it's not going to work. I don't finish the drawing, I don't even wait for her to wipe it away, I wipe it away myself. I look at the white flour; my hand moves, I press my finger down, press it down hard into the board so I can feel the fiber of the smooth wood beneath my fingertip. I want my finger to hurt, I want my nail to leave an imprint in the wood so that what is drawn by my finger will be scratched into the wood forever and can never be wiped away; this will not be a flame now, it will not be a flower or a lightning bolt, not a face that I know only from a photograph; it will not be the face of Grandfather, because I never really saw him—no, this will be something else. The board scrapes beneath my nail, small clouds of flour dust swirl up white around my fingers, and I draw the face of Father in the flour; he looks angry, but I know he's not angry at me, he's angry at the others, he loves me. I know that behind the anger there is a smile; I know I could also scratch that into the flour, but I don't, I just watch, and next to Father I scratch Mother's face as well; not only my finger is hurting, but my entire arm, my back, and my legs are aching; I'm pressing down on my finger so hard that every part of my body is hurting; Mother's face is sad, but I know that it's not because of me, I know that behind her sadness there is joy somewhere; I look at them, and they look back at me.

Grandmother says that I've understood the most important thing, or I always knew what it was. Pain helps us to remember, but in such a way that we not only remember the part that hurts, but everything, because we must remember everything, because there is only that—what we remember—because what we forget is no more, it disappears from the past, it vanishes from the world.

She gives the board a nudge; her ring strikes against the wooden edge along the lower edge of the table, causing a wave to run all along the flour; the faces disappear, the flour is once again smooth.

Grandmother says I should know that it's easy to forget. It's possible that I believe I will never forget anything, that I will always remember everything, but it won't be like that. Even the most important things can be forgotten, the best things and the worst things, the greatest of pains and the greatest of joys —everything, everything.

She looks into my eyes, and she says that forgetting is like a curse, a curse that sits on everyone's back, on my back and on hers, only it sits much more heavily on hers. Once when she was still young, she felt such a horrific sorrow that she nearly died from it, and she forgot everything, everything that had happened to her up till then, and it was Grandfather who taught her how to remember again, and I should know, she says, that one morning after Grandfather's death, she woke up and realized that it had happened to her again, once again she had forgotten everything, not only the old things but the new ones as well—everything.

YOU KNOW ONLY THAT YOU'VE forgotten everything. Not just the little things, like where you put the sugar bowl or the thimble, which you used to forget sometimes anyway— you have forgotten everything, absolutely everything, you have woken up and you know nothing, nothing at all, not even your own name, not even who you are, not even where you are; you sit up in the bed, look at the small light next to the top of the bed, the bottom part of it is made from cast iron, and it's as if you are seeing it for the first time; you reach out and you touch it and you're amazed at how smooth it is, how hard, how cold; you're amazed that you can pick it up and put it back down again. You sit up in bed, you pick up the light, you pick it up and you put it down, you pick it up and you put it down, you don't know what this thing is, you don't know that it's a light, you don't know that it has a switch, don't know that it can be turned on; your head is empty, everything has been wiped away by sorrow and by forgetting, you don't know what happened to you; you don't even know that you're standing up now, that you're going toward the door, that you're placing your hand on the doorknob and turning it, that you're going into the kitchen. It doesn't matter, what matters is only that at one point you are standing by the round table in front of the kneading board, last night you left the dough to rise for doughnuts, all night you let the dough rise, and you wanted to bake the doughnuts today at dawn, but you don't remember that at all, you don't even know what the leavening board, covered with an apron, is, you don't know what the kneading board is, nor do you know what flour is; you just reach into it, and you let it flow between your fingers, once, twice, then many times over; you stand there caressing the smooth flour, and you have no idea what you're doing, you don't know and it's possible that you don't even want to know; the flour slowly grows warm from your touch, you just stand there running your fingers over it. Then somehow your hand begins to move in a different way; your index finger taps on the board, it draws a line in the flour, and this line makes you think of another line, and the second line makes you think of a third line, and then suddenly you know that this is flour, and you know that the kneading board is a kneading board, you know that your fingers are your fingers, you know that your hand is your hand, because until this point you hadn't known any of this, because in fact you hadn't known anything at all, but then from those three lines everything begins to slowly come back to you, at first your name, then where you are, and then the other things come back too: the joys, the sorrows, the grief—your entire life.

GRANDMOTHER IS QUIET; SHE REACHES into the flour, she lets it flow between her fingers. She says that then she took out the letter that she had received two days previously from the court of guardians; on it was my name and my date of birth, as well as the address of the orphanage; she read it over a hundred

```
                    1000 ?
              Seattle Wa 88
```

ee Computer Number: 1

ee Computer Number:	1
Cashier:	ID #1
Transaction Number:	71
Entered:	03/04/2021 09:07
Exited:	03/04/2021 18:04
Ticket #18448	Dispenser #5

                    Damaged Ticket

Rate:	Area 1
Parking Fee:	**$16.00**
5.00 Special Event (1)	-$9.00
Total Fee:	**$7.00**
Cash:	$7.00

Above amount includes the following tax(es):

Sales Tax	10.10%	$0.58
Parking Tax	12.50%	$0.71

                Thank you for choosing
                Ampco System Parking
                  Have a nice day

times, then on that very day she sat down on a train and came to get me and brought me home.

I've only just come, and she would really like it if I could stay, but if I want to leave, she understands. She knows that I tried, and she knows it didn't work out. If I grab a fistful of flour now and throw it behind my back over my shoulder as I exit the kitchen, then I'll be able to leave, the road will take me to the train station, and I'll be able to find the train that will take me back to the institute.

She is silent; she presses the palms of both her hands into the flour, then raises them: there on the board are the imprints of her two hands, the lines of her palms are visible, the vortex of wrinkles on the tips of her fingers, they become entangled with the veining on the board's surface. She sighs once, not a deep sigh, and it makes the flour swirl up just a little bit, and she says that she's known for a long time that everything can be forgotten, everything will be forgotten, and that a morning will come when, for the third time in her life, she will forget everything, and then in vain will she try to draw something back into the flour, nothing will be there, only zigzagging lines. And that day will be the day of her death.

7

IT'S TIME FOR GYM CLASS, and in the dressing room there are two empty hooks; I choose one of them and hang my gym bag on it, take my tracksuit and my gym shoes out of the bag. It's Mother's old tracksuit, the same exact one that the athletes wore for the Olympics; she gave it to me when I was chosen for the school relay-race team. It fits perfectly, except that since December I've been wearing it inside out so the old embroidered national insignia doesn't show. I pull my school clothes over my head, I'm standing there in my undies and stockings, when Krisztina comes over and says that the spot I picked is too close to hers, because I'm right next to her; I should move farther away and take my things as well. I have to sit next to her in the classroom, she can't do anything about that, but here everyone can choose her spot, so I should go somewhere else, not next to her.

I look at her face, pale with anger; my ankle still hurts where she kicked it on the first day. I pick my tracksuit pants up from the bench, and I say that I too can choose a spot, she should leave me alone, I will get changed where I want. Krisztina says fine, but not right next to her. She rips the tracksuit pants out of my hand and throws them onto the floor; she also grabs my jacket from the hook and throws that onto the floor as well, hissing for me to get lost because if I don't, she'll do to me what she just did to my things. In your dreams, I say. I lean down, pick up the pants and the jacket from the floor, and hang them back up on the hook. Krisztina wants to pull them down again, but I shove her aside before she can. She reels but doesn't fall down; I know she's going to come after me, and there she is next to me, she grabs my ponytail, pulls my hair. I grab a fistful of her hair and pull it as hard as I can; she kicks me, and I kick her, she pulls hard on my hair, and I pull on her hair, but her hair isn't in a braid, so it must be hurting her more; I feel the strands of hair snapping off in my hands. I yell that if she doesn't leave me alone, I'm going to rip all her hair out. And I pull even harder, and she pulls on my ponytail, my entire scalp is burning.

Olgi runs in, crying out that Szálki is coming; she looks at me, comes over, and tells us to stop because if Szálki catches us, she'll punish the entire class, and everyone will get a slap on the wrist. Krisztina keeps on pulling my hair; I keep on pulling on hers. Olgi says: Stop already, did you hear? She doesn't want to spend the entire class running on the dirt track. Olgi shoves me; I look at her, see that the hair on her arms is trembling; she gives us both a really hard shove, we almost fall down. Krisztina looks at Olgi, and she says, Fat sow, you can't even run. Olgi just turns away and shrugs her shoulders.

I put my T-shirt on quickly, then pull off my stockings; next I have to put on the sweatpants. I'm standing on one leg, about to push my other leg into the pants, when Krisztina grabs them out of my hand. The sweatpants turn halfway inside out, revealing the old insignia. Krisztina asks, What's this? and she dances backward, dangling the sweatpants in front of me. I yell at her that it's none of her business. I jump toward her, clutching at the sweatpants, but Krisztina steps back and to the side, throws them above my head. I jump up, but I can only reach the sweatpants with the tips of my fingers, I can't grab them; the sweatpants are thrown against the lamp chain hanging down from the vaulted ceiling, half wrapping around it; they begin to slide down and then stay hanging from the tin-plated lamp-shade. The old embroidered insignia, with its mountains, ears of wheat, and oil-rig towers, is hanging right beneath the light fixture. It's high up; I leap up to grab it, but I can't reach that far. I try once more, stretching my hand toward the light fixture as I jump, but I know I shouldn't even bother, I won't be able to reach it. I will have to ask one of the other girls to boost me up.

I hear a sharp whistling sound; everyone snaps to attention. I've just landed after my jump; I'm standing there in my undies, my arms extended, beneath the light fixture. Szálki, the gym teacher, is standing in the doorway of the dressing room; she just finished supervising morning gym practice after leading the singing of the national anthem in the courtyard. From close up she looks even taller and sterner; her hair is pulled into a bun at the top of her head. She's wearing a tracksuit; she looks at me and spits the silver whistle out of her mouth. She steps into the dressing room, and in her left hand is a long reed cane; she whooshes it through the air once and asks, What kind of madhouse is this?

I stand at attention beneath the light fixture. I want to say my name, I want to say, Reporting, Teacher, that I threw my sweatpants up onto the light fixture by mistake, but I find I cannot speak. Szálki looks me up and down; the wrinkles deepen around her eyes, and her nose is wrinkled too, between her eyes. She asks if I'm the new girl. I still can't speak, so I only nod; my thighs are prickling from shame, I would like to cover myself, I know that I'm wearing my old undies with the heart pattern, the ones with the frayed hem. I feel everyone looking at me and the threads hanging down from the sides of my undies.

Szálki slowly raises the reed cane, extends it toward the

light, reaches my sweatpants, hooks them with the reed cane precisely where the old insignia is; she pulls them down from the light fixture and holds them in front of me. She asks who threw them onto the light. I say, Reporting, Teacher, that it was me. I was chasing away a wasp with my sweatpants, but they flew out of my hands and somehow got stuck up there.

Szálki looks at the embroidery, and she asks, A wasp, at this time of year? My face begins to burn; I can't speak.

Szálki swings the cane again, and the sweatpants are in her hand; she grabs the insignia and begins to tear it off. It's sewn on quite strongly, I'm thinking that she won't be able to rip it off, but her nails are sharp, and the stitches loosen. Szálki says I should be ashamed, how could I dare to bring this filth here; well, is that why so many died, so that she has to look at this now? I should know, better than anyone else, that the bodies of those killed when the soldiers fired into the crowd haven't been found to this very day because those miscreants disappeared the corpses and buried them somewhere, and no one knows where. I should know because that sanctimonious hypocritical grandfather of mine had something to do with it too — but of course, his corpse never disappeared, of course his corpse was buried in a proper and respectable way. She's almost scowling at me as she pulls on the insignia, the threads ripping apart one after the other; finally the whole thing is torn away, and Szálki tosses the sweatpants at me. I grab them. Get dressed, she says.

She looks at the others and asks: Who threw the sweatpants up there? Come forward. Nobody moves. That's fine, Szálki says, then the cane will speak. Everyone hold out your right palm.

The girls slowly raise their palms, but Krisztina steps forward, standing at attention in front of Szálki, and she says: Reporting, Teacher, it was me, I am the only one who deserves punishment.

Szálki says she should be ashamed of herself, and she strikes the cane on Krisztina's wrist; Krisztina holds out her wrist, and

Szálki hits her three times; there are red stripes where the cane struck her. Krisztina bites her lip, but she doesn't cry, and her eyes don't water.

Szálki turns to me. I know that I'm next; I hold out my palm. The reed cane whistles as it strikes down; I look at my hand, I see the trace, on my ring finger, where Grandmother pricked it with the hairpin; the shadow of the cane slides past the pinprick. Szálki strikes my palm; I don't feel anything other than the force of the blow pushing my hand down. She raises the cane again, she strikes me again, then a third time and even a fourth time; the scarlet stripes cross each other on my skin, it looks like the footprint of a large bird, as if a large black bird with legs of fire had perched on my palm, and as Szálki raises the cane again, I imagine that I'm throwing the bird into the air, its wings make a whooshing sound, it's very close to my face as it flies away; it circles once around the light fixture, then it flies out the small window to the side of the vaulted ceiling.

I look at my palm. I know that the marks of the cane will swell up into small wheals, they will be raised on my skin. And it will hurt, I can already feel it.

Szálki doesn't hit me again. She thrusts the cane underneath her armpit, then places the torn-off insignia in my hand. She says we can go out nicely now and flush it down the toilet. She wants to see me doing it.

The toilet smells like urine. I throw the insignia into the toilet, push down on the handle; the water, gurgling, takes it down; just a few threads remain. I want to tell Szálki that I'm not a Communist, neither was Mother or Father — I kept the insignia only because I do not have many things that belonged to Mother, and this was hers, but I know that she would never understand. The toilet bowl is filled; I push down on the handle again, and the water takes away the last golden-yellow thread. Good, she says. I deserved the raps of the cane, but she shouldn't have cursed me because of my grandfather, because people can't help who their ancestors are.

IT'S COLD IN THE YARD; we have to stand at attention. I find my place, I'm third in line. Szálki stands in front of us; the weekly monitor steps forward out of the line and says, Reporting, Teacher. Szálki nods, and then she says, Basketball.

When we came outside, I saw where the basketball nets were. I'm ready to head over there, but the others don't move. I'm looking at Szálki, and I see that she is rubbing the whistle that hangs from her neck between her fingers. No one is allowed to break the line until she whistles.

She doesn't whistle, but she says, The new girl should step out. I take a step forward, stand at attention. Szálki says: Krisztina too. Krisztina takes a step forward, and the gym teacher says the two of us will stay behind, the other girls will go to the basketball court. She flicks her whistle once; it flies up to her mouth and spins around there, and already she's blowing on it, a sharp, long whistle. The girls start running off in a trot, and we stay behind with the teacher.

Szálki then says that we both know that with her, there's no lack of discipline, no fighting, no disparities — with her there is only order and discipline. We should be grateful to her, because she's teaching us what that means; we should be grateful to her because she's helping to bring us up, but instead, we're angry at her. Even now, she can see in her eyes that we're angry, but that's no problem, because she's going to help us get rid of this feeling. As she speaks, she gestures for us to come with her. She leads us to the long-jump pit at the end of the dirt track, opens the lid of a crate filled with sand, takes out two sacks, throws one to Krisztina and the other to me.

She tells us to fill up the sacks with the sand from the crate. Whoever finishes first gets the advantage of half a turn. Start now, she says.

Krisztina jumps up immediately; she hangs the mouth of the sack from one of the corners of the crate and begins to shovel the sand into the sack with both hands.

I go to the other side of the chest, open my sack, and see that it has black letters printed on it spelling out the word *sugar*, which is struck through with a blue line; below that the word *sand* has been written, but that has been struck out with red wax crayon, and in big slanting letters, it says *anger*.

The sand is cold and clammy; the marks from the cane immediately began to ache as soon as I start reaching into it with my hands. I place my two hands in the crate next to each other; with fingers extended I dig my hands into the sand, and I transfer it to the sack; if I don't curve my palm inward, it doesn't hurt so much. The sack fills up quickly; it's an old sugar sack and not too big, because at one point it was cut in two, then tacked back together with thin copper wire; now its shape is like a long sausage.

Krisztina is quicker than me; she puts her sack in front of Szálki. Szálki picks it up, nods, gives her a piece of wire, and tells her to tie it up. Krisztina winds the wire around the mouth of the sack; in the meantime mine also becomes full, it's good and heavy, perhaps weighing as much as five kilos.

Szálki picks up mine and hands me a piece of wire as well. She waits for me to tie up the opening of the sack, then she gestures for us both to pick up our sacks. Krisztina hoists hers onto her shoulders, and I pick up mine and place it across my neck, so that it's touching both of my shoulders; I hold it steady with my bent arms.

Szálki draws a line with her cane in the sand of the long-jump pit; the line perpendicularly divides the pit in two. She tells us that the sand in the pit is much the worse for wear after the winter, it's time to freshen it up a bit. We're going to help her with that. Our task is to run to the end of the dirt track with our sacks of sand and then back again, good and hard, to loosen up the sand. When we get back, we have to dump all the sand in the pit, then we go again. And this will rid us of our anger. And whoever loses has to ask the other for forgiveness. On her knees. Szálki smiles; she motions toward the dirt track with her cane—the left side is mine, and Krisztina is on the right.

She swishes the air with her cane; Krisztina starts to run. I look at the track; the surface is damp, there are two large puddles reflecting the gray sky.

Krisztina runs leaning forward; I wait for her to get to the end of the track. As she turns, I hear the cane swishing in the air behind my back.

I start running. The sack isn't sitting properly on my shoulders, it keeps sliding back and forth; after a few steps I can feel the weight on my spine, especially lower down, near my waist. I look at the moist dirt on the track, my shoes loudly pounding; the sack of sand slips forward. I need to carry it differently somehow.

Krisztina is already heading back; we pass each other in the middle of the track. Before Krisztina reaches me, she slips the sack off her back, grabs it with both hands, swings it toward me as she's running; she wants to hit me in the head with it. I notice her movement late, I almost can't lean away from it. I hunch forward and I just miss the sack swinging toward me; the weight of my own sack pulls me forward and I nearly fall on my stomach.

I can't stop, and I can't run after Krisztina; I keep on running. I wait for Szálki to blow her whistle or start yelling at us, but nothing happens.

By the time I get back to the pit, Krisztina has already spilled out her sand and she's starting to fill up her sack again.

My legs are trembling as I lower my sack; I untie the wire, I

begin to pour the damp sand into the pit. It empties out. I walk
over to the chest, I fill up my sack; in the meantime Krisztina
has already finished filling hers; she hauls the sack up on her
shoulders, and before she starts running again, she looks at me.
I know what she's thinking, she's thinking that when the bell
rings I'm going to have to kneel in front of her.

I dig my hands into the sand, grab fistfuls of it, throw it
into the sack; the palms of my hand are aching again, but I don't
care, I scoop the sand into the sack just as quickly as I can, and
all the while I'm thinking that I don't want to lose, I don't want
to have to kneel, I don't want to and I'm not going to, no and no.

The sack fills up; I tie it, I swing it back onto my shoulders,
I begin to run. Krisztina tries to hit me with her sack again, I
lean away, think of the sand, of the many grains of sand in the
sack on my shoulder; the sand shakes with every single step, it's
pressing me down.

I look at the track, at my shoes, as my feet rise and then
bang down again, damp specks of dirt flying out from underneath the soles of my feet; the sack of sand is heavy. I'm slowing
down, this is only the second round, and I'm already slowing
down. I can't slow down. I look ahead to the end of the track;
now the sand is not pushing me down but shoving me forward,
every single grain of sand is pushing me with every single step
so that I'll be faster, so that I can catch up with Krisztina and
leave her behind.

Mother once told me that true running is like falling hor-
izontally; the weight does not pull us down but pushes us forward, and the body does not resist but merely follows, and whoever runs like this will be faster than the wind — unconquerable.

I'm no longer counting the rounds, I'm not thinking about
time, I'm only thinking about what I have to do: fill up the sack,
run, lean away from Krisztina's blows, turn around, pour, fill,
run.

I'm going to catch up with Krisztina. I'm going to catch up with her and leave her behind; I'm going to win.

I'm not feeling cold anymore; the air feels warmer and warmer, almost scalding as I inhale, it nearly burns my mouth, my throat, and my lungs, it heats up my entire body, I'm sweating, I feel the sweat pouring down my back, down toward my bottom. I'm thinking about the grains of sand, how they too are getting warmer, they too are heating up, the grains of sand are pouring out through the sack's stitches, but the wind created by my running won't let them fall, it snatches them up and whirls them around, whirls them all around me. I'm running in a cloud of sand, everything around me is murky, I cannot stop, I am a sand tempest.

Krisztina is behind me now, I don't know when I left her behind; panting, she runs after me, I don't look back, and still I know that I'm leaving her farther and farther behind, after the turn I see that I am nearly half a length in front of her; she doesn't try to hit me now when we pass each other.

I get back to the pit, untie the mouth of the sack, pour out the fresh grains of sand on my pile. Hissing, the sand pours out of the sack; I hold it up high, I hold it up and the grains of sand just keep pouring out and pouring out, my pile of sand is getting bigger and bigger, I can see that it's already bigger than Krisztina's, but the sand still comes pouring out of the sack. I hold it up higher and higher, my arms are trembling, my shoulders and my back are aching, but I don't put it down.

In the meantime, Krisztina has come back; she stands next to me, unties her sack so she can pour the sand onto her pile of sand, I know that hers will be bigger, I'm going to lose. Now only a very thin line of sand dribbles out of my sack, there won't be time for another round, I'm going to lose.

I put down my sack, and in that very moment the bell rings. Szálki's there already, standing next to the chest, the cane in her hand; she reaches it out and taps Krisztina on the wrist just as she's about to start pouring the sand onto her pile. Krisztina throws her sack onto the ground.

Szálki looks at the piles of sand — mine is bigger. She points at Krisztina with her cane, touches the zipper at the top of her tracksuit jacket, slowly pulls the cane's tip down along the metal eyes, then she steps to one side, raps Krisztina on the thighs from behind.

Krisztina steps forward, into the sand; she turns to me and kneels down. Her face is completely white as she says to please forgive her. Her voice is very subdued, but she looks at me, she looks straight into my eyes.

I tell her that I forgive her. Now the entire class is standing next to the long-jump pit; everyone's looking at us.

Szálki says she'll only believe it if she sees us embrace.

Krisztina gets up, takes a step toward me, holds out her arms. She embraces me, and I embrace her too; she squeezes me tightly, and I hold her tightly too; I feel how wildly her heart is beating, much faster than mine. Her hair smells like smoke, it prickles my nose.

Szálki says we can go.

Krisztina and I let go of each other, we head off to the dressing room, she doesn't look at me, nor I at her.

Szálki calls after me. She says my name and says that one afternoon she's going to bring me over to the long-distance trainer so he can take a look at how I run. Maybe he'll even put me on the team. She'll tell me when to go.

Krisztina doesn't talk to me all day; in math class my eraser rolls over to her side of the desk. She picks it up with two fingers and gives it back to me. I thank her, and she nods.

At home, when I take the sweatsuit out of my gym bag in order to air it out, I feel that it's heavier than usual. The two upper arms are tied together, and above the knot, the material is bulging out thickly. As I reach over and grab it, the sand rustles beneath my hands. I untie the knot, and the sand pours out in a yellow pile onto the floor of the room. I shake it out all onto the floor, then I squat down next to it and press my hands into it. I think of the smell of Krisztina's hair.

The sand is drier, and the grains are smaller than the school sand; it's silky and warm, yet it makes my hands hurt.

I quickly head to the kitchen, get the broom and dustpan, sweep it up; I don't want Grandmother to see it.

There's a lot of sand; the dustpan is almost full.

I carry it out with both hands, out to the courtyard, I don't want a single grain of sand to fall.

I go to the flower bed, stand next to it; with one hand I put the dustpan behind my back, then, as quickly as I can, I begin to run around the flower bed.

I stop running only after I've circled it for the third time, when the dustpan is empty.

8

AFTER THE LAST BELL I head home with the other girls; we walk alongside each other through the main square, but when I turn off onto the yellow-paved path next to the Castle Barracks, no one walks with me.

In front of the Castle Barracks, there is a man selling chestnuts; he cuts into the tops of the shells with his pocketknife; already on the small stove a bunch of them are roasting. They're roasting very nicely, beginning to open a bit, and inside, the chestnuts are the exact same shade of yellow as the paving bricks.

They smell really good. I pass by him, and I think of Father, how much he loved chestnuts; we always got some if we saw a chestnut seller, and then I realize that I must still have some money left from what Grandmother gave me. I'm thinking of how good it would be to fill the pockets of my coats with piping-hot chestnuts. I think of how they always burned my fingers when I tried to peel off the shell, and Father always said that I had to hold them really tight and squeeze them so they would crack open; this way they'd warm up the palms of my hands, and the skin of the chestnuts wouldn't burn my fingertips so much.

I'm already about ten steps past the chestnut seller, but I can't bear it, so I go back. I stand next to the small black iron stove, I say hello, and I ask: How much are the chestnuts?

The chestnut seller asks me how is it possible that I don't know; am I new here? Everyone knows how much his chestnuts cost. He shakes a string hanging down from the stove; on the string there are tin cups of varying sizes dangling, a number etched into each one. I'm sorry, I say, I didn't know, and I point at a cup in the middle that has the number 5 on it.

The chestnut seller lifts up the cover of a large iron pot at the edge of the stove; in it are the roasted chestnuts. He dips the tin cup into the chestnuts, it clatters, he pours it into a bag, and hands it to me.

The chestnuts are scalding hot; I can hardly bear to hold the bag in my hands. I reach into my pocket for the money. I can't find it, though. I know it was there, but it isn't there now, but it must be there; I scrape at the lining of my pocket, it's not in there—then I think I must have put it in my other pocket, so I look in my other pocket, and it's not there either. As I shift the scalding bag of chestnuts from one hand to the other, I already know that it won't be there; somehow I lost the money, I couldn't have lost it, but still, it isn't there.

I speak very quietly, and I say, I'm sorry, I can't find my money, so I'll give you back the chestnuts. The chestnut seller smiles at me: Take it as a gift, he says. I'm such a pretty little girl, I deserve it, he says, and then he winks at me.

My face is as burning now as the chestnuts. I shake my head, I want to say thank you, but I can't, then I hear somebody speaking behind me, saying that if the chestnuts are free, then he'd like a cupful.

It's Iván, the boy who grabbed my hand in the hallway. He wasn't there a moment ago; he must have arrived while I was looking for my money.

The smile melts away from the chestnut seller's face. He

says, Get lost, little Iván, after what you did last time, there are
no chestnuts here for you.

Fine, says Iván. He shrugs his shoulder so that his schoolbag slides off, but before it falls to the ground, he grabs it by
the strap and he swings it; the bag flies toward the iron stove,
misses the pot with the chestnuts in it but knocks down the
mug holding the change next to the pot. The chestnut seller
tries to grab the mug, but it's too late, the tin cup falls onto
the paved bricks with a great clatter—it doesn't fall over but
remains standing on its base.

The man curses, crouches down to pick it up, while the bag
swings back toward Iván. He grabs it by the handle; I see the
mouth of the bag is half open. Iván quickly reaches in, takes
something white out of the bag, something like a broken piece
of chalk, and throws it into the largest tin cup, then he raises the
cup to his face, spits into it, lifts up the iron lid of the chestnut
pot, places the tin cup inside, right onto the roasted chestnuts,
then slams the lid back down, and the whole thing happens so
quickly that by the time the chestnut seller has straightened up
again with his tin mug holding the change, Iván's bag is back
on his shoulder.

He grabs my wrist and says, Run, orphan girl, and he's already running along the walkway, I'm running next to him; he's
still holding my wrist, pulling me along with him.

We're almost up at the top of the square, by the row of
trees, where the paved brick comes to an end and there's regular asphalt. I don't go any farther; I try to snatch my hand
away, stand still. Iván lets go of my wrist, but he too comes to
a stop; he turns back toward the chestnut seller, and he says:
Watch this, orphan girl! He points toward the chestnut seller,
and in that moment a piercing thundering sound is heard, the
cover of the iron pot suddenly lifts up; it flies up to the sky like
a rocket, and beneath it the yellow chestnuts come showering
down everywhere.

The chestnut seller is thrown back on his bum from the detonation; his fur cap falls off his head, the chestnuts are clattering down all around him on the paved bricks.

Iván begins to guffaw; he yells out, Well, fuck that, I nearly sent the whole kit and caboodle flying up to the sky!

The chestnut seller gathers up a few chestnuts from the ground, and he's still sitting there when he throws them at us, missing, but he's laughing as well as he calls out: Your father's going to shoot you to the moon, Iván, that's how hard he's going to kick you in the ass when I tell him about this.

Iván looks at me, says, That was a good prank, eh? He jerks his schoolbag onto his shoulders and starts running down the walkway.

I stand there looking at him as his bag slips off his shoulder from running. He looks back at me and calls out: Bye, orphan girl, see you tomorrow.

I'm still holding the bag with the chestnuts in my hand. I put it in my coat pocket, then I reach into it, grab one, squeeze it hard. I turn it around; the skin of the chestnut breaks off in pieces, falling off between my fingers.

I keep on walking home, squeezing the scalding-hot chestnut. I will eat it in a moment, it will be hot and sweet.

It really is very good. The skin comes off easily; I eat one after the other, and at the same time I think about how the lid of the pot flew upward, how the chestnut seller fell down, and how Iván cackled so loudly.

By time I get to the gate of Grandmother's house, there are only three chestnuts left. Before I go inside, I turn out all the broken chestnut shells from my pocket, and I watch as the wind grabs them and sweeps them all away from the sidewalk.

I give the last three chestnuts to Grandmother, telling her that I saved them for her: Eat them, they're sweet, I say.

Grandmother gives two of them back, says one will be enough for her, but it's good that I reminded her, because she has some chestnuts put away in the larder, for roasting; one of these evenings we'll cut them up, roast them, and eat them.

I go out into the garden with my last two chestnuts, holding one in each hand, and I walk in a circle around the flower bed and the walnut tree, the chestnuts warming my hands for a long time.

IT'S EVENING, I'M EATING ROASTED chestnuts with Grandmother. We cut open the tops of them together; I use Grandfather's staghorn-handle pocketknife, Grandmother uses her own pocketknife with a fish-shaped handle. The chestnuts are scalding; they burn my fingers. Grandmother says we can't wait, they're good if they're so scalding that we can hardly breathe while eating them.

As we chew, she suddenly asks me if it's true that my mother never, really never, told me anything about her? Not even one word, ever? Nothing about her, nothing about Grandfather?

My hand, with the chestnut in it, stops moving; it's hard for me to speak, but still I say, No.

It's as if the wrinkles on Grandmother's face just deepened; she nods.

I ask what the argument was about. As soon as I say the words, I know I shouldn't have.

Grandmother doesn't answer. She squeezes a chestnut between three of her fingers, it crackles loudly, she slowly turns it around in her palm; the shell falls in tiny pieces onto the oilcloth. She says that I have a right to know, and I will know —later on, of course, she will tell me, but not now, let's not ruin these lovely chestnuts, she says. I should know, however, that she truly loved my mother.

The shell has completely peeled off the chestnut, there's only a smudge-size piece still stuck at the bottom. Grandmother tries to pick it off with her nail; it doesn't come off. She asks me to tell her something about my parents. Something about our old life.

I nod, and I stick my hand beneath the small pillow being used to keep the chestnuts warm; my hand rummages around in the warmth. I remember how one autumn we went biking up the mountain path, going as far as the brook, because Father wanted to teach us fly-fishing, and we were already at the top of the mountain when it turned out that Father had forgotten to put the box of fly lures in his kit bag; by mistake he'd brought a bunch of tempera paints instead, and when we got off our bikes, and we realized this, I saw on Mother's face that she was afraid that Father would start shouting, and it's true that Father's eyes flashed in such a way that I too was certain for a moment that he was going to yell, but instead he just swallowed once, then said, Well, if we can't catch any fish, then let's make some for ourselves, and we climbed over onto a big long rock sticking out from the brook, and we drew the eyes and the fins and the scales of the fish onto the rock with the tempera paint; I remember this. I take a chestnut from the plate, start to peel it, and suddenly I smell the smoky, slightly acidic scent of Father's woolen sweater, and I know I won't be able to tell this story. I can't, and I don't want to.

I look at Grandmother, shake my head, and I want to say, Please don't be angry, I can't tell you about this, but I can't even say that.

Grandmother swallows a morsel of chestnut, and she says that she can tell from the way I was looking at the chestnut that something did come to me, that I was thinking about something, something that I saw very clearly in my mind's eye, but just then I was not able to say it. She asks me if that's how it was.

I nod.

Grandmother says that sometimes it's easier to be silent. But I should know that the more I am silent, the harder silence will become, and so will talking.

She pokes at the pieces of chestnut shell scattered on the tablecloth with her ring finger; the tip of her nail slowly circles around the oilcloth, leaving long spiraling tracks.

She says that she too was once quiet for a very long time, so long that she was almost not able to speak again. She reaches out and touches the closed pocketknife with the staghorn handle; she doesn't open it, merely runs her fingers along its dented white surface. She says that Grandfather helped her then. He helped her by telling his own story, his own stories.

The most painful stories can only be told in such a way that the people who hear them feel like the events happened to them —as if it were their own story. Grandfather knew this, and so he told her his own story, and she too told Grandfather what she could. She will tell me as well—all in good time.

She flicks the knife, and it begins to spin around on the oilcloth. Grandmother looks at it; she is quiet. I too look at it; the golden copper tip of the knife scatters light into my eyes.

When the knife stops spinning, Grandmother says I should believe her when she says that she understands my mother. No matter how much it hurts, she understands that she chose silence. She reaches toward the plate of chestnuts, takes one, cracks it; it bursts out of its skin. She rolls it toward me; the chestnut stops in front of me. Grandmother says I should put it in my mouth quickly, before it cools off.

I chew on the chestnut, and its taste is sweet. I think of Mother's hands. With her finger dipped in the green tempera, she drew scales like half-moons on the damp stone.

Grandmother begins to speak.

THE LITTLE GIRL DOESN'T KNOW who you are, and she doesn't want to know, she wants you to leave her alone, you can tell right away from how she looks at you. You don't even care about that; what interests you is that gesture with which she brushes her hair back, the way her hand runs all along her hair, trembling nervously; you know this movement very well, it's there in your own hand too, wild and angry. You look at her; her eyes are different, set more deeply, darker, but her chin is just as pointy, her nose has that same curve, and she holds her head in exactly the same way, you can't believe it's true, but now you know who you are looking at: it is the daughter of your daughter, there is no doubt. You think of your daughter, of when you saw her for the last time; you didn't know you were seeing her for the last time. Now that you look at this other girl, as she steps into the office, and she comes over, and she stands in front of you, only now you know. You look down, in your hands the coffee cup is empty; you have to squeeze the coffee cup very tight so it won't tremble, you can't keep holding it so hard, it's going to crack; Let it break, you think. The girl utters a greeting, not to you but to the headmistress, her voice is as if you were hearing your own daughter's voice, your own voice. The coffee cup trembles on the saucer, the coffee grounds in it are too black, you cannot bear this blackness; you reach over and with a sudden movement you turn the cup over, placing its mouth down on the saucer, and with the other hand you grab it, you have to grab onto it, the name of the manufacturer is there on the porcelain in blue letters. You look at the girl again; she's adjusting her skirt, pulling it down; you look at her hand, it's different, that must be her father's hand, there's a bruise on one knee, now it's beginning to spread; she sits down next to you in the other armchair. There she is beside you, completely close to you, and she doesn't know who you are. The bitterness of the coffee rises in your throat; you swallow it back, you make a decision. You are going to speak.

9

OLGI SAYS SHE'S GOING TO take me somewhere and show me something I've never seen before. As we walk, I tell her about the prank Iván played on the chestnut seller. Olgi laughs. She says that Iván's father is a big person in the city, he's the head of the local National Salvation Front, so Iván thinks he can do whatever he wants.

We walk through a door into an inner courtyard, then from there into another one, then into a third one, where there is a wire fence. Olgi knows where the fence can be lifted; she picks it up, holds it, I slip through, then I hold it up while she slips through the fence.

We are now in front of two large iron doors. No matter how often I ask Olgi where she's taking me, she doesn't answer, all she says is that I won't regret coming. We are about to see something we've never seen before. She places the palm of her hand on the iron door painted blue and beats out a rhythm on it, not haphazardly, but with three long and two short beats; she repeats this many times.

Nothing happens. I want to suggest that we leave, or if she doesn't want to, then I'll go, but suddenly I hear the clattering sound of a bolt being pulled on the other side of the door, then a second and a third. The door slowly opens a crack; a fat face with a quivering double chin, a stubby nose, and angry eyes looks out at me. A voice, harsh and raspy, says, What are you doing here? But before I can speak, the face changes, a smile spreads across it: Olgika, is that you? So you came, welcome, come in quickly, before they see you here.

Olga greets her—I kiss your hand, Godmother—then she says that she's brought a friend. The fat woman nods. Fine, Olgika, that's fine. She opens the door, leads us into a fluorescent-lit space smelling like mint tea, then she quickly closes the door behind us, pushes the bolts back in place one after the other, and at the same time murmurs in a raspy voice: Oh, but it's so good that you came, my little Olgika, you have to see this, the opening will be on Monday, but everything's prepared already, everything's in place, she says, all while leading us through a labyrinth of crates and boxes piled up on top of one another.

The air is full of strange scents: mint, laundry detergent, plastic, earth, fresh paint, all mixed up together—it's nauseating and cold. The fluorescent lights hiss and vibrate. I know that my head is going to start aching in a moment, as if we had already been winding in and out of these crates and boxes for a long time. From above, from the direction of the ceiling, there is a soft creaking sound, and I see that high above, meters above the crates and the boxes, there are huge puppets hanging down —paper birds with outspread wings, an owl-headed horse with red wings, a many-headed dragon, a violinist with a green head and a black coat, a sun, a moon, stars, clouds, a tractor, a cat wearing gardening pants and a miner's helmet.

I nudge Olgi to look up. She does and is so surprised that she bumps into one of the crates, which then makes a rattling sound. The fat woman looks up as well, and she croaks, Yes, these puppets are still here, and a few of the old stage decorations too, but don't worry about that, because this hasn't been a puppet theater for a long time, it's something much more fantastic now. The whole place has been transformed, the front hall, the theater, everything.

We come out from among the crates, walk alongside a wheelbarrow, then we reach another door. As the woman pushes open the wings of the door, there is soft music; I recognize it, "The Blue Danube," it's playing in some kind of extended electronic version. The woman says, Look at this, you've never seen anything like this before. She grabs our shoulders and pushes us through the door.

The sharp white light blinds me for a moment, then I look around, squinting. I see that Olgi and I are standing in the middle of a large department store. Everything is packed on gigantic shelves, the colored boxes nearly tumbling off; I see large, thick bars of chocolate, packs of chewing gum piled up in heaps, bags of candy, cake packages, canned goods, one-kilo tins of coffee, huge cases of laundry detergent, cigarette cartons, and there are ten, one hundred, one thousand varieties of each item, and fruit juices — orange, apple, lemon, grape — in enormous boxes.

I look at everything; I can't move. I hear Olgi snort next to me as if she has suddenly been hit in her solar plexus. I too sense that I can't catch my breath, I feel that all these items will collapse on me any moment now, they'll bury me, but at the same time I think about going over to one of the shelves, the first one I can reach, the closest one, grabbing a bag of candy, ripping it open, and snatching up its contents, not to eat but because I want to see if there's really candy inside, and if there really was candy inside, then I would rip open another one, and one after that, all of them, and I would unwrap all the chocolate bars and the chewing gum, everything, all the boxes, all the bags, even the ones filled with items I don't recognize, I would open up every single package and rip out the contents.

I imagine how all these things would flow between my

fingers, the colored wrapping papers ripping open, making crackling noises, the *snap-snap* of the cellophane tearing, and all the while I hear Olgi's godmother murmuring behind us, saying that this is a real supermarket, the very first one in the city. There's everything here, everything that exists under the sun, everything, but really everything, thirty different kinds of toothpaste, eight different kinds of butter, fifteen different kinds of cheese, sausages, salamis, hams, and so many types of soap that even if we used a different kind to wash our hands every day, it would still take at least two months before we had tried them all, and there is much more of each item, not just what's displayed on the shelves, but an infinite amount, transported here with trucks packed to the gills.

She talks about the jams, the toilet paper, the tinned fish, the chocolate creams; there is everything, and there will be everything, because from now on there will always be everything; she utters these words as if they are a prayer, as if she didn't even believe it herself, as if she were trying to persuade herself of something nonetheless true. In a hoarse, cracked voice, to the tune of "The Blue Danube," she sings of the milk in boxes and the vacuum-sealed coffee; before she could never have even imagined that such things exist; she sings of cocoa powder that already contains milk and sugar, you only need to add water and it's ready to drink; she chants how she thinks all this plenitude did not come into existence only recently, but that it always existed, even when we couldn't get any of it, even when the shops here were completely empty, and you could never get anything, people were ready to murder each other just for the one kind of plum preserves and tinned fish that you could get, she doesn't want to think about it, but she can't think of anything else, that's why she wanted us to come and see it for ourselves, because she has been among these shelves for almost two weeks now, she stacked them with her own hands, but never will she be able to grasp the entirety of it. Perhaps she's already too old for this, perhaps it's too late for her, because all she can think about is what it was like when there was nothing, when you had to steal and cheat and lie for a bit of cornmeal, and as she says this, suddenly she begins to sob; she sobs loudly, blubbering like a child, nearly choking on the tears, she says that she did it all for us, she did it only for us, so that we could have all of this, so that all of this would be ours.

She steps over to Olgi and embraces her; with her thick arms she squeezes Olgi into her. Olgi embraces her back, she's crying now too, tottering; they stagger in front of the shelves; there is a large bar of chocolate in the godmother's hands, she rips off the lilac-colored paper and the foil, breaks off large pieces and shoves them into Olgi's mouth—Eat, my little dove, eat, she blubbers—she too bites into the chocolate, I see half-eaten currants and hazelnuts in the chocolate, the marks of the godmother's teeth; they both eat the chocolate, clutching each other, tottering.

I turn my back to them, and I walk among the shelves; I'm standing in front of cans of pineapple preserves, there's also apricot, mandarin, and mango. I reach over and take one, let it drop, reach for another one, and I let that one drop as well. I think of the teacher with the red hair who took us girls into the city once, and we stood in front of a small shop, and for the first time I saw that the shelves were full of items, and the red-haired teacher pressed a fiver into every girl's hand, and she said we could buy whatever we wanted. I bought a package of big chocolate balls for four; I thought there'd also be chocolate on the inside, but when I bit into it, it turned out that on the inside there was sweet pink-colored cotton candy, it was sweeter than anything I'd ever eaten, so much so that my tongue and my entire mouth began to ache, and the candy was so dry that I could eat only one—now I feel the exact same sweetness in my throat, the exact same unbearable sweetness. I let the tin cans drop; I will take only one can of orange preserves. I think of the horse puppet with its owl head and its wings that I saw flying above the boxes, I want it to come for me, to put me on its back, to take me away from here. I open my arms wide, and I think that I'm not here; I run on the white tiled floor, among the rainbow-colored shelves, stocked full to the point of nausea.

10

SZÁLKI ACCOMPANIES ME ONLY AS far as the top of Calvary; from that point on I have to go by myself. She tells me to walk along the fence next to the cemetery, then go across the meadow, as far as the tree that was struck by lightning, and from there I'll be able to see the old riding school where Mr. Pali will be waiting for me; he's the long-distance trainer. There's no reason to be afraid of him, it's true that he's strict, but if he cares for someone, he behaves quite properly with them.

I walk along the cemetery; there are fist-sized pieces missing from the concrete wall, you can see the graves through the holes. These gravestones are different than the ones in the cemetery next to Grandmother's house; they're much older, and many more of them are broken.

The tree struck by lightning is very big and very black, much larger than Grandmother's walnut tree. As I walk next to it, I see that it looks as if it were made of pure coal, it also smells of charcoal; its bark is made of black fissures, I don't dare touch it.

The old riding school is a large empty brick building; you can tell that no horses have been inside it for a very long time.

I walk through, imagining the scent of hay, the knocking of the horses' hooves, their snorting.

I haven't even emerged from the building and I can already see the trainer. He's sitting on three plastic boxes stacked on top of each other; when he notices me, he pushes back the little green hunter's cap on his head and folds up the newspaper he'd been reading.

He waits until I get over to him, then he jumps down from the boxes, looks me up and down, and says, Well, now! His face is one big smile.

I say hello to him, and I begin to say that the gym teacher has sent me, that I was looking for Mr. Pali, when he interrupts me, saying that I've come to the right place, he knows all about me, and that's not the important part, what matters is what he's heard about my running; he didn't want to believe it could be true, but he can already tell from how I walk that I have what it takes to become a real long-distance runner. If I would be so kind, he says, he wants me to run a few circles here, without warming up, just around the old horse track, around the boxes.

I don't say anything but begin to run. It's not even a real path, just an irregular oval shape where the grass is a little more trodden down, but it's good for running, I let my legs take me away. The circle isn't too big, and I don't count the laps, I just run, I don't look at the trainer, but I can feel on my back that he's watching me.

Mr. Pali calls out for me to run a little faster; I pick up speed, then he calls out for me to go slower, so I slow down, and then once again he tells me to speed up.

I keep on running, either more quickly or more slowly, my coat hanging loosely down, then something begins to make a rustling sound; there are round stones beneath my shoes. I look to the side, and I see that Mr. Pali is throwing acorns, nuts, chestnuts, round pebbles, and pieces of branches from one of the boxes onto the path in front of me, and I know what he wants, he wants me to trip and fall, but I don't trip, and I don't fall; the tips of my shoes find the ground, I kick the pebbles away, send them flying on.

Good, says Mr. Pali, I can slow down and stop. He's almost smiling: Good, he says, I'm steady on my feet, no more tricks now, he's only curious to see if I have a good sense of direction, because this is the most important thing in long-distance running. He takes a small cane from one of the boxes; at each end there is a horseshoe attached with wire. He walks over to me and says, Watch this well. He raises his arm and hurls the cane. The cane with the two horseshoes spins through the air, making a whirring sound, then disappears among the trees. I know what's coming next; he's going to tell me to find it and bring it back. I note where it came crashing down among the trees, and I'm ready to set off, but Mr. Pali grabs my arm, and he says, Wait a moment, my little dove; he takes his hat off and presses it down onto my head. His hat is so big, it falls down as far as my nose, and it smells like pipe smoke. I can't see anything. Mr. Pali puts his two hands on my two shoulders, he grabs me and spins me around, around, and around. I hear as he croons, Peck-peck, jackdaw, little blind crow, where has the little boy gone? but in such a cheerful voice that I end up smiling. Mr. Pali turns me around and around and around, then he takes the hat off my head and puts it back on his own head, crying out, The little boy flew away, shoo! I squint; everything is spinning around me, the forest, the earth, the sky, the spinning makes me very dizzy, my legs won't take me where I want to go. As if the wind is blowing me around, I lurch this way and that. I think of the small cane with its horseshoes as it flew spinning through the air; I too am turning; I'm lurching as if I were drunk, but I want to run; this is laughable, and I laugh too; my laughter carries me forward, and I'm already among the trees, I almost crash into a trunk. I run around it, ducking underneath a branch, I step over another branch, and then I see it, there is the cane, the end of one horseshoe is sunk in the earth, the other end pointing obliquely toward the sky, I reach over and I pick it up; I start running back to Mr. Pali, and by the time I reach him, I am no longer dizzy. He takes the cane from my hand, turns it around in his fingers, the horseshoe ends of the cane describing silver circles in the air. He smiles, and he says, Good, very good. God created me for long-distance running, he says, the gym teacher had good eyes to see that straightaway.

He smiles at me and asks if I want to come to track practice.

I think of my mother and all the things that she used to tell me about running; I look at Mr. Pali's face as he smiles; I nod, and then I say: Yes, I want to.

He nods too, fine, then, he reaches into his pocket and pulls out a leather strap, at the end of which is a small black medal; he holds it in front of me, the top of the medal flies open, there is a fine white rod floating in transparent liquid. Mr. Pali shakes it, the rod moves, then it points in the same direction again. Mr. Pali asks me if I know what this is, I say: Yes, I know, it's a compass. He puts it in my hands, I take it, I shake it, I watch as the needle turns this way and that, then points in the same direction again. Mr. Pali says I should always wear it and always look at it, as much as I can. I will always know which way is north.

I hang the compass around my neck, tuck it beneath my coat.

Mr. Pali says I can go home now, he will let me know through the gym teacher when training will start. He smiles at me, then he says that I shouldn't think he's going to make any exceptions for me because of what happened with my poor grandfather. He's going to drive me like a horse, because otherwise he won't be able to look my grandfather in the face in the next world.

I touch the strap of the compass, wind it around my fingers;

I pull on it, and I ask why he isn't angry at my grandfather. So far, I've heard everyone saying only bad things, and the gym teacher cursed him.

Mr. Pali says that people are idiots, and they didn't know my grandfather well. He, however, knew him since he was twenty years old, from the time of the riding school; in the end he was his best friend, if you could put it that way. He was always an upright person, and my grandfather disappointed him in only one thing: he'd borrowed his old prewar military map—which depicted these mountains in more detail and more accurately than any other previous map—and my grandfather had the nerve to die without giving it back. It's impossible to get a map like that anywhere, because the Communists, who hated maps, deliberately misrepresented everything. If I see this map anywhere, I should give it back to him.

I ask Mr. Pali why my grandfather committed suicide.

He shakes his head, and he says that he would have put his own hand in a fire for my grandfather. He is one hundred percent certain he didn't kill himself. He was never an informer. The Securitate killed him—that was all.

I look at the ground. I tell him that everyone says something else.

Mr. Pali spins the cane with the horseshoe ends between his fingers. Of course everyone says something else, but I shouldn't care what these idiots are saying, as long as I know the truth.

I think of Father's face, that angry expression as he slammed the glass he just drank from down onto the table. There's no truth, I say, exactly the same way that Father would have said it.

Mr. Pali spits out a huge gob. Of course there is, how the hell could there not be? he says. The only people who say things like that are the ones who can't even see with their own eyes. My grandfather was a hero, he tells me; he got through the war, prisoner-of-war camp, forced labor, reeducation camp, and then he got through them wanting to turn him, a surgeon, into a street sweeper; my grandfather withstood everything, and he could even withstand those people who were maligning him in death today—but there is one thing he wouldn't be able to stand, and that is his own granddaughter talking rubbish about him.

He shakes his head angrily, and he says he doesn't want to hear any more of my doubts about my grandfather because for the love of God, he'll slap me. His face is red from anger; he's shouting now. The bullets were whizzing back and forth in the city, and then they commandeered the hospitals, and they even stole the corpses after they'd stolen everything else, because they're all filthy liars, and my grandfather was the only one who went over to them and told them to surrender, because he thought that those pieces of shit would have enough honor not to raise their hand to their old teacher.

I can be certain of my grandfather, he tells me. As certain as I am that north is north.

AS I WALK HOME I feel the leather strap of the compass around my neck with every step; it's unusual. I don't want to look at it now, only when I'm home, back at Grandmother's house, but I can hardly even hold out until the lower part of Calvary. I pull it out from under my coat, but I don't look at it; first I decide which way is north, and only then do I take a peek between my fingers at the compass needle. Now it's not spinning so much. It's not completely pointing in the direction I was thinking of, but almost. As I look at it, I notice that at the end of the needle there is a bird with a tiny little beak, its wings slung backward and its tail feathers spread out; it's something like a very elongated plunging bird. As I turn the compass around in my hand, the transparent liquid within magnifies its parts, and I see that it's as if every one of the bird's feathers were individually carved, and not only the feathers but the fibers intertwined with the feathers as well. I don't know what kind of a bird it is; I think it might be a falcon or some kind of eagle. I flick the glass of the compass, watch as the bird extends out in the liquid. I watch its beak, and very softly, I say to myself that north is north.

11

I GET CHANGED AT EXACTLY twelve noon. I take off my
skirt and I pull off my stockings in order to put on my house
clothes, and just as I'm stepping from the carpet onto the floor,
my stomach suddenly begins to hurt. It's hurting like it was this
morning during the long recess, only this time it's much worse.
I've never felt anything like this before. I can't move; I stand
barefoot on the floor, feel the pain drawing out. It hurts from
within, squeezing and tightening, sharply convulsing downward. I press my two palms onto my stomach, leaning forward;
I try to breathe, but the pain gets worse, squeezing and pulling.
I look at my toes, and I think that I'm going to sink into the
bench any moment now, up to my ankles, my knees, my waist,
my elbows. I look at the planks of wood of the bench, the veining of the trees, the lines, as they swirl around beneath the soles
of my feet.

The pain lessens somewhat, but then it increases again; I
feel dizzy, the bench is undulating. I look at the lines, how they
run black beneath the varnish; on one of the planks there is a
large black knot, the lines wind around it, avoiding it.

I move my leg; there's a sensation that the knot is not in the wood but in me, inside my stomach. I don't want to look, so I turn my head away and look at the red pillow with the rooster sitting on the woolen blanket, at the fringes around its red piping, I follow the threads as they wind around, and I think that by the time my gaze has circled the pillow, the pain will stop. I look at the fringes on the edge, wonder who embroidered it; it must have been Grandmother. I imagine how the embroidery needle moved across the linen as the yarn was pulled across and back, across and back again, I can almost hear the rustling sounds. When my eyes have gone around the entire edge of the pillow, I feel that my stomach no longer hurts. I move slowly; even then the pain doesn't come back. I begin to get dressed, and all the while I make sure not to look at the planks of the bench.

That evening, I'm in my nightshirt, turning down the blanket, when my stomach begins to hurt again, just as it did in the afternoon. I sit on the bed; it squeezes and pulls. I press my palms onto my stomach, bend down onto the pillow, bury my face in the cold damask. I breathe in the smell of starch; I don't want to notice the pain.

Outside it begins to rain, the wind blowing the drops against the window; they knock on the glass. I imagine the dark water as it flows down the darkened window, and I fall asleep thinking of the rain, thinking how it rains and rains, and it never stops.

GRANDMOTHER CATCHES ME AT DAWN when I'm attempting to wash out the sheet and my nightshirt. The nightshirt is bloody, but the sheet also bloody. I'm the one who got them bloody. I'm very ashamed. I rub it with the laundry soap in vain; in vain do I beat it against the edge of the bath, the bloodstain will not come out.

When Grandmother opens the door to the bathroom, I

want to hide the sheet from her, but there's nowhere to hide it. I put it behind my back, and the water drips down from the sheet onto bathroom tiles beneath my feet.

Grandmother comes over to me, reaches behind my back, and takes the sheet out of my hand. I'm afraid that she will start yelling; I'm afraid she will curse me.

She doesn't shout; she doesn't say anything; she simply takes the sheet over to the sink and squeezes out the water. The water drips down between her fingers into the sink. I look at her ruby ring, not at the water as it's sucked down the drain.

Now, no more water drips from the sheet. Grandmother shakes it out; tiny drops of water fly through the air. There is the stain in the middle. It's not such a deep crimson anymore, but it has become larger, something like a red bird with its wings spread out.

Grandmother looks at the stain, pinches it between two of her fingers, rubs it. She smiles.

She lets it go, shakes the sheet out once again, lifts it with two hands, and with her arms outspread, holds it up, raising it above her head; the sheet is hidden from me, the red stain is now in front of Grandmother's face. I hear as she sniffs it, and the wings of the red bird stir. I don't want to look over there, so I turn my head away, and I stare at the winding pattern on the floor tiles.

I hear Grandmother humming, singing something.

I can't understand the words, but even so I know what it's about, it's about a ruby-colored bird, a great crimson bird. Grandmother pulls hard on the sheet, and I hear the sheet rip with a ripping sound, the bird's wings fluttering; my hair quivers. I feel the wind of the wings on the skin of my head as the bird flies, fluttering around in the bathroom.

Grandmother tells me to look up. I look up, but I don't see the bird anywhere.

Grandmother shakes out the sheet; it's clean and white.

There's no trace of the stain anywhere. Grandmother folds it up, gives it to me, tells me to spread it out in the garden, and once it's completely dry, I should iron it and put it away—this will be the very first item in my trousseau.

AFTER BREAKFAST, GRANDMOTHER TELLS ME that she's proud of me for being a big girl already; she has something to give to me. She pulls out the highest drawer on her writing cabinet, rummages around in it for a long time, then takes out a black velvet pouch and puts it into my hand.

It's tiny; it just fits in my palm. As I undo the string that ties the opening, it makes a ringing sound. I reach inside; there is something round and hard in there, something like a thick coin. As I take it out of the sack, I see that it is a piece of wood polished to a luster, perhaps a section of disk cut from a thick tree; even through the varnish you can feel the furrows of the annular rings. Grandmother tells me not to look at the piece of wood, the important thing is the hairband.

That's when I notice that around the edge of the wooden disk there is a groove, and in that groove there is a thick black hairband, about half a finger's width, and on it are small metal spheres.

I take one and pull it; the hairband snaps away from the edge, making other metal balls ring; they are tiny sphere-shaped bells, but it seems each one has a different tone, and together they make a beautiful sound. I tauten the hairband with three fingers, shake my hand, and I listen to how it rings, and through the fissures cut into the tiny spheres I see that in each one, a colored glass ball the size of a peppercorn makes a cracking sound.

Grandmother says that this was Mother's favorite hairband, she wore it very often, and now I can wear it too.

I pull my braid across my shoulder, pull off the green rubber band that holds it at the end, and put the hairband in its place. I loop it around eight times, doubling it over so it will be good and tight.

As it tightens against my hair, it rings softly once, then, as I drop my braid onto my chest, it rings again, louder this time. The sphere-shaped bells now sound deeper than they did when they were in my hands, and it really is as if every one of the tiny bells rings slightly differently. I hear them all at once, and yet the sound of each one is distinct; the ringing sounds come apart and interweave with one another again, they weave together and come apart again, making me a little dizzy.

I clutch the side of the writing cabinet; the dizziness lasts for only a moment, passing as quickly as it came.

Grandmother smiles at me, says that it has been a long time since she heard those tiny bells, how beautiful they sound, it's easy to get lost in them. If I don't want them to ring with every step or every movement, then I can do what Mother did. She used to stuff some flax into the bells so they wouldn't ring; I should look in the pouch, there surely is some left in there.

I reach into the velvet pouch and at the very bottom my fingers do feel something soft. I pull it out and see thin rose-brown filaments woven together, flexible and soft.

I pick up the end of my braid and place a bit of the filament in one of the tiny bells, pushing it into the opening with the tip of the nail of my ring finger; it goes in very easily, and it muffles the sound of the tiny bell.

I pinch off another bit of flax, and one by one, I stuff the inside of every bell.

By the time I'm done, the hairband has grown completely silent.

Grandmother smiles again; she holds a mirror up in front of me, and she says I should look at how beautiful I am. The hairband suits me.

It's really quite beautiful; the bells gleam, the sunlight flashes into my eyes from the mirror.

Slowly I stuff the remaining bits of flax into the velvet pouch. I shake my braid once, and I listen to the silence.

WHEN GRANDMOTHER COMES HOME SHE puts a black shopping bag on the table in front of me. I look to see what she has brought. The bag is half filled with large gleaming oranges with waxy skins. I've never seen so many oranges at once. I reach into the bag, take out one, press the nail of my thumb into the skin; an oily orange smell emerges, and suddenly I think of the institute. I think of the day when the drunken Swede showed up.

It's afternoon, the sun is shining, all the girls are outside in the courtyard, we're playing in the snow, which has melted a bit; it's easy to make snowballs out of it because it sticks. The snow is almost as tall as the grass poking out of it. We've decided we're going to build a snow house, one that will be big enough for all the girls to fit inside; one after the other we push the large snowballs, building the snow walls. It's not too cold, but I'm freezing, I really don't feel like building the snow house, but I know that if I don't go along with Ramóna and Kinga, the two biggest girls—they were the ones who decided to build the snow house—then they will give me a wash, scrubbing my face till it's red with snowballs rolled until they're hard.

My wool gloves quickly become soaked through, so I roll my snowball nice and slow; it already reaches up to my waist, creaking beneath its own weight. I have to lean against it with my entire body to push it forward. Kinga notices that I'm faltering; she stands next to me, saying that I'm a good worker, this will be the biggest snowball, nobody else is going to roll one as big as mine, and I say yes, but what I really want is for her to leave me alone, the snowball will end up breaking from its own weight; but it doesn't break, it's just very hard to roll. Suddenly I see that the snow is not white but black between my two gloves. At first I don't understand, then I look down at the ground, and I see that we're standing right in the middle of where the bonfire was, we're rolling the snowballs across it, across one large strip where the ground became completely black from the ashes. Kinga yells at me: Look what you've done! I say it wasn't me, we did it together. Kinga screeches, That's not true, you're the one who did it! I shrug my shoulders, and I say, Fine, it was me, let's keep pushing the snowball; the ashes will disappear by the time we get to the wall, and you won't be able to see it. Kinga screams that I'm an idiot, this is impossible, everyone knows what the ashes are from, they're from the burned pictures of the Comrade General; if we build them into the house, the entire thing will be ruined. So then let's not build it, I say, I really couldn't care less, but Kinga keeps on screaming; the others gather around. I know what's going to happen, they will think she's right, and they're going to wash my face with the black snow. I bite my lip; I don't care what they do, I don't care what they want.

Then one of the girls points at the gates, yells that someone is coming, a car, a big car, and really, there's a large red car speeding in along the driveway, the snow and the gravel crunching beneath its tires. Somebody is yelling that they came for her, definitely they came for her; she begins to run toward the car, and all the girls begin to yell, they all run toward the car, I too start running toward the car, I know that they haven't come for me, no one can come for me, but still I run toward the car together with the others. The large red station wagon stops, its brakes squealing, then it reverses, turns across the driveway, but no one gets out; the car begins to tip, somebody screams

that it's going to flip over, somebody else yells that it's going
to hit us, but still we don't stop, and the car doesn't flip over; it
jerks back onto its wheels and comes to a stop.

The door opens; a man gets out, clutches the door. His entire body is trembling, his face as white as a wall.

We stand around him, looking at him.

The man lets go of the door, takes a step toward us; swaying, he says: My God, girls, have you lost your minds? What
would have happened if I'd hit you? Nearly all of you just got
killed, never do that again, do you hear, never again!

Nobody says a word, we just look at him, then Ramóna asks:
Who are you looking for, sir, whose father would you be? Who
have you come to pick up?

The man stands there, his forehead and his face covered in
sweat, still trembling, and he speaks only after a while, says that
isn't why he came.

Kinga then says that if he hasn't come for that, what is he
looking for here? He should leave—we'll call the headmistress.

The man starts walking toward the trunk of his car, saying that he didn't come to take anything away but to bring
something. He opens the trunk, leans in, and pulls out a large
cardboard box. He says that he too belongs here, we should
know that he was born here, and he had to leave here fifteen years ago; that filthy piece of trash chased him all the
way to Sweden so his heart would be chewed apart by those
maggots, and when he saw on television that they'd blown his
head apart, well, for the love of God, he could hardly believe
it, but then when he saw that it really was true, then, well,
he knew what he had to do. He went and packed his car up
with everything that he could get at home, so much that he
could hardly fit in the car himself, and another thing: he had
driven here for more than thirty-six hours straight without
closing his eyes once, never stopping, but now here he was,
and by the time he got to this point, he had given out every-

thing he'd brought, but then at the very last minute he found out that here, not far away from the city where he had been born, there was an orphanage, so he quickly came here so that he could help us in whatever way he could—help us orphans as well—so here it is, look, this is what he brought, eat up, they're oranges.

As he speaks he opens up the cover of the box and gestures toward us, and it really is filled with oranges. Each one is wrapped up in tissue paper. We look at the oranges; no one moves, then Ramóna steps over to the box, takes one out, takes off the paper and puts the tissue paper into her pocket; with her other hand she raises the orange to her mouth, bites into it, red juice sprinkles and drips down the corner of her mouth. Ramóna spits the skin into the snow, and she says: Very tasty. Inside, the orange is completely red; I've never seen anything like that. Ramóna jabs her fingers into the orange, breaking it in two, the red juice sprinkling everywhere; she rips out the segments from the inner skin.

And then everyone is biting and ripping and opening and eating; the oranges are very cold and very sweet, and as I swallow, I hear the man saying: Yes, girls, eat, because I brought these here out of the goodness of my heart, and as he says this, I'm thinking to myself that it's not really proper, eating like this in front of a stranger.

My face goes warm from the memory of this shame. I turn the half-peeled orange around in my hand. I give it to Grandmother, and I say that maybe she should peel it. The juice from the orange is stinging the sores on my fingers.

NEXT TO ONE OF THE trees on the walkway lies an enormous dog. I've never seen a dog so big, I don't know what breed of dog it is. Its leash is wrapped around the trunk of the tree; it lies there, waiting for its owner. As I walk past it, I see that it's a St. Bernard, but a very old one, its hair is almost completely white.

The dog begins to stir, then stands up. I tell the dog that I don't mean it any harm. I approach it, saying, Don't be afraid, dog, it's just me, but the dog grumbles, baring its teeth, and when I try to pet it, it opens its mouth and latches onto my thigh.

A boy appears next to the dog—he must be the owner—grabs its collar and shouts: What are you doing, Burkus, bad dog, let go immediately! Burkus doesn't let go, it continues to growl loudly and hold on to my thigh, I can feel the pressure of the dog's teeth through my skirt. I know that the dog could bite into my thigh if it wanted to, or rip out an enormous piece of my flesh, but no, it merely holds on to it.

Its saliva drips down between its teeth onto my skirt; its eyes are bloodshot. The large brown irises stare at me; I see my own face reflected within them. Its teeth squeeze my thigh harder and harder; the boy tries to pull the dog aside with the leash. The dog doesn't budge, and its growling only grows deeper.

I tell the boy to let go. My voice is deep and raspy. The boy lets the leash drop.

I look into the dog's eyes; in the corner of one eye there is a bit of yellow rheum that looks like a dried-out morsel of bread.

I speak to it again. I say to it: Good dog, clever dog. Everything's fine, I tell it, there's no problem.

I slowly lower the palm of my hand onto its head, between its two ears, where the broad white stripe that runs up from its nose comes to an end.

Its bristles are warm and soft; beneath my palm I can feel the curvature of its skull.

It's still grumbling, still squeezing my thigh with its teeth.

Once again I look into its eyes, into the exact center of its eyes, into the black mirror of its pupils, and I see myself reflected in them; I see my blouse, I see the hairband with its tiny bells around my braid, I see my face as I try to half smile, I see my own eyes, I see the fear in my eyes, I see that they are green, exactly like Mother's eyes, I see the black spots of my pupils, and I see as well that I'm afraid—the fear pours out of me like black smoke.

I sense that I'm trembling inside and that in a moment my entire body will begin to tremble. I don't want that. I don't want to be afraid. I want the dog to let go of me. And I remember what Grandmother once told me about animals.

I want the dog to listen to me. I want it to serve me. I press my palm hard down on its head, and then suddenly my nose is filled with the scent of acrid laundry soap and washing up; the colors disappear, I see my face from below, my eyes are not green but gray. I grumble, my teeth are hurting, everything hurts, but there's flesh in my mouth, flesh and bones, I want to bite it off, I'm not allowed to, but even so, I must, I can already sense the taste of it in my mouth. This is not permitted. I know that I'm not allowed to do this. I'm afraid; I open my mouth. I release the flesh.

My mouth is gaping; I close it. I come back to myself.

Burkus stands, his mouth wide open, his tongue hanging out; he's panting, his eyes turned upward, white; the palm of my hand is still on his head. I remove my hand. In the corner of his eye there is still that tiny piece of rheum, and with my thumb I wipe it away.

Burkus falls onto one side, his flanks moving quickly up and down.

My thigh is hurting; I grab it through my skirt. I turn away and, tottering, I start off for Grandmother's house. I hear as the owner calls out to his dog: Burkus, my little dog, what's wrong with you? But I don't look back, I don't want to know what happened; my thigh really hurts, I keep on walking.

12

THE WOODSHED IS SOMETHING LIKE a real house, with a tile roof and windows, but it's boarded up, and you can't see into it anywhere.

I'm outside in the garden a lot, and I don't pay much mind to the woodshed. Then one day, when I'm walking past it, it's as if I hear soft crying sounds coming from inside. I walk over to the door and I grab the handle, but I can open the door only a very narrow crack; the lock won't let me move it any farther. I try to look in through the crack, but I can't see anything. I call in: Is there a problem? No one answers, and now I don't hear the weeping sounds anymore. I let go of the handle, and I think that I certainly must have been imagining the crying, or else it was just a cat. Then I call out, Kitty, kitty, but nothing moves. I leave the woodshed and go back into the house.

I'm writing out my lesson when Grandmother enters the room. She asks me what I was looking for by the woodshed. I tell her that I didn't mean to do anything wrong, but I heard someone crying in there.

Grandmother tells me to come with her now.

We go out to the garden. We stand in front of the woodshed. Grandmother looks at me. For the last time, she says, she's telling me not to go near it. No matter what I hear—I should never go near the woodshed.

I say, Fine, I won't go near it. But I definitely heard a crying sound.

Grandmother says I was just imagining it.

Then she says that it would be better if, for safety's sake, we put a fence around the woodshed. She reaches into her pocket, takes out a small plastic bag, and tells me to hold out my hands, then she pours tiny white pebbles into my palms. They are smooth and not very heavy. Each one is carved into the shape of a tooth.

Grandmother takes one and tosses it on the ground. She tells me to throw one on the ground as well. I throw a tiny pebble in the shape of a tooth next to the one that Grandmother threw.

Good, Grandmother says, now let's go around the woodshed in a nice little circle, and with each step we will throw one of these small stones.

We set off, dropping the pebbles one after the other. And all the while I'm looking at the woodshed, and I'm watching it, just in case I hear something—but all is silent.

We circle back to the first pebble. Right at that point I run out of stones to toss.

Grandmother tells me to note this well: I must never step across the pebbles we have just thrown down. If I ever do, she will know.

Fine, I say, I won't step across them. Grandmother nods, and she tells me not to bother anymore with the woodshed.

ONCE AGAIN I'M OUTSIDE IN the garden, and again I hear the crying.

Now it's much louder. I'm certain it's the sound of crying. And I'm just as certain that it's coming from the woodshed.

I want to go over there, but when I try to step across the stones with one leg, the sole of my foot begins to hurt. A lot. As if it had been bitten by something.

I stand on one foot; drawing my breath in sharply, I pull my leg back. I pull off my tennis sneaker and my sock — on the sole of my foot there are tiny red teeth marks. I rub my sole with the palm of my hand, and it stops hurting. I put my sock and my shoe back on.

Once again I hear the crying.

I look up at the walnut tree; one of its branches extends out above the woodshed. I've climbed up it once already; a large section of bark is missing from its trunk, you have to use that as a step to grab onto the lowest branch.

I jump, grab the branch, and pull myself up.

I'm already up by the big fork in the tree, then I climb to the end of the branch, where I'm above the roof of the woodshed.

I look at the mossy roof tiles; I don't dare try to climb down them.

Once again I hear the sound of weeping. I take a deep breath and lower myself onto the roof.

Now the sound of crying is really loud.

I grab hold of one tile, dig my fingers underneath it, pull it to one side, then do the same with a second and third tile. The gap is wide enough, I can pass through it.

I climb in through the opening in the tiles.

I'm in the loft of the woodshed, and it's dusty. Beneath my legs is a thick layer of broken walnut shells; they make cracking sounds and prick my hands as I place them down. Crouching, I climb out next to a large suitcase; I move in the direction of the weeping. I come to a ladder, and I climb down. I'm afraid.

The weeping sound stops.

The woodshed is filled with odds and ends: I see a wheelbarrow, bicycle wheels, a large chest, gas canisters, earthen crockery, tied-up sacks. Next to one wall there is a stack of cut wood; above the wood on the wall there is a spade and above that a miner's helmet.

I turn all the way around to try to see where the crying might have come from. In the back, in front of the window, there is a small table, and next to the table is a cradle carved from wood.

I speak to it. I say, Everything is all right.

I walk over to the cradle. Inside it is a large doll made of rags. Its face is round, its two eyes are two buttons, its mouth is drawn with lipstick. It is smiling.

My heart is pounding. I pick up the doll, lift it from the cradle. It's heavy, but still, I can hold it. I embrace the doll, and I whisper: Shush, now, everything will be all right.

It feels good to hold the doll. It smells like talcum powder.

I hug the doll tightly, I rock it, I calm it down. I can sense that my heart is already not beating so loud.

My chest is tingling. I feel thirsty, and I realize that I'm much too big a girl to be playing with dolls, and yet still I don't put the doll back in the cradle; I hold it and I embrace it.

I squeeze it closely to myself, and suddenly I feel that something is piercing me.

Frightened, I put the doll back down. Once again, I hear the crying. Everything will be all right, I say. I undo the doll's dress, and I see that its body is made up of a large ball of yarn twisted into the shape of a number eight. The yarn is thick red wool, with two large knitting needles thrust crosswise into it.

Oh, you poor thing, I say, reaching down; I pull out both of the knitting needles.

I button up the doll's dress again, and I say everything's fine now, go to sleep. And I sing to myself: Rock-a-bye, baby, in the treetop . . .

Before I climb back up to the roof, I hide the two knitting needles behind a wooden plank in the loft.

I put the roof tiles back, and I brush the dust off my clothes.

I look up at the walnut tree—the sun is shining through the branches. I reach out, grab the branch, pull myself up. I begin to climb back toward the trunk of the tree along the branch. I look back at the roof of the woodshed—there's no trace at all that I was there.

As I climb down from the tree, once again I sing to myself: Rock-a-bye, baby, in the treetop . . . Otherwise there is silence, only the humming of the wind in the tree branches.

IN THE LARDER, IN A large opened suitcase, there are all the walnuts from last year, I can eat as many of them as I want. Their shells are paper-thin, and they're sweet inside. Grandmother says that there are no tastier nuts anywhere in the city. Grandmother tells me to eat them up, they'll make my bones good and strong, stronger than iron. I have to eat walnuts with apples and honey, it's good for both body and mind, a person can survive on this for days, for weeks, for months, with nothing else. I often get this for my afternoon snack as well, two pieces of bread with thinly sliced apple rounds between them, smeared with honey and sprinkled with walnuts.

One morning I'm out in the kitchen as Grandmother is preparing this for me, spreading honey on the bread, putting the slices of apple on it, then spreading honey on that and sprinkling walnuts onto the honey, and suddenly I notice that her hand is trembling; the pieces of walnut are falling next to the slice of bread, knocking against the plate like hailstones. I ask her what the problem is, but Grandmother shakes her head, saying it's nothing, something just crossed her mind. As she pinches up the pieces of walnut from the plate with her nails, the porcelain rings with a sharp, false note, making goose bumps rise on my arm.

Grandmother places the two pieces of bread together; as she places the sandwich on the tea cloth to wrap it up, a piece of walnut once again falls out, the honey glistening on it. Grandmother taps it with the tip of her ring finger; the piece of walnut clings to her skin. She raises it to her mouth, slowly nibbles it off her finger, then licks the rest of the honey from her skin.

IT'S BEEN REALLY WARM FOR two days. I sit down in the garden on the bench, trying to get some sun on my face. I lie down on the bench, and I think about how in the summer I'll sunbathe here. I turn onto my stomach, and on the ground, under the branch, there are lines of marching ants. They too have felt the warmth. They're carrying something. I reach down, place the palm of my hand in their path, and they climb across my hand. I turn my hand to the side, press the side of the palm of my hand into the ground, but it's too high for them, they can't climb across it; instead they go around and keep on marching. Once again I turn my hand; the ants climb into my palm, all across my fingers. The skin of my hand tingles; it tickles.

I sit up, hop down from the bench, squat, and look at the ants close up.

One of the ants is dragging a tiny filament. It gleams blue and black, I don't know what it could be. I hold my index finger out in front of the ant, let it climb onto my finger; the tiny thread that it is holding is something like an eyelash, but I know it can't be that. I blow the ant away from the tip of my finger.

I want to see where the ants are coming from. I press my hand onto the ground—it is almost lukewarm. I kneel down, and I begin to crawl backward along their path, trying to imagine what it would be like to be so small, but it's hard.

The ants' path leads to the flower bed, and as I arrive there, the smell of earth shoots up from beneath the bushes.

I crawl along farther; the ants' path goes around the flower bed, between the woodshed and the walnut tree, and out next to the four pine trees by the dried-out ferns. I don't like the ferns, but now I stand up and brush off my knees in order to walk between them.

And there, far in the back, at the base of the firewall with its chimneys, I come upon the ants' plunder. Beneath the wall, on the concrete edge, lies a jaybird, completely covered by ants. Its tail feathers are black and shiny. Its eye still glitters; inside it's black, circled with blue, the same colors as where the feathers of the wings take their root. I look at it.

Slowly, I reach over, touch one of its quill feathers, whisper, Jaybird, jaybird. The feather is pliable; it bends beneath my fingertip. I press down harder; the strands of the feather separate, trembling, and the tip of my finger touches the quill.

Jaybird, jaybird, I whisper again, and I pull out one of the rustling fern leaves, sweep the ants away from the bird's wing. I throw away the fern and stand up. Underneath the bushes, dug into the earth, I see Grandmother's gardening trowel. I walk over and pull it out.

I pull out the root of the fern; it comes out of the earth only after much effort, I have to pull it with both hands. Its roots are white, covered with soil, gnarled. I press down with the trowel where I pulled out the fern, digging a small hole. I take hold of the wings of the jaybird, drag it onto the spade; there are still many ants on it. And, like this, the bird covered with ants, I drop it down into the hole, sprinkle earth upon it, and I bury it with the ants. I pat the earth on top of it down with the trowel. The ants are running along the concrete edge as if they were tracing the impression of the bird's wings.

I go back into the kitchen, open up one of the upper cabinets. I take out the paper bag of sugar and I pour a large handful of sugar onto the trowel. I come out holding it with two hands; I don't want to spill it.

I avoid the ferns, walk straight back to the concrete edge. Already there are fewer ants.

I pour out the sugar for them at the base of the tree; I reach over and with my fingers I spread out the grains of sugar all along the concrete. The gray concrete is visible between the tiny white specks. I reach over, and with my index finger, I draw the form of a bird; I press my hand down upon it; I wipe it away.

I stand up and look at the ants, then I turn away. I do not wait for them to turn the trace left by my hand completely black.

IF I'M OUTSIDE, I LIKE to look at the firewall and its bricks, uncovered by plaster; it's best to look at them from farther away, and often I lean against the trunk of the walnut tree, and I look at the wall. Each one is brick-colored in a different way; there are ones that are pale pink, and there are ones that are so dark crimson they're almost black. The grains of the bricks are battered; the wall is covered with protrusions and dents; there are deep round holes all over it; here and there it's as if soot were seeping through the wall, and you can see the lines where the chimneys are. There, the bricks are darker, and the wall looks slightly swollen.

Many times I have imagined what it would be like to climb up that wall. I would look and see where the road leads. I would have to start off beside the chimney and from there go straight until about a third of the way up the wall, then to the side, then diagonally upward, right up to the roof, and there I would have to grab onto the tin edge, and I'd be able to pull myself up to the top of the firewall.

I stand and look at the bricks, then I walk over to the wall slowly. I stand at the foot of the wall, place my hand upon it, run my hand along one of the bigger cracks. I trace its line; it leads my hand to a hole; I press my hand down upon it. I imagine that it's a bullet hole, but if that is so, there have to be shattered black pieces of lead in its depths. I dig my fingers into the hole, scratching along the edges, but only brick dust flows between my fingers.

I stretch myself upward, examining the wall; I caress it, searching for a handhold. When I find one, I feel that all I would have to do is propel myself up from the ground, fasten myself to the wall, let my fingers work their way into the crevices, and my body would know the rest. My arms would pull me, my calves would thrust me upward, my toes would find the right toeholds, I would nestle into the wall; I would clamber up it quickly, like mercury.

I stand there, I lean against the wall. I tilt my head back so far that the back of my neck begins to ache, so far that I can see the heavens above the bricks and the blurred streaks of the plaster; I do not move, I just stand, and I keep looking.

13

MY MUSCLES ARE STRAINED FROM running. I'm standing
next to the walnut tree, doing my stretching exercises. With
one hand I lean against the tree, with the other I grab my ankle, and I pull it upward; I stretch it back, imagining that it's
the thick branch of a walnut tree. My other hand slides along
the tree trunk; I lean on it and stretch my back muscles in the
other direction. I try to think about running; Mr. Pali said that
running has to be there when you're stretching, and that when
you're running, you have to be stretching.

I crouch down, slowly extending one of my legs; now it's
not a branch but the root of a walnut tree, reaching out far. I
pull the leg back and switch legs; I extend my toes, trying to
imagine that my leg is lengthening and growing longer, when
I notice that something is moving in the grass. It looks like if a
tiny white pebble is rolling through the blades of grass.

Slowly, I pull my leg in; I step over to the pebble, and as
I crouch down, I already know what it is. It is a small tooth-
shaped pebble, one of the pebbles that Grandmother had me
throw on the ground when she wanted to fence off the woodshed. Sharp pain shoots between my toes; I look at the ground,

and I think it's not from the tooth-shaped stone but because I crouched down too quickly after stretching.

There are ants all around the pebble; they're carrying it, that's why it is moving. They surround it completely, weaving into one another, transporting the tiny stone, coiled around one another, moving toward the walnut tree.

Nausea slowly rises in my throat. But I'm not going to be afraid, I'm not going to be repulsed. I place my hand on the ground in the ants' path and I watch as they approach; they touch my skin and, scrambling, make their way upward; they climb up onto the palm of my hand. They push and pull and drag the tiny white stone across my skin, diagonally across the lines of my palm—the head line, I whisper, the heart line, I whisper—I think of Olgi and how she laughed when I wanted to look at her palm; she said that these were creases in the skin and nothing more, only there for us to know that no fate was written into them and never could be.

As the ants carry the stone, it turns in my palm, and I see that there's a crack in it. I raise my hand very close to my face, and I see that there's not just one crack but many. This is neither stone nor bone—it is merely a morsel of dried-out bread.

I reach over with my other hand, and with two fingers, I pick it up from among the ants; they stop, stretching out their antennae. I rub the tooth-shaped piece of bread between my index finger and thumb until it disintegrates into crumbs; I sprinkle them down to the ants, back into my palm. Then I think that I can sweep the whole thing onto the grass, but no, I wait until they carry down the last morsel; it tickles and makes me wants to laugh.

THE NEXT DAY AS I'M going to school, I see Olgi's mother coming toward me, and on her coat, above her heart, there is pinned a golden bird perched upon a small sprig of golden rain. Yes, it's a Little March, a special pin for the first of March. I think of the very first one I ever got; one morning Father took it out of his pocket when we were leaving the house for kindergarten, it was three tiny golden horseshoes tied together with a red thread; he crouched in front of me and pinned it onto my coat, and when I asked him what it was, he said that this was called a March pin, that girls always got them from their fathers and of course from boys who liked or had fallen in love with them.

Olgi's mother passes by me; I greet her, and she greets me back. I look at the golden bird, and I say how beautiful it is.

Of course, today is the first of March. I place my hand on my red quilted winter coat, above my heart, and I think that I shouldn't have come outside in this coat; instead I should have asked Grandmother to get me a nice spring coat, or I should have just stayed at home, I should have lied to Grandmother and said that I was ill or that my stomach was really hurting.

No one is going to pin anything on this wretched coat of mine.

I don't know if it's the custom here, but in my old school in the morning, we would hang our coats on the hangers, and on March 1, the boys, during recesses, would pin the March pins onto our coats, and we pretended we didn't notice, looking at our coats only when it was time to go home. But then we didn't look only at our own coats but at the other girls' coats as well, to see if they had gotten prettier pins or if they had gotten more pins, and whoever got the most would always show them off, saying look, look at all the pins she'd gotten. And the girl who didn't get even one would run home crying.

I never had to cry, because my coat never remained without a pin. I always got a new one from Father, and in addition to that, I always got a couple more — once I got a silver flower with a red stalk with a beautiful silver ribbon, and I loved it so much that every year I would pin it on my coat again.

I still had it last year, and I got other ones as well; I kept all of them in a small lacquered wooden box. Quite a few of them had accumulated over the years: flowers, birds, stars, bells, lucky horseshoes, silver pussy willows, little chicks. I don't know what happened to the box. I imagine that the flower pin might be on someone else's coat—but no, I would prefer not to know.

The coat racks are by the back wall in the classroom; I'm the first one to hang up my coat, on the very last hook, in the corner right next to the window. During recess, all the girls quickly go out to the courtyard, pretending not to even look at their coats, but they're all watching them from the corners of their eyes. I too glance over at mine, and I don't see anything, only the battered fabric on the back of it.

WHEN THE LAST BELLS RING in school, the girls stand up all at once and run to the coat racks—I stand up and walk over slowly. There won't be anything on my coat; everyone will see that there's nothing on it. I stand next to my coat, not even looking at the others; I hear how enthusiastic they are, showing each other their pins.

I've already realized that I hung up my coat in the worst possible place, because mine is the farthest away from the door. I will have to walk in front of everyone else, and everyone will see that there's nothing on my coat.

I don't even have to go over there, I don't even have to take my coat off the hook, I realize. I could go home without my coat —it's warm enough today, I could just leave the coat here—but everyone would see that as well, so there's really nothing else to do, I have to go over there, I have to pick up my coat, and if there's nothing pinned on it, I will still smile, and I will walk in front of the others as if I had received the most beautiful of March pins.

I'm standing in front of the coat rack. I take down my coat. It's not empty of pins—there is a great golden flower pinned to the chest, luminous and beautiful, as if the sun were shining from the middle of my coat. My face is burning up; I smile, and I look at the large golden flower.

It's not even a flower; it's a great yellow star. Its points are made out of golden paper, and in the middle is a yellow marble. This isn't like one of the March pins sold at the tobacco shop; somebody must have made this by hand, by hand and especially for me. Someone cut out the cardboard and smoothed the golden paper onto it with his nails, glued the marble to the middle, and all the while, he was thinking of me, thinking of my name, that he was in love with me.

My face is burning, and for a moment I think that I'm just imagining the whole thing. I reach over, and I touch one of the points on the star, then I touch the marble—no, I didn't imagine it, it's really there.

I take my coat, I take my bag, and I leave the classroom. The star shines on my coat, and as I step out of the school gates, the wind blows in my face with its scent of water; it feels very warm. I throw my schoolbag over my shoulder, I jump once, then I jump again, and I already know that I'm going to take the long way home, going toward the main square and then along the walkway, so that everyone can see what a wonderful March pin I got.

I STEP INTO THE KITCHEN. Grandmother is sitting at the table; she's playing solitaire.

I say hello. Grandmother just nods, looking at the cards. I put my bag on the small stool next to the door, and I'm just about to take off my coat when the sun shines into the kitchen through the window, right onto my March pin, and the marble in the middle is illuminated, filling the kitchen with the light.

Grandmother looks up, straight at my March pin. She opens her mouth but says nothing; her face turns completely white. She pushes back her chair, the chair tilts but doesn't fall to the ground, Grandmother is now standing in front of me; without a word, she grabs my coat, rips off the March pin—with a ripping sound, the cardboard is torn away from the safety pin.

The March pin is between her fingers; suddenly, wildly, she rips it in half, her nails sharply cutting into the golden paper; I hear it rip. I yell at Grandmother, What are you doing, it's mine, give it back!

Grandmother crumples up the pieces of the golden star, throws them onto the floor; she doesn't even look at me as she shouts: Are they not ashamed of themselves, these murderers? The heel of her slipper rises as she stamps down on the golden paper; next to the paper there is the yellow marble, the slipper once again rises, and the heel stamps down on the marble; it doesn't break, but white cracks begin to spread out from the middle. I know that if she stamps on it one more time, it will break into shards. I don't want it to break into pieces. I throw myself onto my knees; I place one hand on the marble and the pieces of golden paper, and with my other hand I push away Grandmother's ankle; the heel of her slipper almost stamps down on my hand but instead knocks against the floor. I yell at her that this is mine, what is she doing, I'm not giving it to her.

I stand up and I want to turn around, I want to run into the room or out into the courtyard, anywhere, just far away from here, but Grandmother grabs my hand.

I'm clasping the pieces of the March pin; I yell at her to let me go. Grandmother yells at me too, she screams, You stay here! I sense I can't move; Grandmother hisses at me to immediately give her that abomination, to give it over to her and tell her where I got it from. Her fingers, wrapped around my fingers, are strong; the palm of my hand is beginning to open; I'm thinking of my coat, I'm thinking about how I saw the star shining upon it, no, I'm not going to let go, no way.

I yell at her to let me go, I didn't do anything wrong, it's just a March pin, whoever I got it from has nothing to do with her, I found it on my coat, I don't know who pinned it there, but even if I knew I wouldn't say who it was, and Grandmother should be ashamed of herself for asking such things, and she should be ashamed for what she did, because if she knew what it was like to stand there in the classroom and look at the coats, waiting to see whether or not I got a March pin when everyone else already had one, then she wouldn't be doing this to me, because now look, she's ruined the whole thing, and now I know that what everyone said about her is true, she's crazy, insane, but even so she should be ashamed of herself.

My voice is trembling; I can feel in my throat that I'm about to cry; I don't want to, but a tear is already forming in the corner of my eye. I clench my teeth, I want the tear to stay there, I don't want Grandmother to see it, but the teardrop slowly rolls down my face.

Grandmother suddenly lets go of my hand, says, Don't cry, you poor thing. Her voice is completely soft, the cadence in it almost exactly like Mother's, the cadence and her voice as well, this is how Mother would always begin consoling me: Don't cry, you poor thing, she would say, and she would embrace me, and of course that made me cry harder, and Mother would then caress my head, my throat, and my back, and then I would nestle into her neck. I would hide my face in her hair, the locks of her hair would stick to my face, and I breathed in the scent of her hair, and I embraced her, and I heard as somewhere deep in her throat she began to croon and sing; it was always the same song, the lullaby she would sing to me when I was a little girl, about the bird with the yellow legs and blue wings who eternally waits, just eternally waits.

Grandmother does not embrace me; she clasps my shoulder, her touch is soft. I can hear that she's beginning to sing that song about the bird, singing so softly, singing, Oh, what a wondrous bird, what a wondrous bird; the palm of my hand opens up completely, the pieces of the March pin fall onto the kitchen table, at first just the pieces of paper, but then the cracked marble as well. Grandmother reaches over, but now her hand is moving differently, there's no anger in her movement, just sadness, a great sadness; the nail of her index finger reaches the golden paper, it begins to turn and push the pieces on the oilcloth covering the table, the pieces of the March pin are beside one another now; she turns them, pulls them apart again, puts them together again; the paper rustles, and slowly the star is reassembled. Grandmother leaves the cracked marble for last, and then I reach over there and together we push it into place, right in the middle of the March pin.

Grandmother sighs, and then she says that of course, I could not have known, how could I have known. To me, this is a March pin, but to her, it is a yellow star; to her, and certainly to the one who pinned it onto my coat—Grandmother has seen this kind of star before, and she never thought she would see it again.

I look at the torn paper, at the cracks, at the golden points of the star; my mouth is completely dry, and the song keeps fluttering in my head: Oh, what a wondrous bird, wondrous bird.

In the silence, Grandmother begins to speak. Her voice is dry; it sounds like tapping, it has to be listened to.

IT'S SPRING, THAT DAY WHEN *the yellow stars appear on the coats, suddenly they're just there, from one moment to the next. You're going along the tree-lined walkway, and you see your best friend, Bertuka, coming toward you, you recognize her beautiful dark cherry-red coat from far away; she designed it and sewed it herself from gorgeous shiny taffeta; it's really beautiful and very French, Bertuka saw the coat in a fashion magazine being modeled by an actress, and that's where she got the design from.*

Bertuka doesn't walk toward you as she usually does; somehow she is stumbling and leaning forward as she walks, and you can see from far away that there's a problem, her hair is undone, whereas usually she wears it coiled high into a severe topknot, and when she reaches you, it's as if she doesn't even notice you, she wants to go on, and all the while she's fumbling with her hair like someone who is disturbed. You stand next to her and you ask her: What's the matter, my Bertuka? and Bertuka doesn't even want to look at you, she doesn't want to stop, she only says: Nothing, and really it looks like she's about to go on; you grab her wrist, and once again you ask: What's the problem? And then Bertuka finally looks at you, and her face is completely gray, and she says: Everything, and at the same time she shrugs, and from the movement the locks of her hair rise and fly back behind her shoulders, and then you see the star on her chest, sewn nicely around the edge and made of yellow satin. When she sees you looking she wants to run away, but you're still holding her arm, and you yell at her to wait, you ask her to please not run away, and you try to pull her back toward you, and then Bertuka stops, and then you go sit down on a bench there at the edge of the tree-lined walkway where you both have sat so many times before, but this is different; now for a long time you both say nothing, and then Bertuka suddenly says that she thought that if she made it really beautiful, if she sewed it all around with a pretty embroidery stitch, then she would love it, then it wouldn't hurt so much that she had to sew it onto her coat, but she'd worked on it so hard in vain, because it still meant the same thing, and she didn't think that people would really look at her differently because of this ugly scrap of fabric, but they did look at her differently, she felt it as she walked along the main square, everyone was looking at her differently, you know, everyone, even your papa, who, even though he always said hello to her, didn't say hello to her this time; he just looked at her as he had never looked at her before, ever.

You want to tell her that it's not true, that she's just imagining it, that it was certainly only because of the brain hemorrhage, it's impossible that Papa wouldn't say hello to her, but you can't say the words; you just embrace her shoulders, and you tell her not to cry, but Bertuka isn't crying, she's just sitting there on the bench poking at one of the tips of the star. When she speaks again, her voice is so cold and smooth, like glass, and she says that she knows that they're going to take everyone away, her, Miklós, even Bátykó, and her parents too, her whole family, and all the relatives, and everyone else as well, they're going to take them away and destroy them, she heard what her parents were talking about at night, they said that it was only a frightening rumor, but it certainly wasn't just that, because even Bátykó said so, that's why he escaped here, that's why he came here from Poland, because what happened there already was going to happen here now, and nobody wanted to believe him, but she knew that he was telling the truth because she had dreamed of everything in advance.

Bertuka falls silent, and you want to say something again, you want to tell her not to be afraid, that there will be no problems, but you can't speak; you just sit there, next to your very best friend, and you're silent, and you see how Bertuka's fingers are fumbling with the star, how her nails are scratching at the beautiful thickly embroidered edges of the star; one thread begins to fray, then another one. Bertuka speaks again—it's complete idiocy, she knows that everything is ending, but what hurts her the most was that she had to baste the star onto the coat, and because this material was made of such thick fibers and such a fine weave, afterward the trace of the stitching would always remain.

GRANDMOTHER IS SILENT; IN MY mind I still hear the melody of the song, but only very softly now, it is mixed up with

Grandmother's words, as if what she was talking about had happened to me. I see the intertwined locks of hair as they rise and fly across Bertuka's shoulder, as the points of the star, embroidered with golden thread, peek out from under the locks of hair; I feel beneath my palm the cold caress of the coat sleeve; I see the traces of the needle in the cherry-colored fabric.

I want to ask her what happened afterward, but I can't speak. I think about how I walked all along the tree-lined path in my battered coat, and I look at the star, torn apart and reassembled on the oilcloth, and now even I cannot see it as a March pin. I reach over and sweep it beneath the table, and I hear as the marble knocks against the bulrush wall covering, then it falls onto the floor, rolling somewhere behind the flour bin.

Grandmother tells me that she wanted to walk home with Bertuka, but Bertuka wouldn't let her, she wanted to be by herself, she asked her to leave her alone. Grandmother got up and left, and then all the way down the path, she stopped and looked back, and she saw that Bertuka was still sitting on the bench; the sun shone down on her face, with her closed eyes, on her two hands clasped in front of her stomach, on her slowly swinging feet, and above her heart the star gleamed yellow.

Grandmother stares into space, her right hand resting on the table; her fingers move, drumming on the oilcloth, she doesn't even look down at them, a quick rap-rap-rap, like a fluttering heartbeat.

14

I'M WALKING HOME FROM SCHOOL, swinging my bag back and forth. On the hairband at the end of my braid, the silver bells, pearl-like, ring very softly. With every step they ring, and with every step they ring out a little differently. As I exited the school gates, I immediately picked out the flax because I wanted to hear the ringing. My braid hangs down in front, beneath my breasts; if I look down, I can see the little bells.

No one else is out on the walkway; on the bench next to the statue sits the photographer. Every afternoon he's out there on the bench, even when the weather is bad, even when it's raining, and he looks at the two-hundred-year-old linden tree at the end of the walkway. Every day he photographs it once, but only once a day, and so he looks at it for a long time, waiting for good light. I know this because he told me once. I asked him to show me at least one of his photographs, but he said he couldn't. The girls from my class say that he's crazy, that there's not even any film in his camera.

I say hello to the photographer, and he greets me in return. He smiles at me, and I smile at him. I pass by, swinging my bag. I grab my braid, toss it across my shoulder so it will hang behind my back; the bells ring a little differently then; they sound a little deeper.

I'm about ten steps past the photographer when he calls after me, saying my name.

I turn around; he stands up from the bench, camera in his hand, a large black box with two lenses placed one above the other. He's holding it in my direction, and—snap—he's already taken my picture.

He tells me to stop for a moment while he takes my picture again.

I stand still, and he takes my picture again.

He tells me to come closer, to look off to the side, back in the direction of the linden tree, and again he takes my picture.

I don't look at the linden tree; I step toward the photographer, and I tell him to stop. I hold my bag out in his direction in order to cover myself, and he takes a picture of that too. I sense that my face is turning red; it's burning. I lower my bag, and I say, Please no, stop, I'm asking him politely.

The photographer lowers the camera.

He tells me not to be angry, it wasn't his fault, he had to take my picture. Because, he says, I'm very beautiful. This makes my face burn even more, and I say that it's not even true.

But it is, says the photographer. He tells me that I'll see when he shows me the pictures. In a few days, when he develops the films, and he enlarges the pictures, then I'll see.

I tell him that there's no film in his camera, everyone knows that.

The photographer says: Don't move. He raises his camera, and he takes my picture. He says my face is really beautiful. How my eyes flash, it's really beautiful. He has to preserve it.

He says that I should believe him; later on I'll really be grateful to him, when I'm an old lady, I'll be grateful to him for taking this picture of me as a young girl.

I tell him that I'm already past the age of thirteen, I'm not a little girl anymore. I say this loudly; I'm nearly yelling, my hand gripping the handle of my bag; it occurs to me that I can break his camera, I can knock it out of his hand with my bag.

The photographer says he didn't mean it like that. Of course I'm no longer a little girl. Of course not. He takes my picture again.

I tell him to stop, and I swing my bag in his direction.

The photographer steps to one side, and he says fine, he'll stop, he'll stop right away, but he's asking me very nicely to do one more thing, to undo my braid, because he'd like to photograph me with my hair loose.

I ask him what on earth he's imagining, that's out of the question, but he's already grabbed my braid, he's pulling it, I can feel burning pain running up the strands of my hair, all the way up to my scalp.

I yell at the photographer, saying that it hurts, it really hurts, let go of me immediately.

The photographer says nothing; he's holding my braid with two hands, his fingers already by the little bells undoing my hairband.

The camera strap hangs around his neck; the two lenses look at me like the eyes of a head turned sideways.

I let go of my bag; with one hand I grab my braid and clutch it hard so he won't be able to pull at it; with my other hand I grab the photographer's hand, and I try to pry his fingers away from my hairband; I hear as the little bells knock against the pearly glass spheres in the hairband; he's beginning to pull it off my braid. I let go of his hand and my braid as well, and with all ten nails I claw into his hand as fiercely as I possibly can. My nails sink into his skin; the photographer cries out, jerks his hand away with my hairband still in his palm; it had already slid off my braid with a few strands of hair that broke off with it. I sense burning pinpricks on the top of my scalp and on the side, above the nape of my neck, but I don't care, because I see the hairband is in his hand; I reach for it, my index finger locks around it, and I pull it toward myself. Give it back! I yell at him. The hairband stretches out, the bells still ringing, then the hairband snaps; it slips from the photographer's grasp, flies away from my fingers, falls onto the ground; the tiny glass pearls roll onto the ground, onto the asphalt, rolling in every direction.

Now look what you've done, I yell at him, and I jump toward the glass pearls, kneel down, reach after them with both my hands; I sweep them toward myself; the bells ring on the asphalt with a cracked sound, and from that I know that they're all there, not even one was lost.

The photographer's holding his camera, standing next to the bench; his face is completely pale. He says don't be angry, he didn't mean to cause harm.

I put my hairband into my pocket along with the bells and the small glass spheres, and I stand up.

The photographer says again that he's very sorry, he's really very sorry. In the back of his hand, where I dug in my fingernails, there are many small pearls of blood.

I grab my braid at the root, and I comb through it with the fingers of my other hand until all the strands are untangled.

The photographer looks at his hand as if he has just then noticed the scratches on it; he hisses and grabs his hand to his mouth.

I undo my hair with quick movements; the cold locks of hair slide between my fingers.

My hair is now undone; I shake my head, look at the photographer. I'm waiting.

The photographer takes his hand away from his mouth, wipes it on his trousers, then lifts up his camera.

I look off to the side, up toward the crown of the great linden tree; I throw my head back a little bit. I'm smiling.

✳

IN THE CREDENZA THERE IS a tablecloth that we never take out. It's completely white, cool and smooth to the touch, and when I open up the credenza, I always run my hand along it. Once Grandmother sees me, and she asks what I'm doing daydreaming there.

Nothing, I tell her, it's just that the tablecloth is so smooth, I have to touch it. And I ask her why we never put it on the table.

Grandmother says that is because it's not a tablecloth for meals but rather a strudel cloth. It's used for making strudel.

She calls me over, extends her hand, her fingers spread out, and she tells me to hold up my palm against hers so she can see if I'm a big enough girl now. With her other hand, she takes the silver chain from her neck.

Grandmother's palm is cold; her skin is smooth and very soft.

My hand is almost as big as hers, only my nails aren't as long as hers.

Grandmother presses the palm of her hand against mine; she looks into my eyes. She asks me if there's a boy I like.

No, I tell her, but I can sense that I'm turning red.

Grandmother tells me not to lie. With her other hand she weaves the silver chain between our fingers, pulling it by the lizard-shaped pendant at its end.

The tiny silver eyelets of the chain touch the folds of skin between my fingers; it tickles; it makes the entire back of my hand tingle.

Grandmother asks: Is he handsome?

I nod and very quietly, I say, Yes.

Grandmother asks: What's his name?

To that I say nothing, I'm not even thinking of his name, I'm thinking of something else, about sitting on the swing outside beneath the walnut tree, my head thrown back; I'm swinging and swinging, back and forth, looking up at the crown of the tree.

Grandmother slowly pulls on the chain between our fingers, and she asks if the boy likes me.

I tell her I don't know.

Grandmother pulls the silver chain out from between our fingers, and she says that if he liked me, I would know. Then she says that it's time for me to learn how to make strudel. But first she wants me to go to the bathroom and wash my hands. Nice and thoroughly.

When I get back to the kitchen, the tablecloth is already laid out. Grandmother tells me to help her straighten it so that it's exactly in the middle of the table.

I take two corners of the tablecloth, lift them up, and then I notice that there are two eggs in the middle. One brown and one white. As we straighten out the tablecloth, the eggs begin to move, knocking against each other; Grandmother waits for them to roll right into the middle of the tablecloth, then we set it down, allowing it to land on the table with a rustle.

Grandmother tells me to take the eggs while she goes into the pantry to get the kneading board, the lard, the flour, and the vinegar.

I pick up the eggs, hold them in my hand. At the top of each one there is a word written with indelible pencil. On the white egg, the word *joy* is written. On the brown egg, the word *sorrow*.

Grandmother pours flour onto the board; in the middle she presses out a hole with her fist and tells me to break the eggs into it. First the white. In the meantime, she measures a large spoonful of lard into the flour.

I crack the eggs, pour both of them into the indentation in the flour; their yolks are dark orange in color, and in one of them I see my own face reflected as well as the wall of the kitchen with its many colorful plates. Grandmother pours the vinegar on top of it, and the image blurs.

Grandmother tells me to knead the flour. And not to think

about that boy while I do. I can think of anything else, but not him.

I begin to knead the flour; at first, the flour sends up small clouds of dust and sticks to my fingers, then it begins to come together; I knead, the flour is cold to the touch, slowly warming up. Grandmother watches as I work, and she says: Stronger, harder.

With the heels of my palms, I flatten the flour against the board; I press down hard, push it away from myself, push it toward myself, push it away from myself again.

I've grown very warm. I knead the flour, paying attention to nothing else.

Suddenly I sense Grandmother's arm on my shoulder, and she's saying fine, that's enough. I take my hands away from the flour; it is smooth and silky. I look at Grandmother; a drop of sweat rolls from my forehead all the way down my face and drops onto the kneading board.

That's no problem, says Grandmother. I should know that it happened to her very often, that she kneaded the flour while crying.

I want to tell her that I'm not crying, but I don't speak.

Grandmother covers the flour with a cloth napkin, and she says we need to let the dough rest now.

Then we make the filling. We pour out the liquid from two jars of cherry preserves, and we mix the walnuts, crushed with a fork, into the fruit.

In the meantime, the dough has risen nicely. Grandmother says that's exactly how it should be. She sprinkles flour onto the tablecloth, and with her thumb she draws a flowery pattern in it. I recognize what it is, three tulips joined together at the stalk, the kind of embroidery pattern used on pillows. Grandmother places the dough in the middle of the pattern. She takes my hand, presses my palm down, and begins to smooth the dough with it, slowly, as if I were smoothing it down. The dough flattens out; it's as if it is throbbing warmly beneath the palm of my hand.

Grandmother lets go of my hand, then goes to the other side of the table. She says I should do exactly what she does, as if I were her mirror image.

She places the dough beneath her hand, and she begins to pull it. I too grab the dough, and I pull it toward myself. She steps to the side; I too step to the side; slowly we walk around the table. We stretch out the dough, it becomes thinner; we walk around and around, and I begin to see my two hands beneath the dough as we stretch it out more and more.

The palms of my hands are on the tablecloth sprinkled with flour, beneath the dough; I pull with the back of my hand, just as Grandmother does, and at the same time I step over to the side. By now the dough is very thin, as translucent as frosted glass; as I gaze through it, I see the long, interwoven, swirling traces left by the palms of our hands in the flour sprinkled on the tablecloth. Grandmother says not to look because I'll grow dizzy, but it's too late, I can sense the kitchen spinning around me; the dough undulates. I think of the boy's name, I think of his name and his face, of his fair skin, I stumble into one of the corners of the table, but the dough does not break, it begins to slide down from the table. Grandmother quickly thrusts her two hands beneath it, presses down on it with her two palms; she grabs it, and she says that she told me not to look at it and that I should bring the filling already.

I step over to the counter, lift up the porcelain platter; Grandmother motions with her head, saying that I should pour the filling into the dough in long strips. Beneath her palms, the entire thing is undulating and convulsing.

I pour the mixture of cherries and walnuts onto the edge of the table. Grandmother says fine, she smiles at me, and she says: Iván. She raises her palms from the dough; the tablecloth undulates once, and the dough begins to coil up by itself, then it moves as if it wants to slide off the tablecloth.

Grandmother then grabs the fork that we used to mix the filling, thrusts it into the coiled-up strudel, and she says that it has to be pierced thoroughly, so that it won't split open. She lets go of the fork for me to try.

I take the fork, pull it out of the dough, then I thrust it back in; I pull it out, then I thrust it in again, and I hear Grandmother talking about how the way to a man's heart is always through his stomach, but I'm not really paying attention.

THE NEXT MORNING, BESIDE MY school snack, there is a little angular aluminum foil packet. I don't unwrap it, but still, I know what's in it. It contains three pieces of the cherry strudel that we baked together, and with it a pretty bird-patterned handkerchief.

Grandmother is reading a newspaper, sipping her coffee audibly from the orange leaf-patterned porcelain cup; she's in her housecoat, looking up at me from time to time, watching as I pack my schoolbag.

It's a beautiful morning; the sun shines into the kitchen; the waves on the silver cover of the sugar holder glimmer like real water.

I put my schoolbooks and my notebooks in my bag, then my pencil case, then a plastic bag with the bread spread with honey and apple.

I leave the aluminum foil–wrapped package for last, placing it on the very top of my books, so it won't get crushed. Grandmother watches as I carefully close my bag and fasten it. She tells me to be clever. Her coffee cup clatters as she puts it down on the table; she stands up and goes into the bathroom.

As I walk along the street, I keep thinking about the aluminum foil package, the strudel in it, the cherries, the chopped walnuts.

Grandmother didn't tell me, but I know what I have to do with it. I will take it out during the big recess; I have to unwrap it and offer some to Iván.

I imagine that he will smell the vanilla sugar; I picture him standing in front of me. I imagine that he'll look at the unwrapped package, then at me; he'll ask me what it is.

It's cherry strudel, I'll tell him. With two fingers I'll pull back the aluminum foil so he can see all the better what it is, and with my other hand I'll extend it toward him, asking, Would you like some?

I imagine how he'll reach into the package, take a piece of strudel, raise it to his mouth, and bite into it, and I'll watch as he chews and swallows. I'll look at his face, his eyes, as the sun shines on him from the side; at other times his complexion is dark, but right then it will look olive; he'll raise his fingers to his mouth, and he'll lick off the powdered vanilla sugar, then I'll speak to him, say that I was the one who baked it. I won't tell him that it was for him, I baked it only for him, because he will know even without me saying so, and from how his face will change, I will know that he knows.

And he will look at me as he never has before.

He will love me almost as much as I love him.

I smile; my face is burning, my throat is warm; I see his face as clearly as if he were right in front of me.

I go along the walkway, beneath the linden trees and the acacia trees, and when I reach the new branches sprouting out of the trunk of an acacia tree that was cut down, I pull off an acacia leaf as I do every morning.

The acacia leaf is already in my hand when it flashes through me that today I shouldn't have pulled one off.

I repeat the rhyme I learned from Mother — He-loves-me,

he-loves-me-not—I say it once, then I repeat it; I should throw the acacia leaf away, I should let it fall from between my fingers, let it drop, but I can't bear to; I begin to tear off smaller pieces, and I repeat the words within myself, one after the other. My throat is constricted by the time I get to the two-hundred-year-old linden tree; I can sense I'm about to start crying; my schoolbag is falling off my shoulder; now there is but one small leaf left on the long stalk, and I say out loud what has to be said, He-loves-me-not, and I know that it is true. This is the truth, everything else is a lie, a lie and a deception.

I'm at the end of the walkway, beneath the linden tree that is two hundred years old. I step away from the sidewalk, walk over to the tree. I walk around it, throw my bag down onto the grass. I kneel at the base of the tree trunk, dig my fingers into the earth between the tree's roots, dig out a handful of earth, then I do so with my other hand as well. I begin to dig with both hands like a dog; the earth is moist and black. The hole quickly becomes deeper, I stop digging.

I open my bag, take out the aluminum foil package, place it into the hole; I press it down good and deep, below the roots of the linden tree.

I push the earth onto it. The clumps of earth knock against the aluminum foil; I don't want to hear it, and I keep repeating within myself: He-loves-me, he-loves-me-not.

I smooth over the earth.

I stand up, swing my bag over my shoulder, and head off toward school.

15

I DON'T HAVE TO LOOK at the map because even without it I know where I am and where I have to go. I already found two of the points, the plastic horses are in my pocket—Mr. Pali uses them to mark the points—and now I only have to find the last one.

I stand up, and I don't take out the training map, marked up with indigo ink by Mr. Pali; I hold on to my compass through the material of my sweatsuit, but I should know my directions by now even without that. I sniff the wind, and I think of the blurred black lines on the map. I have to run up the ridge of the hill; the next point will be there somewhere amid the trees. And if it's there, then I just have to get back to Mr. Pali, and after that, I can go home.

I run through hazelnut bushes, then I reach a ravine, then I run down, avoiding the jutting tree roots and stones.

The path diverges slightly from the direction I need to go, but I stay on it, because it will take me up to the ridge of the hill. I try to run as Mr. Pali told me to, taking a larger breath only with every fifth step, but even then not too deep; the rhythm that Mr. Pali taught me swirls in my head—*Small-small-small-*

small-big—and it works too; I can keep going without getting out of breath.

The forest thins out at the top of the hill, and far away I can see the thick red scarf, tied around the trunk of the tree, that Mr. Pali used to designate the next point.

I run over there, touch the trunk of the tree, and come to a stop.

A piece of twine hangs down from the scarf; at the end of the twine there is a small noose, and in the noose is a brown plastic horse; in the saddle sits a red plastic Indian with a feather headdress and a tomahawk.

I pull the horse's head out of the noose and put it in my pocket, next to the other two horses. Those horses have no riders; their saddles are empty.

Now I just have to run back to Mr. Pali. I adjust my sweatsuit so that the horses won't dig into my stomach; I touch the compass; then once again I begin to run.

I run all along the ridge of the hill as it gently slopes down —I hardly have to watch my breathing—then I reach the steep slope where there are very few trees; tall dried-out grasses grow there, reaching up to my knees, almost to my waist.

I don't like to run in such high grass where you can't properly see the branches or the stones, it's very easy to trip, but I don't care about that now because I just want to get home as soon as I possibly can. I can feel that my knee socks are sliding down; I don't bother with them; I lean forward, letting the impetus carry me; I run until the earth underneath my shoes begins to make squelching sounds; the ground at the bottom of the hill is always boggy. Here the grass doesn't grow tall. I reach the old concrete road, then I run all the way to the path, and then I'm at the riding school.

When Mr. Pali sees me, he gets up, closes his book, puts it back with the others on the trunk with the thick blanket. He says I ran a good time today; he holds a small bucket in front of me; I reach into my pocket, and I throw the three horses into it. Mr. Pali looks into the bucket, nods, and says, Good, all three are there, we're done for today.

I say goodbye and turn to leave, but then Mr. Pali says to wait a minute, where am I rushing to, and he asks me — as he asks everyone after every single run — if I saw anything peculiar or unusual while I was on my run, any people or any kind of freshly turned earth, anything at all. I tell him that I didn't see anything, and I turn to leave again, but then Mr. Pali speaks to me, telling me not to run away and to look at my legs. My knee socks, crumpled up around my ankles, are covered in thistles; Mr. Pali says that it will be a job picking out all of those prickly thorns, but I should at least pull my sweatpants up to my knees.

I pull them up; Mr. Pali motions for me to place one leg on the book-filled trunk. I see now that my calves are covered with small black spots. Mr. Pali tells me that they are ticks, and I have to take them off quickly, before they suck themselves full of blood.

I reach over, touch one of the small black spots; it's smaller than the head of a straight pin, and hard, as if it were made out of plastic. I'm overcome by nausea, so much so that my head starts to spin.

Mr. Pali grabs my elbow, and he says there's no reason to be so afraid; if I could see how pale I am, like wax. Haven't I ever gotten a tick on myself before?

I shake my head. Mr. Pali says well, in that case, I've had it easy till now, but there's nothing to be afraid of, he'll show me how to get them out, and his pocketknife is already in his hand. When I see it, I want to jerk my leg away, but Mr. Pali grabs my ankle with his other hand, and he says there's no reason to be afraid or fastidious, my dear little star, this isn't a snakebite, and the knife snaps in his hand as he opens up the saw-toothed blade; the knife will be cold, he says, then he smooths it against my skin, pushing the end of the blade beneath a tick; there it is, caught between the last two teeth of the blade; the knife is cold; I have goose bumps over my whole leg. Mr. Pali presses down on the tick with the nail of his thumb, then he flicks his finger on the blade. The tick jumps up from my skin, a tiny red spot in its place. Mr. Pali says you see, it doesn't hurt, it's less than a fleabite, then one after the other he begins to flick the other ticks away from my skin as well.

By the time he's finished, my calf is covered with small red spots.

Mr. Pali gives me the knife and tells me to do the second leg by myself. When I get home, I should ask my grandmother for rubbing alcohol and rub my legs with it all over; there won't be any problems, I'll see. This comes with long-distance running, there's nothing we can do about it. But my blood must be very sweet if the ticks like me so much; it's unusual to see so many of the bastards at once.

Once I get home, he says, I should have a look around and see if I can find that old map. Now he really needs it because he's looking for something, and he doesn't think that he'll be able to find it without that map.

GRANDMOTHER HAS THREE IRONS; SHE keeps them next to each other on one of the shelves in the larder. Two of them are electric irons—they both look the same—and the third is made out of black cast iron; I've never seen one like that before. Even its handle is made of iron, iron and blackened walnut wood, it's good and heavy; in the front there's a small ornamented handle that lifts up the iron plate at the back. The plate is something like a small guillotine; it creaks as I pull it up. I dig my hand into the inner part of the iron and grope around in the soot-scented dark cavity; I can sense how sharp the plate's lower edge is. Something makes a rustling noise between my fingers; I

grab hold of it and pull it out. In my hand is a dried-out cigarette, and through the cigarette paper I can feel that the tobacco
inside is broken and crumbling, nearly dust. I think of Father's
hidden cigarettes; he would always hide them behind his paintings so that later he would have something to smoke. If he had
extras, he gave me a couple to hide as well, so he wouldn't find
them right away, and he'd have something to be happy about
when all his other cigarettes ran out.

This cigarette is longer and thinner than the ones that Father used to smoke; its paper is thinner and makes more of a
rustling sound, and it's nearly transparent enough to see the
grains of tobacco through it. I roll it slowly between my fingers, and I think about how the last three cigarettes that I hid
from Father must still be where I left them, In the plastic pipe
stopped up with a cork beneath the bathtub; this was the one
hiding place that I came up with all by myself, and the only one
that neither Father nor Mother ever figured out.

I roll the cigarette between my fingers; the golden letters
inscribed around the filter blur together, a fine tobacco-scented
menthol dust arises from it, and I think about how Grandmother doesn't smoke cigarettes, so this cigarette that I found
in the iron can only be Grandfather's.

I've never smoked cigarettes, but now I try to imagine what
it would be like. I put the filter end in my mouth, I try to imagine that I'm holding it in a flame. I inhale; my mouth fills with
bitter menthol dust, making my tongue rough and dry.

I cough, then I shove the cigarette back into the iron. As I
pull my hand out from its inner chamber, the iron door slams
shut by itself with a loud clattering noise.

GRANDFATHER'S CIGARETTE CASE ALWAYS SITS on the
porcelain platter on the bureau. The case is made of silver with a

large green lizard resting across it slantwise, a completely life-like leather inset; I like to touch it and run my fingers all along the tiny indents of its scales. Perhaps it's made from lizard or crocodile leather. The lizard lies stretched out with closed eyes, and before I touch it, I always imagine that it's moving; it will open its eyes and, scratching with its small clawed legs, it will run across my hand, between my fingers, and into my palm.

I know the case is empty, but still I snap it open. Inside are black elastic bands, undulating silver indentations where the cigarettes should be placed. Nine cigarettes fit into each half of the case. I think about how I could place the cigarette that was hidden inside the iron inside this case, but I know that I won't.

The silver inside of the case is tarnished; I can see my face in it only very indistinctly, the surface is full of scratches, drawing wrinkles onto my skin — as if it's not even me, as if I don't even know the person staring back at me. Slowly I move my head back and forth, and I watch as the wrinkles shift on that other face.

Next to the case is Grandfather's cigarette lighter; it's about as big as a matchbox, made out of brass. The same green scaly lizard that was on the cigarette case is on the lighter too, only this one is made not of leather but enamel; it's slightly warmer to the touch than the brass. The lizard pattern wraps around the entire cigarette lighter, and at the top the lizard bites into its own tail with tiny white teeth that look something like ant eggs. This lizard's eyes are open, two yellow dots like two pinpoints, and right in the middle of each one there is a tiny black speck of dust, so tiny it makes your eyes hurt.

I flick the lighter open; the upper third of the metal box lifts, the spring snaps firmly, the blackened wick extends out through the perforated metal chimney. I turn the spark wheel; it sends out yellow sparks and the wick catches fire, burning with a large yellow hissing flame. In the middle of the flame tiny black spots dance, each smaller than the head of a pin, exactly like the lizard's eyes.

I reach over, slowly draw my finger across the flame. It doesn't burn my finger, and I think about how there's nothing else as smooth to the touch in the whole wide world.

AMONG GRANDFATHER'S PHOTOGRAPHS, THERE ARE very few where he is visible. I find only one in the box where he is pictured by himself.

He's very young, and not wearing glasses; his eyes make me think of Mother's eyes, he resembles her.

Grandfather stands at the top of the mountain, his arm lifted, proudly waving. I look at the contours of the mountains behind him for a long time, the ridge of the mountains covered in snow, the chasms in the cliffs, the clear sky, and I think about how the air must certainly be thinner up there, because it's so close to the sky. Perhaps it would be harder to breathe, but everything else would be easier. Everything else would have to be easier.

I GO OVER TO GRANDFATHER'S vocabulary notebook; next to it is the pocket French dictionary with the blue leather case. It's a proper comprehensive dictionary with forty thousand entries but shrunk to such a teeny size that it's more like a pack of cards, and the words can't be read with the naked eye. In the case there's also a large rectangular magnifying glass, the same size as the dictionary itself, in a thick black plastic frame; one side of the frame is covered with convex leather. When the magnifying glass stands next to the dictionary in the case, it looks like a thin companion volume.

I look through the magnifying glass; the room begins to flow obscurely in many directions, and I think about the map, I think about where Grandfather might have put it. I take the magnifying glass away from my eyes, and I look at my palm through it, at the enlarged creases of my fingerprints, the tiny nooses in the center of my fingertips.

THE GLASS-FRONTED BOOKCASE TAKES UP half of the wall in the living room. The two sheets of glass are hard to move in the metal grooves; they squeak as I try to pull on them, and sometimes they get stuck. When that happens I press the palm of my hand against the glass, try to lift it up to pull it farther, and usually I'm able to.

On the lower shelves, there are old newspapers, bound together and ordered by year; I love these most. Their paper is fragile and yellowed, with the scent of dust, although they are not even that dusty. There are also old French newspapers, and in those I sometimes come across words underlined in pencil and sometimes notations in the margins. I recognize Grandfather's handwriting.

Grandmother doesn't mind if I look at the books, but she doesn't like the shelves to have any gaps by nighttime, so every evening, every book has to be back in its place. If I forget, then she puts it back without putting in a bookmark; she tells me to take note of where I left off.

In one of the old bound volumes of newspapers, I found a serialized novel about a lady dancer. I read it; it was pretty exciting.

I go over to the bookcase so I can take that volume out; there it is among the others, with the title and the year embossed with gilded letters on the spine.

I touch the glass and try to pull it, but it won't move at all.

As I lean in closer, the glass suddenly darkens; at first I think that I've leaned in too close, that I'm seeing the condensation of my own breath on the glass. I reach over to trace a pattern in it with my nail, but I see that I can't, because the vapor on the glass is not on the outside but the inside.

I move back, looking at it.

There are two oval-shaped clouds of vapor on the glass, blurring into each other obliquely; it makes me think of winter when the steam rises up from your nostrils in the cold air. I step back even farther; the two spots grow and expand, and from them a blurry figure begins to emerge, as if it were standing behind the glass, leaning down with a bent back, resting two hands there, and between the hands a face is pressed up to the glass, trying to look out.

The spines of the books loom through the whiteness, but still I can see it, a white face drawn from vapor on the other side of the glass, unshaven, old. The face has thick-framed eyeglasses on; I know who it is—it's Grandfather. He looks at me, squinting, maybe even winking, then he turns his head and looks to the side; his left hand moves, he takes it away from the glass. At first the palm of his hand disappears from the glass, then four of his fingers, then only his index finger remains there, a tiny blotch of vapor. I look at it as it moves toward the highest shelf; it points up there, to a thick volume sitting on the very top shelf. Now I see more than the tip of his finger; the vapor is also delineating his arm, his shoulder, his entire form; he stands there on tiptoes, his arm stretching toward the highest shelf, but he can't reach that far, he misses it by a few centimeters.

I step over to the glass, but as I touch it, suddenly the vapor disappears from the other side. The glass is clear, as transparent as if nothing had ever been there, tepid beneath my palm.

I pull on the glass, and it now slides smoothly in the groove. I reach up; I can't reach all the way to the upper shelf. I stand on my toes, but even so, I can't reach it. I crouch down and I pull out four large bound volumes of magazines from the lowest shelf, make a tower out of them on the floor, step onto the top of it, grab onto the shelf, and once again I stretch upward, but even so I can't reach the top shelf. With one leg, I step onto the edge of the second shelf; only my big toe can fit. I push myself up from the pile of books, I reach up, and I realize I should have used a chair; I grab at the edge of the highest shelf, and with my other hand I reach out, touch the book that Grandfather had been pointing at, I try to pull it off the shelf, but it won't budge; I clasp it from higher up, reach the top of the book's spine; I pull on it, it won't move, I pull and I pull on the book, and suddenly the book comes off the shelf, the pile of books slides out from beneath my legs; I know I'm going to fall, I'm already falling; in the glass of the bookcase I can see the fright on my own face, my loosened hair fluttering in the air all around it.

I fall on my back onto the Persian carpet; the air squeezed out of my lungs simmers into hissing gas from the shock of the fall, making my chest explode; recoiling, I try to catch my breath; there is no breath, there's only steaming white gas, dizzying white gas, and through that I see that the book that Grandfather had been pointing at is now in the air with its pages opened; it's plunging down, rotating on its spine, then it falls next to me on the carpet. I turn my head toward it; from among its pages something with worn edges, something like a brochure, slides out; immediately I know what it is—it's that old map that Mr. Pali has asked me to find twice already. I lean up on my elbows; my back is still hurting. I look at the cover page of the map patched up many times over with clear tape —in charcoal pencil a tiny cane is drawn on it, and at each end is a horseshoe.

16

IT'S DRAWING CLASS. IN MY old school, I was never any good at drawing cubes, apples, or nuts. Here the assignments are much more difficult; the drawing teacher has draped a starched white damask cloth behind a platter of fruit. He tells us to observe the light, both the light and the shadows, and to draw so that the light will unfold from the shadows.

We're not sitting at our benches but in a half circle around tables; the teacher strolls behind us and looks at our sheets of paper.

I think of Father, how he worked with a brush and a scraping knife and how I used to watch him so much while he was working; if it was just the two of us at home, I could go into the living room, into his studio, where one of the corners was mine; it had two dolls and a dollhouse that we had drawn together on the wall. I played a lot with that dollhouse; the dolls had their own bathroom, and in the bathroom there was even a mirror, a real pocket mirror that Father had bought for me, and we glued it up onto the wall, and while I was playing, I always watched Father in the mirror as he worked. I don't want to think about

Father now; better to think about the blankness of the white paper in front of me.

Everyone is busy drawing, I'm the only one who hasn't started yet. I look at the sheet of paper; it's completely blank. I think of the flour sprinkled onto the kneading board, I think of Grandmother's fingers as she traced the patterns. I raise my pencil several times, but I don't dare touch the paper, I don't want to leave any mark on it. I want it to remain white.

The green apples glisten in the light; I look behind them, at the folds of the damask handkerchief, and I see darkness swirling within the depths. I'm just imagining it, but still I can't not look.

I'm squeezing the pencil in my hand; I raise it, and I begin to draw. My hand is moving, but I don't look down at it, I don't look at the paper, I look only at that swirling blackness there in the depths of the white damask; it's like the large pupil of a large eye, as if something were on the lookout, gazing through a hole. It's there, it's watching me. It sees me, and it wants me to see it.

I look at it. My wrist and my lower arm and my shoulder are all hurting, my entire arm is stiff from pain; the pencil presses down onto the paper, tilts sideways, draws the shaded parts; I look at it, and there on the paper is that darkness. It's not even black but gray, I see the black of the eye and the iris all around it, and above it the eyelashes, and the eyebrows jumping forward, the arch of the eyebrows as they give way to the nose; I see the entire face; it is a man's face. I see his mouth as well, and at the corners of his mouth is a tiny, superior smile; his gaze is cold and severe. He is familiar, and yet I know that I've never seen him. My hand moves; I'm going to draw him, his image will be on the paper before me in a moment.

Somebody calls out my name; it is the drawing teacher. He stands behind me, he puts his hand on my shoulder, and he says: Very good.

My hand stops; the pencil no longer moves. I look down at the half-drawn face, the deep wrinkles emerging from the corners of the mouth. The drawing teacher looks at it too. Very good, he says, I have an incredible imagination. He takes his hand away from my shoulder, raps the tip of the pencil at the edge of the drawing, and he says I should continue, but I shouldn't try to look beyond things, that isn't the assignment now. He grabs one corner of the paper, and with a calm movement yanks it out from beneath my pencil; the pencil leaves a thick black line on the paper, cutting the half-drawn face in two diagonally.

The paper rustles as the drawing teacher turns it over, it rustles as he places the clean side of the sheet of paper in front of me; he tells me to look at the fruit, to look at the damask folds, and that I should only draw what is really there.

I look down at the piece of paper; it is thick, but even so, my drawing on the other side looms through. I don't want to see it. The drawing teacher suggests I try using charcoal. He takes a black pencil out of his inner pocket; it's thinner than a regular pencil, and the inner part is completely black. Courage, he says, and steps away from me. I look at the apples; one of them is bruised at the top, near the stalk, there is a brown splotch extending out in the shape of an oval. I look at the splotch, and I think about the apple, about how beneath, the flesh is softened and brown—whenever I eat apples, the very first thing I do is to bite out these bruised parts and spit them out onto the ground.

I think about the slightly sour taste of winter apples; I know I'm not supposed to be thinking of tastes and fragrances. I look at the bruise, its form, I must not think of what it resembles—it doesn't resemble anything.

I press the tip of the charcoal pencil on the sheet of paper, and I begin to draw the bruise; it's a bruised part of an apple, nothing more, nothing more than an apple with another apple next to it; beneath the apples is a yellow earthenware plate, and around the plate is white damask, arranged in folds. That's all it is, two apples on a plate with a starched, ironed white cloth arranged in folds around it.

I look at the apples; the end of the stalk of one of them is slightly enlarged, with a very small piece of tree bark still attached to it; in the sharp afternoon light it shines white. I draw all around the light on the sheet of paper, the forms of the pieces of fruit unfold from the sharp black contours. I'm not looking up, I'm looking only at the paper, at my fingers holding the pencil, as they move above the paper. I don't have to look up, I know exactly what apples look like, I know exactly what the platter looks like—I look at the lines on the page. It's as if I weren't even moving my own hand.

When the bell rings, there, on the piece of paper in front of me are the two apples and the platter and one fold from the drapery. It's a good drawing. I look at it; my face is burning, and my heart is pounding loudly, pounding even faster than when I'm running. A lock of hair falls loose, and as I push it out of my eyes, I can feel that my forehead is covered with sweat.

The drawing teacher stands next to me; in his hand is a large leather portfolio into which he's putting all of the drawings; he's already collected everyone else's, leaving mine for last. He doesn't even look at me as he takes the drawing; the sheet of paper rustles as he places it in the portfolio. He snaps it shut, tucks it beneath his shoulder, and turns away.

I hold out the charcoal pencil, speaking to him: Teacher, please, here is your pencil.

The drawing teacher stops, turns around, and tells me that I may keep the pencil. And that every Tuesday at three p.m., after classes, there is a drawing club upstairs in the turret room; he expects me to be there from now on. He doesn't await my reply but leaves the classroom.

I don't look at him but at the rounded tip of the charcoal pencil. I'll have to sharpen it later.

ON THE TABLE, ON THE large porcelain platter next to the tape measure, the large tailor's scissors, and a ball of string, is a sea snail. It's a large, prickly shell; its innards are pinkish and white and its mouth so wide that four of my fingers, maybe even my entire fist, can fit into it. If I poke only my ring finger into the shell, I can feel how it narrows and curves; my finger, though, is not long enough and not thin enough to go very far, and it can reach only up to the second spiral inside the shell where the thread of the spiral becomes very narrow; I can feel its curve, but no matter how I try to stick my finger farther in, I can't, and the tip of my fingernail scratches against the shell's smooth surface.

From the outside, the scratching sound cannot be heard.

When I hold it up to my ear, at first I can't hear anything, then I begin to hear a very distant crackling sound, as if I were listening to something very far away; slowly it grows louder, then becomes softer once again, then louder again, then softer and then louder. I can't stand to listen to it for very long; my head starts to hurt from the humming noise and always in the same place, at the back of my head near the base of my ponytail, and it radiates out from there to my throat, and from there it climbs up to the root of my tongue and bitterly climbs out to the tip of my tongue, as if I could sense, on the tip of my tongue, the buzzing sound that lives in the shell, its biting, salty prickling.

Even though I know that afterward I'll feel worse, still, almost every day I take the seashell into my hands; I press down on its pointy surface, I caress its grooves, I stick my fingers into it, I place it in my other hand, I hold it up to my ear, I press it against my ear. Every day it's the same.

At one point, Grandmother comes into the room just when

the scratching sound is at its loudest. She looks at me, waits for me to put the shell down, then she asks if I know what I'm listening to?

I tell her that I don't, but I'm sure that it's not the sea. And it's not the same as when the blood is rushing in my ears.

Grandmother takes the shell out of my hands, and she says I have a good ear. It really isn't the sea. She holds the shell to her mouth, closes her eyes, and she blows into it; I see that her face swells and turns red, the wrinkles around her mouth smooth as she blows more and more air into the shell. I watch her—there's total silence, nothing can be heard at all.

Then Grandmother lowers the shell; on her face, above her mouth, is the red imprint of the edge of the shell; as she opens her eyes she totters for a moment, then she grabs the edge of the table. She puts the shell down on the glass surface of the table, then pushes it toward me. I watch as the shell slides along the glass tabletop.

I take the shell, I pick it up, I hold it to my ear, I press it to my ear. I immediately hear the buzzing sound, and I notice that it doesn't sound like it usually does—no, it's no longer buzzing, it's more like a whispering, but the words are running together; it's impossible to understand them.

It's an old voice, not the voice of Grandmother; it whispers quickly, as if it were afraid that somebody might hear; it's speaking an unknown language of which I cannot understand even one word. It falls silent, then it begins again, the same voice; at first I think that it's saying the same thing again but not at all, now the words have meaning: it speaks of a sack, of a strap that was used to tie up the mouth of the sack, it talks of how that strap had to be pulled hard, it had to be pulled tight, so it wouldn't come undone, so that no one would ever be able to climb out of it, and it talks about how hard it was to carry it to the forest, it talks of how no one ever would have thought that such little beings could be so heavy, and how hard it was, after the exhaustion of dragging the sack to the forest, to dig the ditch, and how easy it was then to push in the sack with just one kick of the foot, and then how hard it was to shovel the earth onto those sacks, without glancing at them even once so as not to see that something was moving beneath the burlap, and how easy it was then to flatten down the earth and to cast dried leaves onto the earthen mound, and then how easy it was to go home and to answer, when the children asked—to say no one knew, surely they must have wandered off somewhere, because nobody had seen any of them for days now, and how after that, nothing was ever said about it ever again.

The voice falls silent, then it starts up again, speaking in that unknown language, but now I understand, now it says everything from the end to the beginning, speaking backwards, beginning where it had left off.

I put down the shell; never has my head hurt so much before. Grandmother looks at me, she asks what I heard; everything is buzzing, and I can hardly hear what she is saying.

I tell her that in the forest there is a ditch that has been filled in with earth. I tell her I know where it is, and I tell her that we should go there and dig it up, we should unearth the sack, and we should untie its mouth, but even as I'm speaking I know that it's already too late, it has been too late for a very long time, I'm looking at the shell, I reach for it so that I can hurl it at the wall with all my strength, but Grandmother is faster than me; she grabs it from the tabletop, thrusts it behind her back. I yell at her to give it to me right now, give it back right away; the pain on the tip of my tongue is sharp and acidic.

Grandmother says there would be no point in us breaking the shell; nothing would be changed. What I heard had certainly happened a very long time ago. Who knows, maybe I would be able to make use of the shell one day, and perhaps one day I too would wish to say something into it.

I shake my head. And I say no, and at the same time I'm thinking that no matter how Grandmother tries to hide it, I'll find it. I'll find it and I'll shatter it.

Grandmother smiles at me, and she says I can look for it all I want.

I'M AT HOME ALONE. I take my drawing board out to the garden along with a bunch of drawing paper and the charcoal pencil that the drawing teacher gave to me. I walk around, looking at everything, trying to decide what I could draw. I sit down next to the garden table; the oilcloth has water on it, the small puddles show where the indents on the tin tabletop are. I place my drawing board on the bench, sweeping away the water with my palm; the drops of water send out sparks as if I were scattering pearls onto the grass.

The sun is shining. The oilcloth on the table will soon be dry.

I look at the walnut tree as I lean back on the bench, my face warmed by the sun.

The leaves of the walnut tree are just now emerging from their buds, just beginning to grow; they're still not covering the branches properly, and I can still follow the forking branches right up to the very top of the tree, up to its very thinnest branches.

A thrush alights on the top of the tree, perches on the highest part of the very highest and the very thinnest branch, which hardly bends beneath its weight. It sings, its beak open wide to the sky; I watch it.

Slowly I place the drawing pad before me. I don't look down, and I begin to draw. I want to start with the bird's beak,

I'm looking for one single thickening line that will go from the beak of the thrush right down to the very roots of the tree.

I look at the sheet of paper, I see that it's no good; I turn it over and try again, that's no good either; I crumple it up, take a new sheet of paper, that one isn't any good either; I turn that over and try again, and that one's no good as well. I take another sheet of paper, I try again; the thrush is still on the branch and it's still singing, I see its contours, I know that if I can draw these contours as I see them, everything else will be easy; after that I will start from the bottom moving upward, my hand will move quickly up and down, up and down, and at the end the thrush will exist on the piece of paper, and the walnut tree too, its trunk, and its crown, in its entirety, everything, there will be the light between the branches, and behind the crown of the walnut tree, the sky.

I try once again, and again it's no good. I want to think about the line, not about how it isn't any good, not about how won't be any good, not about how it's not going to work.

The line must be sharp. I see how the sheet has to be divided in two by black. A line, a cut, the earth below the tree, the thrush on its crown; I close my eyes, I turn my face entirely to the sun; beneath my eyelids there are green and orange-yellow and purple orbs. I prepare for the movement; my drawing teacher said that the paper is white, the charcoal is black, and that's it, that's all you have to know, that's all you need in order to make a good drawing.

The charcoal is on the paper, the movement is in my hand, and I know that it will be good, this line will be good, it will be what it has to be, and I know that I shouldn't be thinking about this, I shouldn't care if it comes out good; if it comes out bad, I do have to care about that, but if it's good, then it doesn't matter, that only means that I can't stop. The paper is white, the charcoal is black; the drawing teacher never explained what this meant. I draw, and as the gnarls on the trunk emerge from the lines, I understand. It means that you have to be stupid—while you're drawing, you have to be stupid, not blind and not vain, just stupid enough to accept that a line is just a line, even if it wants to be more.

The lines weave into each other, breaking the sheet of paper into shards, just as the branches break up the heavens; I feel light, I have understood something that the others have not, that's what comes to me, that I will go and seek out the drawing teacher, and I will tell him that I understood, and I will show him my drawing, and he will see that really, I have understood the lesson.

There is the walnut tree on the paper; like a dancing woman with one thousand arms, it has just now found its way back to the earth after a great leap, it is carried by the motion, winding its arms around itself so that it won't fall down. I look at the tree, look at my drawing. This walnut tree is mine now.

17

DURING HISTORY CLASS THE TEACHER is asking questions and calling on individual pupils to answer; luckily, he hasn't called on me once so far. I peek under the sleeves of my pullover, look at my watch; there's only time now for one or two more pupils to answer, but Curtains, the history teacher, has been leafing through the pages forward and backward in his class roster for a while now; the pages rustle beneath his fingers, and everyone sits in silence, no one moves, no one wants to be the one to answer, and neither do I, my stomach always contracts when he turns the pages toward the back of the class roster because I'm the very last one listed there, not where I should be according to the register. I look at Curtains's fingers as he turns the pages farther and farther toward the back of the class roster; now he really will be turning to the very last page, and for sure he's going to call on me.

As Curtains turns the pages, the movement stirs up a breeze that makes his pomaded lock of hair move—he always brushes it across the bald patch above his forehead. Everyone knows he got his nickname because of this lock of hair, because even if it were plastered to his head, it wouldn't hide his baldness, it's like a badly hung curtain, and the skin of his bald head shines through it like the sun through curtains. I watch as the lock of hair trembles, wishing it would fall down right in front of Curtains's eyes. I know that the entire class is watching that same lock of hair, and everyone is hoping for the same thing.

I was supposed to be studying the great French Revolution, but I didn't, I didn't even open up the book, I was out in the garden the entire afternoon trying yet again to draw the walnut tree; I drew on at least a hundred sheets of paper, but not one of my drawings was good.

On the bench in front of me is my pencil case; I reach for it very slowly, grab my compass, and pull it out; in the meantime, Curtains has thumbed to the very last page, and he's looking at it, I'm sure he's going to read out my name, I see it in his eyes. In a moment he's going to open his mouth and he's going to say my name.

I press my thumb to the tip of the compass; it pierces my skin. I press even harder; it goes in deep. I feel a sharp fiery pain, it makes my eyes water, but I don't blink, I keep looking at Curtains's hand. I want him to turn the page again, to turn away from that page and back to the middle of the class book, away from the page with my name on it.

Curtains does not turn the page, he keeps looking at that last page; there could be no greater silence than there is right now in the classroom, everyone is holding their breath. The teacher licks his mouth, and suddenly he thrusts his other hand between the pages of the book, he claps it open somewhere in the middle, and he's saying a name, loudly, almost yelling. He slaps his palm down on the book and the chalk dust rises up in a white cloud from the platform.

It's not my name; I don't care whose name it is, the only thing that matters is that it's not mine. In the second row of benches, a desk opens with a snap, and a black-haired boy with eyeglasses stands up; it's Gazsi, I don't know his last name, I've never spoken with him; often during recess he stays inside in the classroom, always reading thick books, and even sometimes during class he reads in secret beneath his desk.

I pull out the tip of the compass; the pain sharply spreads throughout the entire tip of my finger; now not only the spot where I stabbed my finger hurts, but my entire finger. I look at it, and I see that there is a large dark drop of blood where I pricked my finger. With my other hand, I reach into my pencil case and I take out the blotting paper. As I press it onto my thumb, the drop of blood is so large that I can almost see myself in it. The blood quickly soaks into the blotter; there's a stain in the shape of a half-moon. I twist it onto my finger, wind it around twice, good and tight, so that the pain will slowly dissipate.

Gazsi is answering the teacher's question, speaking without interruption like flowing water, and that way he recites the Estates General of 1789, Danton and Robespierre, speaking so quickly that it's almost impossible to understand him, I don't even pay attention. Slowly I unwind the blotting paper from my finger; it doesn't hurt anymore, and it's not even bleeding, there is only a tiny red spot where I pricked my finger. I rub it with my index finger; I know that it will be visible for maybe two or three more days, then it will disappear, and there will be no trace of it left.

Suddenly I hear that the class is grunting. Gazsi is silent, Curtains is standing up next to his teacher's desk, staring fixedly at Gazsi, asking him what was it that he just said and where did he get it from —this was not in the book.

Gazsi swallows once; I see his Adam's apple moving; then, inhaling a huge gulp of air, he speaks, he says that it's because it's not in the *b-b-b*—and here he gets stuck, he cannot utter the word *book*, it's as if he is choking or has a mouthful of food that he can't spit out; his face distorts, he clutches at the edge of his desk with one hand, he tries again and again to pronounce *b-b-b-bo-b*. Curtains steps down from his platform, walks among the row of desks, and he asks, What's wrong, my son, can't you speak? You're trying to contradict me, and you can't even speak?

Gazsi's hand is clutching the edge of his desk; he is silent, then he begins again: It's because it's not in the book, that's what makes it true — that's what he says, he doesn't even say it, he shouts it, it bursts out of his mouth and saliva spurts out as well.

Curtains waves his hand in the air; he says that as long as he is the teacher here, some shitty seventh-grade schoolkid is not going to decide what is historical truth and what isn't, they have to learn and they have to recite what's in the textbook, word for word and sentence by sentence, is that clear? Fine, that's enough, you get an F and can sit down.

Gazsi doesn't sit down; he steps out next to the desk, he's saying n-n-no, no, he cannot accept this, he knows the great French Revolution well enough to get an A plus, he said it all, and if he h-h-has to — here he stops, and I think he's going to fall silent again, but no, he pulls himself together and continues to speak: If he has to, then he'll say the whole thing again, the entire class heard how much he knows, and there's no way he can get an F.

To this Curtains says but of course he can get an F, Curtains is the teacher and he can give an F to whomever he wants; if that person does not say what's in the book, then he will get an F, and that's it, or he can even get an F minus, and now Gazsi will get an F minus because, one, he didn't know the material, and, two, he was insolent. If he doesn't want to end up with an F, well, then, here's his chance, and he can say what's in the textbook. Curtains waits with folded arms and looks at Gazsi, whose fingers are nervously gripping his jacket.

Gazsi licks the corner of his mouth; he's speaking with difficulty, I can see that he's afraid he's going to start stuttering again, but then he doesn't stutter at all, he says he doesn't care if he fails, he will no longer recite what's in the Communist textbook, you old Commie, you should be ashamed of yourself.

Half of Curtains's face distorts in anger, and he slaps Gazsi's face with the back of his hand. From the movement of the blow, the lock of hair falls down from his forehead and hangs in front of his eyes.

Gazsi collapses onto the desk; blood is flowing from his nose, gurgling; he says something, but I don't hear what, because in that very moment the bell rings.

Curtains turns away, tries to plaster the lock of hair onto his forehead; he grabs up his class roster from the teacher's desk and leaves the classroom.

Blood is still flowing from Gazsi's nose, someone gives him a handkerchief. He presses it to his nose, sits down, leans his head on the desk behind him.

The blood quickly soaks through the handkerchief. Gazsi is trembling as if he were crying; the boys try to cheer him up, Gazsi blubbers for them to leave him alone, everything's fine, they should just leave, he'll follow after them in a minute, he's just going to wait for the bleeding to stop. They leave him there; slowly, everyone else exits the classroom.

I too stand up, pressing my thumb against the edge of the desk, but in vain, because it doesn't hurt anymore. I look at Gazsi, lying on the desk with closed eyes, still pressing the handkerchief to his nose. I look at the blood spreading between his fingers, and I think that I should have been the one to answer the question. I want to go over to him, I want to tell them that I'm sorry, I didn't want this. I even take a step toward him; the floor creaks loudly beneath my feet, and Gazsi opens his eyes, looks at me. I know that right now I should speak, and yet I don't say anything; I see that his eyes are moist; he quickly covers them and turns away.

I turn my back to him so fast that one of the bells in my

hairband begins to clink, I reach for it and push the flax back into it, then I leave too, as fast as I can.

IT'S THE LONG RECESS; I go to get a reader's card from the school library. Olgi told me that the librarian is really nice, I should get to know her. She had been in the hospital for two months and there was no one to take her place, but now she's back.

The library is on the second floor, above the assembly hall; you have to cross through double-winged glass doors. The doors are open. As I walk in, the librarian is pouring boiling water into a teacup. She looks up, sees me, and is so startled that she pours the water onto her hands; the cup slides out from beneath her fingers and falls onto the desk. It's as if she's seen a ghost.

Her hair is cropped short; it's not yet fully white, but rather silvery gray, and it doesn't even make her look old; it just makes the lipstick on her mouth shine even redder. Her face is very smooth, her eyes very blue; she looks at me, her mouth gaping open, as if she cannot speak or can't catch her breath; next to her ear a long lock of hair curves sharply around her face, reaching almost as far as her chin.

She just looks at me and doesn't even move; she says nothing, there is silence as the boiling water flows, steaming, from the fallen teacup onto the carpet. I look at the tea bag as it floats slowly, on the surface of the water, to the edge of the table. I know it won't fall off.

I can't bear this silence, I have to say something, so I say my name. The librarian moves; she comes around the table, her skirt rustles, she stands in front of me, holds out her arms, embraces me, and she says she knows who I am, as soon as she saw me she knew, she would recognize me among a thousand other pupils, it was exactly as if she were seeing my mother, exactly as if my mother were standing in front of her, and of course I look like my father too, oh my God, we've come back, she never thought that this day would come.

She squeezes me tightly; I'm surrounded by the cold menthol and lemony scent of her eau de cologne mixed in with the scent of powder.

No, I tell her, we haven't come back. I slip out of her embrace, step back, look off somewhere next to her face, and I say that I have come only by myself, they aren't here, because they died in an accident, both of them, Mother and Father.

The librarian's face becomes tense, as if it were made out of glass. It's going to break in a moment, in a moment she's going to start crying. I'm not going to, though, not even a bit.

I look off to the side; at the corner of the table is her handbag, sewn together from colorful patches of leather, black, red, yellow, brown, purple, and green leather patches, they bulge out like the enormous eyes of a beetle, looking at me. At one time Mother used to sew bags like that, she tried to make a little extra money that way.

The librarian sniffs once, takes a deep breath, tries to compose herself, then all at once bursts out weeping, not weeping but sobbing; her entire body is shaken by sobs. She collapses, supporting herself with one hand on the back of the chair; she raises the other hand in front of her face, and she sobs, deeply, with repressed moans. Her splayed fingers smear her makeup. I watch her and I want her to stop. And I even say to her, Stop that already! Harshly, using the second person singular, and as I hear my own voice, I know that this is Father's intonation; he always spoke to me that way if I was crying a lot, and I always stopped, and I would just blubber dryly with my tightened throat. The librarian also stops weeping, or at least she tries to.

She looks down at the table, picks up the cup, and, holding it with two hands, takes a few sips of the boiling water. She takes out a handkerchief, and sniffing, wipes her face and eyes.

She looks at me and says that I shouldn't be angry, she didn't want to cry. If I'm not crying, surely she has no right to cry, even though I'm a young girl, I'm very strong—then she falls silent, not finishing the sentence; once again she wipes her eyes, smearing her makeup even more.

She says that I'm looking at her as if I didn't know who she was.

I tell her that of course I know who she is, she's the librarian.

She says that's it, that's all I know about her, when she was my mother's very best girlfriend? Mother never told me about her?

I shake my head, saying no, never. Her eyelashes tremble; I don't want her to start crying again so I keep talking. Mother never told me anything about herself, about her childhood or her youth, and if I asked, she always said that she would tell me one day when I was grown up. I knew nothing about her at all, she never even told me how she came to meet my father or that she was from this city, nor did she tell me that my grandmother lived here. I didn't even know I had a grandmother until she came to get me from the institute.

The librarian puts away her handkerchief, says: Let's be friends. And that I should call her Anka.

I look at her mouth; the lipstick has smeared all around the edges, it makes her look like she's smiling on only one side.

She's waiting for me to say something; I nod slowly, and I say: That's fine with me.

She turns the chair around so that its back is facing the table; she takes another chair that was beside a shelf, pulls it over, takes my arm, sits down, and has me sit down too.

She says that she knows how my parents met. Do I want her to tell me?

My voice is rasping as I tell her that I really don't care one way or the other. As I utter the words, I can feel that they are not my own; my teeth are chattering, I'm beginning to tremble, but still, I say it. Because it really doesn't matter now.

The librarian takes my hand, she grabs my wrist, she clutches me, and she says it's not true, I shouldn't say things like that, not me, because it will never be something that doesn't matter.

The powder has come off half her face; now I see the spider's web of her wrinkles. She speaks quickly, babbling, at first I can't even grasp what she's saying, instead what I said to her keeps swirling around in my mind. it doesn't matter, it really doesn't matter anymore. I look at her, but I don't want to hear what she's saying, it doesn't matter, and yet her words still force their way in through all the it-doesn't-matters.

The librarian says that it was through her that they met. At that time she was hoping to become an actress, at that time she still believed that she had enough talent, she pleaded for a chance to be in the theater, she worked as an extra, and she accepted one-word roles. Then my father turned up, he wasn't from around here, he was placed here as an assistant transporting stage decorations, a wild Jewish boy with burning eyes who wanted to be a painter, and she saw right away that he would get in trouble and bring trouble to others as well. If he drank even a little, he began to talk about how he was going to change the history of painting, he was not going to do what people expected of him; he always sat in the pub with the others, all the others who imagined themselves to be painters, writers, actors, but among all of them the one with the biggest mouth was my father, cursing the regime loudly, saying he had nothing to lose, he was not going to bargain with these ones, he asked nothing from them but he also wasn't going to give anything to them; if they didn't allow him to paint what he wanted, then he would paint in his head, and really for a long time he painted only in his head. He never showed his drawings to anyone, but he could talk about what he was going to do in such a way that you had to believe that he was genuinely talented. The librarian falls silent, her eyes grow cloudy, and I know that in her mind's eye she sees Father; in a flash she has seen Father's hands — his fingers tensing and clutching the shoulder of his black sweater while he smoked a cigarette, as he did every morning, standing out on the balcony and shuddering, one arm crossed in front of him. At times like that you couldn't talk to him; he was tired because he had been working all night in the artificial fertilizer factory, and he was trying to clear his head to paint, because mornings were his real work time, when he could finally make his own art.

The librarian speaks again, and she tells me that my eyes are exactly like my father's, exactly as black and with the exact same gleam, my face, however, is my mother's, my face and my hair as well, but my mother's gaze was much colder; she could look through boys as if they weren't even there, and not because nobody courted her. The librarian introduced my parents to each other, it was a house party, my mother's leg was broken at the time, and she was angry that she couldn't dance; she teased my father so much that he drew a lynx on her cast with a piece of charcoal, but my mother just laughed and she said it was fine if he didn't want to sweep her off her feet right away with a drawing of a stag drinking in a forest brook.

The librarian breaks into a smile and she tells me that my father, at first, was offended by this, but then of course he began to court my mother, drawing something for her every single day on wrapping paper with charcoal, drawing how she stood, how she looked, how she danced at the ballet barre, and as she sat on the ground cross-legged, massaging the soles of her feet, as she adjusted her hair, as she wept—the librarian falls silent; she reaches toward her own hair, twirls a lock around the finger, pulls her finger out of it, sighs—it took months for my mother to break down, she says, then it became a great love.

I think of the ballet shoes wrapped in newspaper that I once found in the cupboard in the vestibule, I think of the movement with which Mother snatched them out of my hands, and then how she angrily wrapped the newspaper around them again, telling me to stop snooping around, there was nothing for me to see there.

The librarian keeps on talking, talking about my mother and my father, about how they were a beautiful couple and how they really loved each other; her voice grows deeper, it becomes mellow and indulging, and once again I just wish she would stop and be quiet, I don't want to know, not from her and not in this way, I would have wanted to learn all this from Mother and Father, I would have wanted for them to tell me their own story; Mother should have told me why she came to love Father, what she saw in him, what she wanted from him, I should have heard about all of this from Mother, then it would have been my story, but like this it's just gossip, a stupid tale, I don't want the librarian to tell me any more, I want her to be quiet, I want her to stop talking.

I look at the table; I look at her bag; one of the black leather tassels flutters on it, then it moves and climbs backward, and I see that it's not even a tassel but a fly, a great big carrion fly, climbing across the leather patches, up along the strap of the bag to the copper ring attached to it; it climbs up onto the metal ring, it stops, and it rubs its two front legs together. Its belly gleams; I see its segments as if it were made out of metal, out of metal or glass.

The librarian is still talking; now she's talking about Father's first illegal exhibit—it was composed of the pictures he had painted in the reeducation camps and held in the ruined brick factory; it was up for one hour only, and nobody ever dared talk about it, people hardly dared to even look at it, so terrified were they when they saw where he had invited them.

Suddenly the bell rings; it clatters sharply and hoarsely, it rings much more loudly here than in the classroom, and it means that there are only five minutes left in the long recess. The librarian shudders at the sound; the fly starts up, it begins to circle around us. The librarian says that the bell for class will ring in a moment, I should go now, and she'll tell me the rest later.

She becomes quiet as if she wants to say something else, as if she is waiting for me to ask. The fly is no longer buzzing around; it set down somewhere. I walk toward the glass doors; I'm not going to ask anything. I'm by the door when I stop and ask what happened after, why did they leave this town?

The librarian says that my father tried to organize a second exhibit of his own work, up in the forest in the ruins of the chapel, but somebody reported him; the police went out there, they confiscated his pictures, and they also took him away; as far as she knew he was in prison for a year or two. At the time my mother was pregnant with me; she gave up everything, she left everything here, she followed him, she moved to the city where the prison was so she could be close to him. That's all she knew, and she'd heard later on that my father had been released and that they'd both gone abroad, she thought to Israel, but this obviously wasn't true. If it had been true, then I wouldn't be here.

I turn away; I think of one of my father's drawings, a drawing of prison bars; it was different than the others because on it there was one single tiny splotch of light amid the many black prison bars; he often took it out and pinned it up on the wall and looked at it while rubbing a piece of charcoal between his fingers; at such times I was afraid that he was preparing to fill in that splotch of light as well. I notice the fly as it climbs up the glass of the door; behind it I see the face of the librarian, reflected. I ask her who reported them.

The librarian grimaces and says she has no idea. Better for me to ask Grandmother one day.

18

WHEN I COME HOME FROM track practice, the house is empty. Practice was strenuous today; every single part of my body is aching.

I stand in the kitchen and pour myself a large glass of water. I know I shouldn't drink it all at once, but nice and slow. I try to drink it as slowly as I can, and suddenly I think of the story Mr. Pali told about one of his friends and the alcohol that makes hair grow, and laughter bursts out of me, so much that I snort water into the glass and soak the oilcloth cover on the table. I take the towel and I wipe it off, my sides aching.

Today Mr. Pali had us do lung-expansion exercises; we had to stand in line at the foot of the hill and he flung iron-tipped canes up the hill, as high as he possibly could, and we had to run up the hill, find them, and bring them back to him so he could throw them up the hill once again. And all the while Mr. Pali stood at the bottom of the hill and told us jokes; every fifth round we had to stop and listen to one, which was good, because by the fourth round, I felt as if there was no air left in my lungs, but it was also bad, because Mr. Pali's jokes were the kind that made you guffaw, if only because he laughed so loudly himself it was infectious, so my sides ended up hurting much more from laughing than from the air being trapped in my lungs.

I drink the rest of the water, and suddenly I feel that I'm very hungry. I go into the larder, wanting to cut myself a piece of bread that I will then spread with butter. I'm just about to take the top off the breadbasket when I see, on the top of the fridge, the tube of sweetened condensed milk that Grandmother always puts in her coffee.

I take it and screw off the top; the cap gets stuck, and I tell myself that I'll just have a lick, I'll just have a bit to see what it tastes like.

As my tongue touches the tube, for a minute there is a cold metallic taste, then suddenly a thick sweetness spreads across the tip of my tongue, so sweet it almost stings; it's sweeter than anything, sweeter than honey, sweeter than jam, than chocolate, than Turkish delight.

My stomach makes loud growling noises. I press my lips around the tube, and I begin to suck the sweetened milk from it. I know I shouldn't, I know that I should stop and put it down, but my hand isn't obeying, it's clutching the tube, squeezing hard; the thick sugary cream has completely filled my mouth, I suck it and swallow it, I can't stop, I'm sucking it so forcefully that my face hurts; I squeeze the cream out of the tube with two hands, it completely flattens between my fingers, but there's still some left; I suck it out and I squeeze, and I can't stop, the metal of the tube knocks against my teeth.

I swallow the cream, and then suddenly I think of one of Mr. Pali's jokes, the one where the Comrade General enters hell, and the devils allow him to choose the bottomless pit where he will atone for his sins for all eternity, and they show him all of the different tortures, then they get to a cave where the people are sitting up to their necks in pee and shit, but there are planks floating on the surface, packed full of all kinds of delicacies, and everyone is guzzling enough for two, and of course the Comrade General chooses this hell; in the end you can get used to the stink, the main thing is that there's something to eat, and they put him there, and he is just beginning to eat when a siren sounds out, and the devils start yelling: Grub time's over! Dive!

Now somehow it seems even funnier than when Mr. Pali was telling it; my mouth is still filled with cream, I can't swallow it properly, I laugh so hard that it ends up running all down my chin and my face, I'm laughing and sputtering at the same time. Mr. Pali slapped his knees with two hands, his face red, and repeated the punch line several times over: Dive, dive, dive!

I laugh and I laugh, so much that the floor shakes; empty jars clatter against one another on the shelves, and then I hear that someone else is laughing with me. It's Grandmother. She's standing in the door of the pantry, her hands on her hips; she's looking at me and laughing: So, my little cat in the cream, did I catch you in the act? Well, what punishment is good for greediness? After she asks this, she clicks her tongue, and a cardboard box falls from one of the shelves and lands on its side; its lid opens, and something like fifty unopened tubes of condensed milk fall out of it, rolling directly in front of my feet.

Grandmother isn't laughing anymore; she says that once when she was a little girl, she ate some honey in secret, but her father caught her, and he made her eat a whole large glass jar of honey; she had to eat it with a soupspoon until the entire thing was gone, and ever since then she hasn't liked honey. As she says this, her face becomes severe; she looks down at the tubes of cream.

I look at them too; on the tubes are smiling red cows, their mouths gaping open. I know what's going to happen. Grandmother is going to make that tsk-tsk sound again, then the caps will fly off one tube, and another one, and then I will fall to my knees, and another one, and then my mouth will open as well, and another one, and then I'll be catching this or that tube in my hands, and with both my hands I'll press the cream into my mouth; my stomach is churning, I see Grandmother's hand moving, I know that she's going to click her tongue again, *Dive*, I think, *dive*, but Grandmother doesn't click her tongue.

There's just a handkerchief in her hand; she extends it to me, she tells me to wipe my chin, because it's a mess. Then she crouches down and begins to throw the tubes back into the box. She speaks to me over her shoulder, tells me to help, what am I waiting for.

I can't bear it, so I ask her why she has so many tubes of cream. Snorting, Grandmother chortles, saying that Grandfather liked his coffee best with this kind of cream in it, but it was such a rare treasure that he could only permit himself to have it on Sundays, and they could get a hold of it only very rarely; then one time, she went into the city, into the new shop, and she saw tubes of cream standing there in piles; she couldn't resist and bought as many as she could carry home alone.

I'M SITTING AT THE KITCHEN table, writing my lessons. There was a lot today; I leave my math homework for last, but I'm almost finished with that as well, I'm working on the last problem when the tip of my pen suddenly makes a loud scratching sound, and as I raise it, it spits a great big splotch of ink onto the paper. I quickly reach into my pencil case, grab the crumpled-up blotter, and press it onto the splotch, but I know it won't help; because of the stain I'll have to rip the page out of my notebook and write the whole thing over again.

The ink stain slowly seeps into the paper; at first its edges appear, then the middle part; it looks like a face, a face or a lion's head. I press the blotting paper down more firmly on the page; the lion's mane grows, it spreads out, it's no longer just a head now but an entire beast, a dog or a fox; it has a pointy face, ears pressed back; it yelps, grimacing.

I remove the blotting paper; around the new ink stain there are bunch of old ones, dark blue and pale blue ink stains, among them are stains of dried blood, and black ink prints extending out. They abut each other, they clutch at each other, the blotting paper is filled with them.

I turn the paper on its side, and I look at the forms weaving into each other, for many of them I do not know what they are the traces of. I think that I should just crumple it together and throw it out, but I know that I won't; instead I'll go to the pantry and bring out the large iron, and with it I'll smooth out the blotting paper. The iron is very heavy; it will smooth out all the creases, and then I can put the blotter into the folder with my drawings.

THAT EVENING I DREAM OF running. Even in my dream I know that it's because of track practice. I'm in a race; I reach down for the compass dangling from my neck, the map placed in the nylon sheath, but there is only a heavy silver chain there, there's no compass hanging from it, no small pouch for the map, no cross on it, no medal. I let it go; I'm not standing now but running, I run as far as the forest path, the ground is supple but not too soft, I jump across the puddles and the muddy tire tracks or I run around them. The path slowly rises, it will take me to the top of the hill; there I will have a good look around, and I'll figure out where I am. When I get that far, I'll also be able to find the next point where I have to stamp my running card—and then I'll know where the goal lies.

I look down at my feet; my head is bent, I'm running with slackened shoulders, easy running should always begin with loosened shoulders, if your shoulders are tense, then your entire body will become rigid, fatigue will come more easily, and your muscles will fill with lactic acid. I run, I jump across the black roots poking out from the earth; the path is ever steeper, I know that in a moment, I'll be at the top of the hill.

I look over to the side, and I see that the trunks of the trees are black. It's as if the entire forest has burned down; they could have been enormous pine trees, but they're all cindery and dark, swallowing every sound within themselves.

The path rises more and more; I think it'll never come to an end, I'm never going to reach the top of the hill, but then I see that above, among the trees, the sun is shining through. I imagine that the goal is there, up the top of the hill. I run with open arms; leaping, I run.

And then at once I'm at the top. I stop, I'm panting, I wipe my forehead, I unzip my sweat jacket halfway down, pull my braid out from beneath it. The fire must have been much greater on the other side of the hill, there is nothing there but black ash. I look to the left, and I see that a huge crater has ripped through the side of the hill, on its edge lies a blackened tree; something dangles from one of the branches, and I know that it can only be the stamp.

I'm already in front of it, I reach for it, then I remember that I don't even have my running card, but it's too late, I've already grabbed it and pulled it toward myself. The earth moves below me, collapsing into ashes, a black whirlwind pulls me down, down into the depths of the crater. I fall down, but I'm looking up at the sky, I would like to see the sun one last time.

I wake up feeling that everything is hurting, my entire body; I feel as if I'm made of earth, the soles of my feet hurt, my ankles, my calves, my bottom, and my back too, all along my spine, right up to my shoulders. I haven't felt anything like this for a while. I think of Mother, of how she taught me to stretch. I haven't stretched in a long time. When I was little, Mother stretched with me every morning, she said it would help me grow.

I hear Grandmother out in the kitchen as she putters

around. I lie there and I feel that I won't be able to move at all. I am made of earth, of ashes.

I think of the dream, I think of how beneath the covers, my arms are cindery branches; for a moment I just lie there, I don't even dare move my hand from beneath the blanket. I look at the white wall and try to think about stretching; I pull my arms up very slowly from beneath the covers, very slowly I pull up both my arms, upward to the ceiling, I imagine that the pain is tepid sand beneath my skin, dense and moist, it fills up my body.

I stretch my arms out as much as I can; my elbows crack, the sand moves within me, slowly it begins to flow along the inner part of my arm down back into my body, filling my chest, making me groan; it feels good, I stretch some more. I bend my arms back a bit, enough that my shoulders and back are taut, I stretch my thighs, I stretch myself out—Father always said that I should imagine that I'm growing. I'm not imagining that now; rather, I'm imagining the sand flowing out of my body through my back and my bottom, hissing; it falls out of me, flowing across my bed, down through the floor, flowing back into the earth.

I look at the wall, I see the shadow of my outstretched arm, the shadow of my hand, it doesn't look the same as before, the edge is gray and blurry, only the middle part of it is black, as if it were an x-ray, as if I can see the bones in my arm, in my hand, and in my fingers, a skeletal hand drawn from shadows on the wall. I look at it; I squeeze my hand, then I spread my fingers out, I look at the skeletal hand, the bones in the fingers opening and then closing, I'm not imagining this now, and I'm not dreaming, it's really there, the shadow of my other hand is also a bone shadow.

It can't be there, this wall next to the window, and there can be no shadow on it; cold goose bumps run all along my arm, then I understand—on the wall facing the window hangs a glass mirror with wavy silvering, and that's what is reflecting the pale morning light so strangely, making the shadows faint and indistinct.

As I sit up, I reach toward the ceiling and I think for a moment that perhaps I might see my own skull on the wall, the vertebrae of my spine, the gangrenous black ribs in my chest, but no—on the wall I am nothing more than a pale-edged blurry shadow.

I stand up, feeling the stiffness in my body, but now it doesn't hurt so much. I fold up my blanket and begin to make the bed.

19

DURING GYM CLASS I HAVE to wear my hair up in a bun. When class is over, I take off my gym clothes, and put my skirt and my blouse back on. I pull out my hairpins, unwind my bun, undo it, quickly comb it out, and once again I plait my hair. I take the end of the braid and reach into my skirt pocket for my jingling hairband, but today it's not there. I dig around in my pocket, but I don't find it, there's only my handkerchief, the stub of a pencil, half of a walnut, and a razor blade wrapped in paper that I brought for drawing class.

I remember very clearly that I put the hairband in my pocket when I put on my gym clothes, then twisted my hair into a bun and pinned it with the hairpin, but the hairband isn't there anymore. I take everything out of my pocket, place it all on the bench, I turn my pockets out, but I can't find the hairband anywhere.

I crouch down and I look to see if it fell behind the bench, but it isn't there either.

I ask Olgi if she by any chance has seen it anywhere? She says no; the other girls are already headed out, chatting among themselves, the hairband is nowhere to be seen.

In the meantime, my braid has come half undone. I plait it again, and I pull the black rubber band that I use during gym class from my wrist, wind it around the end of my braid, but as I pull it, it breaks and flies into the corner.

The bell for the next class is ringing, the girls have already left, and I'm alone in the dressing room. I know that I have to hurry, I can't be late for geography class.

I don't have anything to tie my hair back with; for a moment I stand there, I don't know what to do, and I look down at my shoes, at my white shoelace.

I take out the razor, unwrap it from the wax paper, I cut a piece off my left shoelace, and I use that to tie up the end of my braid.

I run along the corridor to get to class on time, but all the while I'm only thinking of my hairband and where it could've gone.

I get to the staircase, grab the banister, take the stairs three at a time; I definitely put it in my pocket, I couldn't have lost it, so that means that only one thing happened—it was stolen. Someone was jealous of my beautiful hairband, and so she took it from my pocket.

I make it to the classroom right before the teacher does, not even getting to my own desk by the time he comes in.

During geography class I don't pay any attention, I copy everything that's written on the blackboard into my exercise book, but the whole time I'm only thinking of who it could have been. I look at the girls, and I try to figure out which one did it, but none of them are behaving strangely or suspiciously, none of them turns away, none of them bends her head or otherwise avoids my gaze.

The bell rings for the long recess. I don't leave. I unpack my entire schoolbag onto my desk, maybe it's in there, but at the same time I know I won't find it there.

Only the seventh-graders stay inside. Hajni is erasing the blackboard, Olgi is sweeping.

I shake out my books and workbooks, thinking perhaps it slid between the pages, but at the same time I know that it couldn't have slid in there.

I pack everything back into my bag. Olgi puts down the broom, she asks me if I've found it. No, I tell her.

Olgi says she has a stomachache and has to go to the bathroom, she asks me if I can stay inside till she comes back, because a seventh-grader can only leave the classroom if someone takes her place while she's gone. I motion to her that it's okay for her to go. Then Hajni says she has to go too. She leaves the classroom with Olgi.

I'm alone in the classroom. I walk amid the rows of desks, thinking of my hairband, thinking of the small bells, wondering where they could be, in whose desk the hairband is, whose schoolbag.

When I walk next to the teacher's platform for the third time, I stumble on something. I look down; it's the dustpan, and next to it is the little broom. I kicked the dustpan by mistake, and half of the swept-up dust has fallen out of it. I crouch down, pick up the small broom, and begin to sweep it back into the dustpan.

The dust is gray and very fine, there's a lot of it, at least three fistfuls of dust, filling up at least half of the dustpan. I sweep up all of it, then I put down the broom, and I pick up the dustpan to take it to the dustbin to pour it out.

The dust is so fine that it shifts with every step, sliding back and forth on the dustpan, almost as if it were water. I hold the dustpan with two hands, carry it that way. I look at the dust, and I think again of my hairband, of what Grandmother will say when she finds out that I lost it.

The dust moves again as if it had been stirred by the wind; something like an eddy forms on its surface, I see it for a split second and then it's gone, and at the same time I hear the sound of my hairband's silver bells, very softly and very far away.

I know that I'm just imagining it; they can't be ringing, I stuffed flax into them. I stop and listen, I want to know where the sound is coming from, but there is only silence.

I stop near the first desk, and I place the dustpan on the top of the desk.

I look at the dust; its surface is smooth, pencil shavings and sunflower-seed shells are mixed in with paper pellets.

With my left hand I reach in, grab a bit of dust, sprinkle it into the air, and I think of the sound of the bells.

The dust falls in long straight lines, pointing toward the coats. I step forward and reach into the dust, I once again sprinkle it into the air; the streak grows longer, I follow it, I let it lead me, let it show me the way.

As I get to the coats, the streak of dust turns away, moving along the coat rack, alongside the coats, and I reach the second-to-last coat when I run out of dust. I turn the dustpan toward the floor, but there's no more dust in it. I look down; on the parquet floor, dark brown from kerosene, the dust is gray and snaking, and at its end, the triangular tip of a pencil shaving is pointing toward the second-to-last coat.

It's a dark purple quilted coat, I don't know whose it is, but I know it's a boy's, not a girl's.

I throw the dustpan onto the floor. I take the coat from the hanger, I shake it, but in vain, because I don't hear the sound of the bells. I know that the hairband is in the coat somewhere, it must be in there.

I put it down on the last desk in the classroom, I reach into the two outer pockets, then the two inner pockets. I find coins, buttons, a piece of string, and a matchbox, which I open; inside is a slingshot made of green wire as well as round pins bent into U-shapes, their tips stuck into pieces carved out of a white eraser. I look through the pockets one more time, but I don't find the hairband.

I know I don't have much time; the girls will be back in a

moment, I need to hang the coat back up and sweep the dust back into the dustpan. I put everything back in the pockets of the coat. As I pick it up to hang it back up again, I see a slight rip in the lining. It must be hidden there, behind the lining. Quickly I palpate everywhere on the coat; the outer waterproof layer rustles beneath my palm, and there, at the bottom of the coat, well below the pockets, I suddenly sense something hard. It's the hairband, I can tell for certain by the forms of the round bells.

I don't know how to get it out. I think of the razor blade; I'm about to reach for it when I hear the girls coming back. I quickly grab the dustpan and the broom, and I begin to sweep.

I CAN'T FIGURE OUT WHOSE coat it is. During the next recess I stand next to it, the razor in my hands, but there are too many pupils in the classroom, I don't dare touch the coat, and I don't dare to cut my hairband out of the lining.

There still two classes left; I'm not able to pay proper attention during either one of them, I can only think about who that purple coat belongs to. I look at the boys, I try to figure out which one of them it could be.

Iván notices that I'm looking at him; he yawns. I realize that he was actually smiling, but he didn't want me to notice, so he made it look like he was yawning. I know it's not his coat, his coat is green.

AFTER THE LAST CLASS OF the day, as the bell rings, I quickly grab my coat and my bag, and I'm the first to run out of the classroom, the first to run down the steps, the first to run out the school gates, but I don't head into the street; instead I crouch beneath the bushes next to the fence, I crouch down so no one can see me, and from there I wait for the purple coat to come along.

For a long time there's no purple coat. I'm beginning to think there won't even be one, that somehow the boy realized I'm watching for him and instead he climbed over the school fence and went home another way. I'm just about to climb out from behind the bushes to set out for home myself, but then I decide to count to one hundred very slowly; I'll wait until I finish, just in case he heads this way.

I begin to count nice and slow. I'm already at seventy when I see the purple coat beyond the bushes. The purple coat is passing by me; its owner's head is hanging down, kicking a stone and whistling something, but from here, on the other side of the bushes, I can't tell who it is.

I set off after him, but I don't go onto the sidewalk, I'm taking the path between the row of bushes and the fence. Suddenly he kicks the stone from the sidewalk and goes after it into the street; he's having a hard time kicking it back onto the sidewalk, so I'm able to catch up to him, I even pass him, but the bushes are hiding me, so he still doesn't see me. I look back, see his face —it's Gazsi, the stuttering boy.

There is a gap in the bushes, I step out of it—I'm standing in front of him.

He's so surprised that he nearly drops his schoolbag.

The expression on his face is one of such alarm that I have to laugh. I am, however, extremely angry. I'm thinking of my hairband, of the pencil shavings and the dust, and when I speak to him there is no gentleness in my voice. I tell him that he has something of mine—and to give it back.

He smiles at me, shakes his head, and he says b-b-but no, he doesn't have anything of mine. But he's very happy to see me, he was j-j-just thinking of me, in fact.

I tell him not to think about me, to think about the great

French Revolution instead. I'm hoping that will make him stop smiling, but he just laughs. He says there's no need to bother with these old Commies. They all think they're going to come back, but no, they're finished completely.

I shake my head and tell him I don't care about that—what I care about is why he stole something from me and when he's going to give it back.

He takes a step toward me, and he says that he hasn't stolen anything from me, but he would like to. He grabs my hand; his grasp is warm and moist, I'm so surprised that for a moment I can't move or speak. Then he says that he's been in love with me from the moment he saw me, when I stood in front of the blackboard and threw my braid behind my back and I wrote my name on the blackboard, yes, ever since the very first moment. I love you, he says, still holding my hand; he takes a step toward me, all the while licking his mouth; he looks into my eyes, he wants to kiss me, it feels as if this weren't happening to me but to someone else, I see his hand moving, he wants to embrace me, I shout: What are you doing, leave me alone! I tear my hand away from his, I raise my bag and place it between us, and with all my strength I push him away. He stumbles backward; from the thrust the clasp of my bag opens, my schoolbooks and my notebooks fall out, the pages splay out and, clattering, they fall onto the flagstones on the pavement.

My pencil case falls out last, I step over to the side with my empty schoolbag in my hand and I look down. My chemistry notebook is half opened in a puddle, the cover of my pencil case has fallen off, my pencils and pens have all spilled out.

Now look what you've done, I yell at him, and I bend down to gather it all up. Gazsi stammers out that he didn't want to, he didn't mean to do this, he crouches down, he grabs my chemistry notebook, he takes it out of the puddle, it's covered with mud. I want to rip it out of his hands, but he doesn't let me; I pull on it, Gazsi kneels in the puddle, the notebook slips from his fingers, he scrambles to his feet with difficulty.

The edge of his coat is right there in front of my eyes. I know that my hairband is there in the lining, I grab it, even through the fleece and the lining I can feel that it's there. Give it back! I yell at him. Gazsi says he has nothing, but I've already reached into my pocket and pulled out the razor blade, and I cut into his coat. Ripping, the coat material splits into two, inside the coat there is gauze and gray cotton wadding, and in the wadding there is my hairband, I grab it, and I pull it out. So then what is this, I cry out, and I shake the hairband in front of Gazsi's face. So tell me then what this is, I cry out again, and on my hairband, the bells softly ring.

Gazsi looks at his coat, ripped apart, the frayed lining and the wadding hanging down in tatters. On his face is shock, as if he is unable to understand what happened, and then he sees the razor blade in my hand. He says I'm not normal. I'm crazy, just like my grandmother. Everyone knows about her, that she was in the lunatic asylum for years, well, that's where I belong too, I'm an idiotic cunt.

He's almost crying as he yells this out, he turns his back to me and starts walking down the street. I watch him as his hand rummages along the rips on the coat, trying to somehow stuff the wadding back in.

I put my hairband back in my pocket, then I begin to pack my schoolbooks and notebooks back into my bag.

20

THAT ENTIRE DAY I THINK about what Gazsi said to me—
that I'm crazy, just like my grandmother.

When Grandmother comes into my room with the ironed
bed linens in her hands, I suddenly ask her if it's true what they
say about her, that she was locked up in the insane asylum?

She puts the linens into the bureau and says: Yes, it's true.
She ended up there after the war, when, for the first time in
her life, she forgot everything. She was there for a long time
—weeks, months—and that's where she met Grandfather. Do
I want her to tell me the story?

I nod.

Fine, she says. She sits down on one of the armchairs, and
she motions toward the bookcase, for me to look at the jug on
the top of it.

It's a fairly large jug; a rooster with green wings and blue
legs struts around on it, its head thrown back, its chest puffed
out, you can see that it's just about to crow. Its crest is blue, its
beak is yellow, its tail feathers spread out rigidly, and its tiny
black eyes glitter, ready for combat.

Right now, the sun is shining on it; the rooster's beak is nearly shining.

Grandmother asks me if I notice anything unusual about it.

No, I say, nothing, only that the rooster looks like the fighting type.

She smiles, and she says that the rooster is really beautiful, it was no accident that Grandfather really loved that rooster as well, but I should take a closer look at the jug.

I look at the jug; the white glaze sharply reflects the light back into my eyes. I squint, I see the scales on the rooster's feet, I see the outlines of its feathers drawn in black.

Grandmother looks up at the jug too. Then she closes her eyes and begins to speak.

YOU'RE IN THE HOSPITAL, they call it a mental hospital. A lunatic asylum. They say you're here because they found you in the forest, you were living in a hole scooped out of the ground like some kind of animal, you didn't even have any clothes on your body, you had smeared mud all over yourself as if you were made of earth, you were muttering and making rasping noises and scratching, you didn't want to be taken away. They said that you had spent months, maybe even years in the forest, no one knew.

You don't even know, you don't know about this or anything else. You don't remember the forest, you don't remember the hole, you don't even remember the earth, your oldest memory is of the wall lined with white tiles, the cloudy mirror hung upon it, and from within, a strange woman with matted hair stares back at you, you don't even know who she is; you don't even know who you are.

You don't want anything, you don't talk, you let them dress you and then undress you, you let them wash you, you let them put the medicine beneath your tongue, you let them jab needles into your arm. If they ask you something, you don't answer; you don't want to hear, you don't want to understand.

The forest can be seen through the windows of the back corridor. One of the male nurses leads you over there, says, Look, maybe you can remember something, look, because that's where you were living, there among the trees, look over there and try to remember who you are, what happened to you. You stand there looking at the forest, and suddenly you see that there is some kind of darkness wreathing through the trees, calling you, it speaks to you, it's yours. You know what you need to do, you need to rip off the clothes that they gave to you, you need to tear the hairpins out of your hair, the hairpins they pinned into your hair, you need to climb out the window, you need to go across the yard, across the fence, across the meadow, up the side of the hill, you need to go back there, back among the trees. You begin to climb onto the windowsill; in your nose there is the scent of the rotting leaves and the moist earth, between your fingers there is the memory of the soft mud, you know what it's like to smear it on your body, you know by now that everything they say about you is true.

You're going to go back, that is your place, that's where you belong. You don't want to go back, but still, you will go back. You clutch the windowsill, you know that you don't have the strength to stay here much longer. Then someone pushes you. Not very hard, but still you fall against the glass. In the reflection, you see that it's a man carrying a suitcase, he pushed you. You turn away from the window, you look at him go; the pushing motion must have made his suitcase open, because sand is spilling out from it in thin lines onto the floor. You look at it for a while, then you follow its trace. You go to where the line of sand is leading you.

You find him in the courtyard; he's sitting on a bench, in the sunlight. Next to him is the open suitcase with black sand; he's rummaging in it with two hands, he's kneading it, turning it over, forming it into something. All the while he's talking, his voice is like a dry whispering, you don't understand any of what he's saying; it's as if the grains of sand rustling between his fingers are all that you hear. You don't know what he's doing, you don't want to know, not this or anything else, you don't want to think, you don't want to live, and yet you look; then the next day you go back, and the day after that, you stand there every day just a few steps away from him, pressing your back against one of the trees in the courtyard, and you watch him from there.

His movements remind you of something, but you don't know what that is, of course, you just like to look, you like to observe the black grains of sand as they spin through his fingers; you watch him until it grows dark; when dusk falls the man closes his suitcase and snaps the latch, he puts it next to his leg, he waits for a bit, then he stands up, and with the suitcase in his hand, he returns to the sick ward. You step away from the tree, you wait for the nurses who will come and accompany you back to your bed, you don't want to go, you're afraid of the night, it's true it's never dark in the sick ward, but still you're afraid, you would rather embrace the trunk of the tree, attach yourself to it so you could stay there, so that they wouldn't be able to grab you, carry you away.

Days or weeks go by before you notice that in the suitcase there are not only grains of sand, but something else as well; at first you think that it's larger pieces of stone and fragments of bone, then you take a few steps closer to look at it; you are standing right next to the suitcase, and you see that you were wrong, it's actually pieces of crockery. Then you notice the gashes on the man's arms, both of his forearms are covered with cuts; as he moves his fingers, the muscles and tendons stretch beneath his skin, the throbbing pattern of the wounds draws a red net across the skin.

You watch as his fingers dig in the sand; with his hands he suddenly raises two shards from the suitcase; he puts them together, they do not fit; he turns them, they don't fit that way either; he turns them again, they still don't fit; one of his hands is trembling, the shards knock against each other, the shuddering in his voice runs through you, the man drops the shards into the sand; he rummages around, he takes out two different shards, he tries to fit them together; he's trying every possible angle and direction, but they don't fit together, he throws back *those shards, then he rummages in the sand again, looking for two different shards.*

Suddenly he turns his face toward you; he looks off to the side, his eyes are gray-green water; then, with a tiny, birdlike movement, he turns his head slightly, now he's looking at you; he speaks again, and from that point on you know for certain that he's talking to you, he's telling you something. As for what he's saying, you don't understand that for a long time, his words keep running together, as if he were speaking an unknown language, but you can't even pay proper attention, you look at his fingers, at the grains of sand trickling through them.

One day, as you stand there in the sun, and you watch the shards of crockery in the man's hands, you desire to touch the sand. You spread your fingers apart, the sun warms your skin, and you think of sand that has also been warmed by the sun, you know that you too could step over there, you could reach over there, it would be but one single movement, you too could plunge your hands into the sand, you too could search for those two fragments, you too could try to fit them together, you imagine how they touch each other, how they fit, how they go together, how they stick to each other as if you had spread beeswax on the edges of the fracture. For a moment you close your eyes, and when you open them, you see the man once again touching two shards together, they do not fit, but he turns one of them, and then what you just imagined happens: the two shards of crockery perfectly fit together, they stick together; for a moment the man just holds them, then he carefully lays them down on the top of the sand in one of the corners of the suitcase.

You look at the shards, at the pale blue lines that run across the white glaze; you still can't make out the pattern, but you know that something has begun, that the man will find more pieces that will fit together, not immediately, but not too long from now.

Once again he's digging in the sand, rummaging in it, and while he speaks you suddenly are able to understand two words: Frozen earth, he says; your comprehension of these words shoots through your skull like the sharpest of headaches, you grab your head, you press the palms of your hands to your ears, you don't want to hear anything, you don't want to understand anything, but it's too late, his words have already moved into your head, they unravel, one after the other, from unintelligibility. A Y-shaped incision, he says, a spade handle, he says, rose, peritoneum, onion skin, barbed-wire fence, bread, bacon, blood clots.

You look and you listen, now you understand every word, as if you'd always understood, his stories are now swirling in your brain, he's telling them all at once, and always in the middle of the sentences he switches from one to the other, now he is speaking of service at the front, then of a military academy, then about medical school, now he is speaking of being a prisoner of war, then of when he was a tiny child, then of the years he spent in the labor camp. He speaks of long journeys by train, he speaks of waiting, he speaks of the very first time he saw a naked woman, he speaks of what it was like to smoke cigarettes in the trenches, what it was like to fear being wounded, what it was like to wish for death.

He speaks in a mixture of verses, prayers, and songs, with long and detailed descriptions of surgeries and made-up stories. He tells a story about an appendix removal almost until the end, then he begins to talk about how he'd never tasted anything so sweet as the corn that, in his childhood, they would roast by digging them, husks and all, into the eternally burning slag heap behind the ironworks for fifteen minutes, and then the kernels of corn turned brown and they tasted like caramel, then he talked about how in the camp one time they had to dig a canal ditch for eight days without sleeping, standing up to their thighs in freezing water, the men, one after the other, fainted around him into the water, the ones who were lucky were pulled out by the guards and beaten on their chests until they came to and spat out the black water they'd swallowed; then he began to say that once he saw with his own eyes a man escape from behind a barbed-wire fence by cobbling wings together from the bark of a birch tree, straw, and

*strands of hair from his beard, and with that he was able to fly above
the roofs of the barracks, and from there to the guard tower, and from
there up to the heavens.*

*He tells every story over and over so many times that you already
know all of them by heart, and yet you can't stop listening as he talks,
because he tells every story a little differently each time, leaving out
certain details or elaborating on others, he tells a long story about how
over the course of one night he sharpened the edge of a spade with a
croissant-shaped piece of stone, using very slow pulling movements;
it became much sharper than a razor, so that you not only feel the
smoothness of that pulling movement in your hand, but you hear the
soft yet protracted squeaking of the spade's metal edge as it cuts deep
down to your bones, so clearly that you have goose bumps all over both
arms from it.*

*In the meantime, the man has found more shard fragments that fit
together; with trembling hands he places them in a row next to each
other in one of the corners of the suitcase. Already it's clear that what
he's trying to put back together is a large glazed ceramic jug, and you
know why, it's because he thinks that by doing this he'll be able to fix
his hands; if he's able to put the jug together he'll be able to cure himself of that trembling; his movements will be precise; his grasp will be
as certain as it was before, and then he will finally be able to complete
what he set out to do before the war — become a vascular surgeon.*

*You've heard the stories so many times by now that sometimes you
feel that everything that happened to him has happened to you. You
reach your hand toward the suitcase, you look at the shadow of your
fingers, spread apart, as you turn the palm of your hand to the sun, the
shadows extend out, penetrating into the sand like black roots, then you
turn your hand to one side, your hands weave into one trailing vine,
then once again they separate. You look at the palm of your hand, at
the smooth skin of your forearm, and suddenly on that too you see that
web of scarlet wounds, as if they were really there, as if it had been you
who placed your wrists onto the spade's sharpened edge, as if it had
been you who gashed both of your forearms right down to the bone,*

as if it were you who had wanted to die, as if it were you who had wanted everything to end forever.

You stand up, you sense how the air sharply penetrates deep into the wounds, your blood, throbbing, spraying out from them, the blood runs all the way down your palms, between your fingers, it feels neither scalding hot nor cold, simply lukewarm. You're just imagining these wounds, but even so you know that it's true, your life and your strength are flowing across your palms. You feel that if you could stand without wincing, without moving, then everything would really come to an end, you would really die, or if not, then at least you would forever lose the possibility of knowing who you were and how you ended up here.

The imaginary pain pierces your arm like a knitting needle stabbing it; you can't stand it, you cry out, and then suddenly you see that a long needle is indeed stabbing your arm, now you're not imagining it, and this is not the memory of someone else but your own, it really happened, the only thing was it didn't happen to you, but you were there and you saw how it happened—you remember.

Then suddenly everything comes back to you, and just as suddenly as you are able to understand the man's words, now you know who you are, you know what happened to you, and you know what happened to the others, everyone you loved. The names burst out of you, you scream: Mama, Papa, Miklós, Bertuka, Bátykó—the names cicatrize together in one long scream, you can't stop, you stand there, you stand there with your arms extended, and you scream their names over and over, you know it won't bring them back, but you also know that you will never be able to stop.

The man then pulls his hand out of the sand, he steps over to you, he's standing very close, in front of you, you're still yelling, you scream the names into his face, the man reaches over to you and with both hands he grabs your forearms above the wrists, he grabs them and squeezes them, hard, as if he were trying to close up the wound, not one wound, many; he squeezes your arms wildly, as if he knew exactly what had happened to you, and at the same time he is telling you to look at him, look into his eyes, are you listening, look over there at him, his voice is very calm, it's not at all the voice that he was using to tell his stories, can't you hear what he's saying— but you don't look at him, there you are with the others again, you're kneeling in the mud, in front of the woodshed, you don't want to be there, you don't want to be there, but at the same time you hear the man's voice, he's speaking as if he is trying to awaken you from some dream, he is telling you to look at him, stay with him, don't go, he's squeezing your arms even harder, he's pulling you to him, you don't look at him, you look away at the crockery shards placed on the surface of the sand, but that's not what you see, what you see before you is the black mud, the black mud of the earth, you see the imprint of the heavy boot in the mud that is half filled with rainwater, you're going to fall into it face-first, then your nose will be filled with mud and water and sand and clay, your nose, your mouth, your lungs, your body. You want to be filled up, it's what you deserve — this is what you deserve.

Then the man lets go of your arms, and he reaches toward your face, he holds your face on either side with his hands, and he turns your head toward him with such strength that you can't resist, he looks into your eyes, and you look into his, gray water, you think, he's going to hit me, he's going to slap me, and that's what you deserve. He doesn't hit you— he just yells at you: It's not your fault, he yells, do you understand? It's not your fault that you survived.

You're silent, and he is silent, you look at each other; he pulls his hand from your face, then he speaks for a long time, he says: It could have been otherwise, but now it's like this, and now there's nothing more to be done, because you still have to try to live. He turns away, and he goes back to the suitcase, he digs into the sand, he lets the grains run between his fingers, there are two shards of crockery in his hands.

You look at the suitcase— it's not even a suitcase but a soldier's trunk with iron strips around the edges. You walk over to it, you push your hands into the sand up to your wrists. It's not lukewarm— it's cold.

. . .

GRANDMOTHER IS QUIET; SHE OPENS her eyes, and she says that's enough for now, one day she'll tell me the rest. She sighs a deep sigh, she nods toward the jug with her head. She tells me to push a chair over to the bookcase, to stand on it and look at the jug from there, from up close.

As I step onto the chair, one of my hands touches the glass of the bookcase; the glass sheet makes a loud twanging sound, and the bookcase creaks loudly. The jug is shining in the light. I see that it's full of cracks, it really has been put back together from many pieces; all along the surface thin black lines delineate tiny squares, as if someone had drawn mesh all around it to keep it together.

I've never seen anything like this before; at home we used to have a decorative plate repaired with wire, it hung on the wall in the vestibule, but that had broken into only three parts, and it was held together with a piece of ugly thick gray wire.

Grandmother says that it took months to put the jug back together again, but from that point on she was helping Grandfather with it, and by the time it was ready, the Communists had closed down the hospital. They left the hospital together, and after that, they never separated. The jug was properly put back together, don't be afraid, she says, I can touch it without hesitation.

I reach for it, touch the white glaze; the black threads running across the surface touch the tips of my fingers at the points where they cross each other, I can sense the tiny knots in them. I take it into my hands; the jug is warm from the sunlight. I caress the wings of the rooster, its tail feather.

Grandmother tells me to pick it up nicely with two hands and take it down, but I should be careful, because it's not empty.

I have to clamber up in order to get hold of it, but finally I reach it. I pick it up very carefully; it's lighter than I thought it would be. As I lift it down from the top of the bookcase, something in it sloshes around.

I get down off the chair, and as I take the jug over to Grand-mother, I look inside. I see that there's water in it, it's about half filled with water; the inside of the jug is also covered in cracks. As I carry it, the water sloshes around inside in a whirlpool, and the deep, moldy scent of a well wafts up.

Grandmother takes it from me, presses her hands around it, brings it onto her lap, places it on her thigh; she leans over it and looks in. For a long time she doesn't move, and she doesn't say anything, then with one hand she taps the jug; her ring clinks dully against it. She looks up at me with a wry smile at one corner of her mouth. She says that there always has to be water in this jug so that the ceramic can absorb it and maintain the tension in the silk threads, because she and Grandfather put the jug back together without even a single drop of glue, they used nothing else, only a few inches of thread from an old scarf.

I look at the rooster's throat, at its beautiful bright feathers. Even so, Grandfather didn't become a vascular surgeon, I say. Grandmother shakes her head; she holds her hands in front of her, spreads her fingers apart, grabs the air, makes circling motions with her wrists; the sleeves of her sweater bunch up, and she says that these are hand exercises, a part of Grandfather's morning routine as well, he completed them every blessed morning but to no avail, because he was never able to work as a doctor again.

He became an auxiliary staff member at the public hygiene station; he was placed there. That meant that he had to work as a street sweeper, but he swept streets for only one week before his new coworkers realized that it would be better for everyone concerned if they swept and he tutored their children.

The government did not allow Grandfather to teach offi-cially in any school, but he began to tutor in physics, biology, geography, chemistry, Latin, German, French, Russian, gram-mar, mathematics, everything. He could teach anything to any-one; he could explain even the most tedious subjects in such a way that his students would remember them forever. He was intuitively a great teacher, and for thirty years, half of the entire city's population were his pupils; everyone respected and loved him—and yet he never once stepped foot in a proper school.

Grandmother clasps her two hands together; her fingers crack. She asks who told me about the lunatic asylum.

I tell her that one of the boys said that I too belong there. I tell her what happened with Gazsi and my hairband.

When Grandmother hears how I cut apart Gazsi's coat, she suddenly begins to laugh, and she can hardly stop laughing to say, Very good, I did well, he deserved it, that's exactly what my mother would have done, and there's nothing for me to be afraid of because I'm not crazy at all, or certainly not any crazier than all the other idiots around here. As she says this, the tone of her voice changes a bit, and I can tell that it's one of Grandfather's sayings, and I also know that Grandmother will repeat it, and that she'll laugh again, and I'll be laughing too, laughing along with her.

21

AFTER SCHOOL I HAVE TO go to track practice, but everything is hurting, I don't feel like running or training. For once I'll skip it; I have to. The librarian says that I can visit the library whenever I want, even when it's closed. She showed me where the extra key is hidden. It hangs by the door, on a string from a hinge behind the glass cabinet with an old book showing a woodcut of the city and the school.

After the last class, I wait for all the students to leave the hallway and then, nice and quiet, I go up the stairs to the library. It's closed. I look around, then I pull out the extra key from behind the cabinet. I open the door quickly, put the key back in its place; I go in.

The librarian keeps the forbidden books on the highest shelf in the second row. First you have to push the large, three-meter-high rolling staircase over there. It's fairly heavy; you have to push it hard, then it rolls nicely.

Once the ladder is in place, you have to climb up to the top, stand on the platform, and push all the crimson-bound almanacs to one side; behind them are the forbidden romance novels. The librarian once said that nobody writes novels as beautiful as those anymore; these are very old, from the time before the war. There are not only novels but forbidden fashion magazines too. These items are not permitted in the library, but the librarian says that they make life more beautiful.

I love the fashion magazines even more than the novels. I can read only a few words of them, because they're in French, but that's not the point—every one of their pages is glittery and shining, and each magazine is as thick as a telephone book.

I take down my favorite one; it shows an African woman wearing a fur coat reaching down to the ground. My favorite picture is the one in which she's wearing a long silver fox fur; she's drawing it close around herself with one hand as if she were chilly, but at the same time you can see her bare leg right up to her thigh and one of her breasts from the side. I save this picture for last. I look at all the others first, then at the one of a girl standing in a closet filled with fur coats, as if she were hiding among them, when suddenly the librarian comes in.

She closes the door behind her and turns the lock. She doesn't let go of the doorknob; for a while she stands there, turned toward the door. She's weeping loudly, her shoulders shaking.

I don't dare speak; I hunch into myself at the top of the ladder.

The librarian turns around; her face is covered in tears. She goes to the table, pours herself a glass of water from the jug, drinks very slowly, takes a handkerchief, blows her nose, and wipes her face.

For a moment she just stands there, staring into space. I lean over a little and I see that she's looking at herself in the reflection of the window.

She touches her neck; she unties her black and blue silk scarf, takes it off, smooths it out, shakes it, folds it, and puts it on the table. She smooths down her hair, presses her fingers to her closed eyes, sniffles; she tries to breathe deeply, and suddenly she crouches down, pulls out the bottom desk drawer, takes out a large black wooden box, and places it on the top of the table with a thud. It looks like a little suitcase.

She breathes out once, then opens the box.

Stepped drawers raise out from within it, each one filled with jars and brushes and small mirrors; the inside of the cover is a single mirror. I see enlarged, reflected within it, the librarian's chin, her mouth, and her neck.

I watch as she looks at herself, first turning her head to the left, then to the right, then she looks directly ahead; she grimaces. With both hands she smooths down her hair, presses her thumbs to her temples, pulls the skin on her face upward and back.

She grimaces again. She takes out a jar, opens it, smooths cream onto her face, taps the skin of her face with the tips of her fingers. She waits a moment, then she powders her face with a large brush. The powder has a strong fragrance, I can smell it even from the top of the ladder, it has a completely different fragrance than the powder that Grandmother uses. The librarian takes out a different powder puff, and with that she rubs rouge onto her face, then she paints her eyes, but not just with one color eyeshadow, she uses at least six or seven different shades, mixing the hues from golden compacts with many compartments.

She paints her mouth with a brush as well. I've never seen anything like it; she uses a thick brush, then a very thin one; the lipstick is a wine-crimson color, it makes her mouth shine beautifully.

Her face looks completely different now. I see her only in the mirror; if I didn't know it was her, I wouldn't recognize her.

She looks at herself and tries to smile. In the mirror I can see that her mouth is trembling. Suddenly she reaches out with both hands and slams down the top of the box; she grabs the scarf from the table, pours water onto it from the glass, and begins to wipe all the makeup off her face.

I lift up the fashion magazine very slowly; I close it. I want to put it back.

The librarian throws the handkerchief down onto the table; once again she opens the box, making the sunlight flash into my eyes from the mirror's reflection.

The magazine slips out from my fingers. I reach for it, but can't catch it; it makes a huge clattering sound as it falls to the ground.

The librarian turns around at the clattering sound; on her face is fear and anger. The trace of lipstick is still there, and the eyeshadow, dark, wine-colored smears; it makes her look very old. For a moment I believe she's going to yell, but no, she flinches and smiles at me.

She asks if I was there the whole time.

Yes, I say.

She motions for me to come down.

I climb down the ladder, I bend and pick up the magazine from the floor.

The librarian comes over to me. I hand her the magazine, and I say that I'm sorry, I didn't mean to drop it. She nods and says that she'll put it away. With her free hand she suddenly reaches toward me and caresses my face, I can sense the fragrance of the lipstick and the powder on her fingers; her touch is gentle and warm.

She lowers her hand and says that it'd be best for me to go now, but if I want, she'll teach me how to apply makeup.

I think of the tapered lipstick brush, how she dipped it into the crimson pot. I nod, and I say: Thank you.

I PUT MY RUNNING THINGS in the cupboard in the vestibule before heading to the kitchen. Grandmother is sitting at the table, spinning a coin between her fingers; at times it knocks against her ring. When she sees me, she opens up her wallet, throws the coin in, and asks, looking straight at me, where I was.

I tell her I was at track practice. Grandmother shakes her head. She says that I'm a stupid little girl, I've been living with her for months now and I haven't learned how to lie properly.

I say I wasn't lying. I try to think of running, of Mr. Pali, of the paths in the forest, and not about the library, not about the fashion magazines. I can't do it.

Grandmother looks at me, licks her mouth, and she says, Don't lie.

I don't answer; I look at the floor, I look at the black veining on the planks. Grandmother says that the floor isn't going to help me, I should look up at her, look squarely into her eyes.

I look at her. She says she knows that I'm lying. I'm a very bad liar, and that's not the way to lie, not the way to lie at all. I don't say anything. Grandmother asks me if I want her to teach me how to lie properly.

No, I say.

Grandmother's eyes flash for a second, and she tells me not to lie. Then she smiles at me, tells me not to be afraid because she'll teach me, then she kicks one of the chairs underneath the table; the chair slides toward me. Grandmother gestures for me to take a seat. I sit down.

Grandmother picks up her clasped wallet, snaps it open, and spills the money inside it onto the table; the coins and the paper money fall out. I see banknotes of various denominations, ten, twenty-five, one hundred. The wallet is now empty. Grandmother throws it in front of me on the table, tells me to dig my left hand deep inside it. I look at the open mouth of the wallet with its serrations, the drooping yellow-green material behind it. As I slide my hand into it, I feel how cool and damp it is.

The fine teeth of the clasp touch my skin. Grandmother reaches over, puts her hand on the wallet, and presses the serrated clasp around my wrist. It doesn't hurt very much, but it's unpleasant, a prickling, ticklish feeling, as if I had stuck my hand into a nettle bush. Grandmother looks into my eyes, asks me if it hurts. No, I say; the tingling then grows stronger, now the nettles are causing my skin to break out in blisters. Grandmother once again asks if it hurts, and again I say no; the tickling is now a burning, searing pain, the blisters are bursting open, leaving deep craters in my skin. It doesn't hurt, I say, it doesn't hurt, it doesn't hurt, I want to think that I don't even have a hand, I have no fingers, I have no wrist, have no palm, I have nothing that can hurt, but that doesn't work, the pain stabs through my palm, making my fingers splay out; It doesn't hurt, I say, and I see that the leather of the wallet is bulging out where my nails are touching it inside, you can see the pulsing movement of the swelling as the convulsions of pain thrust my fingers apart and force them back together; the leather of the wallet is moist and gleaming, it's eel skin, I recall the words and they make my stomach turn; the pain runs up my arm, runs across my shoulders, it's already throbbing in my spine, in my stomach, making me dizzy, I feel that in a moment I'm going to throw up.

With her other hand, Grandmother is caressing my hair. I'm a very stubborn girl, she says, stubborn, just like she was, just like my mother was, but it's no use, stubbornness won't help me now, neither will the fact that I bear the pain so well. Because now it's not stubborn that I have to be but clever and deceitful, and I should not bother with pain but with lies, with lies and with truth, with the fact that either of them can be exactly like the other; you just have to want it and that's what it will be, one is a white stone, the other a black stone, and it doesn't matter which one I choose because if I squeeze my fingers around that stone and hide it in my palm, it will disappear in my hand and it will be mine, and from that point on only I will know what color it is, and I can do with it whatever I want.

Grandmother releases the clasp of the wallet; she pinches the edge of it between two fingers and pulls it away from my hand, which is clenched in a fist; for a moment it looks older than hers, it's gnarled, the fingers are knotted, I see wrinkles, yellowed nails, dried-out liver spots, blue veins. I open up my palm, I imagine that in it there is a small gray stone; my skin is once again my own — young and smooth.

Grandmother begins to cram everything back into the wallet; she smiles at me, and she says yes, that's the way to do it, like that. She asks me how many times I've lied to her. I think of the lies, two round white stones in my palm, like glass, they are cold and smooth, and I say: Many times, many, many times.

Grandmother smiles and says, Good, very good. She snaps the wallet shut.

IT'S THE LONG RECESS. I take a bite of my bread with butter and honey, and I watch the boys toss the coins in the schoolyard, back by the bald pine tree. I like to watch as the metal coins fly into the small black hole; the boys dug it out themselves in the corner of the yard. Sometimes the coins strike each other, making a ringing sound, and they come bouncing back out of the hole. The boy whose coin is highest up in the hole at the end of the game plays heads or tails and then gets to keep whatever he wins. I've never played it — usually the girls don't — but I once overheard Iván explain the rules to Krisztina, and I noticed that as he did, he was touching her arm.

Iván is also playing. I watch as he throws, I always want him to miss. I don't know why, but his coins land in the hole only rarely, and even if they do, they always end up bouncing out again.

Today, of all the boys, Feri is doing the best; he's getting the best tosses many times in a row. He throws differently than the other boys. He doesn't take the coin between his fingers and flick it; instead, he closes his hand in a fist, slipping the coin between his fingers, then throws as if he were punching something; at the end of the blow his fingers fly apart, and it's as if the coin were flying right out from the center of his palm—it always goes straight into the hole, and it almost always stays there. The others occasionally try to imitate his technique, but no one is able to.

He wins for the third time, then for the fourth. He gathers the coins from the ground, clutches them in his fist and jingles them; he's now getting ready for heads or tails, but before he can say which opponent he has chosen, Iván suddenly knocks all the money out of his hand, and he yells that it's not okay that he always wins, he's a cheater, a dirty cheater.

Feri says that he didn't cheat. Iván says that yes, he did. He shoves Feri; Feri pushes him back and again he says, No, I didn't. They keep shoving each other—Yes, you did; No, I didn't; Yes, you did; No, I didn't—yelling at each other, their faces getting redder and redder. Iván steps back, trips over one of the roots of the pine tree, and falls on his ass. Feri guffaws; Iván jumps up, yelling that Feri cheated, he's lying now too, because he's a dirty swindler. Feri says he wasn't cheating, that Iván is a born spaz.

Iván flares up; he rushes at Feri. Liar, he screams, liar; the veins are bulging out of his neck. I'll strike you dead, you're an informer, a filthy informer, he screams; he's hitting and kicking Feri. That's not true, Feri yells out, he's screaming now; he grabs Iván's knee. You rotten prick, he screams into his face, how dare you tell lies like that, I'm not afraid of you. Iván stumbles back from the push, he kicks his leg in Feri's direction; You are too, he screams, an informer, just like your father, everyone knows about it, all the workers in the leather factory, the entire city, you piece-of-shit bastard, shitty informer, informer for the Securitate!

Feri screams so loudly that I can feel his voice in my stomach. You leave my father out of this, he screams; he lowers his head, and he rushes at Iván, butting his head right into Iván's stomach; Iván hunches forward. Feri butts his head against his chin, punches him in the sides. You leave my father out of this, you kiss my ass, he screams, punching him hard on his ribs. With one hand, Iván pulls Feri's hair, and with the other he tries to block Feri's blows; the boys fall to the ground, wrestling, hitting each other, yelling, their voices break, the dust whirls around them, you can hardly see them.

Almost everyone is there now, the entire class. I hear everyone yelling out at once: Strike him dead! Don't let him get you! Give it to him! That's it! Right in the kisser!

The boys are lying on the ground, Iván below, his face pushed into the dirt; Feri is half kneeling on his back, wrenching Iván's arms behind him with both hands, and with his other leg he's trying to kick Iván's neck: Take it back, take it back, take it back! he yells, gasping to the rhythm of his own kicks.

Iván is also gasping, his face and his nose are covered with dirt; he tries to straighten himself up, to turn around and throw Feri off his back; I can smell the dirt. Feri tries to pull Iván's arm even farther back, once again he's kicking his neck; Iván's head slams down onto the ground, blood is flowing from his nose, drawing dark crimson lines in the dirt.

Next to me somebody starts screaming: Pull them apart already, what are you waiting for? But nobody moves; everyone just stands there watching as Feri digs his knee deeper into Iván's back. I'm telling you for the last time, take it back, if not I'm going to fracture your shoulder, I'm going to pull your arm out of the socket! Iván, in a gargling voice, still yells out: Informer, your father and you too; his voice causes dust to rise up from the ground. Feri's face distorts, his mouth is one huge black hole: Drop dead! he screams, his voice sharp, then with all his strength he pulls Iván's arm backward and up.

Something makes a cracking sound; Iván lets out an unholy

scream; one of the girls begins to shriek. I shriek with her, then more girls start shrieking too. Feri does a backward somersault off of Iván, and for a second I think that he really has Iván's arm in his hand, he really broke it off, he really ripped it out of the socket.

I know this is impossible; I see that it's only the sleeve of Iván's cloth jacket: as Iván gets up on his knees, the lining and the seams of the jacket hang down in shreds. Iván grabs his shoulder, but then he's already next to Feri, Feri hasn't stood up yet; Iván punches him in the face twice; the second time he punches him, his fist hits the side of his neck, which makes Feri's head slam down to one side. Iván jumps on him, sits on his stomach, beats his head. Feri tries to protect his face; he still has the ripped-off sleeve of Iván's coat in one hand, so with his other hand he reaches over to the side, and he finds the concrete block used as a goalpost on the small soccer field. I know what he's going to do, he's going to hit Iván in the head with it— but right then, from the direction of the school, comes a sharp whistling sound. Watch out, someone yells, Eraser is coming, then the drawing teacher is standing right next to the boys; he yanks the concrete block out of Feri's hand, plunges his fist into Iván's hair and pulls him up, away from Feri, and he shouts, What is this—what are you, animals, to be hitting each other like this, no fighting within the school gates! He falls silent, lets go of Iván's hair; now he's not shouting, but he says in a rasping voice: Stand at attention!

Feri slowly gets up, goes over to Iván, and stands next to him; they don't look at each other, nor do they look at the drawing teacher; both of them stare at the ground. In Feri's hand the sleeve of the coat hangs down, black.

The drawing teacher then speaks after a long pause, saying that he doesn't even want to ask who started it, he knows all the same that they wouldn't tell him, no, he's not interested in who started it, nor is he interested in why they were beating each other up, no, he wants only one thing: for them to promise that on the way home they won't smash each other's brains in with, let's say, a brick in a plastic bag. He only wants them to make peace with each other.

The boys don't move; neither of them speaks; they're still looking at the ground. I can't see Iván's face that well.

The drawing teacher talks to them, asking what are they waiting for, now turn and face each other and say sorry — take each other's hands and embrace. It's not such a big deal, and it'll make things easier for them, they'll see.

The boys still don't move; the drawing teacher then steps next to them, says he doesn't have all the time in the world, and anyway it would be much better to get this over with quickly. With one hand, he grabs Feri's wrist, with his other hand he grabs Iván's; he pulls their hands toward each other. The boys' palms are almost touching when suddenly Iván jerks his hand away; he steps back and says he's not going to shake hands with the son of a filthy informer.

The drawing teacher winces, he lets go of Feri's hand, and he looks at Iván. Where did you hear that? he asks.

Everyone knows, says Iván. The entire city, everyone knows.

The drawing teacher shakes his head, and he says that's interesting, because he's just hearing it now for the first time. But even if everyone supposedly knows it, that doesn't automatically make it true. This is a serious matter, much too serious for someone to be mouthing off about it, someone who is much too young to have anything to do with this.

Iván says he does have something to do with it, he does, and so does everyone else. He has the right to know, the right to dole out justice.

The drawing teacher's mouth contorts for a moment. He says, May the good Lord above save us all from the idiots who want to start doling out justice here. That's just what we need.

Knowing—yes, there is a right to know, if there was something to know. If there were tangible facts—but there aren't any.

He shakes his head; he looks off somewhere next to the boys, then he says that he too was there when, on the fourth day, after the soldiers had fired into the crowd, the ironworkers, driving a transport truck loaded with slag and buttressed with armor they'd welded themselves, broke through the fence of the secret police headquarters. He was one of the first to climb onto the top of the truck when it rammed into the barricade formed from concrete sacks in the yard; he was one of the first to run up the stairs alongside Gyurka Diszkosz; he was the first one when they broke into the main entrance, and he saw the sharp-shooters who'd been caught in the attic thrown off the roof. He was there when they pried open the armor-plated door to the room where the archives should have been, and he saw with his own eyes the empty iron shelves; he saw with his own eyes the remnants of the ripped-apart, charred files. They searched the entire building; there were no documents anywhere. There were none—only ashes and flying cinders, and there was even much less of that than there should have been. For days they looked for the secret basement prisons as well as for the entrances to the secret tunnels running below the city—everyone was convinced those existed—but they didn't find anything. So it's impossible to know the truth. Or even to know if there was any truth. What they did know was that wagging tongues said that the secret police had made up the whole thing and spread the rumors themselves. On those grounds, you could determine who'd been an informer by pulling names out of a hat. Or by, let's say, tossing a coin.

He stops speaking, shakes his head, then looks at the ground, at the scattered coins. Of course, he says, maybe that would be the best way. He sees that tossing coins is popular around here.

He goes over to the hole, and with the tip of his boot he

steps on the edge of one coin; it rings and spins upward. The drawing teacher kicks beneath it as if he were spinning a soccer ball; the coin flies up, turning in the air above the boys' heads, and he asks: Heads or tails?

Iván is silent; only Feri speaks, he says, Heads. The drawing teacher reaches up, lets the coin fall into his palm, then he slaps it down on top of his other hand, squeezed into a fist, and he jabs both hands beneath the boys' noses. He says that until now, he didn't care, but now he wants to know who started it. If they don't tell him within a minute, then he will punish the one who loses in this idiotic game of heads or tails.

The boys are silent; they look at the drawing teacher's hand. Iván's face gets redder and redder, and suddenly he speaks, says: Feri cheated at tossing coins.

The drawing teacher nods; he takes his palm away from the coin held on his other fist. Tails, he says, then he punches Iván in the solar plexus. The coin falls to the ground; Iván doubles over, retching; the drawing teacher turns away, but at the same time he reaches over, grabs the end of the coat sleeve, and takes it from Feri's hand.

He pulls it through his fingers with the same movement he uses to wipe the charcoal dust or the tempera paint from his hands with the paint rag, and he says that now Iván can do some thinking about who's the informer. He throws the coat sleeve onto the ground and goes back into the building.

22

KRISZTINA IS WALKING WITH HER palms cupped together; you can tell she's trying to carry it very carefully. She walks over to Aliz; Aliz asks her what she's carrying. Krisztina slowly raises her hands, holds them in front of Aliz's face, and pulls her thumbs to the sides; Aliz looks down into the hole, and she says, Oh, that's amazing. Krisztina walks away, slowly lowers her hands, then looks at me. I don't want to ask what she's holding, but I'd really like to know.

Krisztina stops, leans forward, once again pulls her thumbs apart, and looks into her palms. I see that she's smiling, as if something in her hands is tickling her. Perhaps she has a butterfly or a tiny tree frog. Aliz walks over to her and says, Show me again. Krisztina shows her what she has in her hands again. Aliz giggles, looks at me, and says, You have a look too.

I know I should say I'm not interested, so I do, but at the same time I'm imagining that Krisztina is holding a tiny downy fledgling in her hands, soft and warm, its heart beating so quickly, because it's afraid. I'll caress it, just a little bit, just with the tip of my finger, so it won't be afraid, just so it'll know I don't mean it any harm.

Krisztina is standing there; she keeps peeking into the gap in between her thumbs, smiling beautifully; it could only be a tiny bird, nothing else could make her smile so beautifully.

I have to see what it is, I can't stand it. I walk over there, say, Show me too, show me what it is. I lean forward, Krisztina opens up her fingers a little bit, and I can already see its tiny dark back, it really is a bird, a downy little duck; I'm about to reach toward it to caress it when Krisztina completely opens up her two palms, and there is no bird there, simply two handfuls of black sand. Krisztina throws all of it into my eyes, into my hair, screaming, That's what you deserve for cheating at skipping rope; you won by cheating, she says, cheating pig, now you got it, now you got it, now you got what you deserved.

I grab my eyes; I can't see anything. The sand stings my eyes. I rub my eyes, I hear them running away, and all the while Aliz is chanting: *Had to be, had to be, just like we put salt on meat.* I yell after them that they should be ashamed of themselves, I didn't cheat! I think about how when I jump, my thighs tighten, I jump up and down, I turn the rope, it whistles and spins around me, I jump and I jump and I jump, I don't miss a step, we stand next to one another, all the girls, everyone is skipping rope, we begin all at once, and whoever misses a step has to stop, the one who can keep on jumping rope the longest is the one who wins; one after the other they drop out, but not me, I pay attention not to them but to the whistling of the rope, I imagine that I am standing in the middle of a great crystal ball, it's protecting me from everything, I won't bungle it. I didn't cheat, I yell after them; the grains of sand fall into my mouth.

I lean forward, shake out the sand; I comb my hair with my fingers, shaking my head at the same time; the sand sticks to my skin, making my hands itchy, making my head itchy. I shake out my hair; the sand keeps falling onto the asphalt, it falls and falls, and even when there's no more left to fall out, the itching doesn't pass. The skin on my head prickles as if red ants were climbing all over it.

THE SKIN ON MY HEAD itches all afternoon. I comb my hair, scratch my head, and I rub it with my fingertips, but the itching only gets worse and worse, I can't stop scratching.

Grandmother notices and ask what's going on. Nothing, I say, it's just that my head is very itchy.

Grandmother has me stand in front of her; she reaches into my hair with two fingers, pulls out one strand. She looks at it, then she holds it in front of me so I can see too.

On the strand of hair there are tiny white globules. Grandmother says that I've been infested with lice, these are the nits, the lice eggs. My hair will have to be completely cut off.

I don't want to cry, but still the corners of my mouth turn down. I've been growing out my hair for three years now.

Grandmother smooths my hair down, then takes a thick lock into her hand, she runs her hand along it, pulling it through her fingers, I can feel the pulling on the roots of my hair, but I don't care. She lets it go, and she says that it's beautiful hair, lustrous and strong, it really is a shame to cut it off. Really a shame.

She says there's another way, but it will hurt a little. It'll be a bit unpleasant.

It's no problem, I say. I can stand it.

Grandmother nods and says she'll be back in a moment, that I should brush my hair out very thoroughly. So that it crackles.

When she comes back, she's carrying a green tin canister. She puts it down on the rug, brings the washbasin from the bathroom, puts that on the small table, and spreads a towel on the back of a chair. She has me sit, then lean backward, so that my head hangs into the washbasin. I feel the chilly edge of the enamel washbasin at the back of my neck.

Grandmother adjusts my hair, combing back every strand with her fingers, combing it away from my forehead. One lock of hair gets stuck in her ring; it makes a hissing sound.

She unscrews the lid of the tin canister, and the room is filled with the smell of gasoline; she lifts the canister and talks to me, telling me to close my eyes, then she begins to pour it over my hair.

I sense as the gasoline flows across the skin on my head, penetrating the roots of my hair; it's hot and it stings.

Grandmother says that it really should be done with kerosene, but this will work too; if I breathe in the fumes nice and deep, it won't hurt so much.

I inhale the smell of the gasoline deeply. It's rough, thick, fine.

Grandmother is caressing my hair; from time to time her ring taps against the washbasin. It's as if I were hearing the sounds from ever farther away.

I hear as Grandmother talks to my hair. She's telling my hair to get clean now, she's telling my hair to be strong, she's telling my hair not to be afraid. It's possible that she's saying this to me instead. Don't be afraid, don't be afraid — there's nothing to be afraid of.

Grandmother's ring knocks against the edge of the washbasin; the ruby stone in her ring knocks against the enamel; it makes a ringing sound as it knocks against the washbasin once, twice, many times, I inhale the smell of gasoline, it stings my lungs, Grandmother once again tells me not be afraid. I'm not afraid.

The ruby strikes the edge of the basin, throws out a spark; the gasoline bursts into flame, it burns, scorching and rustling. I see myself from the outside; my hair is on fire, the whole thing is burning, the strands of my hair crackle, they writhe like small fire snakes, I'm lying in a washbasin filled with fire, it's burning, and yet it doesn't hurt.

I breathe in the smell of gasoline, I breathe in the bitter smoke. Grandmother holds her hand above my face, spreads open her fingers; on the tips of her fingers there are tiny flames. Grandmother squeezes her hands into fists as if she were grabbing something. I can sense that the flames around my head are dying down, my hair is no longer on fire.

Grandmother opens her hands; in them is a thick-handled ivory comb; Don't be afraid, she tells me, and she has me sit up. I see myself in the glass of Grandfather's bookcase. I've grown old, I'm much older than Grandmother now, my hair is completely white.

The corners of my mouth turn down, I know I'm going to cry in a moment.

Grandmother smiles. No need to cry, she says. She holds the washbasin in front of me, plunges the comb into my hair, and begins to comb out my hair; the comb pulls on my hair and it hurts. Gray dust swirls around in the washbasin, gray dust smelling of gasoline. Grandmother keeps combing and combing and combing my hair; the washbasin is now a quarter filled with dust, then half filled, then completely filled.

I see my hair in the glass of the bookshelf; it's no longer white, it's black again, and much shinier and blacker than it ever was before.

My lungs are filled with the smell of gasoline.

Grandmother removes the washbasin, puts it on the small table, throws the comb into it, plunges one hand into the dust, and lets it flow between her fingers. I won't have to worry about lice anymore, she says.

WHEN I GO INTO THE garden, I often bring half a handful of sugar for the ants. I sprinkle it onto the grass, right next to me on the bench, or onto the top of the garden table; the ants always find it very quickly and carry it away. I like to watch as, one by one, they pick up a grain of sugar, as more and more of them come, as they swarm, black, over the mound of sugar. Sometimes I talk to them; I tell them about Mother and Father, about my old life.

I always try to make sure that Grandmother doesn't notice me putting my hand in the sugar bowl, but still one time she notices. She looks at me and doesn't ask anything, and I quickly pour the sugar into my mouth, chew it; it crunches between my teeth, and I say that I need something sweet because of track practice. Grandmother pulls out a drawer, takes out a small wooden spoon, and puts it on the table, telling me to use this next time. I can tell by the way she says it that she doesn't believe me.

From that point on, the wooden spoon is always in the sugar bowl. I don't bring sugar to the ants for three days.

On the fourth day, however, I dare to put half a spoonful of sugar in my hand; I take it out back, and I sprinkle it onto the grass at the base of the plum tree. The ants find it quickly and just as quickly they carry it home. I watch them, then I go back to the garden bench, and once again I try to draw the walnut tree in my notebook.

When I return to the house, Grandmother is boiling water in the biggest pot. As she sees me, she pulls the pot off the fire, puts a dishcloth on each of the pot's two handles, and tells me to help her; if we both carry it, it won't spill.

I go over to her; I pick up the pot from the left side, and even though there's a dishtowel on the handle, it's burning hot. We lower it from the stove, and I begin to move toward the bathroom, as Grandmother usually cleans out the drains in the bathroom with boiling water—she says that the boiling water dissolves all the dirt from the inside of the lead pipes —but Grandmother doesn't go that way; instead she moves toward the door. As we go down the steps, she counts out loud so that we step at the same time, so that we don't scald ourselves.

We head out the back, toward the woodshed. I'm thinking that Grandmother wants to clean out the drain, but we don't stop by the gridded drain cover, we go farther out by the walnut tree, past the flower bed; now we're nearly at the back, by the row of cedar trees, where the big anthill is, and I finally understand what Grandmother intends to do. I miss a step; a bit of the boiling water splashes onto the grass. Grandmother reaches over and grabs the pot handle from my hand. I want to tell her not to do it, the ants aren't hurting anyone, but Grandmother is already standing in front of the anthill swinging the pot, and she hurls the boiling water onto the anthill.

The anthill sizzles, collapsing inward; black steam rises up from it; between the clumps the ant paths are visible; the water grows black. Sizzling and bubbling, it disappears in the underground tunnels, flows all around the anthill, sweeping away the frantic ants.

Grandmother presses her foot down on the anthill; she uses the heel of her slipper to turn over the earth and she says, Just look at that, what a gigantic anthill, even all that boiling water is just a drop in the bucket for them. For this she needs ant powder, somewhere she still has half a packet, well, those ants will get it from her. She turns on her heel, heads off toward the woodshed, her first few steps leaving muddy prints in the grass.

I look at the steaming earth, at the ants swimming in the black mud; my chest hurts and throbs, and I know that my heart is beating in the same way, painfully and prickling.

I turn and look for Grandmother; I see that she's disappeared into the woodshed. I crouch down and grab a handful of the warm earth; I turn over a large mud clump, then another, and a third; the ants are swarming in their pathways, clutching each other and their eggs, trying to swim in the mud; they climb up onto my hand, they clamber onto my skin as if they

were marching somewhere deeper, farther into the ruins of the
anthill. I turn over more clumps of mud; the earth here is not so
moist and not so warm, the ant paths lead the water off somewhere else. I find a cavity about the size of half a fist; it's nearly
dry, the water here penetrated only to one corner. The cavity is
filled with ants and their eggs; they swarm in a spherical black
mass, and in the middle I see one big ant, much bigger than
the others, almost as big as the last two joints of my pinkie; it
doesn't move at all, just stands there in the middle of the swarm.

I look back toward the woodshed; Grandmother hasn't
come out yet, she still hasn't found the ant powder. With my fingers spread out, I carefully reach beneath the ants, slowly lift up
the entire sphere-shaped swarm of clutching and clinging ants,
and close my fingers. The sphere in my palm is something like
a huge living bramble. I look around to try to see where I can
hide it; I see, behind the cedar trees, the bucket for collecting
snails with the gardening trowel in it. I step behind the cedar
trees toward the bucket; it's empty; I bend down and slowly I
release the ball of ants into the bottom of the bucket.

I hear Grandmother shutting the door to the woodshed. I
grab the trowel from the bucket, step out from among the cedar
trees, and stand next to the steaming ruins of the anthill; with
the trowel I turn some earth onto the little cavity, then I begin
to dig as if I were looking for something.

Grandmother comes over; in her hand there is a large paper sack folded shut. She opens it up, sprinkles white powder
onto the ground, then she grabs the garden trowel from my
hand, and she mixes the powder into the earth, saying that I
should learn how to do this. She plunges the trowel into the
earth many times, sprinkling the powder in slow spirals onto
the clumps of earth and onto the mud, turning over the earth,
breaking up the clumps with the trowel; she mixes and kneads
the mud and, slowly, it turns gray.

When she's finished, in place of the anthill there is just a large gray splotch with no ant in sight. Grandmother pats it down a few times with the flat side of the trowel, smooths it over, beats it down, then she wipes the trowel off in the grass and looks around; she's looking for the snail-collecting bucket. She sees it by the side of the cedar trees, takes a step over there. I feel my stomach convulsing, but Grandmother doesn't go any closer, she just tosses the trowel into the bucket. I hear the trowel clattering as it falls into the bucket, its tongue striking the edge; it makes a grating sound as it revolves around, I get goose bumps on my arms and back. I must not think about the ants.

Grandmother folds the ant powder packet closed; she motions for me to bring the cauldron, then we go back into the house. She doesn't say anything, and I don't say anything either, but in my head there is only one thought turning around and around: *Poor ants, poor, poor ants.*

THAT NIGHT, THE SKY CLOUDS over; there's thunder, but no rain falls. Grandmother takes her trench coat and gets her umbrella; she says she can feel in her bones that there is going to be a big storm, but she still has to go out. She tells me that if she's not back within half an hour, it means that she'll be back very late, I shouldn't wait up for her, I should have my dinner and go to sleep by myself.

I'm lying on my stomach on my bed, reading. I wait for the time to go by. I wait for three-quarters of an hour; in the meantime, the wind rises, it's making the windows rattle, and I can see even from my bed that the sky has grown completely dark gray.

When I go into the garden, the sky is nearly black. It's quiet, the wind isn't blowing now, but you can feel in the air that the rain will come any moment.

I head straight for the snail-collecting bucket. The ants are still in there, climbing and clambering, going around and around slowly in the bottom of the bucket. I take the bucket over to the walnut tree, hanging it on my arm; I try to climb up, but because of the bucket, I can't really pull myself up along the branches properly.

I put the bucket at the base of the tree and crouch beside it. I pull down my T-shirt, fold it in half, twist it once; the fabric flaps down like a rabbit's ear, it's a small pocket now, precisely the right size for my fist. I take one of the rubber bands from the end of my braid, gather up the twist in the fabric with it, then I pick up the ants from the bucket, lower them down into this pocket, and fold the fabric over them carefully, and with the second rubber band that I've taken from my hair, I gather up the small bundle.

Now it's easy for me to climb up the tree. My stomach is exposed as I pull myself up the branches, my navel is touching the trunk of the tree, the bark is scraping it and it hurts, but I try not to think about it. I head upward, I want to go up to the part of the tree overhanging the wall, by the branch's third fork, where there's a cavity in the stump of a sawed-off branch. As I get to the second fork in the branches, the sky rumbles; I hear a large boom of thunder coming in my direction, then the wind picks up, blowing wildly; the tree is groaning and cracking, the branch moves with me on it. I clasp it tightly with my thighs, pull myself quickly upward.

I'm nearly at the fork when the sky flashes sharp and white and then rumbles so loudly I can hear the clattering in my chest; the rain begins to pour down, wildly beating the leaves above me, and dry bits of wood and leaves swirl all around me as the wind shakes the walnut tree. I'm almost at the cavity; I grab it with one hand, lifting myself higher, then I lean my elbows onto the branch; beneath me the trunk is smooth and slippery, the water is pouring down through the grooves in the bark, but I don't even feel the rain because the leaves are protecting me from it. I rip the hairbands off the little bundle, reach into it with one hand; I feel the ants moving in circles and climbing onto my palm, and as I extend my hand toward the cavity, lightning flashes again. In the sharp light I see how they have marched onto my palm; I thrust my hand into the cavity, open and close my fingers; I wipe my hand on the side of the cavity, trying to brush the ants off. Go now, I tell them, go now.

My voice is swallowed by the roar of the thunder; the tree groans and shakes once; one of my legs slides off the branch, I'm turning around the branch, but I'm able to hold on. The wind blows; my hair is soaked through, it lashes around me like a rope; my hair comes loose, the wind blows into my face, my leg slips off the trunk, the wind tugs at me; I know that if I let go of the tree, it will pick me up and slam me against the firewall.

I think of the ants and how, in my palm, they swirled around, clutching each other; I tense my muscles, turn to the side, and stretch out; I'm hanging down, the wind is making me sway, I swing back; once again my thighs and my arms are wrapped around the branch, it's there, I've got it, I'm squeezing tight. I begin to climb down; the tree is groaning and shaking more and more, but I know now that everything will be fine, I'm not going to fall.

I jump to the ground; the rain is pouring down wildly, dust rises from the earth. I look up, wipe my hair away from my face, and run toward the kitchen.

23

I ASK FOR A PIECE of rag and some buttons from Grandmother; for handicrafts class, we need to do some needlework. I have to sew four buttons onto a piece of fabric, then I need to cut out four buttonholes next to them and finish the edges with a nice, finely sewn overcast stitch.

Grandmother says we certainly have more than enough rags. She sends me into the pantry to bring out the rag sack; it hangs beneath the stairs on a nail.

I bring it out. Grandmother unties the handkerchief from the mouth of the sack, shakes the sack, and pieces of material and other fabrics spill out onto the small table. Grandmother says there are as many rags here as there is trash; she digs in the pile of rags, pulling them apart. There are all different colors: dark blue, brown, gray, yellow, green, red, crimson, black. Grandmother takes one out, and she says, Jersey; she pulls out another one, and she says, Taffeta; she pulls out another one and says, Crepe; then she says, Everything is here — satin, silk, fine wool, linen, bed stuffing, and broadcloth.

Touch it, she says to me, go ahead and pick it up, Bertuka always said that it's not enough just to look at fabric, you also have to feel it, that's the only way you truly know its nature. Bertuka used to say that you could always tell who the serious customers were because they wouldn't just look at the clothes, they would touch them, pinch the material between their fingers, rub it, keep touching it, caress it.

I reach for the pile of fabric, plunge my fingers into the rags. I run my fingers over the fabrics; some pieces already have buttons on them, buttons or buckles or fasteners; I think of how each swatch must have been cut from a piece of clothing and how each has its own story. My fingers follow the gold-stitched contour of a rose stem; it's lustrous, embroidered on blue material; the edge of the fabric has fringes and is cut obliquely, splitting the petals of the rose so that there's only half of it.

Grandmother runs her hand along a cherry-red piece of fabric. She says that Bertuka's coat was this color. Or almost this color.

I want to ask her what happened with Bertuka, but I don't speak. I turn the material over; there's a button on the other side. As I touch it, chills run down my spine, because I realize this is exactly the same kind of button that was used to make the eyes on the rag doll in the woodshed.

Grandmother's finger taps loudly on the table; she's looking at me. She asks if I ended up going into the woodshed even though she told me not to.

I can't speak; my heart feels like it's been stabbed, I feel like it's going to stop.

Grandmother says yes or no, I have to make up my mind, there's no time to think. There is no thinking, either you lie or you tell the truth, nod your head or shake it—yes or no.

I nod.

Grandmother says, Good, you're a brave girl. Then at least she can tell me the rest of the story. Because at some point she'll have to tell it. In the end, that too is a part of the lesson. Everything is a part of the lesson.

She looks off beside me, up above the bureau, above the green-glazed jugs on the top of the bureau; she looks out through the window to the street, and she begins to speak.

IT'S EVENING, SHE SAYS, *it's evening, you're sleeping, and you awaken to the sound of someone knocking on the window; you're so sleepy that you think it's just a dream, you're just dreaming the whole thing, it's just a large white bird knocking on the window with its beak, and it wants you to let it in, let it in already.*

You get up from the bed, and you stand there in your nightgown, you stand in the darkness, you're freezing, and once again you hear the knocking; you go over to the window, you raise the blinds, and there really is a white bird there, it's fluttering behind the dark glass; it opens and closes its wings, it addresses you by your name— no, no, it's not a bird but a palm, a white palm, it's knocking on the glass; you lean over and look out. Bertuka is standing in the street, your best friend, you recognize her even in the pale moonlight. You haven't seen her for weeks, you knew that she was sick, but you couldn't visit her, and now here she is, standing out in the dark street beneath your window, asking you to open it.

She asks you to open the window, to let her in, to hide her. That's all she says— nothing more.

You stand there in your nightgown in front of the open window, you look at your girlfriend as she stands there and waits; she's waiting for you to say something, waiting for you to say yes or no; you can't say anything else, you know you're going to say yes, and you do say yes, but before the word forms in your throat and reaches your tongue, what comes to mind is that you could actually close the window, and you could draw the curtains shut, and you could lie back in your bed; you could pull the covers over yourself, and you could put the pillow over your head, and you could lie in bed facing the wall until the next morning; you could try to go back to sleep, you could try to pretend to be somebody who really and truly was sleeping.

You say yes, and all the while you feel that your face is burning, it's burning because you thought about no, about the possibility of no, you were thinking that you could have said no, you are thinking that you could have stayed in your bed, you could have pretended you never even heard the knocking at the window, as if you'd just dreamed the whole thing, that great white bird beating at the windowpane, everything.

You say yes, and you look at Bertuka, how she is standing in front of your window in the darkness; she's wearing that same cherry-red coat from which you did not rip off the star, she's standing there looking at you, and her two hands are resting on her stomach, the hand that just a moment ago had been beating against the window, and the other hand as well; her fingers are clasped, white, in front of her stomach. You say yes, and you lean out of the window, and you grab her, and you pull her up, and she steps onto the edge of the plinth; this is how you used to climb into each other's windows when you both were little, but now it's not so easy, you have to pull harder, and she has to push herself up harder, and finally she steps up to the windowsill, and then you see that she's barefoot, and there on the windowsill is her long slender foot, you always envied her that, and now you know with complete certainty that you're not dreaming, you pull her, along with yourself, into the room, nearly knocking over one of the jugs on the bureau; you close the window, and you pull the curtains shut.

You pull her coat off, fold it up, and shove it beneath the bureau; both of you are careful not to make any noise, you don't want your parents to wake up in the other room. Bertuka is shivering as if she has a fever, her teeth are clattering as she tries to speak, you whisper to her, tell her no, she doesn't have to, be quiet, you take her and you push her toward your bed, you lay her down in the bed, you cover her up with a blanket; she's still shuddering, still trembling; you lie down next to her; the cold emanates from her body. You embrace her, trying to warm her up, but you too begin to feel cold, then you think you hear something moving in the room next door, so you quickly hide Bertuka beneath the covers, then you climb under the covers with her, beneath the pillows, into the warm, bed-scented darkness.

She wants to say something, and you want her to be quiet; she can't be quiet, she pushes her mouth toward your ear, and she whispers something softly, very softly, into your ear, it tickles, it makes you shiver; in a low voice, hardly audible, she tells you about the brick factory, about how she found out that everyone is going to be taken there, everyone will be moved there at dawn, but she can't go, she cannot allow herself to be taken there, because now she doesn't have only herself to look after; she grabs your hand and she pulls it beneath her nightshirt, and she presses your hand onto her stomach, and she whispers into your ear: There inside, do you feel it? But you don't feel anything, only that Bertuka's skin is smooth and cold. Slowly you pull your hand away from her stomach, and you whisper into the darkness, Don't be afraid, everything will be all right, there won't be any problems, but at the same time your heart is in your throat and it's throbbing that there will be problems, there will, there will.

You lie there and you know that you won't be able to sleep; you listen to the breathing of your girlfriend as it slows more and more. Father and Mother must not see her, they must not know that she's here, you have to hide her, you have to conceal her somewhere.

You only know that you fell asleep by the fact that, at one point, you wake up.

For a moment you think that you've woken to a voice singing, that you were dreaming of a sorrowful song, then, as you open your eyes, you immediately realize that you weren't dreaming, it comes from outside, from the street, you can hear it through the closed window and the drawn curtains, but it's not a song, it is not a mere song.

You don't want to hear it, you don't want to see it, you don't want to get out from under the blanket, you don't want to get up, don't want to pull open the curtain, don't want to peek out onto the street, but still you get up, and still you go over to the window, and still you look out.

Outside it is dawn; everything is cold and gray, the sky and the asphalt and the trees, everything.

The street is filled with people, women and men and children, old and young; they're walking, they are moving quickly, they're being driven by men in uniform, you don't want to see it, you want to close your eyes, but you know it's no use, everything is gray, everything is faded and gray, the clothes and the kerchiefs, the hats and the coats, the suitcases and the bags are gray, the bundles and the rucksacks; gray as well is their skin, their faces, their eyes, their noses, their mouths, the entire world is gray, you don't want to see them, you don't want to know, but already you've seen them, and already you know. Because, from this point on, you will always see them.

You step away from the window, away from the curtains; now here inside the room everything is gray as well, the walls, the furniture, the air, the bed, everything is gray, you feel dizzy, you grab the arm of the chair, your fingers are gray, your skin is gray. You feel nauseated from all this grayness, it's making your stomach churn, you stand there, retching, you press your hand against your stomach.

You look at the bed; beneath the blanket Bertuka is lying curled up, she's curled in on herself beneath the pillow, you see only a few locks of her disheveled hair, and that's not gray, that can't be gray, it's red, because Bertuka has red hair, you could never see it being gray, the dawn light is making everything look like this, it's because the sun has not yet risen. It will rise, and it will shine, it will shine through the window, through the glass, through the voile curtains, through the heavy fabric curtains, and it will shine on Bertuka's hair. Bertuka's hair will be red, the sheets will be white, the glazed jug will be green, the walnut bureau will be brown. Everything will be the way it was before.

You close your eyes, you turn your face to the window, you wait for the sun to start shining on you, you wait for the scarlet and or-ange-yellow and green and purple light to painfully flare behind your eyelids. You stand and you wait, but to no avail, because you know the sun will not rise and it will not shine, it will never rise again, after this everything will always remain gray.

You raise your hand and rub your eyes; you feel your eyeballs mov-ing beneath your eyelids; you press your fingers down them hard so it hurts, so that the pressure will make you see colored lights, but in vain.

You open your eyes, and you think that it's your fault. You never should have woken up, you shouldn't have gotten up. It's your fault, all of this is your fault. If you could go back to bed, if you could silently creep along the pattern on the edge of the Persian carpet, if you could step across the planks of the floorboards, if you could slip back beneath the covers in such a way that the bed wouldn't creak, if you could pull the cover over your eyes, if you could squeeze Bertuka to yourself, if you could fall asleep next to her, then everything would be the same as it was before.

You move; with the first step the floor creaks loudly beneath the carpet, a loud cracking sound, it cuts right through you, you're no lon-ger standing, you're already by the bed, you grab the edge, you want to sit down and climb beneath the blankets again, and then Bertuka moves, she raises her head, her face is gray, she opens her eyes, her eyes are gray, and from how she's looking at you, from the terror on her face, you know that your face looks gray to her.

She half sits up, clutching at you, she pulls you next to her on the bed, and as she touches you, your stomach turns again, the nausea ris-ing up your gullet, it's much stronger now than it was before, you can't keep it down, you start dry-heaving, you think of the gray leaves of the acacia trees; you lean forward, with one arm you reach under the bed, you touch the floor, you grope along it looking for the chamber pot, maybe it's not there, but it is there, your fingers bump into its enamel handle.

You yank it out from beneath the bed; the movement makes the lid clatter; you take off the lid, the gray cracks along the edge of the gray enamel move, you grab at them, and you notice that those are not cracks but a large gray daddy longlegs, but too late, you can't pull your hand away, the spider runs up your fingers, it runs up your arm, it's going to run up underneath the sleeve of your nightgown.

Bertuka reaches over and brushes it off you; as she touches you, suddenly the nausea disappears, even though you see how the spider's body is crushed, its legs tearing off, falling onto the sheet.

Bertuka then convulses; she leans over the chamber pot, she throws up. You put your arm around her shoulders, you hold her, you feel her back tensing and her body convulsing and shaking. You hold her, you embrace her. On the street outside, somebody calls out, a woman's voice, long and loud she screams, she yells out, You don't understand, you don't want to understand.

Bertuka stops vomiting now, she falls back onto the bed, her face and her forehead are covered with drops of sweat, tiny gray glass beads. They move, they roll down her face, down below the cover, below the pillow, below the sheets, they disappear, they disperse, smearing.

Outside someone is yelling again. Bertuka winces, she doesn't look toward the window, she looks at the wall, she looks at the gray and white streaks of the wall hanging, then suddenly she gets up; you want to tell her, Stay here, don't move, but Bertuka is already standing in front of the window; through a gap in the curtains she is watching the procession, holding on to the edge of the bureau with one hand; she's trembling, the jugs and the glasses on the bureau knock against each other, clattering, they strengthen the rhythm of the trembling, you feel it penetrating through your teeth right into your bones, and in a moment you too will begin to tremble.

There's no more time. You have to hide her, you have to conceal her somewhere. You walk over to Bertuka, stand right next to her, and very softly in her ear you whisper for her to come, she can't stay here by the window, she has to hide. Bertuka doesn't move, she trembles and looks at the street; you don't want to look out, and yet you look out — the street is gray and empty now.

You put your arm around Bertuka, you hear as she says: They've taken them away, they've taken them all away. You are trembling just as much as she is, but still you take her, you walk toward the door, slowly, quietly.

You're standing next to the cupboard with the shelves, you hope the door doesn't creak, you open it, it doesn't, from the lower shelf you take out the warm camelhair blanket, you drape it around Bertuka's shoulders, then you put your arm around her; you lead her, slowly, quietly, out of the room, through the vestibule, through the kitchen, out the kitchen door, out into the yard. You're thinking about the silence, just let there be silence, let nothing creak, nothing knock, nothing make any sudden sharp noises.

The yard is gray, the garden is gray, the woodshed is also gray.

There is silence, and yet there's no silence at all, the branches of the walnut tree are murmuring and clattering and crackling, and the wind is mixing voices into it, voices singing, voices weeping, cursing, yelling, the wind is blowing from the direction of Calvary, to get to the brick works you have to cross Calvary.

The woodshed door is closed, but you know where the key to the lock is, it hangs on a string in one of the crevices in the bark of the walnut tree.

You pull out the key and you open the lock. Inside, the woodshed is dark, completely dark, a pitch-black darkness; you go in, and you pull Bertuka in after you. You close the door, then the two of you just stop and look at the darkness, waiting for your eyes to adjust.

You bend over to her ear, you whisper that she will be safe here, no one ever comes in here, no one will look for her here. Yes, she will be safe.

You step over to the woodpile, it's as if the entire woodshed were full of chopped-up pieces of wood, but it isn't, you crouch down and begin to pull out the pieces of wood, and when the hole is big enough, you squeeze through it with Bertuka.

This is Father's secret pantry. On a battered shelf there are apples and quinces, beneath them round cheeses, and beneath the shelf, on the ground, are sacks of flour and a few tubs of honey.

Next to the back wall stands the old wooden grain chest with roosters carved into it; you open it up, it's three-quarters filled with walnuts. You grab Bertuka's arm, you help her climb in. The walnuts make a gentle clattering sound as Bertuka settles down upon them, you put a pillow filled with yarn next to her, she fits in comfortably,

*and you whisper into the semidarkness for her to pull the walnuts on
top of herself so she will disappear among them. Don't be afraid, you
whisper, then with both hands, nice and slow, you carefully close the
lid to the grain chest. Only you can enter here. Mother never comes
into the shed because she's afraid of the dark and the spiders, and ever
since Father had his stroke, he can't crawl through the hole. No one else
knows about this spot, no one will ever find her here.*

GRANDMOTHER FALLS SILENT; SHE SHAKES her head, she
wipes her eyes with the sleeve of her sweater, then she stands
up, goes over to the bookcase, and takes a thick book from the
lower shelf; on it the words *Anatomical Atlas* are inscribed in
golden letters. From among the pages, Grandmother pulls out
an old photograph, its edges cut in an ornamental pattern. She
puts it on the table in front of me. She says that apart from
Grandfather, no one has ever seen this photograph, not even
my mother, she has never spoken to anyone about this part of
her life.

Grandmother is in the photograph; I recognize her. She's
very young, standing with another girl, the girl is wearing eyeglasses with thick black frames. This can only be Bertuka. On
the other side of Bertuka there is a boy, tall and thin, with tired
dark blotches beneath his deeply set black eyes. They stand arm
in arm. There is a fence behind them, behind the fence are wil-
low trees, the photograph might have been taken on a riverbank.
I look at the faces; they're not smiling, it's as if they are grimacing, but no, you can see from their eyes that they're trying to
hold back laughter that's about to burst out, that's what makes
their faces look like that, you can tell that they won't be able to
stand it for too much longer, they're about to start laughing so
hard that it's going to make their stomachs hurt, so hard that
they will double over, clutching each other, then they will lose

their balance, tears will run down their cheeks; they'll barely be able to catch their breath, they'll just cackle, their faces will turn red with shame, because they'll be ashamed of themselves, it's not proper to cackle with laughter like this, they'll be ashamed of the photographer seeing them like this, but it won't matter, this will just make it worse, they'll laugh and laugh and laugh, and they won't be able to stop.

I look at the picture; Grandmother's eyes are gleaming so much that I feel I must smile too, and for a moment I feel that I'm standing there on the riverbank with them, that I too heard the joke that the photographer told them, the cackling is about to burst out of me, I won't be able to hold it in for long, only until the shutter clicks on the camera, then I too will be shaken and tossed about by the high spirits, it will grab me and spin me around and make me dizzy.

Grandmother clears her throat, and she says that they had been celebrating Bertuka's name day; the boy standing next to Bertuka is her older brother, Miklós. They had been drinking elderberry wine and eating poppyseed-walnut pastries; the picture was taken by their cousin, Bátykó, who had come from Poland to visit for the summer. As she says this, her voice is veiled, and I can't decide if there is grief or anger in it.

I ask her if she remembers the joke that made them laugh so much. Grandmother says that Bátykó was trying to say, Watch the birdie! but he kept mixing up the words; it wasn't actually that funny, but still they cackled so much that they nearly pissed their pants, and Bátykó laughed so much that he nearly dropped the camera.

ALL MY CLASSMATES ARE TALKING about how the swimming pool is going to open this weekend, it's already being filled with water. The river is still too cold for swimming, but the pool water will warm up quickly if the weather stays nice; perhaps by Sunday it'll be good for proper swimming or jumping in. The boys vow that they're all going to go to the pool; they talk about who'll jump from which diving board—the three-meter one, the five-meter one, the seven-meter one, or the highest, the ten-meter one.

Many of the girls are also saying that they're going. Krisztina is the loudest, saying that she got a new bathing suit directly from Italy, it's red, and the triangles that hold together the sides and the top part are tiny golden chains; it's very beautiful, and it looks really good on her, she knows it's hard to believe that she could look more beautiful than she does in her fox-fur coat, but we'll all see on Sunday, because she's going to wear her new bikini, and she'll be the most beautiful girl at the entire pool. As she says this, she looks at me, and I can see in her eyes that she thinks that I certainly won't be there because she's sure I have no bathing suit. I turn away, and I see Iván looking at Krisztina, his eyes glued to Krisztina's blouse, and I know he's imagining how she's going to look in that wonderful red bikini of hers.

I don't have a bathing suit; I've never even had a proper bra. I used to have pale blue swimming shorts; Mother bought them for me when I was seven years old and we took a trip to the sea, but I don't even know what happened to them.

When I get home, I tell Grandmother that the pool will be opening this weekend, and I want to go, so I ask very nicely for her permission and for some money for a bathing suit. Grandmother says she doesn't mind if I want to go, I certainly can, but a new bathing suit won't be necessary; she'll have a look because she remembers that somewhere in the house is one of my mother's old bathing suits. Just the other day when she was cleaning up, she saw it somewhere.

I want to tell her that that won't be any good, it'll be old and ugly, but I bite my tongue.

As I'm writing out my lesson, I hear Grandmother rummaging in the wardrobe, and I know she's looking for the bathing suit; I keep hoping she won't find it. I repeat it to myself: *Don't let her find it.* I can't concentrate on my lesson; I turn back to the last page in the notebook, and I write it down: *Don't let her find it.* I write it once, twice, many times over, until nearly the entire page is filled. Grandmother keeps looking, pulling out all the drawers. I start a new page, and it's almost half filled up when I hear Grandmother sigh once and close the doors to the wardrobe.

There is silence; the pen in my hand stops midway through the sentence. I wait for Grandmother to say something. She clears her throat, then says my name, and she says that it seems that she didn't remember well, because she can't find it; as I hear this, I close the notebook, smile, and silently call out: *Hooray!*—but then Grandmother speaks again, saying don't be sad, though, because she found something else, it's a little on the old side, but I'm so lovely it will surely look good on me. Come and have a look at it, she says. I can hardly speak, but then I say, In a minute, I'll just finish my math lesson, and I hear how my voice is completely hoarse. I open up my math notebook, cross out the sentence that I wrote so many times, one line after the other. I clutch the pen in my fist and scribble all over the page; the tip of the pen breaks off; I don't care, I keep scribbling; I look at the page in the notebook, and I try to breathe deeply.

I hear Grandmother asking what's taking me so long, aren't I coming already? I'm coming, I say, and I put down the pen.

The bathing suit is much worse than I thought, it's a one-piece and black. Grandmother lays it across the back of the chair so I can see it better: the shoulders of the bathing suit and the rounded neck opening are decorated with black lace ruffles, as if someone had sewn together a short-sleeved shirt with black underwear; on the chest there are black roses   it's impossible for me not to wince, it's so ugly. Luckily, Grandmother doesn't notice, because she's looking at the bathing suit, saying she doesn't know where it came from, she doesn't remember it at all, it's quite unusual but still very beautiful, she's curious to see how I'll look in it.

I look at the bathing suit; I can't take my eyes off it. When I finally speak, my voice is very quiet, and I say: I think it'll be too big for me. Grandmother says that until I try it on I won't be able to tell, so I should head into the bathroom and slip into it, then I'll see how nice I'll look. I should try it on already and not stand here making faces. Don't think I didn't see you, she says, because I did see you. She takes the bathing suit from the back of the chair and gives it to me.

I don't know what kind of material this is; it's elastic, as if it were made out of terrycloth, but it feels completely different, it's rough and repulsive. I take it into the bathroom, close the door behind me, throw the bathing suit on top of the washing machine. I get undressed, put my clothes on top of the closed toilet seat. I don't take off my underwear. My feet are freezing from the cold tile floor. I stand in front of the mirror and step back to see myself better. I imagine that I'm wearing a red bathing suit, a normal bikini, one held together with tiny golden chains. I grab the two sides of my underwear and hitch up the sides.

I look at the washing machine, at the crumpled black bathing suit. I go over and take it off the top of the machine; I hate even having to pick it up. Then I realize that maybe I don't have to try it on, maybe it's enough if I just hold it up in front of myself. No, that's not possible, Grandmother will want to see it on me. For a moment I don't know how to put it on, then I grab the ruffles at the neck, feel the elastic, and stretch it open. A faint musty smell emanates from the black material. I don't want to feel it on my skin, and yet I step into the suit, balance on one leg, thrust my other leg into the other hole; the material is rough, rubbing unpleasantly against my inner thighs. Good thing I left my underwear on. I look down at the bathing suit beneath my chest, on my stomach; it's just a bunch of crumpled-up black roses and ruffles. The two ruffled sleeves hang down from my waist like two broken bird's wings. I reach down and pull up one of the sleeves so I can stick my arm in; from the ruffles of the bathing suit, a musty, sour smell drifts upward. I pull it up onto my shoulder, then I pull up the other side of the suit; I feel the material surrounding my upper body. My chest tightens; it's not too big and it's not too small — it's just right.

I look in the mirror, then I quickly close my eyes. It's not me standing there. The bathing suit wraps around my body like a bunch of snares; the roses hang down from it like enormous black carbuncles; the black ruffles encircle my thighs, my arms, and my neck. I open my eyes, and I look at the neckline; a long thread is hanging down from one of the ruffles, clinging to my skin. The bathing suit tightens around me; it squeezes me; I can't catch my breath. It's not me in the mirror, it's some old lady with a child's face standing there hunched over and ashamed. I see how my face goes scarlet. I feel as if I can't even move. The suit is squeezing me, it burns. The thread feels like a deep wrinkle on my skin, making my neck itch.

Slowly I pull myself up. The bathing suit is too tight, but I'm stronger than it. Underneath the mirror, on the shelf, is Grandfather's razor. I reach for it, pick it up by its yellow bone handle; from the razor a copper-colored snake's tail stands out. I place my thumb on it and the razor snaps open; its convex blade is golden-colored, only the edge is gray. As I touch the edge of the blade to my throat, I see, in its concave surface, my face reflected upside down, my skin glowing golden. I pinch the black thread between my two fingers; it snaps as soon as the blade touches it, trembling shoots through me. I look at myself in the mirror—my fingers are gathering up the black lace. The blade is moving all by itself as it begins to cut the lace from the bathing suit; the material stretches and makes a cracking noise as the blade appears on its lower edge, then, farther down, the blade slides along my skin, slicing palm-size strips off the bathing suit. I watch as the roses tumble onto the ground, then, from inside the material, my breasts pop out, then my stomach, my belly button, and, finally, my underwear. Everywhere my skin is white and smooth. I look at myself; one of my nipples has hardened, it's grown stiff and pointed; I see my mouth moving, I'm whispering something without sound, I read it from my lips: I'm still the most beautiful girl in the whole class.

I look down; the bathing suit is now nothing more than black ruffles and rags lying on the tile floor. As one of the black roses rolls slightly away, I kick it back into the pile.

I look at the crumpled fabric, something like a pile of muddy washcloths, and I think, That's the end of that, there's no way you could sew anything out of this or put it back together again. I smile. Grandmother will curse me, but I don't care.

The opened razor is still there in my hand; I stick it beneath my underwear on the side. I move it upward; the underwear stretches, drawing the trace of the blade's edge. I tip the blade over a bit and pull it up; the small white elastic threads pop out, then the cut runs all along the material; I also cut open the other side, and the underwear falls to the ground between my thighs, onto the tiles. I step back; I want to see myself from head to toe, my breasts, my stomach, my belly button, my waist, the black triangle of my hair.

I haven't looked at myself completely naked for a long time; my body has changed a lot. I raise my two arms above my head, see how my breasts also rise, how my ribs move beneath my skin. I slowly stand on tiptoes; my stomach tautens. I lick my mouth and smile. No, that's not good, too cheerful. I want my smile to be severe and cold, even more severe, even colder, than Krisztina's—I want to think that I'm beautiful.

Suddenly I sense that someone is looking at me. I see Grandmother in the mirror, standing there in the doorway of the bathroom. I didn't notice when she opened the door, I didn't notice when she came in.

Suddenly my entire body contracts. I place one arm quickly across my chest; with the other one I cover myself below. The opened razor is still there in my hand, and I almost end up cutting my stomach with it, but I know that Grandmother is behind me and she sees my bottom. I try to turn away.

Grandmother looks off to the side, to the black pile of rags, and she says: I see this bathing suit didn't work out.

I feel I'm turning red, and I try to say that I only wanted to cut off that one thread that was hanging down, I didn't mean to ruin the whole thing, but when I speak, I say that I really didn't look too good in it.

A wrinkle runs across Grandmother's nose, then she begins to laugh. She laughs so much that her body is shaking; at the same time she steps over to me, takes the razor out of my hands, closes it, and puts it back on the shelf.

Her laughter makes me feel even more confused.

Grandmother says that nothing has changed; ever since the world has been the world, little girls always want to be big girls.

I want to tell her that I'm not a little girl, but I say nothing.

Grandmother says that if I realized how beautiful I really am, if I could see myself as others see me, I wouldn't be able to catch my breath, I would just stand there and admire myself. She steps over to the toilet, scoops up my clothes, and says she knows what it's like, she didn't believe at the time that she was beautiful.

She presses the pile of clothes into my hands, and she says that I would certainly be a huge success if I went parading around at the pool in my birthday suit, but for now it would be better if I got dressed. The remains of the black bathing suit should be put nicely into the rag sack; they might be good for something later on.

She leaves the bathroom; I get dressed quickly. I pick up my cut-apart underwear from the floor—good thing that at least Grandmother didn't see this. There's no pocket in my skirt, so I stuff the underwear into the sleeve of my pullover.

Grandmother comes back with the rag sack, sets it on the floor, motions for me to put the scraps in. I crouch down, and I don't even look at the scraps of bathing suit as I gather them up. When I'm done, I tie up the mouth of the sack, then I wash my hands for a long time under the tap while looking at Grandfather's closed razor. I notice that the bone handle is decorated with a copper inlay depicting a monkey with side-whiskers crouching on a bentwood chair, and the metal ornament that opens the razor, which I at first took to be a snake, is actually the end of the long winding tail of the monkey hanging down from the chair. The monkey grimaces, scratching its beard with one of its paws.

I take the pile of rags out into the kitchen; it's strange to

walk like this, with no underwear beneath my skirt. Grandmother motions for me to take the sack into the pantry.

FOR THREE DAYS NOW, I'VE been sleeping very badly, and I've
been having very bad dreams. I don't remember what they're
about, only that there is darkness in them, a swirling darkness
much darker even than black.

I think of Father; when I was little, and I'd had a bad dream,
he always said that I could get rid of the bad dreams by drawing
them. I think of Father's black paintings; I never asked him if he
was trying to draw his dreams away too.

I put a piece of white drawing paper in front of me, and I
place the tip of the charcoal pencil right in the middle of it, but
I can't move my hand at all, I just keep thinking that it doesn't
matter, it won't help anyway. I close my eyes, I sigh, I try to sigh
the darkness out of myself. I begin to draw, but not really; I'm
just letting my hand move over the paper.

When I open my eyes and I look down, I see that on the
paper are a bunch of spirals weaving into each other, swirling
and dizzying, but the blackness of my dream isn't there. I fold it
up and rip it apart; it tears into three pieces.

I want to crumple it up and throw it in the garbage can.
Grandmother stands beside me; she reaches over and takes the
paper from my hands. She looks at the drawing, makes a wry
face, crumples up the paper, and says, This won't be enough.

She goes into the inner room; I hear the settee squeaking,
then she emerges with my bed linens gathered in her hands. She
throws them onto the table, and she tells me to take the whole
bundle out into the garden, pin it up onto the laundry line, and
she will be out in a second.

The bed linens are creased and somewhat musty-smelling.
I pin them up on the line, and the wind blows toward me and

spreads the sheets into my face. As I crouch down beneath the sheet, it flutters behind me; I imagine that it's a great white cloak or a very long veil. I grab the laundry line, pull it down, and lean back into it; I look at the sky, how the wind tears at the clouds.

Grandmother brings a large black cauldron and puts it on the ground, then quickly takes off the lid. The cauldron is half filled with glowing embers; atop the embers sits the black iron that I saw in the pantry, and next to it is the red-handled gardening trowel.

Grandmother says that we're going to iron the bed linens nicely, we're going to iron all the bad things out of it. If we do it well, I'll sleep like a baby tonight.

She picks up the iron and as she shakes it, pulling up the metal plate at the end of its inner chamber, I suddenly think of the cigarette, and I want to tell her that something is in there, but Grandmother has already turned the iron downward and is shaking the ashes and smut out of its interior into the bucket filled with glowing embers; the cigarette also slides out of the iron and, spinning, it falls onto the embers. Grandmother winces, tries to snatch it up, but it's too late.

The straw-yellow paper burns off the cigarette, the tobacco catches fire, and then a thick menthol smoke rises up from the bucket. Grandmother leans forward, holding her face in the smoke; for a moment it completely shrouds her head as she breathes it in deeply, panting; she inhales, she blows it out, once again she inhales, the smoke slowly disperses; her face appears from within the smoke once again; her wrinkles have somehow deepened and contracted her skin, she seems very old and worn now. She's still looking at the embers; of the cigarette only the filter remains, then that, too, sizzling, shrivels to mere black.

Grandmother sighs deeply. That's how everything burns away, everything and everyone, she whispers to herself; she shakes her head, Poor, poor Grandfather, she says, and she wipes her face with the sleeve of her dress; when she lowers her arm, her face looks as it usually does.

She picks up the gardening trowel, stirs it once through the embers; I can see in the light of the small sparks jumping up how her gaze has softened. She extends the iron toward me, saying, It's heavy, hold it tight so it won't fall.

The iron really pulls my hand down, I have to hold it with both hands, and even so it trembles a bit. Grandmother uses the gardening trowel to fill it up halfway with embers, pouring them into the iron's inner chamber, then she pushes the opening shut. Now we just have to heat it up, she says. She tells me to hold the iron in front of myself, spinning in a circle on my heel three times, like those—what do you call them again—those hammer-throwers, but make sure not to throw it, she says.

The iron hisses as I circle it around myself. I feel its weight in my arms and my shoulders, and in my waist too, my skirt is twirling around me, I'm spinning so quickly, and I must think of the hammer-throwers, I see before me those huge brawny men as, with reddened faces and panting, they spin the hammers around themselves, but they are all wearing twirling skirts, and they all have irons in their hands, and this image is so funny that I have to laugh; I spin around and I'm laughing, and Grandmother is laughing with me, I know that she's also thinking of the same thing; I've already completed the third turn, the fifth turn, and the seventh turn, I'm dizzy, I'm going to fall down in a moment, but I can't bring myself to stop; I turn and I laugh; the iron is going to go flying out of my hands any minute now; it flies, streaks of embers flying through the air behind it, it's going to fly far away, right out of the stadium, and I won't be able to stop it.

Then Grandmother says: Enough, and then suddenly I stop, and there I am with the dream-scented, creased white sheet in front of me; it's billowing. I know it's because I'm dizzy, but I see that the sheet is swelling out in circles. I hear Grandmother chuckling, and I already know what it is, it's the round cauldron cover, Grandmother is pressing the sheet outward with it, and she's saying: With feeling, gently, with feeling.

I press the iron down onto the sheet, and through the sheet onto the cauldron cover; it hisses, gray steam rises from it, I sense how the cover is moving, and the iron follows it, I know that I should be thinking of the darkness of my dreams, but I can't, my entire body is shaking with laughter, the iron is light in my hands; with that I follow the forms that Grandmother draws onto the sheet with the cauldron lid, it's as if I were painting every kind of letter with an enormous brush on an enormous canvas.

It is dusk by the time we are finished with the sheet, the pillowcase, and the duvet cover. Grandmother takes the iron out of my hands, places it in the cold bucket. My palms are sweaty; I wipe them on my skirt, then run my hand over the sheet; it is lukewarm and completely smooth. Grandmother touches it too, and she says: Take note, this is the right way to iron.

I'M IN THE DEPARTMENT STORE, standing in the staircase on the third floor, right before the glass doors to the toy and shoe departments. I've already gone through the toy section twice and the shoe department once; the shopgirls have long since stopped asking me what I want, they know I'm not going to buy anything.

I've saved all of my money, but it's still not enough for a bathing suit. Olgi said I shouldn't be sad, because I have exactly enough money for two lottery tickets, and if I win, then I'll have enough to buy twelve bathing suits.

The lottery tickets are sold in a booth by the staircase landing, with the new kinds of scratch-off lottery tickets displayed on the counter. When I was little, Father sometimes bought me lottery tickets, although at that time they didn't have this scratch-off kind, only the ones with the tear-off tabs. It always made Mother mad; she said it was a rip-off, you could never win, and we never did win, but Father said that if we never tried, then obviously we would never win. He told me to blow on the ticket before he tore off the tab, but even that didn't work, and we never won.

On every lottery ticket there's the same picture of an elephant lifting a bucket of money toward his head with his trunk, and the many banknotes are beginning to pour out of the bucket right onto his head. I hand over the money, whispering to myself, Money, come rolling to me, then I quickly take two lottery tickets, the middle one and the second one from the right.

I turn it over; on the back there is a small illustration showing where the elephant skin has to be scratched off and the sum of money beneath it — if I get three of the same, I win.

I blow on the lottery card, begin to scratch it, but my nail only scratches thin lines in the gray paint. I step over and put the lottery ticket up against the wall, and I try to scratch it off that way, which goes a little better, as the pigment falls off in wider swaths beneath my nail, and I see the first number, it's a five. I keep on scratching, then I see the number twenty-five, then there's a fifty, then one hundred. I've scratched off nearly half the pigment, but I still haven't found two matching numbers, so I already know I'm not going to win.

I take out the second lottery ticket, and just as I'm about to start scratching it off, a sweet scent of eau de cologne fills my nose. The librarian is standing beside me asking, Whatever are you doing? She grabs the lottery ticket from my hand, says that she sees I'm trying my luck; she leans over, kisses my face, and she says the ending is always the most exciting, let's see, let's see. She goes to the staircase, sits down on the top step, takes her bag into her lap, puts the lottery ticket on top of it, and begins to scratch. I sit down next to her and I watch; the orange-colored polish on her nails gleams, she quickly removes the paint from the lottery ticket with small scratching motions, then she shrieks and embraces me, and she tells me that I've won, I've won fifty! What a lucky hand I have, it's a miracle.

I feel my face burning from joy; the librarian gets up, and I jump up too. I ask her to show me, let me see, the librarian holds the ticket away from me; I see two fifties but not the third one, her finger is covering the edge of the lottery ticket right there, and as I reach for it to take it from her hands, she's already put it into her bag, she says she'll redeem it later, now let's go and celebrate, celebrate the fact that we've won, let's go and get something for ourselves. She puts her arm through mine, and she asks what I want. A bathing suit, I tell her, that's why I'm here. The librarian says that she has an acquaintance in the clothing department who can get me a bathing suit that'll make me more beautiful than the sun itself.

IN THE CLOTHING DEPARTMENT THERE are no other customers. The librarian speaks to one saleslady, offers her a cigarette, asks about her husband. I'm not paying attention, I'm looking at the mannequins; each one has the same black hair and the same mouth painted red, each one is wearing the same cotton dress, one in green, one in yellow, and the third in brown. They all stand in exactly the same position, stepping forward with one foot, as if they were marching somewhere. One of them is missing an arm, a black screw sticks out of her shoulder, and apart from the colors of the dresses, this is the only difference.

The librarian touches my shoulder and says don't stand around here, I should go into the fitting room, and she'll be right there. She shows me where it is, on the other side of the clothing department, beyond the shelves and the coat racks.

I set off, and the librarian calls after me to get undressed, she'll be right there, and she'll bring the bathing suits.

I stand in front of the heavy crimson curtain; when I take hold of it to pull it to one side, a fine dust rises in between my fingers.

The fitting room is quite big, almost like a small room; the walls are covered with the same dusty-smelling red material as the curtain; on the facing wall there is a single large mirror, but it's split in half, as if a chair had been smashed through it. One side of the mirror is unbroken; the other half is fractured into hand-size pieces.

My skin looks completely pale under the sharp white light.

I take the hair clip out of my hair, unwind my braid, and undo it; my hair falls down on either side of my face; now I don't seem so white. I look at myself, stepping to the side, then to the right, then to the left again.

The metal curtain rings make a clanging sound on the bar; the librarian pushes aside the curtain with a huge cardboard box, so big that she has to hold it in front of her with both hands.

She puts the box onto a chair next to the wall, looks at me, and says that this is the entire stock, it hasn't even been put out yet: we can be the very first ones to choose from it. She begins to toss out the bathing suits, all wrapped in cellophane, from the box. They are all different colors—I see the librarian sorting them according to color, stacking them up in piles on the linoleum floor. She looks up at me, and she asks: Oh, dear girl, you haven't even gotten undressed yet?

I stand there, I feel that my skin is burning, I don't say anything, I just shrug my shoulders.

The librarian gets up, stands next to me, places one hand on my shoulder; with the other she caresses my hair. I see that you're ashamed, she says, you're afraid of the mirror, which is an idiocy, little girls always want to hide behind their mothers' skirts. But I'm a big girl already, she tells me, a true woman, and, well, I have no mother.

This should hurt, but it doesn't. I think of the bathroom, I think of how I raised my arms above my head. I begin to undo the buttons of my blouse.

I'M NAKED, LOOKING IN THE mirror; the cracked half of the mirror breaks my body up into a mosaic. It's as if all the pieces had gotten mixed up. Knees, elbows, thighs, stomach, ankles, nipples, shoulders, waist, armpit, pussy. It's me and it's not me. I run my hands through my hair; my locks make swooshing and sizzling sounds as I pull my fingers through my tresses.

The librarian stands next to and behind me, holding a red one-piece swimsuit in front of me. No good, she says, throwing it onto the ground; she holds a golden-yellow top piece in front of my chest, says, No good; she holds black bikini pants in front of my stomach, says, No good; she takes out a top piece with a green-and-white pattern, No good; she holds a black-and-white panther-striped one-piece in front of me, No good; she holds a turquoise bikini top piece against me, No good. Nothing is good enough, everything can go on the ground, golden-speckled bikini bottoms, No good; a blue-and-white circle-patterned bikini top, Come on, already; a light green one-piece, That's not it; canary-yellow bikini pants, Still no good. The bathing suits pile up: No good, no good, none of them are any good, but no problem, there are still plenty in the box, we're not going to stop until we've tried all of them. The cellophane rips open, the paper rustles, everything has to be opened. We need the best, the most beautiful, and if it's not, then bye-bye, onto the ground it goes.

Then suddenly we find it. A dark green bikini with silver clasps on the side, the material printed with a faint scaled pattern like the moon shining on the skin of a great fish swimming deep in the water. The librarian says nothing, but I know right away that this is it. I grab the bikini pants from her hand and pull them on; I take the top part, it fits perfectly; the librarian is doing up the clasp on my back, I'm holding my hands above my head, then I lower them, I turn around to the mirror, I stretch out, standing on my toes.

The librarian says that she wouldn't have thought so at the beginning, but this was really made just for me, the color is perfect for my eyes, the cut is perfect for my figure, and it might even be good in the future if my breasts don't get too big over the next year.

Suddenly I ask her: Am I as beautiful as my mother was? The librarian steps next to me; with both hands she strokes my arm, my chest, my stomach; she steps away from me, and she says: Almost.

25

I GO OUT TO GET some bread. The small shop at the end of the street is closed; there's a slip of paper pasted on the glass door that says *Closed due to illness.*

This means I have to go to the big shop. The sun is shining, I'm happy to go. I'm wearing shorts, I made them myself; with tailor's scissors I cut the legs off an old pair of jeans that I'd grown out of so that there would be a fringe all the way around; it looks pretty sharp, and it suits me too, with every step I feel how the threads tickle my thighs; it makes me smile.

I'm singing about the spring breeze, swinging my shopping bag back and forth. The bottom of the bag is made from leather, it closes with a zipper all around; if the zipper weren't broken, you'd be able to close it, and it would be something like a purse. But I don't mind, I like to swing it back and forth.

I'm walking along the tree-lined path, then I go down the one hundred and one stairs.

I step onto only every second stair, and I don't hold on to the banister even once. I arrive at the bottom of the stairs and head off toward the shop, but then I hear somebody whistling behind me.

I should continue on and not pay attention, but still, I turn around. Next to the staircase, sitting on an old stone bench, is a boy, maybe in the eleventh grade or even older than that. He's holding a bird on his arm, and on the bird's head is a cap.

I've never seen anything like it before. I stop and look.

The boy's mouth pulls into a smile on one side; he motions for me to come closer.

I walk over and look at him.

He speaks: Hello, little girl.

I tell him I'm not a little girl, but I regret this as soon as I say it.

The boy smiles again, and I see that he has a bit of black down above his lips, as if there was a shadow there, that's what it looks like. He says: Well, then, hello, big girl.

The bird flaps its wings, and the boy says: Don't be afraid, it won't hurt you.

I nod, I say that I know that. I look at the bird's beak, it's pointy and black, but as it widens it becomes lighter, and where it disappears beneath the bird's cowl it's almost entirely white.

That's a really beautiful bird, I say. What is it?

The boy says that it's a hunting falcon and that I should take a good look.

He holds out his arm toward me; on it there's a thick leather glove, reaching up to his elbow, and the falcon sits on that. I see its thick, feathery legs. I look at its claws; those too are almost white as they grip the crimson-brown leather of the glove. As the boy extends his arm to me, the bird very nearly takes flight, beginning to spread its wings; its feathers are brown with clear stripes on the edges, creating a mosaic-like pattern, it's really beautiful.

The boy asks me what my name is.

I've already told him when I realize that instead I should have said it's none of his business and not to go whistling after me, but by then the boy is smiling at me, and he says, What a beautiful name, and he tells me his name too, it's Péter. Then he says something, but I'm not paying attention, I'm looking at the bird. I notice that there are short leather straps attached to its legs, their ends gripped by the leather glove.

I ask him where the bird is from.

Péter says that he incubated the bird's egg himself, carrying it in a small cotton sack tied beneath his left armpit for more than a month.

I ask him where he got the egg from.

Péter shrugs his shoulders, and he says: From where, from where, from here or there. I shouldn't ask so many questions, he says, I should tell him where I'm going.

I tell him I'm going to get some bread at the shop nearby.

He reaches into his pocket and takes out a five note. He asks me to get him some tinned fish. Sardines would be best, as long as they're preserved in oil.

I don't reach for the money; I'm looking at the bird, at how the mosaic pattern on its wings shifts with even the slightest movement.

Péter again extends the money to me, asking me to please help him, he can't go into the shop because the falcon never likes to be under any kind of roof; even though it has a hood, it still senses that it's inside somewhere; it will become restless and start screeching.

I take the money.

THERE AREN'T MANY PEOPLE IN the shop. I get some milk and some bread; there are many different kinds of sardines, I pick one in a yellow tin.

When I get back to the bench, Péter is smoking a cigarette. Next to the bench there is a large black motorcycle; I can't decide if it was there before or not.

He sees the tin of sardines in my hands, flicks away the cigarette, and smiles at me.

He takes a pocketknife from a backpack thrown onto the seat of the motorcycle, and he snaps out the can opener from the knife, extends it toward me. He says that he doesn't want to put the falcon down, and he can't open the sardines with one hand —could I do it for him?

I put down my shopping bag, take the pocketknife. It has a handle made from antlers; the can-opener blade is shaped like the head of a bird, and it even has a tiny copper speck for an eye.

I place the tin can on the stone arm of the bench so I can cut around its edge. When the tin is cut all around, I shove the opener beneath the cover, and as I bend the tin back, a bit of oil spills onto the stone. I put down the pocketknife next to the oil stain.

As I look up, I notice that Péter is staring at my legs and my bottom.

He sees that I'm looking at him, and he quickly turns his head away, says thank you for the help; he sits down farther back on the bench and reaches for the sardine tin, but clumsily, nearly knocking it off the bench. I reach over and grab the sardine tin, telling him to be careful.

Péter nods, he reaches for the tin; with two fingers he takes out one sardine, places it on the palm of his glove, and squeezes it; the body of the fish is squeezed out between his thumb and his index finger, the skin of the fish is shiny with oil.

He takes the leather cap from the falcon's head, and he says, Here you go, my little sister, you have something to eat now.

The wings of the falcon flutter for a moment; it steps forward on the glove, grabs up the fish and tears it with its beak, swallows, tears something from it again.

I ask what the falcon's name is. Péter says, Its name is Ré.

That's not a girl's name, I say. Péter smiles, and he says that he named the falcon when it was still an egg; he had no way of knowing it wouldn't be a tiercel. But still it's a beautiful name, isn't it? he says.

I nod. I look at the falcon; the feathers on its head shine, it balances on Péter's fist with its wings outspread, there is a coffee-colored splotch around its eyes, which are very big and very black.

Péter feeds it some more fish; the falcon eats, and I watch them.

When all the fish is eaten up, the falcon screeches once, then looks at me, beats its wings a few times, shifting its weight from foot to foot. Péter says to it softly: Quiet, my little sister. The falcon is still looking at me, and I look at it, its beak and its big black cold eyes, and as I look at it, I'm suddenly very hungry.

I say it's really very beautiful, but now I have to go.

Péter says he's happy he met me, we will certainly meet again. Ré never forgets anyone who gives it something to eat.

I nod, but I'm really not paying attention to what he's saying, because I'm so hungry that suddenly my entire stomach is aching, and my mouth has gone dry.

I grab the shopping bag from the bench, and, running, I go up the steps, taking them by threes, and I feel, with every step, my calves, my thighs, my bottom tensing.

It occurs to me that I could break off just a little piece of the fresh bread, and I could drink a bit of the milk, but I don't want either, even the thought of it makes me want to throw up, so much so that I would happily toss the shopping bag.

I don't throw it away, though, I run all the way down the walkway, in the middle, between the two lines of trees, and I'm already at our street when I hear the rush of wings.

I look up, it's Ré, flying low, beneath the crowns of the trees, and when I turn around it's already flown above my head, then all the way to the end of the tree-lined alley, and where it comes to an end, Ré sweeps across the crown of the tree, begins to fly upward, up to the sky.

I run out of the alley; I look up, I place my palm above my eyes, but even so I don't see anything.

I swallow once, put my hand on my stomach, turn onto our street, and run to Grandmother's house.

AS I ENTER THE HOUSE, I don't take anything out of the shopping bag; I immediately go into the larder.

The tinned fish are all on the highest shelf, next to the cans of beans and peas. There are about fifteen altogether. I stand on the footstool and take one down. It has a ring on it, so I don't need an opener.

I open it up there in the larder, reach into it, and take out a sardine, eat it. I sense how the tiny bones of the fish's spine crunch between my teeth. It feels good. I take another, then another, then, when the tin is empty, I take it into my two hands, and I drink up the salty, fishy oil from the tin.

I place the empty tin on the shelf. With one hand, I grasp at the edge of the shelf, lift up one of my legs, stretch it forward, point my foot; I sense my calf muscles tightening. My socks slide down to my ankles, my calves bulge; they're moist, I see that a tiny bit of oil has dropped onto them. I don't wipe it off.

I HEAD TO THE GARDEN, and I look at one of the pine trees; at the ends of the branches are buds that look like tiny brown eggs.

I lean in very close to them, and I look at them; they all have an eddying pattern, a bit like fingerprints. I take one in my hand; it slides off from the bud as if it were a tiny hat. I pull it onto the tip of my index finger. It's very fragile and a bit sticky; it feels as if a very light eggshell has gotten stuck to the tip of my finger. I take another one, then another one, until there's one sitting atop almost every finger. I look at the buds of the pine tree; they are formed by light green pine needles, they stick together, they look like soft tassels.

I touch one; it's very soft. A few of the buds slide off my fingers, but I don't mind; I rub the fresh pine needles between my fingers; they are pliable and not prickly at all, they have a sweet scent of pine, something like resin but much more subtle. I pull one off and put it in my mouth, I bite it in two; I wait for the taste of pine or resin, but no, instead there is a fresh taste of lemony onion, garlic, but it doesn't sting at all. I chew it and swallow it; in the back of my throat I still sense the taste of pine and a kind of light, smoky bitterness.

I tear off another bud, bite into it and chew on it, and I almost swallow this one too when suddenly I am seized by a wild greediness; I imagine myself tearing off more and more buds from the pine tree, stuffing them into my mouth; my mouth and my throat will be full of them, I know that if I did that I'd never ever want to stop, I would continue eating one after the other, not thinking of anything else, and the taste of pine would grow stronger on my tongue and beneath my tongue, I would just eat and eat, and all the while I would imagine that I was turning into a tree, a tall and straight pine tree, one that could never be cut down. I would stretch my arms up high, I would spread my fingers, and I would become a tree, I wouldn't just *think* I was a tree, I would really become a tree. I press the chewed-up bits of bud with my tongue against my palate. I know that if I swallow it, I will become a tree.

I remember how Grandmother once said that it's no good thinking about something, you just have to act, and I know already that it's too late, I've ruined it. I put my hand in front of my mouth, spit out the chewed-up bits of buds, a green paste with the scent of onions; you can no longer see the pine needles in them. I spread it onto the trunk of the pine tree, then I touch the bark, and for a moment I imagine that my fingers are pine needles, and the breeze is blowing between them.

I DREAM THAT I'M FLYING. I lie down on the wind, I let it carry me away. My hair is undone, and it flies out all around me; it's as if I am floating in very transparent water.

I fly toward the sun; it's large, shining and hot, I sense it on my skin, it warms me through the cold wind.

I turn on my back, spread my arms, spread my legs; I draw in my stomach, I spread my fingers, I stretch them out; I hold my arms above my head, I stretch myself out all the way.

The wind howls through my fingers, smooth and palpable; I grab it, I allow it to spin me around, turn me over.

I see the ground, it's very far away, far away down below me, and yet I still see the roofs of the houses and the trees clearly; I see the trees and the leaves, I see the yellowjackets, I see the ants crawling to the edges of the leaves, I see everything.

The sky is clear, I can see so far — somewhere, something is burning, the wind makes the smoke unfold, turns it white.

Beyond the smoke, high above, even higher than me, is a black spot.

It's coming toward me, growing larger and larger; I know that it will be above me in a moment.

I turn on my stomach, I spread my arms apart, I flee from it.

I can sense it's getting closer; a cold shadow is now cast on me, I descend toward the ground. I see Grandmother's house, I see the walnut tree; my legs begin to move wildly, I begin to kick very quickly with small movements; the wind is scratching my skin, the walnut tree is already close to me, but I sense that something is plunging right onto me, something black.

I throw myself to one side, the air is harder and thicker than water, I burst into it; with my arms spread out, I'm spinning,

I see a huge black bird flying next to me, it's enormous, much bigger than me, it pursues me with outspread wings.

I pull my knees up to my chest, pull my arms tight against my body; I somersault. I see the large firewall, its hard bricks, and below at the base the undulating gray tin, its broad edge.

Suddenly I wake up; the side of my body is hurting like it does after I've been running, when I'm out of breath. It's still dark.

I stretch my arms, grab the edge of the bureau next to the settee, feel for the glass of water on it.

I lean up on my elbows, the side of my body is still hurting.

I drink the water in large gulps. It's cold and rough, like air.

26

WHEN I COME OUT OF the changing booth with the folded-up, brown ironing blanket in my hand, I immediately hear Krisztina screaming. The sound is coming from the direction of the trampoline; I set off in that direction between the large bushes. I've hardly gotten there when I see that she's running straight at me; behind her are the boys from the class, they're chasing her, there are a bunch of other girls running too, they too are screeching, but Krisztina's screeching is louder than anyone else's; all the boys want to get to her.

To no avail, though; Krisztina is very quick, and every time they're about to catch up to her, she changes direction; the boys try to grab her, their hands outstretched, but they can't reach her, she spins and turns between them, her red bathing suit metallic and shining; she evades them, she ducks beneath their arms, she makes them dance in circles, she jumps farther away; she stops as they run after her with her arms spread apart, then, shrieking, she begins to run again. She runs around the trees, she jumps across the benches, she plunges through the sandpit; the boys are running after her, but they never catch up to her.

I arrived at the pool late today; Grandmother made me

sweep out the kitchen and the vestibule twice, only letting me go afterward, and almost everyone else from the class is here already. If the boys catch Krisztina, they'll throw her into the water, then they'll throw in all the other girls as well, one after the other, until everyone is drenched.

I stand behind the bushes adjusting my bathing suit. The scale pattern on the green material is barely visible now; it doesn't shine but absorbs the light, deep and dark, as if it were made of water. When I tried it on in the changing room, holding my hands above my head and sticking out my chest, I stood on my tiptoes, and I thought that no matter how beautiful Krisztina's bathing suit was, mine was certainly more beautiful, and I was certainly more beautiful. But now that I see how she runs and jumps, how her skin glistens from sweat, for a moment I think that I won't even step out from behind the bushes; instead I'll quickly turn around, I'll turn around and wind the ironing blanket all around myself so that nobody will see me, my thighs are too skinny and my skin is too pale, the veins on it are much too blue. My hand moves, beginning to unfold the blanket; a dry smell of iron seeps out.

Krisztina once again allows the boys to approach her, once again she allows them to very nearly touch her, then suddenly she turns, laughing loudly, and steps to the side; just then she's on the path strewn with pieces of tree bark and lined with stones. I keep hoping she'll trip on one of the stones, trip and fall on her stomach, slide onto her stomach on the wood shavings, scrape her elbows and her knees on the stones, and smash her head. I wish she would die.

I look at her leg, her slender foot, the toenails painted crimson, and I know that it will be exactly as I wish, she's going to trip, striking her instep on one of those stones, then that stone will scrape her foot right up to the toes; her hands beating the air, she'll try to regain her balance, but she won't be able to. I think of the stone, the sharp and hard edge of the stone, then suddenly something is making the light flash in my eyes, sharp and strong, making me blink. It's Krisztina's foot that is gleaming, her ankle, there's a thin golden chain around it, I didn't notice it before, but now I see clearly that with every step she takes, it slides a little up her shin; there's also a pendant hanging off it, and now I see that it's a lizard. Her foot curves into an arch, it slides along the edge of the stone, and I know she isn't going to trip. I watch her as she steps onto the stone; she stops, she smiles.

She's looking straight at me; I know that she knows that I'm behind the bushes. She's not running now, she's not laughing, she's not even screeching, she's just standing and looking at me, holding her arms apart. It looks as if she's trying to embrace the air, but I know that's not what she's doing. The boys are running behind her, they're getting to her, they're going to reach her, she's holding her arms out so it will be easier for them to catch her.

The boys get to her; the first one to grab her is András, then Misi and Feri, and then Iván. I see their hands as they touch her body. Krisztina shrieks again, now it's just a sharp little shriek, just a little *Oh my!* Iván grabs the upper part of her left arm by her bra, next to her heart, and it's as if a cold hand were grabbing me, grabbing me and squeezing me.

Krisztina throws herself back, back and up; the boys grab her, they hold her, they lift her above their heads; they're carrying her. Krisztina is lying in the air, her head thrown back, her hair hanging down; she looks at me and she smiles; I see her face upside down; her smile is a grimace wrenched apart.

The blanket drops to the ground, the fabric chafing like sandpaper. I kick off my flip-flops. I want to run after them, I want to reach them, I want to overtake them, I want to jump up and tear that golden chain off Krisztina's ankle.

The earth below my feet turns to dust; it feels like clumps of grass are tearing off beneath my feet, I've never run like this before, I'm not going to overtake them, they're already at the footbath, they've already crossed it, they're already standing there at the edge of the pool, on the blue and white mosaic tiles, they're swinging Krisztina, and they're shouting, Heave ho! Then suddenly they let her go; Krisztina is above the water, her body curved into an arc, she reaches back somehow with her left hand, grabs one of the boys' hands with outstretched fingers; it's Iván's hand, I recognize it. Krisztina tugs on the hand, Iván topples over, and they fall together into the water.

I've just stepped into the flat footbath; I slip, and I nearly fall. The water throws up green-white froth all around them, I see the chain flashing, I see how the pool swallows their bodies, and now I can't even see them. I call out Iván's name, I know that I shouldn't, but it's too late, the surface of the water is a broken mirror, it's throwing the light into my eyes, I know what's happening beneath the surface, I see legs and arms and backs and waists, they're grabbing at each other, they're intertwining.

Already they're swimming upward; in a moment they will surface, their faces next to each other, and they will laugh, both of them will be laughing.

I already hear the laughter, but it's not them, it's the others who are guffawing, and I know that it's at me, I know it's because I called out Iván's name.

I don't want to see them come to the surface. I don't want them to see me crying. I turn, and I begin to run along the footbath at the edge of the pool; the water splashes all around me, my bathing suit gets wet; I look up, and I see that I'm running toward the diving board.

The concrete steps are closed off with a rusty chain; on it there's a black padlock. I reach for it, grab the banister of the stairs, jump over the chain; one of my ankles hits it. I run up the steps. In many places the concrete is crumbling with iron pieces jutting out; I run higher and higher.

I pass the three-meter diving board, then the five-meter, I don't stop, I go farther, I pass by the seven-meter, then I'm standing at the very top, by the ten-meter diving board.

The concrete panels reaching above the pool are, in many places, almost completely disintegrated, they have huge holes in them; as I step onto the board, a large piece breaks off it; for a moment there is silence, then it splashes into the pool. Below, suddenly everyone begins to cry out, everyone's calling my name. I know that everyone's looking at me, yes, they're looking at me and not at each other, that's what I'm thinking as I raise my hands above my head, that's what I'm thinking as I slowly walk out on the concrete diving board, as I walk all the way to the edge, as I stop there, as I stand on my tiptoes, as I look up into the sky, as I fill my lungs with air, as I push myself off from the concrete.

Me—only me.

I FLY THROUGH THE AIR, I'm smooth, I'm a piece of stone covered with slippery green moss. Beneath me is the pool, the water is dark green, almost black; I tense my body, I try to turn forward, I stretch out my hands—too late, I will not reach the water headfirst, the world is spinning around me, I see the diving board, I see the crowns of the trees, I see my classmates standing at the edge of the pool, I see the water and, once again, the diving board.

I turn on my side and plunge into the pool. The sound of my body splashing into the water is mixed with the cries of my classmates; I don't hear what they're yelling, the water punches me between my ribs, it becomes sharpened, stabbing across me, it is a black funnel filling me with pain, dragging me down heavily. Before my eyes, foamy white bubbles swirl around, then

I only see the black water, thick liquid glass, spinning around, crushing me, pushing me farther and farther down.

I reach my arms up, try to kick; the water presses coldly around my ankles and my knees and my thighs. I want to turn, turn upward toward the surface, but the strokes are only pushing me down; the pool is growing narrower, like an upside-down pyramid. Everything is green and murky, then I see the bottom of the pool, filled with concrete debris; placed nearly in the middle is a huge clump of stone and, from it, extending out toward me, are sharp-pointed pieces of twisted reinforced iron, already one of them is by my hand, the sharp strands of wire stand out jaggedly from its tip. I try to pull back my hand but it's too late, the end of the iron bar slides between my fingers, almost touching the palm of my hand, then the inside of my lower arm. I know that I must not hold on to the iron, but I also know that if I don't grab on to it, its tip will slash my lower arm in two, and my blood will become a black ribbon, I don't want to, the touch of the iron is repulsive, slippery and dark, but I don't worry about that, I clutch it, it doesn't cut me, I hold on to it below the tip, but the iron clings to my palm, slimy, and I can't let go of it.

I want to let go of it, I want to let go of it and swim up to the surface, I want to break the surface smiling; with two hands, I want to smooth my watery locks away from my face, swim two strokes to the metal ladder, and climb out of the water nicely; I want to stand by the edge of the pool, leaning on the iron banister, and then I want to ask: Well, girls and boys, who dares to go after me? I think of Iván's face as he smiled when he pulled Krisztina into the water; I know he will never be mine. So who needs him? Let him be Krisztina's.

I can't let go of the iron.

The air begins to warm my lungs, it's pulling me upward; I tense the soles of my feet against the bottom of the pool, throw my head back, look up; I want to propel myself up, up to the surface, up toward the light, but this clump of stone won't let me.

My hair has come undone, it floats before my eyes; there is a burning sphere in my chest; I want to call for help, but I can't, I know that I must not open my mouth.

Still, I must yell. I have to. The air breaks out of me in one single enormous bubble; it stops before my face, a great green glittering sphere. I see myself in it, my face is paper-white; in the middle my gaping mouth is a black hole, the water pours out of it coldly and sharply.

The sphere slowly starts upward, and with my free hand I try to reach after it, and I reach it, but I can't grab it, it breaks up into smaller bubbles, then two whirl all around my fingers, and, gurgling, they float upward.

The deep green darkness closes in over me; I'm writhing, but I know it's no use. I can no longer escape from here.

I'm nothing; I'm troubled waters. I'm just imagining that somebody is embracing me from behind, I'm just imagining that a hand is grasping my wrist, I'm just imagining that it has yanked my hand away from the iron, I'm just imagining that it has begun to pull me upward. I'm also imagining the light, the surface of the water, the air too, and how everyone is screaming out my name. My eyes close.

EVERYTHING IS DARK GREEN, EVERYTHING is black. I open my eyes; through the green and black I see the sky and the diving board; my body is hurting on both sides; I'm lying on my back. I begin to cough, I feel a searing pain from my lungs all the way up to my throat; I turn onto my side, my mouth is filled with water. Coughing and retching, I spit it out onto the tiles. It tastes of puddles and algae.

My windpipe is burning as if boiling tar is flowing through

it; I think that the water will be black, black or scarlet, but no, clear water comes out of my mouth, flows all around me.

I lean up on my elbows, and I look at the water, how it enlarges the cracks in the tiles.

I hear somebody behind me saying that I'm lucky I didn't take in too much water because I easily could have drowned. It's a boy's voice, I don't know whose.

I have to cough; it makes my lungs and my stomach hurt, it's hard for me to speak. But I say that I'm sorry. I turn my head; a boy is crouching next to me. No, it's not a boy, it's Péter. As he moves, something makes a slight clanking noise; on one of his wrists is a bracelet woven from leather, three pierced copper rifle bullets are woven between the strips of leather.

He smiles at me and says what a stroke of luck, he's been certified as a lifeguard for not even one whole day, and look, already here's his chance to try out mouth-to-mouth resuscitation.

Then I suddenly begin to cough again. I lean onto the tiles, push myself up into a sitting position, put my hand in front of my mouth; my face is burning as if it had been slapped. I bow my head; I want my soaking wet hair to fall in front of my face and hide it.

Péter laughs and says he was just joking, I don't have to swallow everything he says. He smooths my hair back from my face with the hand that has the leather bracelet on it. He says that I swallowed a lot of water, he just had to raise up my arms a little bit, that was all, and almost everything came out. He didn't even have to do mouth-to-mouth resuscitation. But even if he had to, that still isn't a kiss. And even if it were, a kiss isn't the end of the world.

I try to stand up; Péter extends his hand, grabs my wrist, pulls me up. He squeezes tight. I wince as I stand up; he lets go of my hand. He looks at me, and now he's not smiling. He says that I could have drowned, seriously, don't jump anymore from the diving board, he says. If I want to die, it would be better for me to jump off the bridge headfirst into the turbine ditch; there the channel bed is full of scrap iron. His eyes shine blackly as he speaks, and I can sense that he really is angry.

I want to say that I'm sorry; I think of the clump of concrete at the bottom of the pool, the touch of the iron. But I don't say that I'm sorry; instead, I ask him: How is Ré?

Péter says Ré's doing very well, but his voice vibrates with surprise, and from the way he's squinting at me, I know for sure that he didn't recognize me. I'm one hundred percent sure that he doesn't even remember my name.

That's good, I say quietly. I turn away, I don't want to look at his face, I don't want him to look at my face. Pain is shooting through my lungs; I begin to cough; I don't look at anyone, and I head toward the changing cabins; the black water, smelling of algae, drips from my hair, flows coldly down my back.

27

CARRYING THE SHOEBOX UNDERNEATH MY arm, I walk along the cemetery fence. Beyond the cemetery flows a brook; a concrete bridge crosses it. I go up to the bridge, stand right in the middle. The riverbed is covered with concrete, the frothy green water runs quickly through it. I step over to the railing and look at it from there. I place the shoebox on the top of the railing.

I don't open it for a while, I just watch how quickly the water runs and how much garbage it carries. I take the lid off the box, throw it into the water. The wind spins it around, it falls into the water on its edge, quickly sinks, and I can just make it out as the water carries it beneath the bridge.

The shoebox is filled with my drawings, crumpled and ripped into pieces. I reach in, dig my fingers into the scraps of paper; they rustle like dry leaves. I look at the lines drawn in charcoal, recognize one of the branches of the walnut tree, the tip of a bird's wing, pieces of my own face, the curled-up leg of a fox.

I spent the afternoon going through all of my drawings. I took all of them out of the linen chest, placing each one on the settee, and I looked at every one of them, thinking all the while of Father, of what he said once to Mother when they were having a big fight—that it was no use, no matter how merciless she was to him, she could never be as merciless as he was to himself.

I clutch the scraps of drawings in my hand; I look at the water.

I think of Father's face: He's standing in the middle of the room, he's looking at the packing paper tacked up on the wall; on the wall is a picture that he's been working on all morning; he doesn't know that I'm watching. He thinks I'm in my room reading, and I am sitting in my room, but with my back to the door opened just a crack. I'm sitting in the armchair with a book in my hand, but between the pages of the book there is my pocket mirror—the one that used to hang on the wall of my dollhouse—and I'm watching Father in the mirror; I'm holding the book so I can see his face.

He doesn't move for minutes on end, he just stands there, looking at the picture, tilting his head a bit to the side, his lips squeezed together, the expression on his face angry and menacing, just like when he's about to start shouting or fighting with Mother, only his eyes are different now, the anger in them is colder and more resolute. His mouth contorts; I know what he's going to do, he's going to step over to the wall and tear the drawing away from it, and he does, he tears it off the wall and he rips it in two, then he rips it into four pieces, then into eight pieces, then into sixteen—I don't want to see this, I don't want to hear it; I turn the pages of the book onto the mirror, I find a sentence at random and read it aloud; the words mean nothing; I read it again and again and again, the words still don't mean anything, but they are spinning and buzzing in my head, and that's good because then I don't have to listen to the tearing sound of the ripping paper or Father's cursing.

On the surface of the water, gray foamy spume dances. I grab a fistful of the paper scraps, and with two hands, I scatter them onto the water. I think of my drawings, I think of how, when they were lying there spread out on the settee, I suddenly wanted to tear them all to pieces so I'd never have to look at them even for a moment again; I thought about how truly terrible they were, but then I looked them over thoroughly one by one, as if it hadn't been me who had drawn them but someone else, and one by one, I judged them: bad, weak, not worth anything—and one by one, I ripped every single one to pieces.

And as I ripped them apart, I repeated the truth about them once again: that they were just like me, clumsy, vain, ugly, awkward, bad, lies, worth nothing at all.

I raise up the shoebox, and I scatter all the pieces of paper into the water; the wind, murmuring above the water, grabs them, makes them fly beneath the bridge. I want to close my eyes, but I don't; instead, I watch how they fly through the air above the water; sick white butterflies. I shake out the last scraps from the shoebox; the box is gray and empty inside, just like the packing paper Father used to paint and draw on.

I pull the box apart in two directions; the glue holding it together loosens, then the box breaks in two. I throw the pieces into the water. Once again I think of Father, how I was always happy when I heard the tap-tap-tap of the hammer coming from the living room, because I knew that meant he'd once again nailed a large piece of packing paper onto the wall—he was going to start again. Again, and despite everything.

The pieces of the shoebox disappear beneath the bridge— my hands press down on the cold iron railing.

I let go of the railing, I turn around, and I run to the other side of the bridge. As I look down at the water, I see the pieces of the shoebox bobbing up and down, surrounded by the scraps of the drawing paper swimming whitely, swirling in a vortex.

I watch and I wait for them to disappear, then once again I say aloud: No. My voice doesn't sound like me; still, I know it speaks the truth. I will not stop, I will continue, once again

I will take out the charcoal, the white paper, I will try again, because I am the same as he was. Merciless.

I WATCH THE WATER UNTIL the very last scraps of paper disappear. Then I turn around, and I see that Péter is standing there, leaning against the other railing.

He flicks his half-smoked cigarette over his shoulder into the water, and he says that I shouldn't be trying to cause myself any harm because of that little monkey Iván. Believe me, he's not worth it, he says. And this is the small brook, not the turbine ditch, there's no use jumping into it, because I won't drown.

I say that I had no intention of jumping in.

Péter shrugs his shoulders, and he says it really looked like it. He saw me scattering all of my torn-up love letters into the water. He was already preparing to pull me back by the waist.

I tell him that those were not love letters. I'm not in the habit of writing love letters.

Too bad, says Péter. Because he'd be happy to read one.

I shake my head, and I want to say that he can wait for that if he wants, but instead I say, These were my drawings. The ones that weren't any good. I usually rip them up, and then here, from the bridge, I throw them into the brook.

Péter asks: Are there good ones as well?

I think of the empty linen chest, and I say, Of course, there's a whole bunch of them.

Péter's not looking at me; he's fiddling with his leather bracelet. I think of what will happen if he asks to look at them, but he doesn't—instead he asks if I know how to skate and if I have a pair of skates.

I've never skated in my entire life, and I've never had a pair of skates on my feet, but I lie and say, Of course I know how to skate, and I have skates, but why is he asking this in May? He starts laughing and he says, What kind of question is that? Don't I know that the very first indoor ice-skating rink in the entire country was built right here in our city? They can make proper ice there even in the summer if they want to.

I realize that I heard something about this when Krisztina was telling the other girls about it, how she'd gone skating on her birthday in her new fur coat with her father and how the fur coat swam in the air behind her.

I shake my head. *I don't know how to skate at all,* that's what I want to say, but I manage to get out only *I don't* before Péter presses the leather bracelet with the bullet casings into my hands while saying that he'll show me if I want. Tomorrow I should be in front of the ice-skating rink at six in the evening, by the statue behind the Great Market.

He doesn't even wait for me to respond; he turns his back and, with quick steps, goes to the end of the bridge. I shake the leather bracelet, call after him: What am I supposed to do with this? He doesn't look back, he just yells for me to be careful with it, because it's one of his greatest treasures.

The leather bracelet is made from black and brown straps; the tips of the rifle bullets are very sharp. It's pretty cool, but still I know what's going on, this is just a cheap trick to make sure I go tomorrow. I should be angry, I should throw it into the brook as well, but I don't.

I SMILE, THEN BITE MY lip; I shouldn't have lied, I should have told him the truth. I really was intending to. Now it's too late, and tomorrow I'm going to have to tell him—no, I can't say that I lied, I have to come up with something else like, let's say, that I grew out of my skates, and I noticed only at the very last minute, when I tried them on before leaving the house.

I keep walking, and I keep repeating that story to myself over and over, but it sounds worse and worse; each time it sounds less true. Péter will realize it's not true; he'll know that I lied to him.

Halfway down the street there's a big puddle in the asphalt, and I don't walk around it, I step right into it, just like when I was a little girl; I plunge my foot into it, the water splashes all around my shoe. Then suddenly I remember one photograph of Grandfather, he's wearing a suit and he's skating, standing on one leg, right on the tip of the skate; he's holding his briefcase, holding it up above his head with both hands, he's smiling, but you can't see his eyes because his glasses are shining so much in the light, it's as if he weren't even wearing glasses but had two shining light bulbs attached to his forehead.

AS SOON AS I GET home, I begin to look for Grandfather's skates. They must still be here somewhere.

I search the entire house, I look everywhere, I even go up to the attic; I look inside the trunks full of books and newspaper clippings, I look inside the suitcases and all the boxes where Grandfather kept his teaching materials and textbooks, I even open the typewriter case, but to no avail.

Finally, I find the skates in the larder, on the highest shelf, behind the jars of preserves. They are in a large black cardboard box that's thickly covered with dust; clearly no one has touched the box in a very long time. The box is heavy, and as I place it on the step, it nearly slides out of my hands; an undulating wave spreads across the dust, then swirls upward, and I see that there's an illustration on top of the box: a polar bear on skates made out of tissue paper. It's wearing a tuxedo and has its arms spread apart, and in one paw there's an icicle.

I open the box; the skates are also wrapped in tissue paper,

they look completely new. I unfold the paper—the black lacquered surface of the skates is so shiny that I can see my face in
them. The blades glitter blue. I pick one up, lift it out of the box,
and I look at the concave groove of the edge of the blade, the
jagged teeth in the front, the bronze-colored fasteners attach-
ing the blade to the soles. I've never seen such beautiful skates
in my whole life.

I take the other skate out of the box, climb down the attic
stairs to the third step, and there I turn around, sit down, and
put on the skates. First I put on the left one, muttering to myself, Don't be too small, if it's too big, that's no problem, I can
put on three pairs of socks, just don't be too small, but I know
that it won't be too small—it won't be too small and it won't be
too big, it will be just right and will fit onto my foot.

And it does. I lace it up, then tighten the laces and tie them;
I put on the other one, lace it up, tighten the laces, and tie them,
then for a while I just sit there, and I think of the picture of
Grandfather, how he held his head in the picture.

I lower the blade of the skates onto the linoleum; with two
hands, I hold on to the banister of the attic stairs, and slowly
I pull myself up. There—I'm standing in the skates. I let go
of the banister, take one step forward, toward the inside of the
larder. I almost fall over, but then I don't; I take a step onto the
battered Persian rug. I can feel its softness beneath the blades.
I'm going to fall, I know that I'm going to fall, my legs will
slip out from under me, I'm going to fall against the shelf or
the refrigerator, I'm going to crash into something. I think of
Grandfather, how he raised his hands above his head in the picture; slowly I stretch my arms and I raise them above my head,
and my ankles buckle, but I tense my calf muscles and I press
the blades of the skates firmly into the carpet, I'm standing, I'm
still standing, I'm standing, and I raise my arms above my head.

I look up; the window to the larder is placed high, right
underneath the roof, a small, dust-covered window. I stretch

my body out and I turn my face to the light. I know that beyond the glass and the dust the sky is gray, but I imagine that the sun is shining, it's shining, and it shines through the window, so strong that I have to squint, so strong it makes me close my eyes. I clutch at the rays of light; they hold me up, pull me up, slide me all along the ice.

I flex my thighs until they tighten, rest my hands on them for a moment, then I let go, and I balance that way, shifting my weight from one leg to the other. I slide across the ice, forward, directly toward the light. The skates are holding me up; I lift my legs, I step to the side, I propel myself forward, the blades of the skates glide, ringing; I hear music, soft, crackling, as if it were coming from a faraway gramophone, something like a lively march. I speed up, I have to hold my hands out to the side, the straight line will soon come to an end, and I will have to turn. The tempo is ever faster, and I too move faster, and I know that Péter is there next to me, together we're moving, only the two of us are on the ice, now once again we have to turn, have to lean into the turn. I put my hand onto my side and I lean into it, but it's no good, I sense my skate slipping from under me, I'm going to fall, but suddenly Péter grabs my hand and he holds me up, we take the turn, but even then he doesn't let go of my hand, and in that way we glide next to each other, hand in hand.

I want to see his face as he smiles at me. I turn to him, and then I see that it isn't Péter at all; it's Grandfather who is next to me, his glasses are shining, they're made not of glass but of ice, and not only his glasses but his head and his neck—he is completely made of ice, pure and transparent. He smiles at me, and the smile causes white cracks to spread across him, the ice turns completely white, then it disperses like fog; once again I've lost my balance, I fall against the refrigerator door, slide onto the carpet. I plop right down on my bottom; it doesn't hurt, but I'm freezing, my legs, my hands, my entire body is cold. I look down; the blades of the skates are completely covered with frost, my hand is freezing the most, I raise it in front of my face, spreading out my fingers; on the palm of my hand is a thin piece of ice, it's transparent, through it I see my lifeline and my fate line.

The ice melts quickly, and as it runs through my fingers, I suddenly smell a stagnant pond.

THE ICE-SKATING RINK IS CLOSED, dark and abandoned. I squeeze the bag with the skates to myself, and I'm thinking that this whole thing was certainly just a joke. Péter wanted to make a fool out of me, and that's why he pulled this prank. Next to the skates in the bag is his leather bracelet; I don't take it out.

In front of the skating rink there is a statue of a goalie; it's welded together from large rusty pieces of iron and iron disks; with his knees turned out and his arms extended, he's trying to protect the goal. He has no face, just a curved rusty grid beneath a helmet the size of a washbasin. In one of his hands he's holding a plate-size hockey puck, shining as if it were made of gold.

I reach up to touch it, but it's very high. I stand on my tiptoes, but I can't reach it, not even with the tips of my fingers. I jump up, and I can touch it; the blades of the skates clang together in the bag.

At the end of the street, Péter suddenly appears, this time he's on his bike; he rears it backward, then brakes next to me and gets off; slightly out of breath, he says that the hockey puck of the Iron Goalie brings luck to whoever touches it, and that's why it's so shiny.

He reaches up and touches it.

I tell him that the ice-skating rink is closed. He nods and he says of course, it's going to be summer soon. He didn't promise it would be open, just that he would show it to me. He takes out a jangling bunch of keys, shakes it, and says, Let's go.

WE GO TO THE BACK of the rink; Péter opens up iron doors and barred gates one after the other. We cross courtyards, we traverse a room full of droning and clattering machines, then we head down some stairs, go along a corridor, and suddenly we're at the edge of the skating rink, on the rubber mat. There is semidarkness in the hall; the skating rink is like a huge lake, emanating its gray cold toward us.

Whispering, I say: Did we just break in?

Péter shakes his head; he takes his skates out of his backpack. Not entirely, he says, his father is the caretaker here, these are his keys.

He gestures for me to put on my skates. I sit next to the bench, and as I take Grandfather's skates out of the bag, the leather bracelet falls onto the rubber mat. Péter picks it up, puts it on his wrist, and asks me if I know what these are. Yes, I say, they're bullets, and he says of course, but they're not just any bullets, did I know that he and his whole gang were there at the demonstrations, they were there at the street battles afterward as well? These are genuine submachine-gun bullets, he gathered them himself from the live cartridges. He could have blown off his arm.

I look at his hand, at his fingers squeezed together as he pushes the leather bracelet onto his arm; his hand is surprisingly small, but his fingers are long and slender. I don't want to imagine what it would be like if, instead of fingers, there were bloody stumps there, I feel the anger churning up inside me, I want to shout at him that I don't care, he should leave me in peace with his idiotic machine-gun bullets and his idiotic heroics, is this why he invited me here, so that he could boast about this garbage? But all I say is, Congratulations. I'm not whispering anymore, my voice is sharp and grating.

I take off my shoes, and I pull on Grandfather's skates.

Péter stands up, and he says that he wasn't telling the truth before, or, that is, not completely; his father doesn't work here anymore, he got kicked out because too much of the cooling liquid was disappearing and they had to pin it on someone. But at least he wasn't here during the revolution.

I stand up too; it's strange to stand on the blades of the skates, harder than it was in the larder. I'm sure I'm going to fall, if not here, then on the ice. I take a step toward the ice, and I ask, What was good about that? I'm not interested in the answer, I'm interested only in making sure he doesn't notice how much I'm tottering.

Péter steps onto the ice, and he says, Because of all the dead people. He says that after the soldiers opened fire on the crowds, the people from the Ministry of Internal Affairs kept the corpses here on the ice for a few days before they hid them somewhere else so they could cover up the entire bloodbath. If his father had still been working here, he wouldn't be alive today.

As he talks, I too step onto the ice. I grab the banister, then I let it go; the skates set off with me. I feel that my legs are going to slide out from under me; grasping at the air, I try to get my balance. Péter grabs my hand, I don't fall; tottering, we glide across the ice.

His hand is warm, he holds mine, and he pulls me along. I'm skating, a boy is holding my hand and I'm skating, I just want to think about that, about that and nothing else. Why is he talking to me about the dead?

He squeezes my hand; I know it's going to happen, he's going to pull me alongside him, and we'll go around and around ever faster, we'll fly along the ice in ever smaller circles, going around and around, he'll spin me around himself, then I'll get completely dizzy, then he'll pull me in and he will embrace me; it will be good.

The surface of the ice is watery; our skates keep sending up spray, it's as if the ice is undulating around us. I think of the monument on the main square, and the pictures pasted there. The ice is gray, it's not even an ice rink but a lake; we're skating on a lake and the cracks are spreading across the ice; I shouldn't think about that but it's too late, the ice is groaning and cracking all around us, it becomes transparent, and I see how there, below the ice, all the corpses are floating; their arms outspread, their hair loosened, they swim with open eyes, the ice screeches beneath our skates as we glide above it; they're all there, the ones who I saw in the photograph, but not just them—Grandfather is there, Mother is there, and Father too.

They are there below—they are watching us. I don't want them to see us.

I snatch my hand away from Péter's, I want to stop; one of my skates turns to the side, beneath it the ice makes a grating sound; the spray from the ice strikes my face; it smells like a puddle, and I cry out, That's enough, leave me in peace, leave me in peace already. I stand there swaying, then I begin to run to the edge of the rink.

The blades of my skates clatter against the ice, carving holes into it; I'm going to fall, my hands, waving wildly, clutch at the air; I'm running, I don't fall, my knees are hurting and my back is hurting too, I'm never going to get out of here, never going to get to the edge of the rink; even though I know that there are no depths below me, it's just concrete, still I sense that the ice is going to open up and I will fall.

At last I jump onto the black rubber mat; I pull at the laces and tear them off, one of them breaks, but I don't care, I kick off the skates.

Péter is there already, crouching next to me, asking what's wrong.

I shake my head, and I say that he never should have brought me here, can he not understand that this is too much for me? I want him to get me out of here, take me home.

I sense that my hand is trembling; Péter holds both my hands to stop them from trembling, he says to calm down, of course he'll take me home, please don't be angry at him, he didn't mean to scare me. He didn't want that, just to dance with me a bit on the ice.

His fingers are massaging my hand, and again he says: Please don't be angry.

I take a deep breath, and I whisper: Let's go, we'll dance another time.

He caresses my fingers, his face flooded with a smile, and he says: That would be really nice.

28

WHEN I'M WASHING THE DISHES, I think of Péter, I can't stop thinking of him. I wipe off the rest of the egg and noodles on the plate, and I think about how he smiled at me. Grandmother takes the plate from my hand, begins to wipe it dry; the plate gleams beneath the rag, but she doesn't stop, she just keeps wiping and wiping. She says I should know that true love is always painful. It's painful, it's hard, but that's what makes it beautiful. She asks me, Is it a more serious boy this time?

Maybe, I say. I nod, and I tip the second plate into the water; I press the sponge onto it, and I wipe off the food scraps. Grandmother says that Miklós, Bertuka's older brother, was her first serious love. From the way that Grandmother takes a breath, I know that she will tell me a story again. I look at the sudsy dishwater. I have to pay attention to Grandmother's voice.

YOU ACT AS IF NOTHING has happened, as if everything is the same as it always was, you walk down the street just as you always did, it's spring, the tulips are growing in their beds just as they do at other times, the pale brown sheaths of the pine trees' buds burst downward as always, the sun shines the same as it always did, your shoes knock against the cobblestones as they always did, and you sing to yourself as you always did, it's just that now the doorway and the windows of the drugstore are broken and boarded up, and Mr. Brenner isn't standing there in front of his shop in his usual place, and he's not saying, Good morning, Miss Emma, but still you walk by as if he were standing there; you think of the fragrance of Chanel No. 5 because Mr. Brenner once blew it onto you; he smiled and he said that it wasn't right for you now, but you'd grow into it in a few years, and then you'd be able to wear it like a beautiful dress, and you don't want to think about this, nor do you want to think about the long procession of people walking, or of the brick factory, or of the barbed-wire fence, or about the fact that Mr. Brenner is at the brick factory now, and he has to sleep on the floor, you cannot think about that, because you must act as if everything is fine, nor can you think about Bertuka, of how she is lying deep within the woodshed in the darkness of the grain chest; you are here in the light, and she is there inside, but you must not think of this, you must forget, and no one is allowed to know, not even you, so now you keep the knowledge that she is there as if you had forgotten all about it.

You walk and the sun shines in your face, and you act as if everything is fine, as if you are in a good mood, you hum to yourself as you walk, you hum to yourself as you walk by the other boarded-up storefronts; humming to yourself, you turn onto School Street; humming to yourself, you go up to the corner of Old Post Office Street as if you aren't even going by there, as if you haven't even noticed the tailor's workshop that belongs to Bertuka's family, as if you just happened to stroll over there, as if your path is taking you there completely by accident; already you're next to the gate, and you can't not read the malicious inscription that somebody has written with tar on the whitewashed planks of wood, you don't think, Now or never, you only think of what Bertuka said, you don't even slow your steps as you place one foot at the base of the fence; you grab the plank, you push yourself up, and you swing yourself over the plank, and on the other side, you crouch down, hunching into yourself at its base.

You look around the empty courtyard; you don't bother with all the objects thrown around, you avoid the small ditches dug into the ground; in one there is deep black water, you don't look into it; you step across a broken plate and a picture frame, its glass cracked; you avoid the books torn from their spines, then you're in the summer kitchen, and by the back wall is the ladder, just as Bertuka told you.

You climb it.

The third rung is broken; you step onto the edge, it creaks but it still holds you, and already you're at the top.

The door to the attic isn't bolted shut; you push the door in, you climb in. As you straighten up, something moves in one of the corners, and you think that maybe it's Miklós, maybe he's hiding, maybe they didn't see him, but it's just a cat, a large cat, its fur scarlet and red; it looks at you, it meows once, then it quickly runs away, it slips through a hole between the tiles, and you don't see it again.

The attic is filled with junk; you see broken chairs, a smashed spinning wheel, piles of newspapers, open suitcases thrown onto each other, and, beneath the peak of the roof, among stacks of bricks, a large pile of sand; as you reach it, you see a small red-handled gardening trowel sticking out, you recognize it, the last time you saw it, it was in Miklós's hand; he was in the back, crouching in the courtyard, digging a large hole, he didn't say hello to you, and he didn't even look at you; by then you weren't surprised by that, but still it hurt, still you stood there and you watched him, and you listened as he hummed something to himself, and you were able to withstand this until Miklós stood up, turned his back to you, and moved a bit farther on, only to crouch down and begin digging a new hole.

You take the handle of the trowel, you pull it out of the sand, and you think of the courtyard, you think of Miklós as he crouched there among the many holes in the ground; you think of yourself as you stood there and watched; the pile of sand moves, it streams down as if only that trowel had been holding it together, black clumps of loam emerge from beneath it, you see the rough contours of an arm, legs; beneath the sand a large black statue lies in pieces, the statue is molded from earth; you look at the chest, the ribs clawed on both sides by fingernails; on the left side where its heart should be, there's a fist-size hole, and it's as if the sand is swirling in it, only the head is missing, your hands seem to move by themselves, digging in the sand, looking for the head, they don't find it, again you think of Miklós, of his high-pitched humming, of how he looked at the earth. That's not why you're here; your hand sinks into the sand, you see the body of the statue from very close up, it is covered with scrawled numbers, formulas and equations flowing into each other, they cover its loamy body entirely. You grab a fistful of sand and sprinkle it onto the body, and you don't watch how it flows down on it.

You go toward the chimney, and once again you're thinking of Miklós, you're thinking of his hand as it held the pencil in the summer when, for two hours every day, he tutored you and prepped you for exams; you think of how sometimes he drew spiderwebs or flowers or birds for himself as he waited for you to solve the problems, how he looked when, after many attempts, you still could not recite without error the little verse about the proof of the Pythagorean theorem and of how once he reached out toward you, completely unexpectedly, and pulled the hairpin out of your bun.

You walk toward the chimney, but you're not there, you're in the small room next to Miklós, he's standing there, the hairpin in his hand, your hair coming undone like a coiled spring; it covers your eyes, but still between the locks of your hair you see Miklós's face as he smiles triumphantly, then suddenly the smile is swept away by worry, as if he had not realized until then what he'd done; he looks at his own hand, the glittering hairpin in his fingers, on his face is the fear of a small boy; suddenly he hands the hairpin back to you, stuttering, he says, I'm s-sorry; you shake your head, you smooth the hair away from your eyes, you smile at him; your face is burning, and you think you're not going to be able to speak, but then you can, and you say: Here, keep it. You're giving it to him as a keepsake, as a gift; stuttering, he says, N-n-no, he c-can't accept it, and the hairpin is there in his hand, a green-eyed dragonfly, the membranes of its glass wings formed by golden threads; it shines as if it were real, as if it were about to fly away, restless; you know that it's only Miklós's hand that is trembling; you suddenly reach over and grab it, closing his fingers around the hairpin, and you say, Don't be silly— this is what he usually says to you when he wants to reprimand you. His skin is soft, his fingers easily clasp around the hairpin, you squeeze his hand tightly, you never realized how small his hand was, it almost fits in your palm; beneath his skin there is still that nervous trembling, making your palm moist. Miklós stands up, pushing his chair back, he wants to yank his fist away from yours, away from your grasp; he says, Don't be angry, but you don't let go, then he grabs your fist hard, he pulls you over to himself; the chair is knocked over, and there you are next to him, as close as possible to him; your hair sweeps across his face, it's as if you both were dancing, your arms held out to one side, your thigh touching his thigh, your chest next to his, your face is very close to his face, your mouth is close to his mouth, your hand moves to hold the back of his neck so as to pull him toward you so you can kiss him, so he can kiss you; he grabs your bottom, you feel his hand through your skirt and your slip, you feel his fingers grabbing you, feel his thigh between your thighs; he's pulling you onto himself, you're pushing yourself onto him, he's trembling as if he were afraid, but you know he can't be afraid because you're not afraid; you grab the nape of his neck, his body convulses from your touch, he moans, his face changes in a flash, joy mixed with dread; he lets go of your bottom. Don't be afraid, you want to say, you want to say there's no problem, but you can't speak; Miklós turns his head, he steps to one side, he pushes you away, his neck slips away from your hand; he says, I'm sorry; he says, I didn't mean to. He yanks his fist away from your palm, the hairpin sticking out of his fingers, the tip of it scratching against your skin. He grabs his bag, he runs out of the room, and you don't go after him; you look at your palm— the scratch made by the hairpin obliquely crosses your fate line and your lifeline, the blood oozing out of it in tiny drops; you raise your hand to your mouth and you lick the wound, quickly.

You go toward the chimney, you're thinking of Miklós, you're thinking of what you felt when you found out that the final-year students from the other school had caught him on the bridge of the Watermill Canal and then, as a joke, decided to baptize him and threw him over the railing, and Miklós almost drowned because he didn't know how to swim, and then, when they pumped the water from his lungs, he didn't open his eyes, he wasn't regaining consciousness, he just lay there somewhere between life and death. You think of the piece of graph paper that you took out three days after Miklós had been pulled out of the water. You didn't dare visit him, it wasn't proper, but still you couldn't bear it, you came here, in front of their house, you stood in the street in front of his window, you held up your pocket mirror, and then you looked in through a crack in the curtains in case you might be able to see him, but you couldn't see him, you only saw the end of the bed, you only saw the motionless white blanket, and you couldn't tell if it was him sleeping beneath this blanket. You put away the mirror and you went home, and you took out the large notebook with graph paper, and you ripped out a page from the middle, and you began to write, one beneath the other, the prime numbers. You think of that piece of graph paper, the scratching of the pen, of the numbers you wrote one below the other in a line. You began at the very beginning, with 2, you wrote it down, you wrote down the number 2, and at the same time you said to yourself: Let Miklós regain consciousness; you wrote down the number 3, and you said to yourself: Let Miklós open his eyes; you wrote down the number 5, and you said to yourself: Let Miklós sit up; you sat at the small kitchen table all afternoon, all evening, and all night, and you wrote the prime numbers one after the other, and you repeated the sentences to yourself one after the other, and each sentence began with the same words: Let Miklós ask for something to drink, let Miklós ask for something to eat, let Miklós blink his eyes, let Miklós smile, let Miklós put on his socks, let Miklós put on his underwear, let Miklós put on his trousers.

You walk toward the chimney; you think of Miklós, you think of how you wrote down the number 997, you think of how you said to yourself: Don't let Miklós die, let Miklós live.

You stand before the chimney, you begin to count the bricks from the very bottom, just as Bertuka told you, you think of how much it hurt when you found out that in vain had Miklós regained consciousness, in vain had he opened his eyes, in vain had he sat up and in vain had he gotten dressed, in vain had he done everything that you had recited, because he hadn't gotten better, you couldn't and you didn't want to believe what they were saying about him, that near drowning had made him feeble-minded.

They said it was as if something in him had broken; he didn't want to look at anyone, he kept shrugging his shoulders, kept making clicking sounds with his tongue as if he were imitating the clapping sound of a trowel; he sang or spoke all kinds of gibberish, no one could understand what he was saying, and even when they could, he made no sense at all, as if he were putting the words next to each other just as they came, with no rhyme or reason.

As you count the bricks, you touch each one; on one there is the insignia of a rooster pressed into the brick, the rooster's body is black, soft soot; this is not the brick you need, but the middle one, twenty-one bricks up from the bottom, it looks just like the others; you press it in, it doesn't move, you try to pull it out, you place the edge of the gardening trowel into the crack between the bricks, and again you think of Miklós, you think of the first time you met him after he'd regained consciousness; he sat at the top of the staircase with one hundred and one steps and he was singing, you didn't recognize him from behind, only when you passed by him; you said hello to him, but he didn't say hello back, he didn't even look at you, he just stared at his hands; you stood in front of him, and you said you were happy that he was feeling better, even then he didn't say anything; you saw that in his hands he held a ball of mud, he was turning it over and smoothing it between his palms, it was very round and very smooth, and as he turned it slowly, it became even rounder and even smoother between his fingers, and it was so black, like the blackest tar or like the toe of a polished shoe, only it didn't gleam; instead, it sucked the light back into itself; you stood there and you looked at him, and you thought of those three simple words, those three words, and if you spoke them, perhaps Miklós would look up, maybe he would look at you, perhaps he would see you, perhaps he would hear you; you stood there and you looked at that black ball of mud as it turned and became rounder and rounder between his fingers; you almost heard your own voice as you spoke, as you said those words, those words that you did not say all summer, those words that a girl must not say first, they were there in your throat, on your mouth, on your lips, but you still couldn't say them; you looked at the ball of mud, you looked at how dreadfully smooth and how dreadfully black it was, and you knew that if you spoke those words and nothing happened, it would be even worse than silence, so you didn't speak at all; you turned away, and you set off, you climbed down the one hundred and one steps, the iron tips of your shoes clattering on the basalt steps louder than they ever had before, all those unuttered words clattered, they rattled in your head, in your throat, in your mouth, but even at the bottom of the steps, you did not dare to speak them, not even softly, not even whispering— in no way at all.

The brick grinds beneath the edge of the blade; sand spills out from the crevice; the brick slides out a couple of centimeters, you grab it, you begin to pull it out, it comes out from the chimney wall; the inside of it is covered with soot, with a black nail knocked into it and a string knotted onto the nail; both ends of the string disappear into the inside of the chimney, and when you grab the string and pull on it, black streaks are left on your fingers and on your palm; then out of the crack two soot-black tiny lizards slip out, one bigger and one smaller, they slip between your fingers, then nestle themselves in your palm. As you rip the twine away from them, the scales of soot swirl off as if they were shedding their skins; beneath the soot the texture of white metal threads emerges, with blue illuminated stones set within, you've never seen anything shine so much. One big lizard and one small lizard — a bracelet and a necklace, they cling together heavy and cold as you squeeze your hands around them, the trembling runs all up and down your arm. You try to think of what Bertuka told you: This was life, the diamond jewelry that was hidden in the chimney meant life, because with that they could get back Miklós, Bátykó, and all the others too. You unbutton your blouse and you shove the jewelry into your bra, the little lizard on the right side, the bigger lizard beneath your left breast.

THE DOOR TO THE WOODSHED *opens without a creak; you go in, you close it behind you. It's entirely dark; if you listen closely, you hear a faint scraping sound: you know it's the clatter of Bertuka's knitting needles.*

You slip in under the woodpile stack, you light the kerosene lamp, and you say that it's you. Bertuka climbs out of the grain chest, crouches next to the lamp, and she asks, Do you have it? You nod, you pull them out of your bra, you slip the jewelry into her hands.

You twist the wick of the lamp a little higher; Bertuka looks at the two lizards curled up next to each other. They're so warm, she whispers, it's almost as if they were real. The lizards' bodies make the lamplight multiply and scatter; they look like they are illuminated from within. They slip between Bertuka's fingers; she holds the palm of her other hand beneath them, she slips them from one hand to the other, she looks at them as they shine, then suddenly she looks at you, she says: You don't know how Miklós regained consciousness. You don't know, because Bertuka hasn't told you yet.

You don't say anything to that; you're thinking of the prime numbers, you're thinking of that piece of paper that you filled with them, you think of how many times you repeated his name to yourself.

The larger lizard winds itself around the back of Bertuka's hand, making her skin red like fire. She says that when they brought Miklós home and they laid him down, Bátykó touched his face, then he burst out crying, and, crying, he said that he wasn't going to come back to himself, you will see that he won't, he will lie there and breathe for three days, but he will only get paler and thinner, and on the fourth day, he will not live to see the sunrise. At first they didn't believe him, and they sent him out of the room, but they sat in vain next to Miklós's bed for three days, relieving Mama, and in vain did they shave him and caress him, in vain did they talk to him, in vain did they sing to him—he only grew paler, and then on the evening of the third day his face was completely gray, and then Mama could no longer bear it, and she called Bátykó into the room and she asked him why he had said what he had said. Bátykó held Miklós's face between his two hands, he bent over him and held his ear to his mouth, and he listened for a long time with his eyes shut, then he sat up and he said that there wasn't much time left, there was only one last thing to try, he was going out to the yard now, and he would be back in a moment, and in the meantime they should undress Miklós and wash him, and when he came back they should not speak a word, they should say nothing and ask him nothing, but they must do whatever he commanded—and they should know that if they spoke even a single word, it would be the end of everything, and one hour later, when Bátykó came back, his clothes were drenched in sweat, and he said: Wind a sheet all around Miklós, because he must be brought out to the yard, and he was so heavy that three people could hardly carry him, but somehow they dragged him across the summer kitchen and out the door, and then they saw that in the yard, by the base of the fence, there was a freshly dug narrow ditch, like a grave, but only one-quarter as deep, and they laid Miklós in that, and they were so terrified that they didn't even dare cry, and then Bátykó began to sprinkle the dirt onto Miklós with both hands, and he gestured for them to help; they started by his feet; and so they buried him nice and slow, and when they got to Miklós's head, Bátykó took out a long-necked wine bottle from somewhere, took a long drink from it, then he offered some to them as well; it was biting, bitter brandy, and they drank it, then Bátykó sprinkled the rest of it onto the mound of earth; he broke the neck of the bottle, and he dug the top into Miklós's mouth; he held it with one hand, and with the other he began to fling the earth onto his face; he motioned for the others to help, and then they helped, and nothing had ever been so hard for Bertuka in her entire life than to sprinkle those few handfuls of earth onto Miklós's face and onto his eyes, but Bátykó didn't stop, so they didn't stop, neither did Mama; they scattered the earth and they scattered the earth onto Miklós until he was completely buried, and then, when everything was finished, and only the broken neck of the bottle stuck out from the earth, Bátykó had them kneel on both sides of the ditch, and he knelt by Miklós's head, and he slowly sang, but without words, softly, as if he were imitating the sound of the violin or as if he were howling, and then they sang with him, and they were there all evening until dawn, and they only stopped when the base of the sky began to turn red; at once they grew silent, because Bátykó held out his hands, his fingers spread out, toward them, and then the silence became great as they knelt there in the gray dawn light, and then Bátykó slammed his left hand down onto the earth, and then suddenly they heard a kind of choking coughing from beneath the earth, and the earth started to move and undulate, and then Bátykó reached over and grabbed the glass stump and flung it aside, then he scratched at the earth with both hands, they too began to scratch the earth with Mama, and there was Miklós's arm, where it was supposed to be, beneath the loosened clumps of earth; they grabbed it, together with Mama they grabbed one of his arms, and Bátykó grabbed the other arm, and they pulled Miklós from the earth, and he wasn't entirely out before he suddenly opened his eyes and he looked at them, but it was as if he were seeing them for the very first time, then, with racking coughs, agonizingly, he spoke, and he said that he had slept very badly, and he had had very bad dreams.

Bertuka is silent; she's holding the clasp of the necklace in one hand; she raises it, the necklace is one long serpent, it slowly swings from side to side; Bertuka's gaze follows the rhythm of the swinging, then she speaks again. Bátykó told him then that it wasn't a dream, and that made Miklós start coughing again; he knelt next to the ditch, and, nearly choking, he coughed for a long time, so much that if they hadn't held him, he would have fallen. Bátykó slapped his back; Miklós, lean-

ing above the ditch, was retching, you could hear that something was bursting from his lungs, and then he began to spit thick black muddy spittle onto the upturned clumps of earth.

You're looking at the lizards. Bertuka raises them slowly by their tails, holding her other hand beneath them; she lets their tails go, the necklace and the bracelet fall into her palm, and once again the diamond scales are shining on them. You want to think about the prime numbers, you think about Miklós talking about their truth, cold and irrefutable. You ask Bertuka what she's going to do now.

Bertuka clasps the jewels in her fingers, says that she's going to use them as they were intended; she will go to the old chief engineer, the older brother of the commander of the gendarmes, he knows her well, has known her since she was a little girl, because he always had his suits made at her parents' workshop; she's going to give him one of the lizards, and she will get Miklós and Bátykó out of the ghetto, and Papa and Mama too, she's not going to let them be murdered. She has to do this, only she can do it; if it weren't for her, Bátykó would have left a long time ago; he decided to stay here only because of her, and if they had believed him, they all would have left; Bátykó had told all of them in advance what was going to happen here, but—as they were naive—they didn't believe him, and now it was too late.

She has only one question left for you: If she is able to bring them out, can they too stay with you? Not for a long time, just for a bit, just until she can use the other piece of jewelry to arrange to get them across the border somehow.

You think of Miklós, you think of his touch, and you nod—there's nothing else you can do.

GRANDMOTHER IS SILENT; SHE WIPED the dishes bone-dry and put them back in their place a long time ago, and now she's standing in front of the open cutlery drawer with a polished soupspoon; she looks at herself for a long time in the reflection, she's not paying attention to me. I turn away, I go into the other room, I hear the drawer being shut loudly. I sit down on the bed. I want to think about Péter, but all I can think about is the broken bottle neck sticking out of the ground.

29

PÉTER SAYS HE CARVED THE wooden bird by himself, then glued pigeon and magpie feathers onto it; its beak is formed by a hooked nail that has to be latched onto the slingshot's elastic strap.

I squeeze the iron handle of the slingshot with all my strength; Péter tells me to support my elbow, so my hand won't tremble. I should tense my arm and, pulling the band as far back as I possibly can, take aim at the sky, then release the tail of the wooden bird.

I tense my arm. I pull back on the elastic strap.

It slides out from the hooked nail.

The second time I hold it a little differently, but it still slides out.

Péter says to do it delicately, with feeling.

I have to pull the elastic so hard that my arm almost breaks; I don't know how this can be done delicately. Then I try it the third time. As I let it go, I wish for the bird to fly.

This time it works.

The wooden bird ascends and ascends into the sky, then for a moment it's as if it has stopped in the air, then it turns, head down, its wings beating; on its back a small trapdoor opens, a tiny silk parachute rises, and, slowly, spinning, the bird begins to fall.

Péter then puts two fingers into his mouth. I expect him to start whistling, but he doesn't, he makes a shrieking sound.

Ré is up there too, high in the sky, circling so high we can hardly see her, but now Ré begins to plunge toward the tiny parachute; there's a gray wind, a flash of brown, now Ré is above the parachute; with her wings spread she swoops down on it, the wooden bird is already between her claws, now it's next to us on the roof of the railcar. Ré presses it against the roof and begins to tear its feathers off.

Péter crouches next to Ré, calls out her name, puts a shred of meat into her beak, sits her on his fist, and gives her another piece of meat. Ré eats the meat, then paws impatiently at Péter's glove. Péter throws her into the air again.

Lying on our backs on the metal roof, we watch Ré fly higher and higher. The sky is pure blue, there are no clouds in sight, it's warm.

I take some of the cherries the other boys brought, put half a fistful into my mouth at once; the cherries are a little sour and watery, but they taste good. When there are only the pits left in my mouth, I lean forward on my elbows and spit them out from the roof of the railcar.

We're in the switchyard of the railway station; this is the headquarters of Péter's gang. He says there are more boys here than at home. There are six railcars hooked up behind a large old-fashioned steam locomotive. Péter says that this train isn't going anywhere; as far as he knows it's been sitting here for forty years.

The others boys are beyond the railway bed, playing soccer next to the turbine ditch; there are more than ten of them, each with a gang name based on an animal. Péter tells me their names: Cobra, Falcon, Wolf, Jackal . . . I don't remember them all, and I don't know who is who, I only notice the one named Zebra, and that is because he wears a fringed vest made out of zebra skin instead of a T-shirt. Péter tells me that Zebra found it in some railcar along with a bunch of other animal trophies, but by the time they went back for the others, the railcar was gone.

The sun has completely warmed the roof of the railcar. I place my arm under my head, and I watch as Ré flies higher and higher in the sky in ever-widening circles. Péter says if she wanted to she could leave, she could fly away forever, she would never have to come back, she can do whatever she wants to, but still she always comes back and alights on his fist, lets him put the hood back on. He used to ponder this very often: Did Ré know that she could leave? Did she come back to him because she wanted to, or did she come back only because she didn't realize she had a choice?

Ré is nothing more now than a tiny gray speck; if I didn't know she was up there, I probably wouldn't even be able to see her. Slowly, I reach out my arms, I spread them apart, I press them down onto the roof of the railcar. I stretch; the sun warms me from above, the roof of the railcar warms me from below.

I know that if I want to, at any time I could imagine what it's like to fly, to lie on the wind and see the city and the world from above, but I don't want to think about that now. I want to just lie here, I don't want to think about anything at all. I close my eyes, and when I open them again, I don't even see Ré, only the empty blue sky. I stretch farther. It feels if I don't even have a body; I'm light, I want the sun to keep shining, to warm my skin even more, to always stay like this, for everything to always stay like this.

Péter is still talking about Ré; he tells me how before he puts the hood on her, he looks into her eyes, he looks and he tries to figure out what she's thinking, if she's thinking anything at all;

he wants to understand, although he knows that this is impossible, but even so he wants to understand why she comes back when she could leave—he would like to know.

Péter falls silent as his heel taps restlessly against the tin roof, and from that I know that he's waiting for an answer, he's waiting for me to say something. The sack makes a rattling sound as he reaches in for the cherries, the pits make a knocking sound as he spits them out.

I say it doesn't matter why, the main thing is that she comes back. That she always comes back. My voice is sleepy, deeper than it usually is; I feel as if I could fall asleep, and I'm going to, not deeply, just a little. Just let Péter keep on talking quietly, let him say what he has to say, and he keeps on talking. I hear his voice grow sharp, and he says of course it matters, I have to understand that if Ré comes back because she feels that she can't do anything else, it's not the same as if she comes back because she *wants* to come back, I have to see that.

Yes, I whisper, yes, I see that. My eyes are half closed; through my eyelashes, the sky looks somewhat darker, as if the cottony fluff of poplar trees were floating in the air. I feel a gentle breeze on my face; it really is floating in the air, the cottony fluff of poplar trees; the breeze blows from the direction of the water where the row of poplar trees is, it's bringing the cottony fluff from there, I could reach out and grab it, but I don't, why bother? The thumping sound of the soccer ball and the cries of the boys playing soccer sound ever more distant, and Péter's voice too sounds ever more distant. He is still speaking about free will, his voice growing ever fainter and fainter.

WHEN I OPEN MY EYES, I see a dark cloud growing right above me in the sky; it's so black that I think I must be dreaming.

I sit up.

The cloud is still there; already I know this is no dream, and I'm not imagining it, above me the sky has gone completely black. A thick black cloud of smoke is coming from the direction of the old locomotive, at the front of the row of railcars; not only is the chimney of the locomotive smoking, but the soot-black smoke is wreathing, billowing out of the windows; already I can taste the bitter acrid smell.

Péter cries out, My God, they've set the locomotive on fire! The others start yelling too, they scream, War, death to the ironworkers! Then they scream, Victory! Shrieking, everyone runs toward the locomotive. Péter leaps up next to me; he too begins to run toward the locomotive; he runs along the roofs of the railcars; when he gets to the end of one, he jumps onto the next one, then runs to the next. From the direction of the locomotive there's the sound of detonations; the smoke is pouring out of it; I've never seen such thickly swirling black smoke, it floats in columns toward the sky, the columns intertwine, winding around each other, creating an even larger cloud of smoke. Péter screams at the top of his lungs, You idiots, bring water, don't you hear, bring water, fill up the rowboat and bring the water in that.

The others stop and begin to run back toward the turbine ditch. I don't know what they're going to bring the water in; I would look over there, but I can't take my eyes off the smoke, it's so thick, as if it were liquid, and it grows toward the sky like an enormous black bush.

Péter is swallowed up by the smoke, I can't see him any-more, I only hear his voice, crying out, Hurry, quickly, hurry!

The boys are carrying a tin rowboat, it looks something like a bathtub; the water splashes around as ten boys hold on to it and try to run. They get to the locomotive. Péter is there al-ready; together they raise the rowboat, and together they pour the water onto the locomotive. I hear Péter as he yells, Smoke bombs! Then he shouts, This is a trick.

From the corner of my eye I see movement within the swirling smoke. I look over, and I see that on the other side, some boys are jumping down from the fence and running, crossing the old tracks overgrown with weeds.

I'm sitting on the roof of the very last railcar; they're running right at me. I see how one boy running in front has a large ax, the others have sticks, and as loud as I can, I scream at the top of my lungs, Attack, over here, attack!

Péter and the other boys throw down the tin rowboat, they're on the other side of the locomotive, they vanish into the smoke as they run around it, then they're also running in this direction; in the meantime the others have reached the railcar and are beating it on the side.

I know what's happening; Péter told me that his gang is at war with the ironworkers. During the revolution, they fought together, but then afterward they had a big argument about the weapons they'd confiscated that were supposed to be handed in.

Screaming now, they hit one another, but I can hardly see anything in all the smoke. I don't even want to see it, I just want them to stop, to not do this anymore.

The smoke slowly disperses, and I now see that all of them are standing in a large ring; in the middle, Péter and the boy with the ax are circling each other. Péter is holding a large iron pipe. They swing the weapons toward each other, making hissing sounds in the air; the ax and the pipe clang together, and all the while they're cursing each other. The boy with the ax screams at Péter that he's a thief, a traitor and a thief, everyone knows that he didn't hand in all his weapons, everyone knows they're hidden around here somewhere; Péter hisses back that that's a lie and that he answers only to Eraser. He did exactly what Eraser told him to do.

Eraser is the drawing teacher, I realize; he's the one who told us about how the men broke through the fence of the secret police headquarters, but I don't care, I just want this to stop.

Once again they clash, I don't know what they're doing. Then I look down and see the slingshot.

I grab hold of it, take a fistful of cherries, and scream at them, Stop already, you idiots, do you want blood, then you'll get it! I fire half a fistful of cherries at them, then another and another. The cherries hit their targets, splattering scarlet stains all over their clothes; it looks like blood flowing, as if they're standing in the middle of machine-gun fire, and scarlet wounds are opening up on their chests, their heads, their backs.

For a second, there really are expressions of deathly fear on their faces, then they realize what's happening; they begin to guffaw, and they put down the weapons, but I don't stop, I keep shooting the cherries at them. It might hurt them, because, hissing, they try to duck the cherries, but at the same time they're still laughing like crazy men; cursing, they keep yelling for me to stop, but I don't stop, I keep shooting at them until there are no cherries left.

I PLACE THE CHARCOAL ON the paper, and I think of Péter, and I think of Ré. I want to draw Ré, I want to draw that moment when she spreads her wings with the wooden bird in her claws, but it's no good, the movement of her plunging isn't there, so I stop drawing. Then I think of the blackness of the locomotive and the smoke, swirling, reaching up toward the sky; in one corner of the paper I quickly sketch the locomotive, then I begin to draw the smoke pouring out of it. The contours become entangled with one another, whirling, eddying.

I lick my fingers, rub the lines into each other, then draw newer lines onto the darkness. The cloud slowly appears on the paper; there are the columns of smoke, coiling; they come apart and knit together again. I lick the paper, I scratch it, I rub it with the back of my hand and then with my palm, not knowing exactly what I want. But no, I do know what I want, I want my drawing to be exactly like that smoke was.

Suddenly it's just finished. I look at it; it's as if I didn't even draw it. I prop the drawing against the wall, I step back, I look at it, trembling. I clasp my hands in front of my chest and I hunch over, but I'm still trembling, my teeth are chattering.

I want to cry. I know that's idiotic; I can't cry over my own drawing, I made it myself, it's just charcoal and paper.

I think of Father's picture, how I'm standing in front of him and I'm looking at him, and I'm afraid. I'm still very little, maybe three or four years old, I haven't started kindergarten yet. Father's picture is really big, I know the title of it too, because I heard Father telling Mother that it's called *Glade*. It takes up half the wall; one of its corners is still blank, that's where the clearing is supposed to be, but in the middle there is a forest, dark and black, full of shadows, and in the forest it is evening, in the sky only the halo of the moon can be seen, but not the moon itself, the moon isn't in the picture because it didn't fit in, but from the shadows of the trees you can tell that it's shining. Ever since this picture has been on the wall, I haven't dared cross the living room. I'm afraid to look at it, I'm afraid to look into the dark between the trees, because I know that someone lives there. The owl with a pig's head lives there; it's huge, as big as a bear or even bigger; one day it's going to come out from among the trees, it's going to grab me and devour me. Ever since the picture has been there on the wall, I don't dare cross that room, I don't dare go out to pee, but I must, because I'm big already, for a long time now I've been too old to sit on the potty, I have to cross the room. I don't want to look at it, I want to pretend it's not there, but I have to look at it, I know that it's lurking there in between the trees, it will come out from the trees and it will devour me, it will devour me, Oh, please don't devour me, that is my wish, please don't devour me, I'll be good, I'll do anything, just don't devour me, please don't devour me this time, I promise I'll be good, I'll behave and never jump in the street again, I'll never step in a puddle ever again, but the pig-headed owl says nothing in reply to this. I know it's only waiting for me to turn my back to it, to walk toward the toilet. I look at the trees—it's there, there behind the trees; I stop, I can't move. Suddenly Father is there beside me; he asks, What's wrong, my sweet little kitten, and from that I can tell that he's not angry, when he's angry he never calls me that, he calls me Emma. I can't speak. Father asks, Are you afraid of the drawing? I can't bring myself to say yes; I bite my lip and nod; I want to nod only once, but I nod twice, then a third time and a fourth time, I can't stop nodding, and then Father crouches down next to me, and he looks at the picture, and he says that I'm right, it really is a frightening picture, he is going to take it down and take it out of there, somewhere far away, and while he says this he hugs me; he squeezes me to himself and he lifts me up, but right then I feel the warm pee filling my underwear and my stockings, I can't hold it in anymore, I peed myself because I had to go so much. I'm afraid, I think that Father is going to be angry at me, he's going to throw me down, he's going to say, Oh, yuck, Emma, look what you just did, but he isn't angry, he doesn't throw me down, he just says, Oh, my sweet little kitten, and he embraces me even more, and he strokes my back and my hair and he says, Don't be angry, and he says that he didn't want to trouble me, and he says that he loves me more than anything else in this entire world, and he says, Don't worry.

I never saw the picture ever again, and I never even thought of it again, until now. I look at the locomotive; my hand is no longer trembling.

GRANDMOTHER ENTERS THE ROOM, BRINGING in the freshly laundered linens; as she opens the door, I quickly flip the drawing over. She stops and asks, What is that? I think of Father, I flip the drawing back, and I hold it out in front of Grandmother.

She looks at it; her face hardens. She asks, Did you draw this? Yes, I say, I drew it.

She says it's exactly as if my father had drawn it.

I ask her if it's true that she was the one who denounced Father to the secret police.

Grandmother doesn't answer; she takes the drawing out of my hands. I let her. Let her take it.

She holds the drawing out in front of her and examines it. I think that any moment she's going to rip it in two, crumple it up. But she doesn't.

She said she was very afraid that my father would bring trouble to the family and that Grandfather would be sent to the labor camp again because of him. This is true. She had spoken with my mother about this, asking her to somehow influence my father so that he wouldn't cause problems for them if at all possible. This is also true. But she also knew just how much my mother was in love with my father, and I should know that never in her life would she have wanted to cause her own daughter pain.

She places the drawing on the table, presses her fingers down on the smoke, begins to follow the lines of its labyrinth. Never in her life, she says again, her voice is so quiet, I can barely hear it.

30

IT'S SATURDAY; I'M HEADING HOME from the market with Grandmother. We're standing in front of our gate. I wait for Grandmother to take out her key and open it.

She takes out the key, but she doesn't put into the lock; she hisses once, as she stands there with the key in her hand, she's looking at the gate.

On one of the wings of the gate, somebody has drawn, with white chalk, a pale snail shell, the size of the palm of a hand. Grandmother just stands there and looks at it, her mouth sharp as a blade, the way it always looks when she's extremely angry; she shakes her head, making her hairpins clang. May God strike the heavens down upon them, she says; she raises her left hand to her mouth, licks her thumb, and with quick, angry, wild movements, she rubs the traces of chalk from the iron gate.

ON SUNDAY IT'S STILL DARK when Grandmother wakes me up; the sun hasn't even risen yet. My muscles are aching,

I'm sleepy, I tell her, there's no school today, let me sleep, but Grandmother says not today, today we have to clean.

I tell her I don't want to, we'll clean in the afternoon, let me sleep, but Grandmother says, No sleeping today. She slaps her hand on the end of the bed so hard that it makes the entire bed tremble as if it's been struck by lightning.

I sit up, feel the sleep vanishing from my eyes. Grandmother sticks a mug of hot cocoa under my nose, and she says I must drink it right away, before the sun rises, because today we may not drink or eat anything else until the sun sets; we must work hungry and thirsty today, because only in that way will there be true cleanliness, only then will there be true order. Only in this way and only then.

The cocoa is thicker and sweeter than usual, and the mug isn't the usual one, it's bigger and rounder. Grandmother watches as I drink, and she says I should drink it up nicely, it will give me strength.

Then, for the entire day, we clean, we sweep, we scrub, and we scour; we beat the dust out and we vacuum; we wipe up and we polish. By the afternoon my hands are hurting, as are my arms and my elbows and my knees; everything hurts but still I don't feel tired, I work without stopping, I do everything that Grandmother tells me to do. Grandmother is working much harder than me, she doesn't stop for a moment, not even long enough to wipe the sweat off her brow, and I don't stop either, I try to work just as hard as she does.

When we're finished with the cleaning, we begin to wash. We wash everything in the kitchen, we wash and we dry everything, then I have to clean the silver spoons while Grandmother cooks; she kneads the dough and then makes potato soup, with chicken paprika and gnocchi for the second course, and by the time that is ready, the dough has risen. Grandmother rolls it out, puts a pot on the stove, fills it halfway with oil, lights the burner, then takes a glass and cuts circles out of the risen dough for doughnuts. On the glass there is a large emblem made of two parts, I see it between Grandmother's fingers; on one half of the shield there is a man with bent knees and outstretched arms, and on the other, there are white tulips in a green field. I've never seen this glass before.

I watch as Grandmother cuts with it; it's as if the man with the outstretched arms were flying, he descends and then he rises, he descends and then he rises up again; the edges of the cut-out doughnuts don't remain sharp even for a moment, the soft dough swells up as soon as Grandmother places the glass onto it.

Grandmother uses the spoon to place the doughnuts into the oil; the oil spits and hisses. Grandmother doesn't worry about the drops of oil falling onto her arm; she turns back to the table, kneads the rest of the dough, rolls it out, and cuts disks out of that as well, and finally there's just a tiny bit that is too small to be cut into a circle. Grandmother kneads it again, forms a small bird out of it, and throws that into the oil.

I polish the spoons; each one is shining and glittering, but I can't stop, I must keep rubbing them with the buckskin cloth, and while I do it, I watch the doughnuts frying. They smell delicious, but I'm not even hungry, I don't know how we're going to eat all these delicious treats.

Grandmother turns the doughnuts over in the oil; they're puffing up nicely, bubbling on the surface, they're brown and crimson like fox fur; a tiny pinkie-size white ribbon runs around their sides as if painted on with a brush.

Grandmother places a cloth napkin on a large porcelain platter with a flower pattern, and she places the doughnuts on that, making a pyramid out of them. She goes into the larder, brings out a jar of plum preserves, then she takes the silver gravy boat from me and spoons the preserves into that; she sticks a silver spoon into it, looks at it, and adjusts it.

The oil has begun to smoke on the stove. Grandmother

turns to the stove, takes the pot from the flame; the oil undulates within it, nearly spilling over. Now only the bird formed out of dough bobs up and down in the oil; it's burned. Grandmother reaches over and picks it out with her hand; she hisses, throwing it from one palm to the other, there's no ribbon on it, only a tiny white spot where its wings should be, its head is nearly burned black. Now for sure it's not so boiling hot. It's lying there in Grandmother's right palm. Grandmother dips the nail of her pinkie into the plum preserves, quickly dots two eyes on the bird, then draws its wing and tail feathers. I can see from the wing feathers gleaming blue that it's meant to be a blue jay. Grandmother puts drops of plum preserve on the bird's legs, and she uses that to attach it to the top of the doughnut pyramid, then adjusts it so the jay is standing nicely; she lets go of it, and suddenly the pendulum clock begins to strike.

One of the weights on the clock descends, clattering and rattling; I look at it, the clock strikes, ringing out, many times, I don't count the number of strikes, the flour-covered kneading board has disappeared from the table, I didn't even see when Grandmother took it back into the larder, I must have been looking at the silver, I was looking at my own face in the glittering silver. Only the glass that Grandmother used to cut the dough circles is still on the table; now it stands on its base, I can see the emblem on it. The man with the outspread arms in the field filled with white flowers isn't flying, he's not even alive — he's dead, he's strung up by his legs; he hangs from a beam beneath his knees, only the smile on his face remains the same.

I'm seized by nausea. I look again at the wall clock, it's still striking, loud and buzzing in my head, it's making my head ache, the throbbing pain begins at my temples, goes back to the nape of my neck, right to the base of my plaited hair.

· · ·

THE CLOCK STOPS RINGING; THERE is silence; it echoes for a while in my head, then that too dies down. Grandmother speaks, says the evening star has risen, we're ready just in time. She praises me, saying that I worked as one must, and she's very happy with me.

I'm pleased that she has praised me, but I can hardly pay attention, I feel very tired, extremely tired, as if the entire day's work were piled up and poured onto me. I feel it clinging to me and pulling me down heavily, like liquid mud, I can't move at all.

Suddenly my nose is filled with smells—the scent of the rosemary of the potato soup mixes with the onion and lard and paprika scent of the chicken and the scent of the vanilla sugar melting on the doughnuts. I'm very hungry, and the hunger is made even stronger by the fatigue. I imagine myself dipping my spoon into the soup, and before I even swallow it, I've already put another spoonful in my mouth, then another and another, and that's how I'll greedily eat up the chicken paprika as well, and the doughnuts; first I will split one open with the edge of the little spoon, and then I'll fill the inside with plum preserves. As I bite into it, the thick gluey sweetness will spurt into my mouth, and I'll just swallow and swallow, stuffing one doughnut after the other into my mouth; the powdered vanilla sugar will stick to my mouth and my chin but I won't wipe it off, I won't even stop long enough to do that.

I'm waiting for Grandmother to speak, to tell me to put out the cutlery and the plates; I'm waiting for her to say it's time to eat. I look at the bird standing atop the doughnut pyramid, and I think maybe Grandmother will give it to me. I'm going to eat that right away, just as soon as we've finished off the chicken paprika.

I look at the doughnuts, I look at the vanilla sugar melting on the doughnuts; the handle of the spoon stuck into the plum preserves scatters the lamplight into my eyes. I look at Grandmother, ask her to let me try one of the doughnuts, I promise her that I'll eat my soup properly too, and the second course, just let me try one of the doughnuts first, because I really have been wishing for that.

Grandmother says that's not possible. She says she sees how I'm looking at the food, but I can't have any of it, not any of the doughnuts, not the chicken, not the soup, it's not possible, neither of us can have a bite of it, not even one bite, not even one morsel, because the entire thing is for the guest.

I ask her, my voice cracking, what does she mean for the guest, what guest? Grandmother says not to think about that, I don't need to worry about the guest, that's not my problem. She knows I'm very hungry, she knows it's not good to sleep on an empty stomach, but there's nothing else to do, this is how it has to be. She tells me to go and put on my nightgown, lie down, turn to the wall, go to sleep, and don't wake up, not until tomorrow morning. And she says that if I wake up, I shouldn't get up, and under no circumstances should I leave the room.

I want to yell, I want to yell in her face that this isn't right; I could reach over and grab one of the doughnuts and stuff it into my mouth, and she wouldn't be able to stop me, but Grandmother looks at me, and she says, Don't even try. Her face is severe, but not as it usually is; beneath the severity there is something else too, something I've never seen in her expression. As she picks up the glass she used to cut the dough, it knocks a little bit against her ring; I look over and I see her hand is trembling, she has to squeeze the glass with all of her strength so her hand won't tremble, and already I know that Grandmother is afraid.

GRANDMOTHER TAKES THE GLASS INTO the larder. When she comes back into the kitchen, she is carrying a round green-glazed, two-handled vessel with a large cover on it; she holds it out to me and says to take it. I take the bowl from her, it's good and heavy. Grandmother lets go of it, she says I certainly don't know what it is, well, it's a chamber pot, a proper chamber pot for grownups, because there used to be such things in the old days when there were no bathrooms, that's how people took care of their business so they wouldn't have to go out in the snow and the freezing cold across the cold courtyard to the outhouse. She tells me to take it into my room and put it underneath my bed, and if I have to, then I should do my business in that, because I may not leave the room, not even to go to the bathroom, do I understand? I nod. I look down at the cover of the chamber pot; it makes me feel ashamed. I turn away, and I head toward the other room, I don't wait for Grandmother to speak to me again.

I put the chamber pot next to the settee. I know I'm not going to use it. I know that with one hundred percent certainty. I'm thinking of the guest, wondering if he'll be able to eat the enormous amount of food. I think of the doughnuts again; my stomach growls.

I lie down in my room, I turn out the light. I want to think about Péter, or about Ré, or about nothing at all, but I just keep thinking of that guest. Who could it be, why is he coming here, and why is Grandmother so afraid of him? I realize that if I peek out of the window I might possibly see him coming, but suddenly I feel so sleepy, so sleepy that I can't move. My hands are heavy, my legs are heavy, my body pulls inward and sinks down into the bed; I feel my eyes closing, I'm falling asleep.

Outside, the sky is thundering, I hear it from far away; the windowpanes rattle as the wind rises. There's going to be a storm, I think, and I think of how much we worked today and of how tired I am.

I fall asleep.

IN THE MORNING, I DON'T dare open the living-room door immediately; I stand, and I wait, and I listen. I hear a kind of faint whistling sound, but I don't know what it could be. Very softly, I call out to Grandmother, then louder, but she does not reply.

I open the door.

Grandmother is sitting there in the armchair fully clothed, with her head leaning to one side; she is sleeping. Her breath whistles as she breathes in and out, there is saliva in the corner of her mouth.

On the small table all the food is still there, exactly as I saw it yesterday, without even one tiny bite taken out of it.

The powdered sugar has melted onto the doughnuts; I want to reach over and take one. Now it won't be as crispy or as warm, and the dough will be a bit rubbery and sweet; that's no problem, I'd still like to have some.

Grandmother suddenly wakens; she stares cross-eyed for a bit, then, groaning, sits up in the straighter in the armchair and slowly looks around the room.

I ask her what happened to the guest.

Grandmother yawns. It seems the guest didn't arrive, she says, then she yawns again. Then I have to yawn as well, and for a moment I feel extremely sleepy.

I point at the doughnuts, and I ask her, So can I have one now?

Not even one bite, says Grandmother. But if I want some so much, she'll make me another batch. Now I should go and get dressed.

When I come back out to brush my teeth, Grandmother is in the kitchen; she sweeps all the doughnuts from the platter into the waste bin, then she begins to pour the chicken paprika over it.

My stomach churns; I quickly go to the bathroom. I put

twice as much toothpaste as usual onto the brush, then I brush my teeth for a very long time.

I WASN'T DREAMING OF THE thunder or of the wind. There really might have been a great storm last night. All around the walnut tree, the grass is full of green walnuts. I try to break one open; I place it onto a large smooth stone, then I tread on it with one foot; the walnut slips out from beneath my gym shoe and cracks, leaving an oily green streak on the stone. I put it back, step on it again, and now I tread on it with my heel just as hard as I can, the walnut shell cracks again, but then it flies out from beneath the sole of my shoe.

I look for it among the other walnuts in the grass. Its shell is cracked and scraped; I dig my fingers into the crack, forcing it open. The inside of the walnut is mucus-like and gelatinous, its core is light brown, thin, and soft; I can press it open with my finger. There's already a walnut kernel inside of it, spongy and white. I pick it out with my nails, put it into my mouth, and chew it. It's oily and bitter, but in the middle it's sweet and crunchy.

I rub my palms together; a thick scent rises from them. I inhale. It scratches my throat, almost like vapor from gasoline.

I take out the snail-gathering bucket from behind the cedar trees, and I begin to throw the nuts into them. There are many walnuts; soon the bucket is almost half filled.

I stand in front of the woodshed, reach into the bucket, and take two walnuts, one in my right palm and the other in my left. I whisper to myself, *Ready, set, go,* and I throw both of them onto the roof of the woodshed; the walnuts knock against the firewall, then they roll down the tiles. The roof is covered with dry branches and moist bunches of leaves, tossed there by the storm, the nuts make cracking sounds, get stuck, speed up again, it's impossible to know which one will reach the ground first.

It's a race; one of the walnuts is me, the other one is, let's say, Aliz—but no, the other one is Krisztina. Whoever loses the race will have to die.

My walnut leads the way for a long time, rolling nice and smooth down the roof tiles. I'm going to smash apart the loser, not with my foot, but with a brick, I'll smash it apart and eat its center. My walnut is already by the edge of the roof when suddenly a large branch stops it and slows it down. The other walnut has bumped into a bunch of leaves; it jumps across the branch and falls from the roof, causing a stone to flick in my direction; it rolls on the ground, and there it is already, right in front of my foot.

My walnut is still behind the branch. I look at it, now I want it to stay there, but no, it slowly rolls out from behind the branch, then it too rolls across the ground and stops in front of me.

I lost. There is no mercy. With the tip of my shoe I flick my walnut into a cavity in the stone; I go over to the firewall, take a brick from the pile. I hold it with its edge facing down, lift it up high with both my hands, and smash it down on the walnut. It splits apart with a deep, dull crunching sound.

I take the gelatinous kernel of the walnut; I know it will be bitter, but still I must eat it, I must, I deserve this, because I wasn't better, because I wasn't cleverer.

I put it into my mouth; it truly is as bitter as bile. But I don't spit it out.

I pick up the victorious walnut from the ground and look at the bucket; for the second match I'm going to take out the largest and the roundest walnut, and the next time I won't let myself lose.

I'm just about to reach into the bucket when I hear Grandmother's voice. She's already next to me, holding my hand, taking the walnut out of it. In her other hand is the open penknife; she begins to cut the walnut in two in her palm. She presses down on the knife so fiercely that I think she's going to cut her hand open, but she doesn't. She snaps the blade back and throws half of the walnut into the bucket.

She presses down on the other half as if it were a lemon; it sweats out a greenish-brown oily substance. Grandmother sticks her ring finger into it; at first she sniffs it, then she licks the moisture off it. She says it's good and bitter, it's very good that I gathered these walnuts, this is exactly what we need.

She picks up the bucket from the ground, shakes it, and heads off toward the kitchen. She motions for me to follow her.

IN THE KITCHEN, SHE FILLS up the porcelain tureen with a rooster on it with water, then she pours all the walnuts from the bucket into it. She gives me a sponge and tells me to wash them all off nicely while she gathers what she needs. Be careful, she says, not to damage the shells.

The walnuts are slippery in the water; they slip between my fingers. I turn them over here and there underneath the sponge. I don't know which ones I've washed and which ones I haven't, but I don't stop, I keep rubbing every walnut that turns up in my hand.

Grandmother brings in a wide-mouthed mason jar, two knitting needles, the sugar bowl, and two full bottles of vodka.

She sets everything down on the table, then she sits down.

She reaches into the porcelain tureen and takes out a walnut. She takes one of the knitting needles, scratches something into the shell of the walnut, then throws it into the mason jar.

The walnut clatters around in the jar, then it rolls around the bottom and stops in front of me. Grandmother has scratched a long, arched line into it, something like a very flat half-moon, extending from the stalk of the walnut to its bottom, and from its convex section, there are smaller lines standing out obliquely; altogether it looks as if it could be a caterpillar. I don't like to look at it.

Grandmother extends one of the knitting needles to me, and she says it's my turn. I should take a walnut and scratch out the same thing, as nicely as she did.

I take the knitting needle and a walnut from the tureen. As I press the end of the needle onto the walnut, it nearly flies out of my hand. I draw the long contour, the body of the caterpillar. I slide my hand down lower on the knitting needle, then I draw the legs as well. The longest line is the deepest, and an oily brown drop trickles from it; I think that it looks something like a teardrop, and then suddenly I understand that what Grandmother scratched into the walnut shell, and what I'm also scratching into the walnut shell, is not a caterpillar at all, but a closed eye.

I imagine that the eye will spring open and look at me; I can almost see its pupil, furrowed like the walnut shell; its gaze is fearful.

I quickly throw the walnut into the mason jar; it leaves an oily streak on the inside of the jar as it clatters around inside.

Grandmother looks at me and says there's nothing to be afraid of, and I shouldn't forget that I have the knitting needle in my hand.

She takes another walnut from the water and begins to scratch the closed eye on its shell; she motions for me to continue as well.

I take a walnut from the tureen; now that I know what I'm drawing, I can pull the knitting needle along the walnut shell without trembling.

We work in silence. Then, suddenly, Grandmother makes a hissing sound and plunges her knitting needle into one of the walnuts. I hear the squeak of the needle; when she pulls it out of the pierced walnut, I don't look.

When I take the next walnut from the tureen, I think that what I'm going to scratch into it will not be an eye but a caterpillar standing on its back legs.

When we've finished with the walnuts, Grandmother folds in all of the sugar from the sugar bowl, then unscrews the lids of the vodka bottles, pushes one toward me, picks up the other one herself, and together we start to pour the vodka onto the sugared walnuts.

When we finish, the mason jar is two-thirds full. Grandmother stirs it once with the knitting needle, and in the jar the liquid begins to form a whirlpool, the nuts swirling within it, the air filled with a thick, biting nut smell.

Grandmother takes the tin lid and screws it onto the jar. She shakes it once and says we'd better hurry now.

She steps over to the credenza, pulls out a drawer, and takes out a folded-up piece of fabric; I see that it's the same material as the window curtains. She unfolds it; it's good and big. She spreads it out on the table, places the jar on it, and tells me to help her wrap it around the jar.

We quickly wind it around the jar. Grandmother takes one end of the rolled-up fabric; she motions for me to take the other. We pick it up, move next to the table, and we begin to swing the jar in the fabric, at first delicately, then faster and faster. Grandmother is muttering something; at first I think she's counting, then I hear that she's saying, over and over, the word *awaken*.

Even through the fabric you can hear how the liquid is seething back and forth in the glass jar, the walnuts thudding and dully cracking.

I don't want to think about the walnuts, but still I have to imagine how, one after the other, the eyes scratched into the walnut shells are bursting open.

Grandmother pulls so hard on the fabric that the end slides out of my hand; it opens, and the glass jar falls onto the kitchen carpet, but it doesn't break, it bounces against Grandmother's leg, then it begins to roll toward me on the carpet, the green whirlpools swirling within it. I look at it; there's something in the middle of the jar.

Grandmother looks at the jar too, then she holds the fabric in front of my face and yells at me to close my eyes. I do; beneath my eyelids the darkness is green.

I sense, from the wind that has been stirred up, that Grandmother has yanked the fabric away from my face, I hear her groaning as she crouches down to retrieve the glass jar, muttering.

I think of the caterpillar; I think of how it's crawling there now in the glass jar.

I don't know how much time is going by. Then, all at once, Grandmother says that everything's fine, I can open my eyes now.

I blink, and I see that Grandmother has gotten up from the floor; there in her hand is the glass jar with the fabric wound around it. She's squeezing it with one arm firmly under her armpit, humming a lullaby to herself as she carries it into the larder.

31

ONCE AGAIN GRANDMOTHER WAKES ME at dawn, and I know from how she looks at me and how she sticks the mug with hot cocoa beneath my nose that this is once again one of those Sundays when we're expecting a visitor. Once again we will work for the entire day, from the moment the sun rises until evening, without stopping and without rest, continually.

I know what this means: Once again we will pull the furniture to one side, we will roll up and take the carpets out to the courtyard, once again we will scour the floor with water and vinegar, not just haphazardly, but every single floorboard individually, and once again we will wash the windows, on the outside and the inside too, and we'll wipe down the frames between the windows; once again we'll rub down every single window with newspaper three times and then twice with the buckskin so that not even a speck of dust remains; once again we will take the pictures and the plates down from the wall, we'll wipe off each one with a moist dusting cloth, in front and in back, and we'll dust the entire wall behind them with the feather duster, and only then will we hang everything back in its place, then, in the courtyard, we'll beat out the carpets, and we will vacuum every single one, two times, three times, or four times, until the vacuum cleaner bag is completely full, then we will brush them with a moist cloth brush, and only then will we bring them back into the house, and then, when we're finished with all that, and we have scoured the tiles in the bathroom and scrubbed the grouting between the tiles with a small nail brush, and put everything back in its place, and hung everything back where it has to go, and Grandmother has gone around one last time and looked to make sure not a single speck of dust remains anywhere and that all of Grandfather's things have been put back properly in their place, even then we are not going to rest, because then we will go to the kitchen, and then Grandmother will cover half of the round table with a clean damask cloth, and on the other half she will put out all of the pots, all the frying pans, all the plates, all the cutlery, and all the glasses, then she will let boiling water run into the sink, and she will pour lukewarm water into the washbasin, then she will place sodium bicarbonate in it, and she will wash, one by one, every single pot, pan, plate, cup, and glass, and my job will be to dry each one of them and polish them till they shine, and we won't stop until every glass is glittering like crystal, until the very last plate is glittering like a mirror, and then when we're done with that and we've put everything away, even then we won't stop, because then Grandmother will begin to cook. Once again she will make potato soup, and chicken paprika with gnocchi, and for the last course she'll make doughnuts, and while she cooks, I will need to be there with her in the kitchen, and I will need to shine the silverware, and for that I'll get a pair of white cotton gloves and a shoe-polish container filled with polishing cream, an old bone-handled toothbrush, and a very soft handkerchief, and I know that I will have to rub and polish every single knife and fork and tablespoon and teaspoon until I can see myself reflected in each one. I will need to be able to see my own face reflected clearly and without any distortions, and if I can already see myself reflected in the silverware, then I need to polish it as if I want to rub off the reflection of my face; I don't bother with the fact that the more I polish, the better I can see it, I know that I have to do it as if I want to rub away my own face, around and around, around and around and around, I can't stop because the silver will never be clean enough and never be glittering enough, no, I must polish and polish and polish until the evening star emerges in the sky above.

I drink the cocoa with closed eyes, I feel my body filling with strength; I know that by evening it will be filled with fatigue, I know I will be hungry, hungry and tired, but I vow to myself that tonight, I'm not going to fall asleep. I will muster all my strength, and I will remain awake.

WE DO EVERYTHING JUST AS we did before. When the clock begins to chime the hour, Grandmother again goes out into the larder, and I know that once again she's going to bring out the chamber pot, and she does bring it out, but not just that. In her hand there is a wide-mouthed crystal carafe, and underneath her arm is the mason jar wrapped in the fabric.

She takes the fabric off the mason jar. Inside, the walnuts have grown completely dark; they swim in cloudy brownish liquid. She places the chamber pot on the floor, and she tells me to hold the liquor carafe above it while she fills it up, this way none of the liquor will spill onto the floor.

As she pours the liquid, it's as if the liquor is changing colors; now it looks brown, now dark green or black. When the bottle is filled up halfway, Grandmother shakes the glass jar once, and three or four walnuts plunge into it.

Grandmother puts the stopper in the bottle, places it on a silver platter, puts liquor glasses next to it, and takes it into the living room.

She tells me to go and wash my hands well, then go straight to bed. I should take the chamber pot too. I should change quickly into my nightshirt and turn toward the wall. And fall asleep.

I'M LYING IN MY BED, the fatigue is pulling me deeper into sleep. I'm not going to fall asleep. Not even for one second.

Before I lay down, I pinned a large packing needle into the seam of my nightgown; now I pull it out, and I prick my finger-tip. Once, then once again, and then a third time, nice and deep, so it will hurt, so it will bleed.

I put my finger into my mouth; the pain shooting through my finger is keeping me awake. It hurts as much as if I had pierced my finger all the way through; tears fall from my eyes; I turn my head to the side and wipe the tears on the pillow.

There is silence.

Slowly, very slowly, and quietly, very quietly, I fold the blanket back. I sit up, then I get out of bed. I don't want the bedsprings to squeak or the floorboards to creak.

The chilliness climbs up my legs, slips beneath my nightgown, making my thighs and my bottom freeze.

I go over to the window, stand there, and hold the edge of the curtain. Very slowly I pull it to one side, but just the heavy curtains, I don't dare touch the voile. I peek out through the crack; outside it's dark, only the street lamps are shining; light filters out from the houses across the street, the street is empty.

I stand there and I look outside—there is silence, nothing is moving.

Then suddenly there is darkness. The street lamps go out, and in the houses too, the lights go out; not even the moon is shining, there is as much darkness as in the old days when there were power cuts.

I place the palm of my hand on the voile curtain and through that onto the windowpane. I look out, I see nothing, it's as dark as if my eyes were shut. I think of Mother's cube-shaped red pocket flashlight; when she brought me home on winter evenings from the swimming pool, she would allow me to carry it to light the way, only I had to be very careful not to shine it in anyone's window because its light was very strong and went very far.

Afterward, Mother gave me the flashlight so I wouldn't be afraid in the dark; she even attached an elastic holder onto it for extra batteries, so it would last longer, and the light would never go out. I don't know what happened to that flashlight; I didn't even have it with me when I went to the institute.

The lights go back on. I see an obscured pale face beyond the window, and in my fright, I quickly pull back the curtain. The face undulates for a moment, but I already know that it was my own face I was seeing, it was the curtain that made it pale and blurry.

I don't know how long the power was out for; maybe half a minute, maybe fifteen seconds. Maybe not even that long.

On the other side of the street, underneath one of the acacia trees, there is a van, I can't recall if it was there before or not. It looks gray in the lamplight, there are mud tracks on its side. I feel as if I've seen it before somewhere, but I can't recall where or when. I look at the mud splotches on the van; my stomach begins to hurt.

I turn back toward the bed, I hear the clattering of silverware, of a spoon clanking against a plate, and from the rhythm of the sound I can tell that somebody is eating soup.

I want to see the guest.

Light shines through the keyhole of the closed double-winged kitchen doors. I know that if I were to simply look into the room through the keyhole, Grandmother or the guest would notice the glimmer of my eyes, and they would know that I was spying on them.

Still, I want to look through the keyhole; I want to see them.

I go over to the door, stand there, then I crouch down, but I don't place my face against the door; instead, with both my hands, putting one behind the other, I form a telescope, and in that way I look through the keyhole.

I see a hand, it's holding a spoon. It disappears, then it appears again, it's spooning up the soup. It is simply a man's hand; I see neither ring nor birthmark, and the nails aren't even grimy.

No one is speaking, neither the guest nor Grandmother. For a moment I see Grandmother's hand as she exchanges the soup plate for a dinner plate; now in the guest's hand there is a fork. He stabs a piece of chicken with it, then a gnocchi, and dips them both into the gravy.

It's no good like this — I can see only his hand. I lose sight of the hand, then I can see his knee and his shoulder, he's wearing a gray suit. He eats, not saying a word.

Now I really want to see him, and despite everything, I press my eye right up to the keyhole.

In the armchair sits a gray-haired man. There's nothing frightening about him. I don't know what I was expecting, but it certainly wasn't this — just an average person, not too thin or too fat, not too old or too young, his hair not too long or too short. I see his face only in profile, but it has no scars, there is absolutely nothing peculiar about him at all.

The man eats a third doughnut, then bites into a fourth. Grandmother puts the shot glass in front of him and fills it.

The man does not reach for the glass; he wipes his mouth with the napkin and leans back in the armchair.

Grandmother then says that he's eaten here for the last

time. He will now nicely pick himself up and leave — and never come back here ever again.

The man throws the crumpled napkin onto the table and says he thought Grandmother would be happier to see him.

Grandmother again says, Go. Why did you come back here? Leave now.

The man says he didn't come back; he never left. He was here until the end, he and the others too, they were here, and so they too will remain here.

Grandmother says she doesn't care about this — but he will torture her no longer. She's a widow now, and there's nothing that he can blackmail her with. Get out of here, she says.

What an interesting world this is, says the man; a few hundred kilometers from here a general was shot in the head, and now all the dogs think that they can command their old masters just as they please. That's just how the old professor sounded too, always acting as if he were our Savior, God the Father Himself, as if he were the incarnation of the oppressed, that's how he went around preaching to everyone.

The man briefly falls silent, then continues, his voice deeper, his chest swelling: The dead have the right to their final rites, and the living have the right to know the truth. At the end of the statement he laughs loudly, as if he has told a hilarious joke.

I know that he was imitating Grandfather's voice. I press my eye even closer to the keyhole; now I see Grandmother too, she's biting her lip and looking at the guest, her face completely pale from anger, and she snarls: Enough of that.

The man shrugs and is quiet; he takes a doughnut from the platter and begins to eat it.

Then he says: In the end you have to admit that in one respect the professor was right, the truth is really a huge thing. It can change the world, and it can particularly change people. The professor just needed a little piece of the truth to make him not even want to live anymore. The stupid ass.

The man stands up. I no longer see his face, only his hands as he reaches into the inner pocket of his jacket; he takes out some folded-up gray papers, and he says that he didn't come here to preach, he'll leave that for the others. No, no, he came here only because he had promised the professor something. And he was so magnanimous that he promised him not only one thing, but two. First, he promised him that he would destroy these pieces of paper, he says, and he rattles the papers in Grandmother's direction. Do these look familiar? he asks her.

Grandmother reaches out for the papers; the man pulls them away from her. Well, he says, you calm down now, and he slaps Grandmother's face with the back of his hand.

Grandmother falls onto the armchair, her bun coming half undone from the blow. My throat contracts. I look at Grandmother, I want her eyes to flash with anger, I want her to knock her ring against the table, but she doesn't.

The man takes another piece of paper from his other pocket, and he says, to put it briefly, for the second promise, he'd given his word to the poor old professor that he would pass on these few lines of farewell to his dear beloved wife.

He shakes that piece of paper at Grandmother as well. *Promise* is a beautiful word, he says as he neatly stacks the papers, folds them up, then suddenly rips them in two, then he rips them again and again and yet again; he crumples up the papers, he tears them apart, ripping them to pieces, I see how they become scraps in his hands. Here you are, take them, he yells, scattering them in Grandmother's direction.

Grandmother shrieks; she tries to reach for the shreds of paper, they swirl around her in the air, gray grimy snowflakes; she grabs a couple of them, the rest fall to the ground. Grandmother is already on her hands and knees, her hair completely undone, covering her face, and, crawling on the carpet, she tries to gather them.

The man steps forward, and he says a dog will always remain a dog, the master will always remain a master. He bends down, picks up the shot glass from the platter, and makes a wry expression; revulsion is on his face, he's going to put it back, I know that he will put the glass back, that he's not going to drink from it.

Then I want him to drink it, to drink all of it. The needle is still there in the hem of my nightgown, I take it out, stab it into my finger, and pull it out.

The man drinks the glass of vodka in one gulp; he makes a clicking sound with his tongue, throws the glass onto the floor. We will meet again, he says; he turns away and exits the room, slamming the door behind him.

The door makes such a large banging sound that I hear the glass of the bookcase trembling, the ceramic jugs on the bureau ringing together. The brown liquid swirls in the liquor glasses; one of the walnuts slowly drifts to the edge of the glass, it turns, and I see the black lines of the eyelid and the eyelashes scratched into it. The eyelid springs open; an illuminated angry green eye looks out.

32

WE PILE UP THE FUEL for the bonfire in the middle of the flower bed. Grandmother brings the large walnut-tree branches from the woodshed, the old newspapers, and the kindling.

Beautiful white and crimson roses are blooming on the bushes in the center of the flower bed. When Grandmother begins to strew the newspapers, rolled up into balls, and the kindling among them, I ask her if this isn't a shame for the flowers, but Grandmother says not to worry, they will sprout again, and the ashes will be good for them.

She tells me to help her place the kindling so that it's spread out everywhere. I help Grandmother set out the kindling.

Grandmother slowly walks all around the flower bed, thrusting brushwood in among the thick branches and leaves of the boxwood, while she sings to herself in a murmuring voice.

Once she has walked around the flower bed, she reaches into the pocket of her apron, pulls out an old sardine tin, takes from it a large white piece of chalk. She breaks it in two and gives me half.

The chalk is exactly like the kind we use in school; it even has the red and white tissue paper around it.

Grandmother tells me to write everything I want to be freed from on the branches.

She shows me how to do it. She picks up a branch and writes on it *Sorrow*. She asks if I understand.

Yes, I tell her. I grab a thick branch and write *Headache*.

Grandmother nods; she says, That's right. She says that as for what I'd like to receive, I should write that backwards; she shows me how to do that. She writes out the word *Venom*.

I pick up a branch, and I write *Taoc ruf xof.* Grandmother looks at me and smiles.

We write things on the branches until the chalk is completely used up.

Then we place the branches in the middle of the flower bed. We make a nice big pile of them, as if we were building a hut.

When we're done, Grandmother says that the fire's house is now built. It's time for it to move in.

Once again she goes into the woodshed; she brings out the gasoline canister, then she brings out two milk bottles, then she brings out a large black sack. The sack is so big and heavy that Grandmother drags it on the ground. I say that I can help her, but Grandmother says she doesn't need any help. Not yet.

She fills up the milk bottles with gasoline and gives me one of them. She tells me to pour it on the walnut-tree branches. But not just any old way. I have to do it the way she does.

She stands with her legs spread, her back to the flower bed, and she begins to sing *Come-joy-leave-sorrow;* she pulls her skirt up above her waist, with two hands she grabs the milk bottle, she bends down, and she swings the bottle backwards between her legs, dousing the branches with gasoline in thick streams. She's not wearing underwear; the hair between her legs is completely white.

I too stand with my back to the flower bed. I pull up my skirt; there are goose bumps on my thighs. I too begin to sing. I think of the fox-fur coat. I grab the milk bottle; I'm afraid that

Grandmother will tell me to take off my underwear, but she doesn't say anything. I'm also afraid that I'm going to spill the gasoline on myself or spill it on the ground, so I energetically swing the milk bottle backwards.

The gasoline glides like a green glass snake out of the bottle. When it reaches the branches, it breaks up into drops; it falls and spills in many directions.

Grandmother straightens up and lowers her skirt. She takes a newspaper and twists it, then she gets a match, and she lights the end of the newspaper.

She motions for me to come over. She doesn't even have to say anything, I know what she wants: for me to take the paper as well so we can both throw it among the branches.

THE BONFIRE BURNS IN THE middle of the flower bed. The fire crackles yellow between the thick walnut-tree branches, the flames snatching at the sky; the words that we wrote on the branches flare up, then grow pale; it's good to watch them.

We both crouch down next to the fire. We watch it. Grandmother is singing, and I'm singing with her.

Then Grandmother gets up, goes a bit farther back, takes the sack that she brought out of the woodshed, and pulls it over next to the bonfire.

She grabs a branch from the fire, and with that she draws a rectangle on the ground. She begins to tear out the grass within the lines of the rectangle. She motions for me to help her.

I help her tear out the grass.

The ground is dry, it's very hard to rip out the clumps of grass and the other weeds; luckily there isn't too much of it. We throw the clumps of grass and weeds into the fire.

The last bunch of grass is really hard to pull out; I grab it with both hands, my fingers clutching it, and I pull slowly;

when it finally comes out of the ground, it's as if the clump of grass lets out a short sharp cry. I turn it over and look; the grass has long slender white roots, with bits of sandy earth clinging to them.

I throw it into the fire. It falls onto a thick walnut-tree branch, clings to it; at first the grass flares up, and the roots simply twist, white and hissing, while the grains of sand in the smaller clumps of earth crackle and spin outward like black sparks. Then the roots contract, turn black, and catch fire, twisting in the flames as if they were small beetles' legs; above them the clump of grass smolders cherry-red—it looks like a huge hairy spider made of embers, running along the branch. It skirts around the flaming letters, stops at the very top of the branch, and raises itself up as if it is looking around, first at me, then at Grandmother, then at me again; then, hissing, it contracts, and I can tell it wants to jump out of the fire and nest in my hair.

I'm filled with fear, and I don't know what to do.

Grandmother sees what's going on.

She quickly reaches down, picks up the iron poker lying on the ground, and, without a word, puts it into my hands.

The iron poker is scalding; it was too close to the fire, and in my hands, it makes a hissing sound. The pain makes the fear dissipate; now I'm angry.

As I strike at the fire-spider with the iron poker, I know what I have to say. I have to say the word *netene.*

Netene! I say. *Netene!*

The spider shatters into sparks; the sparks fly up toward the sky, and the walnut branch that it was sitting on makes a cracking sound as it collapses into the fire.

I look at the sparks, then at the fire. I throw the iron poker onto the ground. Well, then, I say, well, then.

My voice sounds exactly like Grandmother's.

*   *   *

GRANDMOTHER SLIPS A FOOT OUT of her slipper and places it where we cleared the grass and the weeds from the rectangle of earth. It's tepid, she says, you try it too.

I go over to where she's standing. I pick up a handful of earth; it really is tepid. Grandmother tells me to take off my shoes.

I unlace my white tennis shoes, take them off, then I pull off my terrycloth socks, roll them up in a ball, and put them in one of my shoes.

Grandmother raises the sack that she brought out from the woodshed from the ground; she unties it and begins to spill out its contents.

In the sack there's dry earth; it breaks up into smaller flat pieces and clumps and turns to dust as Grandmother pours it out.

She strews the rectangle of earth, now cleared of grass and weeds, neatly with the contents of the sack.

She steps carefully into the rectangle as if she were walking into water; she pulls her skirt up above her knees. Her legs sink into the earth almost up to her ankles. She stands there, watching the fire, then she looks at me. She calls to me and says that it's clay, and it's nice and warm.

I step into the rectangle; it feels as if I am stepping into sand warmed by the sun.

Grandmother turns to face me; she grabs my elbow. I grab hers too. It's bony and pointy.

We stand there, facing each other, holding each other. The fire crackles.

Grandmother whispers very softly that I can look at the fire, but I may not look down at the earth. Not at the earth or at my own feet.

I nod.

Very good, Grandmother says in an undertone. She clears her throat, spits on the ground, then begins to sing. She doesn't open her mouth, but she makes a sound vibrate deep within her throat. It vibrates in my throat as well; it traverses my entire body.

I sing along with her.

She clasps my elbows firmly. And I clasp hers firmly.

At one point, Grandmother begins to move. She takes a step to the left, and I move with her, taking a step to the left. Then she takes a step back, then to the right, then forward.

At first she steps slowly, then she speeds up. The song also speeds up. It's quicker now, the rhythm sharper.

The soles of our feet sink into the clay, beating against the earth ever more quickly, ever harder. I feel it growing warmer.

We keep on dancing.

The flames of the fire extend higher; the bonfire burns high and golden.

Grandmother closes her eyes; her hair comes undone; she sings in a very loud voice. I sing along with her in a very loud voice.

The clay beneath my feet is scalding now, the soles of my feet beat down on it hard. The earth reverberates beneath us, cracking and clattering.

Then it becomes even louder. It rumbles like drumbeats.

Suddenly I feel that the soles of my feet are sinking into the earth. I want to stop, I want to see what's happening, but Grandmother opens her eyes and looks at me, shakes her head no, and all the while she's still singing and dancing, and I remember what she said at the beginning, not to look down, to keep on dancing.

I feel the mud around my feet squelching and burning, and I even slip at one point, but Grandmother grabs me and holds me tightly, and then later on when she slips, I grab hold of her, and I hold her.

My throat is burning and dry and tastes like smoke from all the singing. My voice is deeper, raspier, hoarse.

We keep on dancing.

Suddenly I sense that there's something hard beneath the soles of my feet; I almost trip over it. Grandmother holds me tight. It makes my leg slip; it could be a branch or a thick root, I don't know how it got there; I want to look down, but I don't dare, so instead I look at the fire; the branches have almost completely turned red-hot; they burn crimson, cracking, they slowly sway between the flames, I see that in a moment the bonfire will collapse in on itself.

Grandmother looks at it too, then she looks back at me; we're still singing, but now we're no longer dancing, we're only jumping, and beneath the soles of our feet there's no longer any mud, the clay has hardened, it's as if I am jumping on stones or very hard earth, and I don't look down.

And then suddenly I'm not jumping together with Grandmother; we're alternating—first she jumps, then I jump, then for a moment we both just stand there, then once again she jumps, then I jump, thump-thump-thump, I can feel in my chest that this is the rhythm of my heartbeat, we're jumping to the rhythm of my heartbeat.

I'm covered in sweat; my T-shirt is muddy, and my hair is drenched. I feel the sweat pouring down my back, my waist, my thighs.

We're jumping ever faster, my heart is beating ever faster, then suddenly I feel something moving beneath my feet; it pushes me off, throws me up high.

Grandmother and I jump up very high, out of the clay and onto the grass, next to the bonfire.

I'd like to look back, but I don't dare.

Grandmother crouches down, I crouch next to her; both of us panting, we look at the fire.

Grandmother reaches her hand out toward the fire, and she says, *Now.* Cracking, the bonfire collapses.

Grandmother puts her hand into the fire, grabs something and pulls it out.

She shows me the palm of her hand and the glowing embers on it, the size of a walnut.

She doesn't say anything, only motions, and from that I know what I must do. I turn, and Grandmother turns with me; I look down at the ground, Grandmother also looks down.

In the loamy mud rests a figure; it has a body, a head, hands, and feet. It is made of earth, it is made of clay, I see the imprints of our feet on its chest and on its head.

It has no face.

Grandmother bends down, and with the nail of her pinkie she draws a mouth on it; with her ring finger and her middle finger, she presses two nostrils above the mouth; with her index finger and thumb, she pokes two eyes above the nostrils. Then she says, *Netene.* And I see that the embers are still in her hand.

She gets up, steps across the figure lying on the ground to the other side, then she crouches down again; with the palm of her hand she presses the embers into the figure's chest, on the upper left-hand side. I hear a hissing sound; Grandmother scratches the earth on top of it, and once again she says, *Netene.*

Then with two hands she grabs the left hand of the figure. She motions with her head for me to help her. I grab its right arm by the elbow; the clay is heavy, hard, and warm beneath my palm.

Grandmother tells me to pull. She too starts pulling; it's very heavy, but it slowly begins to move.

I keep pulling on the figure, and Grandmother keeps pulling as well. I know that in a moment it will rise up from the ground, it will stand up.

I look up to its face, to the traces of Grandmother's fingers. Its face is fearful; I want to let go of its arm, but I don't dare.

Grandmother speaks to me, telling me to pull and not be

afraid. It's only a clay man, and its name is Earth Bone. It will be our servant, it will live in the woodshed—we have called it forth to watch over us.

I don't say anything. I grasp the arm of the clay man; it's firm, as if there really were a bone inside. I grasp its arm and I pull hard.

33

I'M OUTSIDE IN THE GARDEN, leaning against the board of the swing; I'm not sitting on it but standing on my tiptoes between the two ropes of the swing and trying to step back as far as I possibly can. I lean backward, I grab the two ropes, and I look at the tree, counting the walnuts. I keep losing count, and so I begin again. I'm thinking of Péter, of the letter that I found under the brick; he wrote that he wants to show me the stars tonight. If I want to see the rings of Saturn, I should wait for him outside the gate after eleven p.m. The breeze rises, shakes the crown of the tree; a single walnut falls onto the roof of the woodshed, rolls along the tiles, gets stuck on one, and remains there on the roof. I want it to keep rolling, but it doesn't move.

Suddenly Grandmother is there next to me; she too is looking at the woodshed. She touches the rope of the swing, and she says it's gotten very old now, I should be careful that it doesn't break under me. By the way she's looking at the woodshed, I know that she's going to continue telling me the story. I don't feel like paying attention. I want to think about Péter, I want to think about tonight, I want to think about where he wants to take me and what he wants to show me. I want to think about whether or not I'll go.

Grandmother clears her throat; her nails fiddle with the threads of the fraying rope. She begins to talk; I don't want to pay attention, I'm looking at the walnut, now I don't want it to roll anymore but to stay up there on the roof. Grandmother's voice is sharp, and there's a kind of sadness in it that means that I can't not listen, I can't not pay attention. The walnut moves; slowly it rolls down the roof, falls onto the ground, and rolls into the grass. I look at Grandmother, and I listen.

EVERY OTHER DAY AT DAWN, you go out to the shed to get firewood, and you always bring them two large glasses of water. If you can get some milk, you bring them that too. You stand in front of the high woodpile, you pull out, from the pieces of wood, two empty glasses concealed there, and in their place you put the full glasses, and as you fill the basket with wood, you ask, in a whisper, if they are all right, if everything is okay. It's always Bertuka who answers, and she always whispers, Yes, for the time being, yes. As the basket fills with wood, you whisper the news to them, and you try not to think of what it would be like to sit there for days and for weeks in the dark — to sit, to wait, to be afraid.

One morning, after you bolt the woodshed door behind you and pick up the basket filled with pieces of wood, you are suddenly seized by dread as never before, and for a moment you know with complete certainty that they will be found, that is certain, they will be found, they can't hide here forever, they will be found and killed, and the whole thing will be your fault, all your fault.

You stand there grasping the handles of the basket; you try to steel your body, you try to be stronger than the wild trembling that is emanating from your stomach; if you have been brave until now you can't suddenly turn into a coward, nothing has happened, everything is the same as it was before, you can't let yourself be so afraid. Your body lightens and grows stiff, now you're not trembling, it will pass, you know it will pass, and it almost does pass, but then suddenly your head begins to hurt. Enormously— with a sharp, vertiginous, lacerating pain, so lacerating that the basket almost falls out of your hands; you take a few steps, but you know that in a moment you're going to fall; either you will faint or you will die, your head is exploding. You take a few more steps; you're standing next to the walnut tree, it's as if the basket is being dragged to the ground; you put it down with a jolt, you're going to fall, you're going to fall right onto the basket, one word is swirling in your head, stroke, you think of Papa, of half his face hanging down, it can't be, this can't be a stroke, you're much too young for that; you straighten up, you step away from the basket, grab the swing hanging down from the walnut-tree branch; you try to breathe in deeply, and you're thinking that this isn't a real headache, just fear. But in vain. The headache doesn't pass it grows stronger; you're forced to sit down; you sink onto the swing, clutching at the ropes; you haven't sat down on it for years, it was Father who tied it up to the tree branch; you grasp the rope and hold yourself up like that, you feel that in a moment you will begin to retch from fear, but it can't be a stroke, no, it can't be that.

You sit down, your hand squeezing the rope; your head jerks back, you look at the walnut-tree branches and, between the branches, the sky —the sky is moving, it sways back and forth, and the swing is moving with you, it's not you pushing it, you're not alone, somebody is sitting next to you on the plank of the swing; you look over and you see it's Bátykó, he's whistling something very softly to himself, bending forward and backward from his waist, he's making the swing go faster and faster. He wasn't here a moment ago, and he's not here now, you know you're just imagining it, but you both hardly fit on the swing's seat, his torso is pressed against yours, and his clothes smell like smoke and earth.

Your head is hurting even more now, you feel that in a moment you won't be able to catch your breath; the rope of the swing is beginning to slip from your fingers, you're going to fall on your back, you're going to break your neck, you try to grasp something, but you can't.

Bátykó then reaches across your back, grabs the swing's rope, and you lean into his arm; he holds you— he's really there, he's really sitting there next to you, but he can't be there, because just a moment ago he was in the wooden chest behind the woodpile, you heard very clearly as, murmuring softly, he said something to Miklós.

Bátykó speaks; he says, You don't have to hang on like that, don't worry, you're not going to fall.

You let go of the rope; your hand falls into your lap like it isn't even yours.

Bátykó says that when he first saw you, he knew at once that you were a very brave girl, he saw it in how you held your head up and in how you stood up straight; there was defiance and arrogance in that movement, but mainly there was courage, enormous courage.

You want to shake your head, and you want to say that it's not true, he's mistaken, you're not brave but cowardly, doesn't he see how you're about to die of fear— but the pain of the headache won't let you speak.

Bátykó says that you should believe him, he's thought a lot about what cowardice really means. Of his whole family back in Poland, of all of his relatives, he's the only one left, only him, everyone else was taken away, and because he's already stopped dreaming about them, he thinks they're probably not alive anymore. His father gave him a diamond the size of a hazelnut so that he could remain here; his father chose him of all the siblings, of the children and the elderly, of everyone in the family; he told him that no matter what happened, he, Bátykó, had to survive. His father told him that he had to be brave, and he was cowardly enough to act as if he believed him.

Bátykó suddenly puts his palm on the back of your neck, and through your hair you feel his fingers pressing hard on the nape of your neck. He says he meant to stay here only one day, just long enough to warn them, and if he hadn't met up with Bertuka he wouldn't have stayed here at all, but from the moment he saw her, he knew that he *didn't want to go anywhere without her; he begged Bertuka and her family to leave with him when there was still a chance to flee, but no one believed him, they said that what was happening in Poland could never happen here—there would never be a ghetto here, people would never be loaded onto cattle cars here.*

Bátykó says he can never thank you enough for what you've done for Bertuka or for what you've done for both him and Miklós, he can never thank you enough for your courage, and not to be afraid, because they will bring no trouble to you, he knows what you're afraid of, and you're right—they can't remain here any longer.

Suddenly he pulls his hand away from the nape of your neck, and another kind of pain cuts through you, penetrating and sharp, as if somebody has pulled forcefully on your hair, but this pain is quick, it disappears almost immediately, and with it, it takes away that other pain as well, the other pain that almost made you die.

In its place, there remains a light dizziness; you sigh, then you inhale the air deeply—it is sweet, pure, cold.

Bátykó holds his hand in front of you, his fist closed tight as if there is something in it, and he says that it's possible to die from fear, it's possible to be so afraid that the heart breaks and the brain cracks, it's possible, but it's not inevitable; he opens his fist a bit, you look at it, at first you see nothing in it, then something is moving there, between his fingers; you see that his palm is filled with swirling, eddying gray sand. You both look at it, you want to reach over to touch it, but before you can, Bátykó snatches his hand away; with a wild gesture he scatters the contents of his palm behind his back, and he says I'm sure you never imagined pain or fear to be anything like this.

You're sitting on the swing; suddenly you feel very tired, you want to ask what that was, and if it's so easy, then why couldn't he heal Miklós properly.

Bátykó slowly rubs his palms together, and he speaks very softly; he says that once when he was so little he didn't even know how to walk or talk, one time he was playing in the mud, he was kneading tiny birds and beetles and frogs out of the mud, and he was giving them names, and he saw how they shook the earth off and they flew away, climbed away, or jumped away. He looks at his palm, and you see that his nails are caked with soil and mud. He says that he shouldn't have thought about anything, shouldn't have wanted anything, he should have just let everything take its course. He shakes his head, and he says that if he had as much strength now as he had back then, he could make everything better, he'd be able to save everything and everyone. He would be able to revoke every bad thing that had happened, he'd be able to heal every illness, he'd be able to change the world—to redeem it. Sometimes he feels that just a little snap of his fingers would be enough for everything to be made right again; other times he feels that everything is hopeless, because what once had been his knowledge and his strength was forever past, forever gone from him, and he was now the mere shadow of what he might have been.

He falls silent, jumps off the swing, looks at you, and says that the worst thing is that sometimes there are moments when he doesn't know if he even really loves Bertuka or if he's just lying to himself so that he can stay here in hiding and in that way be closer to those whom he abandoned to their fates. He knows he shouldn't think this way, but still, these days he can't help but think that he never should have left Poland, he never should have allowed his father to pick him out of everyone in the family. He should have remained with the others there. He should have let happen what had to happen. He should have resigned himself, and that was all.

Bátykó speaks as if he is relieved to be saying this; he stands hunched over in front of the swing. You think of Bertuka's wildly beating heart, her anger, that resolute motion as she squeezed the diamond necklace and said that she would leave and get them out of the ghetto; and it's as if fire is blazing up within you, and suddenly you slap Bátykó across the face, you tell him he should be ashamed of himself, he can't speak like this, if he knew how much Bertuka loved him, how she would do anything in the world for him, he would never speak that way, he has to pull himself together.

The slap makes a loud clapping noise; Bátykó grabs the side of his

face, and with a clumsy smile, he says that considering that just a mo-
ment ago you were on the threshold of death, that wasn't too bad. And
you shouldn't think that he's a coward, because he's not. If you were in
his place, you'd know how he feels.

GRANDMOTHER FALLS SILENT; HER HAND runs all along
the rope of the swing right up to my hand; she caresses the
back of my hand, looks down at the ground, then says maybe
she shouldn't be telling me these old stories. Maybe it would be
better if she just allowed herself to forget the whole thing. She
turns away and tells me to go in, she'll prepare something for
dinner.

I grab the rope of the swing, step back one pace, then jump
onto the plank. The branch trembles, the rope groans beneath
my hand, but I know that it's not going to break; the swing
moves forward. I thought I felt a headache stirring at the back
of my neck, but it's possible I'm just imagining it. I breathe in
deeply, I throw my head back, I wait for it to either disappear
or intensify.

I TURN OFF THE SMALL light, pull the blanket over myself,
close my eyes, and pretend to fall asleep. I must not think of the
letter, I must not think of when Péter is going to come for me or
why he's coming for me. If I don't want Grandmother to know,
then I have to forget the whole thing. I need to think of sleep,
of dreams, and I think of sleeping, I think of my breath being
nice and even, I think of sleep and dreams, but I also know that
I must not fall asleep.

I hear the clattering sounds first, the noises that come from
the house, the creaking of the floor, the groaning of the beams

in the attic; I hear the tops of the pine trees murmuring in the wind, their trunks slowly and softly creaking but differently than the attic beams, and I imagine Grandmother's house as if I were seeing it from above—the yellow light from the kitchen window pours out onto the stones in the courtyard. I hear Grandmother groan once and get up; suddenly the light is extinguished. Grandmother shuffles into her room; now from the window of the living room an elongated yellow rhombus is cast onto the street. Grandmother's clothes rustle as she gathers them and puts them in the bureau; she pulls out a drawer, takes her nightgown out, and opens the divan, making the springs of the Epeda mattress clang and reverberate off-key; the down pillow emits soft thuds as she fluffs it up. I hear her muttered prayers, I hear her lying down in the bed, and I hear the click of the light as she turns it off.

I picture the house from above as the light from the living-room window is extinguished; the house is now completely dark.

I hear Grandmother clearing her throat, I hear the mattress springs groaning beneath her body now and then.

I think of sleep, I think of how Grandmother should sleep, I think about how she should fall into deep dreams.

I hear her wheezing, and I adjust my breath to the rhythm of hers. I lie there thinking of dreams, thinking of Grandmother's dreams.

I move slowly; slowly I sit up, slowly I get dressed, and all the while I breathe with Grandmother, in and out, in and out, in and out.

Grandmother is sleeping, she's sleeping deeply, she is dreaming.

She doesn't hear the chair creaking when I sit down on it and pull on my shoes, she doesn't hear me zipping up my tracksuit jacket, she doesn't hear me going out into the kitchen, she doesn't hear me opening the kitchen door, she doesn't hear me going out into the courtyard, she doesn't hear as I cross the paved entryway, she doesn't hear me opening the large courtyard doors, she doesn't hear as I close them behind me.

Before I take my hand away from the black handle of the big double doors, I wish for Grandmother not to be awakened by anything other than the first crows of the rooster at dawn. I let go of the handle; it doesn't spring back up again, but remains pressed down. I want it to move back into place, but it doesn't move. I breathe in deeply, I don't breathe out, I wait; the door handle remains pressed down. It's dark outside, I can hardly see anything, so instead I just imagine the lock with its black chestnut-leaf insignia and the handle itself, formed in the shape of a bent and gnarled tree branch; just a moment ago it was beneath my hand. I can't touch it again; it will spring up, it must. The black air sits in my lungs, black and thick like smoke, I support myself with both hands against the door, stand there. My heart is beating very slowly, ever more slowly, it's going to stop in a moment. I hear the bell ringing in the chapel at the end of the street, reverberating slowly and deeply; as if it were the wind, it makes the door shake; the door handle still doesn't move. I know that the sound of the church bell has entered the house, entered the kitchen, the small room and the living room; the ringing of the church bell has entered Grandmother's dream, and she will hear it, she will hear that it is ringing too loudly, she will wake up, she will sit up in bed, she will call out my name, she'll call out my name and she'll ask where I am; that's not what I want, I want her to keep sleeping, to sleep until dawn no matter what I do, just to keep sleeping. As I think about this, beneath my hands, the wood of the door moves; my fingers follow the cracks in the planks of the doors, painted black; my hand reaches the iron strap that runs across them at eye level and the angular nails holding it in place; the third nail is very pointy. I press my thumb into it, I feel it piercing my thumb, the skin splitting; the blood pours out, scalding, from my finger; I pull my hand away from the door, tighten it into a fist, squeezing my fingers around the wounded thumb; it throbs in the middle of my palm. I know that I must not think of the pain, I don't want it to pass. I must think of Grandmother, of her sleeping deeply. I spread my fingers apart; pressing my hand onto the door, softly I whisper, *Sleep, sleep, sleep*, once again the bell begins to ring, then it rings again and again and again, the eleventh hour is struck, it's as if with every toll of the bell, the pain in my hand is increasing, sharp and biting.

The bell stops ringing; it has struck the eleventh hour, *Sleep*, I whisper for the eleventh time, for the last time; the door then moves beneath my palm, and the door handle springs upward loudly; in the depths of the metallic creaking the words, scalding, hiss: *So it will be.* I let go of the door, and I say: *So be it.*

IT'S NOT VERY CHILLY, BUT I'm cold, everything is silent. I don't know how much time has gone by, I don't want to check, and I can't see anything in the dark anyway. I don't want to know how long I've been waiting.

I'm standing in the dark, not looking at the end of the street; I don't even know what direction he's going to come from—from the cemetery or the tree-lined walkway—so instead I look down at the sidewalk in front of me, at the asphalt and my shoes.

Surely he will come, he promised me that he would. I'm thinking of the rings of Saturn; Péter told me that once he looked into a telescope that was so powerful that you could see the grains of the rings, the tiny rocks they are composed of; in reality, of course, the rocks that make up the rings aren't tiny but enormous, unimaginably enormous, yet through the telescope, they looked like pebbles.

He's not going to come; I'm going to wait here until dawn,

he isn't going to show up. I must not think about this; instead, I think of the astronomical chart, I think of Grandfather's old sky atlas, I think about where Venus might be, maybe toward the west, in the direction of the cemetery. I raise my head, look up at the western sky; it is completely dark, not even one star is visible. I slowly turn around; the sky is black, with no stars at all, even the moon has disappeared, it is completely dark.

Péter is not going to come; on a night like this there's no reason for him to come. As I think this, I feel how dry my mouth is. I breathe in the bitter black air.

It's possible that even if the sky had been clear he wouldn't have shown up. He wrote the letter as a joke, he doesn't want anything from me, he was just playing with me. I'm still too much of a little girl for him. There's no point in waiting anymore. It would be best for me to sneak back into my bed. I feel the chill air slipping beneath my dress, at first in the back, stroking my thighs, then farther up, on both sides of my bottom, up to my waist, and I know that in a moment I'm going to start shivering from the cold.

Suddenly somebody grabs my arm. I look over; it's Péter, there he is beside me. He's holding a rectangular pocket flashlight, it's shining onto his face, he's smiling. I see that he wants to say something, but before he can speak, I whisper to him, Shh, don't say anything, be quiet. I know that if he speaks, Grandmother would instantly hear him, even in the deepest sleep, and if she heard him, she would wake up, she would wake up and she would sit up in her bed, and she would call out my name, and I would hear her calling for me even through the walls and the curtains, and I wouldn't be able to move at all, and neither would Péter, we would stand here on the sidewalk like two black statues, and then suddenly Grandmother would appear right in front of us — she never needs a flashlight, she would be able to see us clearly. She would look at me, her eyes flashing angrily, then she would look at Péter, and she would step over to him;

she wouldn't say anything, she would simply pull a long black knitting needle from the sleeve of her black sweater, and she would step behind Péter's back, and she would stab the knitting needle into his back, stab it right into his heart, and Péter wouldn't die, there would be no problem at all, but a black birthmark would remain on his skin where the knitting needle had been, and he would immediately forget all about me. He would forget me, my name, and he would also forget that he'd ever even seen me. I would never enter his thoughts again.

It's not true, Grandmother would never do anything like that, I don't know why I'm thinking this. I recall her touch as she caressed the back of my hand, as she looked at me sadly earlier today. I don't care. I'm looking at Péter, I hope my face doesn't reveal how confused I am.

Péter smiles widely, he doesn't speak, just motions with his head toward the cemetery; he turns off the flashlight, takes my hand, and pulls me with him. We walk very quickly with bowed heads, we're practically running, the palm of Péter's hand is almost scalding hot, it warms my hand.

We reach the end of the street, turn left, and run along the cemetery fence. We get to Péter's motorcycle; it's there beside the fence. Péter grabs my waist, lifts me up, puts me on the seat, and sits in front of me; then he reaches back, grabs both my hands, and pulls them forward. I know what I have to do, I have to hold on to him, hold him around his waist, just like last time.

Péter sets off and we're driving down the street. He's going fast; I feel in my thighs how the motorcycle leans in on the turns; I lean with it, the wind is blowing in my face, I squint my eyes.

When we come to a stop, everything is undulating. I'm so dizzy I can hardly stand. I look up at the sky; it's black and empty. I speak to Péter, say that we won't be able to see anything, nothing at all. My voice is very deep; it sounds unfamiliar.

Péter asks me if I was afraid.

I don't say anything, but I nod.

Péter says there was nothing to be afraid of. If he promised stars, then there will be stars.

AS HE POINTS AROUND WITH the flashlight, I see that we're in a large building under construction. Péter says that this is supposed to be new housing for the ironworkers, but work stopped almost a year ago, and now they're saying that the ironworks are not going to be expanded anyway, so he doesn't think this building will ever be completed.

He says that he knows where we can get across the fence.

He grabs my hand, lighting the way with his flashlight. We walk on planks placed across ditches, we tramp on bricks and stones placed in the mud, we enter through a concrete staircase. Péter opens up a wire-reinforced door, takes me into a wooden booth encased in iron bars, and he says don't be afraid; he pulls on a lever, the floor beneath my feet begins to move, clattering and groaning—we're going up.

Péter says that this is the workers' elevator. It takes us right up to the sixteenth floor. In many places, the building's outer wall panels are still missing, but even so, the building is structurally nearly complete.

The elevator shakes and quivers; we ascend quickly. At the top there are only a couple of concrete walls; it's windy. The sky is dark, and the city is too, but not completely; in a few places the lights are still on, they reveal the outlines of the prefab housing estates and streets. Péter grabs my hand, leads me almost all the way to the edge, and says that the view is the most beautiful from here, you can see the entire city, it's a shame that he can't bring me here during the day because of the ironworkers.

The height at which we're standing seems much greater in the darkness; the palms of my hands are growing moist. I realize how tightly I'm squeezing Péter's hand; I pull my hand away from his, then cross my arms in front of my chest.

Don't be afraid, says Péter, everything will be fine.

At the base of one wall there are two overturned plastic buckets. We go over there; the wall acts as a barrier from the wind. Péter points to one of the buckets and sits down on the other one. He takes something out of his pocket, a match flares in his hand, then he lights a small gas burner; the flames burn, seething in a blue circle.

He takes out a bottle, rips off the foil and wire from the top, and once again he says don't be afraid; he shakes it once, the bottle shoots out the cork with a bang, and the liquid spills out, foamy and frothy, onto Péter's hand. He laughs, and he says, To your health, and he gives me the bottle. I take it, and I say, It's not my birthday. He says that's not why he said it, he's just happy that he can be here with me, happy that we're alive.

As I raise the bottle to my lips, I recall that the last time I drank champagne was two years ago, on New Year's Eve, with Mother and Father. I don't want to think about that now. I raise the bottle; the champagne, bubbling, pours into my mouth, it's sweet and very sparkling, it goes straight to my nose, making me sneeze and laugh. Péter takes the bottle from my hand, drinks from it as well, puts it on the ground, then he looks at my face; I don't know what it must look like in this blue hovering light. Suddenly he says, You're beautiful.

My nose is still filled with the bubbles of the champagne, my laughter is loud and sharp, but at least I'm not giggling; I laugh, and I smile, looking at Péter. With a clumsy movement he picks up the bottle and takes a huge gulp.

As he puts down the bottle, I think about what he's going to say now. I quickly ask him, What about those stars? I don't see even one.

Péter says that he has a telescope in his bag, but it's possible that he might not be able to show me the rings of Saturn tonight. This time of year, in August, the most beautiful thing to see are the falling stars.

He reaches into his pocket again; it's chock-full of sparklers. He divides the bundle in two, gives me half. There's no point in bothering with them one by one, I should just hold all of them at once into the flame of the gas burner.

The blue flames lick all around the ends of the sparklers. I watch them as they slowly turn red, then white; in a moment they will ignite. I look down at the city and I can't bear it anymore, so I stand up, I swing my arm around, and the sparklers, making cracking sounds, begin to throw out their sparks. As I fling them into the air, on the ground far below us, the bells of the great temple begin to ring; they strike half past; my sparklers are flying; Péter throws his own sparklers among mine, and I hear as he cries out, *Saturn, Saturn, Saturn, I love you, I love you, I love you.* I cry out with him, I look at the sparklers' streaks of orange and white and yellow, they are blinding, but I don't even blink.

Then Péter turns toward me, and I know what's going to happen, he's going to kiss me on the mouth, he's going to embrace me.

I see the beginning of his movement, I know it's going to happen — I'm going to want him, I will let him. I won't be afraid, I won't snatch my hand away, I won't close my mouth, I won't clench my teeth, I won't hide behind my crossed arms, I won't hide my breasts, I won't cross my legs. I won't turn my head away at the very last moment, I won't push him away. I'm going to kiss him back. I will embrace him back.

He pulls me toward himself, he kisses me, he squeezes me tight.

His kiss tastes like smoke, like sparklers.

I let him — I want him.

.   .   .

THE FLAME OF THE GAS stove is still burning. Finally the moon has peeked out from behind the clouds. From somewhere far away the wind brings the sound of thunder. Péter turns in that direction; he listens in the darkness. He says that it's a rifle going off. If you've ever heard that sound, he says, you will always know it. It could be the ironworkers; it seems like they were able to get hold of some weapons again from somewhere.

He gazes into the darkness. He says that it was good during the revolution, because during those four days, he at least knew who stood with whom.

He says that he will never in his whole life ever forget that feeling when they broke through the gates of the secret police building. In that moment he knew exactly what freedom was. And what it meant.

Now, however, he says, he's not so sure. He thought he was fighting so that no one would ever have to go without again, so that no one would have to be afraid anymore. Not so that people like Iván's father—people who weren't even there—could slowly but surely buy up half the city. He's heard that he has bought not only the tannery but also the ice-skating rink. He shakes his head; why does anyone need such a huge business like that, an entire factory? He'll never be able to understand. And how can a factory even belong to anyone? He certainly had not faced death so that all of this would belong to one single person.

I ask if he wasn't afraid he might die.

Péter says no, he wasn't afraid at all. He smiles, he licks his mouth, then his face grows serious; he looks at me, then he says that it isn't true, what he just said a moment ago isn't true. He was afraid, he was so afraid that he pissed his pants, literally, and when Feri, one of his best friends, who was running beside him was shot in the chest, he was so afraid that he thought he was going to collapse, as if he were the one who had been shot. He was more afraid than he'd ever been in his entire life.

I reach over to the nape of his neck; I allow my supple fingers to run through his hair. I caress his head; the tips of my fingers touch his scalp. Everything's fine, I whisper, don't worry.

Péter takes my hand; his eyes flash for a second, and he says, Don't think that I'm a coward.

I smile at him, and I say that I know he isn't. I know he's very brave.

I don't believe you, says Péter. His face grows tense, and he says he can see it in my eyes—I think he's a coward.

Don't be ridiculous, I say.

I'm not, he says, this is really serious. He tells me to look into his eyes and tell him sincerely that I think he's a coward.

Stop it already, I tell him, I'm sorry I even asked.

Too late now, he says. I should tell him the truth.

As he speaks, his voice is trembling.

Once again I tell him not to be an idiot, not to do this to me.

He's not doing anything, he says, I'm the one who is doing it. He was sincere with me, and I'm not being sincere with him.

I ask him to please stop.

He says that there's nothing to stop, because he didn't start anything, I started it when I said he was a coward.

I tell him I never said anything like that. I would really like it now if he would stop. And I have no idea why he's doing this.

He says it's because he's not a coward, he is in no way a coward, he never was one, and he will never be one, and I should know this.

It's as if he isn't speaking to me but to someone else. I sense that no matter what I say, it won't be any good.

He jumps up next to me, knocking over the champagne bottle; the last of the champagne pours out, foaming up, onto the concrete. Péter says that if I don't believe him, he'll show me, he will prove to me that he truly is afraid of nothing. By then he's standing on the balcony, which has no railing; he's standing on the very edge of the concrete platform, then he steps out above the depths, and he's standing there in the air, in the void of the darkness.

I feel like I can't catch my breath; my lungs are full, but I can't expel the air, it's as if I am standing there on the edge, and I have to look down into the darkness. I think of flying, I think of that dream in which I flew above our darkened neighborhood, but now the depths, heavy and giddy, are dragging me down, he's going to fall, I know he's going to fall, and I feel the plunge in my own stomach.

The champagne bottle rolls to the edge of the balcony; Péter looks at me, and slowly he holds out both his arms; he is still standing there in the void, he still hasn't fallen. This is impossible, I think, and I look at his legs—he's standing on something, I see it now, from the concrete panel of the balcony there is a long iron tube extending toward the depths. I know what it is, it's a water-drainage pipe, we had one on our old balcony; Péter is balancing on that.

Slowly, he raises both his hands above his head; he's standing there like a dancer, and he smiles at me.

My stomach is convulsing in fear; he's certainly going to fall; the champagne bottle rolls to the edge of the balcony, slips over the edge, and disappears, but I don't hear the sound of it shattering on the ground, because then Péter steps to the side, off the pipe, out into the void, and plunges down like a piece of stone.

I shriek, I don't want to see this, I don't want it to be true, but it is true, it really is true that Péter stepped off the pipe, plunged down beside it, then, at the very last moment, he grabbed hold of it with one hand, and there he is hanging by one hand from the balcony on the sixteenth floor.

He snorts once; he reaches up with his other hand, grabs the edge of the concrete balcony, slowly pulls himself up, changes his grip, turns onto the side, puts one foot up onto the concrete edge, and climbs back. He crouches, gasping for breath, at the edge of the balcony; he looks at me and then stands up.

I feel the anger tingling all the way from the roots of my hair all across my face. I grimace, yell at him: You stupid idiot! I want to attack him, I want to punch him in the stomach, I want to slap him, I want to tear him apart, pinch him, kick him, bite him. And I want to tell him to never do anything like that to me ever again, he has no right to torture me. It won't make me love him any more. I stand there and I watch as he steps toward me —You stupid idiot, I say, you absolutely stupid idiot.

34

ON MY THUMB THERE'S A small brown scar where I stabbed it with the packing needle. My other wounds healed quickly, but this one didn't want to heal at all; it was still forming pus, then Grandmother saw how I was scratching it, so she gave me some common gypsyweed to put on it. Now it's completely healed; it just itches a bit from time to time.

I'm alone; outside it's raining, the weather is chilly, as if it isn't the end of August.

I want to make some tea for myself; I'm going to put a lot of sugar in it and a bit of rum too, that'll warm me up nicely.

The tea tin is empty. As I put it back on the credenza, I see that in the back, on the same shelf, there is a much bigger tin box with the same kind of tea inside.

I take it and open it, and I see that there are no tea leaves inside but pieces of paper torn into tiny scraps.

I know what this is. It can only be the papers that the guest ripped up. I grab a handful of them; I didn't know they were still here.

I take the box to the kitchen table, and I look at all the

scraps of paper. I see tiny black letters, pale typewritten letters; I pour it all out until it stands in a small pile.

I spread out the scraps of paper on the oilcloth; one by one I turn them over so that the sides without writing face upward.

And at last the entire table is covered with them.

I lean on the table with my elbows, I look at the torn strips, their creases.

They are gray, white, and yellowish pieces of paper, I look at them, and I don't know what to do with them.

I reach over, clear a small space for myself on the oilcloth; with my index finger I move a scrap of paper into the middle of the table, then another one, and I place the first next to the second—they don't fit together.

I select another scrap, then a third, fourth; none of them fit together. I place more scraps in front of myself, push them with my hands. I create patterns, circles that then create spirals, and then they extend into stars, growing tentacles; the tentacles intertwine, the pattern disappears; I begin again, the oilcloth murmurs as I shift the scraps of paper here and there, none of them are fitting together.

I recall the jigsaw puzzle that I got for my sixth birthday. Mother found it somewhere, and when it was all put together, it formed the image of a painting; on the box there was a picture of it, showing many village children playing a whole bunch of different games.

It had more than a thousand pieces, and for a long time I didn't even dare open it; I just looked at the box, I looked at all the children, wondering what they were doing. There was a river on it, and on the bank of the river sat two little girls wearing big round skirts, and their skirts were spread out all around them, but you couldn't tell what they were playing. I liked to look at them the best; I imagined that once I put together the puzzle, I would be able to tell what they were playing, but I didn't dare begin.

Then one day, when Mother wasn't home, Father saw me looking at the box, and he asked me if I had put the puzzle together yet, and I said I hadn't, and then Father said let's do it together. Father said I would see what a good puzzle it is, I should bring it into the living room, he was coming too, he was just going to get himself a beer. There wasn't enough room on the small table because it was filled with books and newspapers and empty bottles, but we pulled away the carpet next to the divan, and we opened the box, and we dumped the puzzle pieces onto the floor, and I sat cross-legged; Father lay on his side next to me.

I quickly reached into the puzzle pieces and began looking for those pieces that showed the two girls, but I couldn't find even one of them. Then Father said that wasn't the way to do it, just randomly, that first we had to find the sides of the puzzle and the corners, assemble the edges of the picture, and then when that came together, we could begin to work inward. He showed me how to find the pieces that had at least one straight side. From that point on we looked for those pieces, but I still would have preferred to find the pieces that showed the girls in the round skirts sitting by the bank of the river. Then, once we had collected all the edge pieces and the corner pieces, Father said that we could start putting it together, and we began to, but somehow none of the pieces fit together. Father had finished his beer and sent me out to the kitchen to get him another, and now he'd also finished his second beer, but the perimeter of the puzzle still wasn't complete, only one corner was, and Father was trying to fit the small pieces together with increasing anger. I saw how a whole bunch of them really didn't fit together at all, he had to keep forcing the rounded tabs of the puzzle into the slots with his thumb; I saw how angrily he was holding his head, just like when he shouted and yelled, so I tried to help as best I could, but no matter how much I tried, the pieces wouldn't fit together, and when they did fit together, the edge of the picture didn't form a straight line, so I had to take them apart again, and then I noticed, in the pile, two pieces of one of the girls in the round skirt. I reached over and grabbed them, and they fit each other perfectly, there was half the body of one of the girls, and a big piece of her skirt; then I saw half her head, so I reached over to take that as well, and then Father yelled at me, asking me what was I doing, hadn't he told me that we had to complete the edges before working on the center parts? And he reached over, and, with an angry movement, he swept the pieces of the girl back into the pile with all the other puzzle pieces, and I thought that I would never find them ever again, and I began to cry; I didn't want to, but I couldn't stop myself, and then Father leaped up from the floor, and he yelled at me to stop bawling already, but I could see that he would be only too happy to give a good kick to that pile of puzzle pieces, that's how angry he was; still, though, he didn't kick it, he just turned around and crouched down next to me and told me now it was time to stop. He really smelled like beer, and he was holding his head in such a way that I knew he was going to start yelling again. I squeezed my mouth together and I swallowed back my tears, I wanted it to pass, and it did pass, and then Father said, That's the way, good girl.

I look at the scraps of paper now; I think of the puzzle, and I think about how I never took it out again, I shoved it into a secret hiding place behind the drawers of the linen chest. I'm thinking of the girls as they sat there in their swirling skirts on the banks of the river.

I wipe my eyes with my fists; the scraps of paper are spread out all over the oilcloth, and I know that I won't be able to fit even one piece with another.

I squint, wipe my eyes again, and then I see that one of the scraps of paper is moving. It's slowly turning in a circle; I know

I'm just imagining it, but then I see that another scrap of paper is moving too, it's heading toward the first; they reach each other, they circle around each other; they join up together; they fit into each other perfectly. Then a third scrap of paper moves. I lean in closer, and I see that among the scraps of paper there are tiny black dots moving. They are ants — many tiny black ants.

Ever since Grandmother poured boiling water on the anthill, I haven't seen any ants in the garden. But now here they are again, they're faster and blacker. I watch how they arrive, climbing up one of the table legs. I push back the chair but don't stand up; sitting, I lean to the side, supporting myself with one hand on the floor. The ants are climbing out from the cracks in the floor, then climbing up the table leg and onto the oilcloth.

Now the entire table is full of them. They clamber between the scraps of paper; every scrap is moving, around each other, above each other, below each other; they slowly move here and there, they turn this way and that, they merge together, then they come apart again, the scraps of paper make rustling and swishing sounds. I watch as they move, I don't dare touch the table; the slow swirling of the scraps of paper is making me dizzy, I feel as if the kitchen is moving around me, and I have to lean on the table; I sense something scratching the side of my palm. I look down; next to my hand a gray scrap of paper is moving. I see that two of its edges are straight, it's the corner of one page; as it turns, its tip once again touches the side of my hand, then it slowly sets off for the middle of the table to another gray scrap of paper; it stops beside it, they fit together perfectly, there's a third one already right next to them; slowly the edge of the paper comes together; I keep watching, getting dizzier and dizzier.

THE SCRAPS OF PAPER ARE whirling in my head; sometimes I touch one or the other with the tip of my finger, let it carry my hand. Outside there's thunder, there's lightning too, then the rain begins to pour down. I hear the wind dashing the drops of rain against the windowpanes, and yet I can't look away from the table.

I hear the large courtyard doors opening outside; suddenly the ants come to a halt on the table, they look like many motionless black poppy seeds. The door closes, and the ants suddenly head to the edge of the table, all moving in one direction; it's as if the table has been tilted and black water is running along its surface, pouring down the table leg, flowing back into the cracks of the floor.

On the table, five sheets of paper—once torn into shreds and now reassembled—lie next to each other; every scrap of paper is in its place. My head is buzzing, full of the rustling sounds of the ants.

THE KNOCKING OF GRANDMOTHER'S SHOES against the paving stones is even louder than the rain. She comes up the three steps leading to the kitchen door.

I have time—I could quickly hide the pieces of paper.

But I don't.

Grandmother steps into the kitchen and shakes the water from her half-closed umbrella, then she clatters it open, places it on the old carpet in front of the larder, takes off her trench coat, hangs it up on the nail next to the door, and only then does she look at me, and only after that does she look at the table.

When she sees the pieces of paper, she loses her balance for a moment, and I think she's going to faint, but only her face turns gray. She steps over to the table, looking at the reassembled scraps, and she whispers that she had asked Grandfather to help her with this, to no avail. He wouldn't.

I'm silent; I don't dare say that it wasn't Grandfather.

She goes to the credenza, and when she comes back, she has a roll of tape in her hand; she searches for the end of it, scratching with her fingernail. She finds it, grabs the end, pulls it out; the tape, rasping, winds off the roll; she holds it up for me to cut it. I can't find a pair of scissors anywhere, only the big knife, so I cut it with that. Grandmother tapes it to the back of one sheet, then she pulls off another strip, and I cut that too.

By the time we're done, we're almost out of tape.

We stand there and look at the pages, now taped together; the big knife is still there in my hand, its blade now covered with adhesive, my thumb is sticking to it. As I put it down, I sense that the scab is coming off my finger. It hurts for only a moment; I look down, and in its place there is a tiny black spot, like an ant beneath my skin.

Grandmother reaches for the papers; she puts her hand on each of them, she moves each of them. The tape is holding them together; every sheet remains in one piece and they slide here and there beneath Grandmother's fingers. She asks me if I know what these are.

I lick my mouth—I could lie to her now, and she would believe me. But I say yes, I know, because that evening I was spying on the guest who came to visit.

Grandmother nods, then, one by one, she turns the sheets over.

The adhesive tape is holding them together, but the scraps don't fit together perfectly. One sheet of paper is slightly different than the others. I recognize Grandfather's handwriting. The words, half legible, jump out from the sheets of paper: *always*, I read; *eternally*, I read; *truth*, I read, then I think, That's enough. I turn my head away; this was not written for me and it's none of my business.

On the other sheets of paper, typewritten lines are mixed in with handwritten lines, a creased and broken mosaic; I feel that I don't want to read even one word of these pages—suddenly I wish that I had just fallen asleep that night at midnight, I wish I'd never reached for the tea tin, I wish I'd never poured out the scraps of paper and that I hadn't saved the ants. I wish I had never come here.

Grandmother reads Grandfather's letter, then she puts it down, throws down the other sheets of paper on top of it.

I'm waiting for her to start crying, but there's no sadness on her face; instead, she just looks extremely tired.

She looks at me. She says that I can't understand something like this when I'm so young, and I mustn't understand, but still, if I want to try to know what it would be like to understand, then I should pose one question to myself, and that is this: What would I do for that boy about whom I'm thinking so much these days—what would I do for Péter?

She falls silent, shakes her head, and says that no matter how sincerely I might ask myself this question, I still could never know. The answer to something like that emerges only when someone has to decide, when someone has to say yes or no. The purpose of Grandfather's entire life was for him to say no, but for him to do this, somebody else had to say yes in his place. He never would have escaped from them. They would have let him teach for a year, then they would have blackmailed him. They would have forced him to inform on his own students. And it wouldn't even have mattered if he said yes or no; he would have died of it one way or the other.

All she'd wanted to do was to spare him this. And all she'd wanted was for Grandfather to live. That's all she'd wanted, and she couldn't even do that.

Again she's quiet; she looks at me, waiting for me to say something. I see her hand is trembling.

I can't speak, I'm looking at her hand, at the red shadow

trembling on her wrinkle-covered hand cast by the small ruby in her ring.

Grandmother then says that if I want to, I can leave. She let me go once before, now she's letting me go for the second time. I can go just as my mother did. For her it's enough that she could be with me for almost an entire year.

She pulls the ring off her finger and hands it to me, tells me to take it. To keep it and to hold her in my memory. This is all she wants—she asks nothing else.

I look at the ring, still seeing it on her finger; there's a name engraved on the inside of the ring that I can't read.

And now I must speak. The skin on my thumb begins to tingle as if that black tiny ant were climbing in circles within the whorls of my thumbprint. But I know that I've already decided, I've already chosen, and there are only two words I can say: I'm staying.

35

WE'RE OUTSIDE IN THE GARDEN, making plum jam. Grandmother says I have to learn how to make it properly so I'll be able to eat delicious preserves when she isn't around anymore. My job is to mix it. The wooden spoon is so big that I have to hold it with two hands. The wood is entirely black and you can tell it's very old — so old that maybe Grandmother got it from her own grandmother.

Grandmother asks me to climb up onto the walnut tree and throw a chain around one of the branches; we hang the big washing pot on that, and we build a fire beneath the pot. The plum jam is cooking, it's two-thirds common plums and one-third greengage plums, the mixture is thick and black as tar, with bubbles breaking open on the surface; they burst, the mixture seethes, it's getting harder and harder to stir. As I stir, I have to grip the spoon tightly so that the preserves don't wrench it from my hands.

I also have to keep an eye on the fire. The flames can't be too strong, but they can't go out either. From time to time I have to add more wood. And yet I can't stop stirring for a moment.

Right now, Grandmother isn't here. She took the sickle and

went to gather some herbs. Those are also needed for the preserves, she said, to make them as delicious as they should be. If
we put in only the plums, it will be tasty, but it could be even
better.

She didn't say where she was going, and I recall that once
she said that the best herbs grew in the cemetery, because the
earth was greasiest there, then I recall how she laughed out
loud when I said, Really?

The preserves are getting thicker and thicker, so much so
that when I lean down for another piece of wood, I can easily let
go of the handle of the spoon; it stands up in the mixture and
turns as if it were stirring the preserves all by itself.

I watch it as it turns, and I whisper, *Go to work, spoon;* the
spoon slowly turns in the preserves. I take hold of it, I push it a
little, then once again I let it go and let it turn by itself.

That's exactly what I'm doing when Grandmother comes
back. She flicks me on the neck, but lightly, so I know that she's
not really angry at me. She says that she didn't tell the spoon to
go to work, but me. The wooden spoon makes a sloshing sound
as she pulls it out of the preserves; it draws a strip of tar in
the air, stretching out like rubber. Grandmother puts the spoon
back into the preserves, and she says it's almost ready, just keep
on stirring nicely.

I nod and I take the spoon.

Grandmother hangs up the sickle on the nail sticking out
from the walnut tree; she puts the bundle, which she tied up in
her apron, onto the trestle table next to the freshly cleaned mason jars and ceramic jugs.

Grandmother undoes the bundle; it's filled with herbs and
berries and mushrooms. She pulls one of the tin lids toward herself and begins to tear up the grasses and leaves and put them
in it. While she does this, she sings. I don't know these herbs.

Grandmother finishes ripping up the herbs. She lifts up the
metal lid and approaches me.

She tells me to stir the preserves as quickly as I possibly can.

I try to stir the mixture quickly; in the pot, the plum preserves are swirling in black whirlpools, my arm is getting tired, it's so difficult, my shoulder is aching, my neck too, and I know in a moment my head will start aching as well.

Grandmother nods and says, That's good. With one hand she holds the metal lid in front of me; she points at the herbs with her finger, recites the name of each one; I have to repeat each name after her, and I do, but I'm not paying too much attention, I'm watching the swirling preserves.

Grandmother begins to sing; I know this melody, but I don't sing with her, I watch as she turns the contents of the metal lid into the middle of the whirlpool. She motions for me to stir it even more quickly.

A somewhat tart scent drifts up from the cauldron. Grandmother leans over, her mouth gaping open, and inhales it in deeply, then she continues singing in a soft guttural voice. Her hair is undone, nearly hanging down into the preserves.

I keep stirring. The preserves are very thick now.

Grandmother straightens up, her face completely red from the heat; she grabs the spoon from my hand, again pulls it out; she presses her thumb into the boiling preserves, then she shoves it into her mouth and licks it off her thumb with a smacking noise. She closes her eyes and nods.

She wipes her hand on her sweater, and she says the preserves will be good. I'll see later on how sweet they will be and what sweet dreams they will bring. Never will I eat anything so good in my life.

I nod. I look at Grandmother's undone hair; the end of one of the locks touched the preserves, and there is a large dark drop sitting on it; it looks like the thickened resin on a cherry.

IT'S THE LONG RECESS; WE'RE outside in the yard, the sun is shining and there are no shadows in sight, it's extremely hot outside. Krisztina and her friends are playing jump rope, right now Aliz is jumping across the long elastic bands, she's quite good at it; a lot of us are watching, and at the same time I'm talking to Olgi; she's telling me about her cats and how she likes to play with them.

I'm thirsty. I ate my bread spread with plum preserves greedily, Grandmother sprinkled chopped-up walnuts between the two slices of bread, and it was tastier than the finest pastry. I'm thinking about going to the girls' bathroom to get something to drink, and Olgi is explaining how she figured out that one of her cats is left-handed because it always bats the skein of yarn with its left paw first.

First I see one boy running out from behind the corner of the school building, then following after him is a second boy, then a third; they're chasing each other, the ones at the very back are shouting, We'll catch you, we'll get you, the other boys are running after them, right toward us, there are many of them, not just from our class but from the higher grades as well.

As the first boy reaches Olgi, I see that there's something in his hand; his shoe squeaks and sheds dust as he stops next to her. I recognize him, he's a boy from the seventh grade but I don't know his name. For a moment I think he's going to fall or push Olgi over, I yell for her to be careful, but he doesn't fall; half crouching, he bends down; there's something red flashing between his fingers, but already he's shoving it beneath Olgi's skirt. I yell out to Olgi, but too late, Olgi shrieks, the boy laughs, and at the same time I feel someone pulling up my skirt, feel ice-cold water being sprinkled onto my thighs. My skirt is soaking wet, and so is my underwear, this is really bad; I shriek. You stupid prick! I yell. The boy yanks a dripping water pistol out from beneath my skirt; he smirks, shouts that I peed myself, Hey, hey, hey, she peed herself! He points with his water pistol at the puddle around my shoes; the other boy also screams out that we peed on the ground like horses, like horses; they jump and run all around us, yelling, Pee-pee girls, what did you do, pee-pee girls, what did you do. Olga is crying, her face completely red; she crouches down, picks up a piece of asphalt, and throws it at the boys, but she doesn't hit any of them.

By now, the other boys have also gotten to us; each one of them has a water pistol, they try to drench the other girls beneath their skirts, they aim the water at their legs, at their faces, at their necks; someone sprays water at my neck; the water flows coldly down my back and beneath my armpit. I'm filled with rage; I grab the hand of one of the boys; I want to take away his water pistol, but I just grab the sleeve of his shirt and pull it hard, the shoulder seam splits apart with a cracking sound; the boy yells at me, You idiotic stupid cunt, look what you did, let go! But I don't, I pull even harder, I want to rip off his entire shirtsleeve. In the boy's other hand there is a water pistol; he raises it and sprays it into my eyes; I let him go; I try to scratch his face, but I can't reach it. My face is wet, I don't see anything; by the time I've wiped it off, the boy is gone, him and the others, they've all gone. Emőke says it's because they ran out of water, but when they fill up their water pistols again, they'll be back.

Krisztina's hair and her clothes are drenched; she says that everyone should gather up stones, so that when they come back they'll get something they'll never forget. She bends down, picks up a water pistol from the ground, says that some idiot dropped it and left it here. She reaches into her skirt pocket, takes out a medical syringe, attaches a huge needle onto its end, hands me the water pistol, and says, Help me; hold it. I take it by the funnel, holding it in front of myself; Krisztina shoves the syringe into the handle of the water pistol and begins to suck out the rest of the water from it. I ask her what she's doing. Krisztina says that this is a syringe for cleaning ears, she stole it from her grandfather's medical bag; if the boys come back, she vows that she will spray water into their eyes so hard, they will be seeing double for days.

I have to laugh at this, and Krisztina laughs with me. Her hair has loosened in the back, and for the first time I see her as beautiful without any feelings of envy; she looks at me—perhaps after all we can be friends.

The syringe is completely full now, and there's still a bit of water left in the pistol. Krisztina pulls out the syringe. I squeeze the handle of the pistol between my hands; after the syringe is extracted, the rest of the water sprinkles out between my fingers, almost spraying Krisztina. Krisztina steps back, saying that I should wait for the boys, don't waste the water. It's one hundred percent sure that they're going to come back, and then we'll show them who's the stupid cunt.

WE'RE AT OUR DRAWING CLUB right now. The drawing teacher waits for everyone to sit down, then he walks around the classroom handing out large blank sheets. Then, without a word, he sits down, pushes back his chair, stretches out his legs, clasps his hands behind his neck, and looks at the ceiling. In the corner of his mouth, instead of an unlit cigarette, there's a small toothpick; as the chair slowly tilts back and forth, the toothpick moves back and forth.

Everyone is looking at the blank sheets of paper, waiting for him to say what we have to draw.

The drawing teacher doesn't say anything. Now he's not even looking at the ceiling because he's closed his eyes, and only the toothpick moves from time to time in the corner of his mouth.

We sit motionless, everyone looking at his or her own sheet of paper; no one moves, no one draws anything.

I look at the drawing teacher's legs, stretched out in front of him, at his boots, jutting out from beneath his trouser legs, his legs crossed at the ankles. On one of his shoes the battered metal tap shines; it's missing from the other one.

The boys begin to hiss; one of them gestures in front of his forehead to show that the teacher is off his head, another opens his mouth, gaping, and makes a motion like he's drinking from a bottle, squinting and grimacing all at once; he stops, pulls off a piece from his sheet of paper, rolls it into a pellet, puts it in his mouth, spits it out into his palm, then throws it, covered in spittle, at one of the girls. It doesn't hit her, so he tears off another strip of paper.

I watch the drawing teacher, I wait for him to get up and start yelling at us, I wait for him to set something on the table for us to draw, but nothing happens. Somebody, whispering, tells a joke, guffawing loudly at the punch line; even then the drawing teacher doesn't get up, he's still leaning back fully in his chair, his two legs stretched out, crossed at the ankles, and now even that toothpick in his mouth isn't moving.

Once again I look at his heavy shoes. I put down the charcoal and pick up the graphite pencil; I begin to draw the drawing teacher as he sits there in the chair, his head thrown back and his eyes closed.

I try to draw him from a foreshortened angle, as if his shoes were dangling off the sheet. I imagine that the metal tap on the sole of his shoe is shining, scattering the light into my eyes so that I can't even see his face; I'm paying attention to the light, and I try to capture the shining metal shoe tap, the deep teeth of the treads of his shoes, the pieces of mud stuck on the side.

It's as if the drawing teacher has fallen asleep; he's not moving at all. The others are now speaking loudly. I don't pay attention to them; I pay attention to the light.

Suddenly, the drawing teacher clears his throat, jumps up, grabs his chair, and with all his strength slams it down on the ground; the chair makes such a loud banging noise that I think it's going to break into pieces, but no. The drawing teacher yells, Silence, order, discipline!

Everyone jumps back into place, and suddenly there is silence, such a great silence that it is broken only by the sound of a pencil slowly rolling across one of the drawing tables.

The drawing teacher says that he thought that the students who came here liked to draw, that they were the kind of students who could work independently, not only when they were being told what to do. The kind of students with ideas of their own. But it seems that we know only how to bellow and play the fool like a bunch of idiots. And it seems that no one here has any idea of what to do with freedom.

As he speaks, he walks around the classroom, gathering everyone's drawing paper one by one, he doesn't even look at them; with other every step, the metal tap on his shoe strikes the floor.

He says that he personally risked his own life so that this country would no longer be governed by idiots and their idiotic commands, but if we want to be idiots, then so we must be. Then we'll all deserve to have them sitting on our necks again, and if we end up here with the same thing we had before, we have only our own selves to blame. And it will be all our fault.

He stops, shuffles the sheets of paper together in his hands, and he says we certainly have heard that not everybody thinks there should be free elections. That we are not yet mature enough for freedom.

His face twists into a bitter grimace; he falls silent; the papers rustle as he flips through them in such a way that we can all see what's on them. Most of them are blank; there are two sheets with drawings on them. The drawing teacher grabs these two pieces of paper, looks at them, and holds them up. This is how many there are, he says, from twenty-five students there are only two who tried to do anything at all.

One of the drawings is mine; you can't see anything of the

light on it, just two ugly shoes crossed over each other; the toe tap is overdrawn, it looks like there's a huge hole dug into the piece of paper. Nobody's looking at my drawing, though, everyone is looking at the other drawing: It's a sketch of the drawing teacher, but with a donkey's head, big, bristly, drooping ears, smirking buckteeth, and an enormous smoking cigar in his mouth; his jacket and his trousers are made of tattered rags; from one of his pockets a brandy bottle is sticking out, in the other one is a fly swatter; at the end of his crossed legs there are two iron-shod hooves, and a long horse's tail hangs down to the ground beneath the chair. Flies are buzzing all around him.

For a moment there is silence, then everyone breaks into laughter. The drawing teacher bellows once, then he too begins to laugh with a neighing sound, he heehaws as if he really were a donkey, his face turning red. Suddenly he stops, and he says with the exception of two people, we all deserve to be kicked to hell in such a way that our legs would never touch ground ever again. But we shouldn't worry, there will be no punishment, because there is at least one person here with some blood in his cock. And we all have him to thank.

36

THE GROUND BENEATH THE BUSHES is covered with leaves; the full moon shines white, scorching the branches. It's so bright outside that you could read a book. Krisztina climbs in front of me; the ground is cold beneath my hands as I follow her. I press down on dried flowers; they crunch as I climb over them, my nose is filled with a pale scent of jasmine.

Ever since Krisztina squirted the water in the eyes of one of the seventh-grade boys when they tried for a second time to shoot water pistols underneath her skirt, we've been on good terms. We often talk during the big recess, and we've gone to the movies together twice. We've just come from there now; we saw a French police movie.

Krisztina pulls her coat beneath herself; sitting cross-legged, she takes out a cigarette and matches, and as she shakes the matchbox, the shadows of the branches cast by the moonlight on her hand look like black lace. She says that this is her spot and her spot alone, nobody knows that she comes here, and it's the best in the summer when it's really hot; sometimes she spends the whole afternoon here, reading or looking up at the sky between the leaves.

She says that she didn't like the movie, and I should know that a whole bunch of girls from the class are in love with Alain Delon—not her, though.

She lights the match, holds it up to the end of the cigarette, and inhales. The end of the cigarette smolders; it's so scarlet red that for a moment, her face behind it disappears into the dark, then slowly emerges again, the skin on her face is now a dark crimson mask. She blows the smoke toward me, and she asks me if I remember the last time I saw my mother and father.

I thought she was going to say something bad about Iván—she's been very angry at him ever since he started going after that big-chested girl from school no. 14—or ask me if I liked him; I was already formulating the response in my mind. I shake my head; I want to think about Alain Delon, about how he lights his cigarette, how he lies in bed and looks at that female gymnast; I don't want to think about Mother and Father, I don't want to remember, but of course I do remember, I've thought about it so often that I can't not remember. There I am in my room, sitting on my bed with my knees drawn up, I'm trying to read, but I can't pay attention to the book because I can hear that they're fighting, as they do now before almost every single departure. Mother got dressed too slowly again; once again she forgot to iron Father's single cuff-linked shirt; they're fighting in subdued voices, whispering so I won't hear, but still I hear. Mother is saying that she doesn't want to go, she wants to stay here, and she explains why too, it's because she knows that Éva will be there, and she doesn't want to have to see how Éva looks at Father, and she also doesn't want to see how Father looks back at Éva, with that hypocritical half smile, she doesn't want to see it, because she knows all too well what that look means, what it always means. I press my hands over my ears, but still I hear as Father, in a wheedling voice, mollifies her: You're just imagining it, my heart, my love, you're just imagining it, you know it's only you I love, only you. I press my hands hard over my ears, I don't want to hear it, because I know it's true, and I also know that Mother doesn't believe it; she wants to believe it, but she doesn't; if I were there, I would see that cold smile on her face as she hisses back, Of course, of course. Then Father says, If, however, you didn't keep guzzling away at the white wine the entire night, one glass after the other, if you didn't always have to get so dead drunk — and by now he's not whispering anymore, and I know that in a moment he's going to start yelling. Mother isn't whispering either, and she says that it's not even wine but vinegar, sour and bitter vinegar, and she says, Even if I drank twice as much as I usually do, I wouldn't understand how you're able to flirt with her, especially with her, when you know that she's a stinking informing whore who is going to write every single one of your words in her report for the secret police, and then Father yells that that's exactly why, that's exactly why, because at least he doesn't have to be suspicious of her, if you don't understand this, he says, then you don't understand anything. Father is cursing; I hear a loud clanging sound, I know what it is, Father has thrown the old ashtray at the wall, I know that movement of his, I've seen it before: the cigarette butts fly everywhere as the ashtray smashes against the wall and falls to the ground, a cloud of ashes remains in the air; it hovers in front of the wall and then, swirling, slowly disperses. I look at the paper, I look at the letters printed on the page of the book, and I think of the ashes and how the ashes will cover everything. I don't hear them yelling anymore, I only hear them call me to come and give them a kiss, because they're leaving. I go out into the vestibule where they are standing arm in arm, elegant and perfumed. Hello, I say, have a good time. Mother says that if there are no power cuts, I can stay up reading till eleven; they certainly will be coming back late tonight, I shouldn't wait up for them. Mother bends down to kiss me; her face smells like powder, and it's still burning from the argument; I kiss Father too, and although he's closely shaven, his skin is still rough and bristly when it touches my face; once he said that his beard was so wild that no razor could ever tame it. They go out the door and down the steps; their clothes rustle, their shoes clatter loudly on the staircase. I close the door, I close it and lock it, I don't go with them, I go back to my book, back into my room. It was then. That was the last time I ever saw them.

Krisztina's cigarette smolders; she's still waiting for me to answer.

I'm silent.

Krisztina blows out the smoke and says that she was with Réka, her twin sister, to the end, and she's there with her now too, out there in the main square, they're standing next to each other in the crowd, hanging on to each other, singing with the others, they're singing that lies are dead, long live truth, servitude is dead, long live freedom, evil is dead, long live happiness, hurrah! The entire crowd is singing, everyone, for a long time, a very long time, until the soldiers arrive, until the soldiers have lined up with their tanks and their trucks at the upper end of the square, and then they begin to sing to them, to the soldiers, they sing to them: Open, open, open your hearts, open, open, open the prisons, open, open, open your eyes, hurrah! They stand on the square and they sing; it's cold, but they don't feel the cold, they lean against each other and they sing, their throats are hurting, their lungs are hurting, but they don't stop, neither does anyone else, they stand there and they sing, and Krisztina is thinking about fear, thinking that she should be afraid, that not only is it not permitted to sing these words; it is not permitted to even utter them, not even softly, in no way at all; it is not even permitted to think them, to think them and at the same time know that the others are thinking the same thing, Réka and all the others too, and this makes her sing even louder, so loud that it's impossible to sing any louder; her throat is hurting so much that she has to throw her head back all the way, as if she were looking up at the sky, the sky and the large snow-white clouds; open, open, open your eyes, open, open, open the prisons, and then suddenly she feels a kind of contraction in her stomach, in her abdomen, and not just her, everyone else feels it too; the entire crowd suddenly contracts together; somebody screams, then somebody else, and somebody else as well, and the sounds of the screams are sharper than anything, you can hear them through the singing, she will never forget that; first she heard the screaming and only after that did she hear the detonations; a huge explosion cuts into the crowd like thunder from the heavens, but she knows that it wasn't thunder from the heavens, because above, the clouds are frozen in the sky, and from this point on she remembers only Réka, she remembers how she is squeezing her arm with all her strength, and Réka is squeezing her arm with all her strength too, for a split second everything is motionless, everything and everyone; above the square, the detonations and the screams tangle together, echoing, and then she thinks that this is the end, the end of everything, of singing, of everything, once again she will have to be silent, and now she will have to run away from here, run home, away from the square, and as she thinks that, she immediately feels ashamed of herself, and the shame makes her squeeze her sister's arm even harder; somebody falls down right in front of them, an old man, he was shot in the neck, the bullet forces him down onto one side, his hat flies off his head, the blood spurts out from his neck, she looks and she sees the blood is dark, completely dark, almost black, it's thick and black like oil; she doesn't want to see it, but she can't not see it, and she knows that Réka is also looking at it, looking at the black blood, and at the same time she knows that the bullets are flying all around them, but she doesn't hear that, she doesn't hear anything, it's as if she's grown deaf or as if somebody has covered her ears. They stand, clutching each other; everyone around them is running, but they can't move, they squeeze and embrace each other, then suddenly she feels something wrenching Réka out of her arms, wrenching her, lifting her, tossing her away, and in the next moment Réka is lying there in the cobblestones, her quilted winter coat covered in blood, her face covered in blood, her hair covered in blood; she stands there above her sister, with both hands she grabs her wrists, tries to pull her up, she tugs at her wrists, she wants to pull her up from the ground, *Come on, get up, stand up and live,* but Réka doesn't move; everyone around her is yelling, tugging, elbowing, and pushing, they carry her with them, away, out of the square; Réka's wrists slide from her grasp, she doesn't want to let go, she squeezes, her ten fingers digging into Réka's skin, but she can't pull her up, she can't move her, she can't hold her, she lets go, and she never sees her again.

Krisztina is silent; she inhales, her face is drawn into the scarlet light of the cigarette. She says that since then, all she can think about is that it wasn't like that, it didn't happen like that, but instead the opposite happened, everything is the opposite: She's the one lying on the cobblestones, she's the one whose throat was torn apart by the bullet, she's the one from whom blood and life flows out, and it is Réka who stands above her; it is not she who is grabbing Réka's wrists but Réka who is grabbing hers; it is not Réka's skin that is as cold as bone but hers; it is not Réka who is dying but her, and everything that has happened since then is just something she's imagining — me, the bushes, the earth and the sky, the entire world, everything, because in reality she's still lying there on the cobblestones, and she sees her sister leaning above her, and she sees the horror in her sister's eyes, and above her sister's head she sees the sky and the gray clouds.

The tip of the cigarette smolders. Krisztina says look, if I don't believe her, then look; she pulls up the sleeve of her sweater, takes the cigarette out of her mouth, and presses its burning end onto her left wrist; I hear as her skin sizzles, and all the while she's looking at me, and she says she feels nothing, do I understand, she feels no pain whatsoever, and that's how she knows that she's not even alive, do I understand, she's not even alive; she lifts the cigarette from her skin, then presses it onto her arm again, she presses it down again and again, I smell her sizzling skin, I yell at her not to do this, stop it, have you gone mad? Krisztina doesn't stop; she presses the smoldering cigarette into her skin over and over again.

I reach over; I want to knock her hand away, I want to take the cigarette out of her fingers, but she pulls her hand away; her fingers grasp my wrist, she squeezes it, but it doesn't hurt, and she says, You're not alive either; then she lifts the cigarette to her mouth, she inhales; I know what she's going to do, and I know that with my other hand I can knock the cigarette out of her hand, but I don't; instead, I let her press the ember into my skin.

I think of Father and Mother again; they're standing there in the vestibule, and I'm there with them, not wearing my old, stained tracksuit but my denim skirt, my leather boots, and my green-grass-colored sweater, Father says how beautifully I am dressed, I'm a big girl now, Mother says I can go with them, they're taking me too, together we leave the apartment, together we go down the steps, together we get into Uncle Egon's Trabant. Father sits in front, I sit with Mother in the back, it's dark, we drive across the city; Uncle Egon is telling an old joke to Father, but I can't hear it properly, even though I'm leaning forward because I too want to laugh; as we reach the winding road and take the first turn, Father is still laughing at the joke; I see that beyond the turn there is a large truck approaching, its headlights sweep across the bushes, the lights are not yellow but white, just like moonlight, then we're right in front of it, the headlights are shining into my eyes, I don't blink, I don't even close my eyes, I see as the truck switches into our lane; Uncle Egon tries to twist the steering wheel to one side, Father cries out something, Mother grabs me, the white light blinds me completely, it's much stronger than moonlight, it's white, white, I know we're going to die, we're all going to die, I'm not afraid, Father's voice is in my ears, I understand what he's yelling, my name, he's yelling my name and not Mother's; I am both happy and ashamed of myself; I feel Mother squeezing me tightly, I want to reach over so I can embrace her back, but it's too late, I can't.

The ember of the cigarette is poised against my skin, Krisztina presses the cigarette down; it hisses. I really don't feel it. Krisztina lifts it from my skin, I know that in a moment she's going to press it down again, and once again she's going to say that we're not alive—neither she, nor I, nor anyone, that's what she's going to say, and then I am going to embrace her, and I'm going to say the same thing, because it's true, and then Krisztina really presses the ember into my skin again, and she whispers that we don't deserve to live, and as I hear this, I suddenly feel the pain on my arm, white and glowing it cuts, burning, sharp; it pierces through my arm, through my skin, and down to my flesh, down through the bones, ulna and radius, these words come to mind, Father taught them to me. I suddenly cry out, Leave me alone! My throat fills with the scents of moist earth and jasmine leaves; I yank my hand away so quickly that the cigarette flies out of Krisztina's hand, pulling a streak of light in the air and extinguishing in a red cloud of ash. I bring my wrist to my mouth, press my tongue to the burning blister; my skin is bitter and rough and burning, it's hurting so much that my eyes fill with tears.

Krisztina says that still, it's all our fault, and I should know that they died for us, all the bad things happened because of us and only because of us, it's useless for me to think that I can't do anything about it, because I can do something about it, I should know I can do something about it, that everything happened because of me, and only because of me, that I'm the one at fault.

I bite my skin; the burning blister, salty and painful, bursts into my mouth; I spit it out onto the ground; in the meantime my arm is moving, I'm slapping Krisztina, the slap rings out on her face underneath the palm of my hand. I yell at her: Stop, shut your mouth, do you understand, shut up, we're not the ones at fault, we can't do anything about it, not about them dying, not about us surviving, that's how it was and that's how it is, there's nothing more to do, life goes on.

I yell it really loud, because I want it to be true.

Krisztina presses her hand to her face, and she says I can lie to myself if I want to, but she won't lie anymore, she's had enough, the time has come for her to tell the truth. She leans forward, begins to scratch the earth with her two hands, quickly and wildly, like a fox, like a dog, and, panting, gasping for breath, she tells me that when she and Réka were little, they played at being princesses, and they always fought about which one of them was the firstborn, because no matter how many times they asked, their father never told them, he always said that even the question itself was foolish, they shouldn't worry about that, the whole thing took two minutes, two minutes is nothing, they should consider that they were born at the same time —Krisztina is silent; she stops digging, grabs something, pulls it out of the earth with both hands, it's a crooked black root, no, it's a black plastic bag; she shakes off the clumps of earth clinging to the bag, then puts it down before me and continues speaking—she says that on their seventh birthday, she woke up with a doll lying on her pillow; it was placed there so that it would be the very first thing that she would see. It was a princess, and at first she couldn't even believe it was there and not a dream, but it was real, it was really there, and the princess was so beautiful, with a ruffled silver dress and little silver shoes, and she had a crown too, and she had lace gloves, and a necklace, and a bracelet, and a belt, and earrings, and everything was made from silvery, shiny plastic; even her hair was silver, it was the most beautiful doll she had ever seen in her whole life. For minutes she just looked at it, not daring to move, not daring to blink, because she was afraid it would disappear, then she took it and sat it up, and the doll's eyes sprang open, and she had blue glass eyes, and until that very moment she hadn't thought of what Réka might have gotten, and it was only when she saw the doll's eyes spring open that she thought of it, then she suddenly wanted to know, and she leaned up on her elbows in the bed and looked over at Réka's bed. Réka was still asleep, and on the pillow next to her head there was also a doll, a doll exactly the same as hers, only much more beautiful, because its clothes were not silver but gold, and the doll didn't have silver hair, but golden hair, and not silver shoes, but golden shoes, and from that she knew that Réka was the first and she was the second, it had always been that way and it would always be that way. And then she got out of bed, softly, so no one would hear, and she went over to Réka's bed, and she exchanged the two dolls, she exchanged the silver doll for the golden one, and the golden one for the silver one, finders keepers, losers weepers, and then she lay back down in her bed, and she pretended to be asleep until Réka woke up.

Krisztina reaches into the plastic bag and pulls out a doll by its hair; its crown has slipped to one side and it's broken, but the crown and the dress glimmer in the moonlight anyway. I can't tell if this is the silver doll or the golden doll, I can only tell that it's very beautiful, a real doll that can open and close its eyes, and I think of how much I would have loved a doll like that, but Mother was never able to get one for me.

Krisztina says that Réka never knew that she switched the dolls, she never was jealous, she acted as if they were completely the same, as if the whole thing didn't matter at all; it did, however, matter, it really mattered, because now she knows that she exchanged her fate for Réka's, and so it was she who was responsible for all the bad things that happened, and she tried to punish herself, but it never worked, and as she says this, she shakes the doll by its hair, the doll's eyes open, then they close, then they open, then they close again, and in Krisztina's other hand there is a large glass syringe with a long injection needle at the end. I didn't notice when she took it out or from where, but I recognize it, it's the same ear-cleaning syringe with which she almost poked out the eyes of that boy from the seventh grade, the one who squirted water under her skirt.

Krisztina clasps her fingers around the syringe and plunges it into the doll's stomach, she pulls it out again and thrusts it into the doll's stomach again, holding the doll by its legs; she stabs it, muttering, Useless, worth nothing, nothing, nothing at all. Pain shoots through my stomach, I know I'm just imagining it, but it hurts. I speak to Krisztina, tell her to stop, I try to reach over; I want to grab her wrist, I want to twist the syringe out of her hand.

The doll falls to the ground; I force open Krisztina's fingers, she claws at my wrist and I claw at hers, we tear at and yank each other's hands, somehow I get hold of the syringe, I pull on it, but it's just the inner part, it slides out, and the syringe fills up with air.

We're facing each other, kneeling, underneath the bush; each of us grasps half of the pulled-apart syringe with one hand and clutches the other's wrist with the other; we're panting. Krisztina begins to pull the syringe toward herself. Help me, she says, I have to help her, don't I see that she can't do it by herself, she's not brave enough, but if I help her, then it'll work, then at long last she'll get what she deserves. The needle is already at her throat, its tip is about to touch her skin, she says that if we plunge it in together and squeeze the air into her artery, that will be enough, that will be the end, she read this in a medical encyclopedia. She wants me to do it, she wants me to help her.

Krisztina closes her eyes, bends her head to one side; her neck extends white in the moonlight. I see how the needle casts a shadow on it, the black line on the white skin, I know that somewhere beneath her skin the blue vein is running, it has to be there, it's there even if I don't see it. Krisztina is stronger than me, I feel it now, just a little bit stronger, but it's enough, she's going to do it, we're going to do it, I'm going to do it. I look at her face as she lifts it with closed eyes up to the moonlight; I've never seen her like this before, frightened and determined and angry and very beautiful, I know that I have to say this, just two words — *You're beautiful*—if I could say that to her the way that Péter said it to me, she would let go of my hand, but I can't speak; panting, I tense my arm, but for nothing; the tip of the needle has already touched the skin, it's about to pierce through, and as I think of this, my mouth opens, but I don't speak, instead I begin to sing, and I sing, Lies are dead, long live truth, servitude is dead, long live freedom, and I sing the whole thing, I'm not really singing it, just humming it softly, as if it were a lullaby.

Krisztina doesn't move; she doesn't open her eyes, she doesn't say anything, but I see that tears are running down her face, I feel the grip of her hand loosening.

By the time we put down the syringe, she's racked by sobs. I know that I'm going to cry too; clutching each other we will cry for Father and Mother, for Réka and all the other dead, and for ourselves too, for the entire world. I think of Father and how he said that crying isn't good for anything, it's not worth anything, but I don't care, I've held out till now, the end; I let Krisztina embrace me, I embrace her back, I hold her, I squeeze her, clutching each other, we fall to the side, we're lying on the dry leaves, our tears are flowing—we're alive.

37

IT'S OCTOBER 24, GRANDFATHER'S BIRTHDAY. Grandmother doesn't reveal how old Grandfather would have been, but she says that we're going to observe his birthday. At midnight, as if it were New Year's Eve, because this is her first celebration with me, and we won't be celebrating New Year's Eve.

From the radio, I hear a concert; it could be an operetta, because a subdued man's voice occasionally conveys in a whisper what's happening onstage; the audience frequently claps during the music, it's pretty irritating, but it's hard not to pay attention to it.

Grandmother is sitting next to the table with the damask tablecloth; she is playing solitaire. I look at the pendulum clock —it's only half past ten.

I don't know why we're doing this; ever since Grandmother read Grandfather's farewell letter, I haven't seen or heard him in the house even once. I want it to be midnight already, I want to go to sleep.

Grandmother quickly lays out the cards; they rustle between her fingers. Sometimes she stops, looks at the tablecloth, then continues, the cards clicking as she lays them on top of one another.

Now she's trying it for the third time, and I already know she won't win. She runs out of cards. Grandmother looks at the columns of cards, then she blows the air out of her mouth once, gathers up the pack, shuffles the cards. I sense that she's looking at me, but I don't look back at her, I'm looking at the clock, at the weights, in the shape of pinecones, dangling at the ends of the chains.

She doesn't deal out the cards again but puts the pack on the table, goes over to the radio, and turns it off.

Again she looks at me. She says that she knows that I'm angry at her. I chose to stay here, but still, I'm angry at her.

I bite my lip; I don't answer. I want her to leave me alone, I want to go into my room to read. Or to sleep, or even just to think. What do I know?

Grandmother says if only she knew how much time we have left together.

I say nothing to that.

She waits for a little bit, then she asks me to go into the living room and bring the green kerosene lamp from the bureau.

For a moment I think that I'm not going to do it, but in the end I get up.

The glass in the kerosene lamp is placed at the wrong angle; as I lift it, it wobbles, nearly falling out, but I catch it at the very last second.

When I come back into the kitchen, Grandmother has placed a small wooden box on the table, next to the porcelain washbasin. She takes the glass out of the lamp, lights the wick, puts the washbasin in my hands, and tells me to go outside and gather three handfuls of pine needles from the tree.

I go outside without even putting on my coat. Everything is clear in the moonlight; I can see the pattern at the bottom of the

washbasin, the three black roosters chasing each other, and if I
wanted to, I could even count the number of feathers on their
wings. The long pine needles prick my hands; they break off
from the branch with short sharp sounds. I toss the pine needles
into the washbasin; I look up at the moon, at the stars; I look at
the Big Dipper, and I think about the rings of Saturn.

I hear movement in the garden, I look over—a white cat is
standing in the grass, looking at me; I see its face in the moonlight. I bare my teeth and meow, loudly, angrily, as if I were a
cat too; the cat meows back at me, its eyes flash green, and it
disappears among the bushes. I place the washbasin back under
my arm and return to the kitchen.

Grandmother asks me if I saw anything or anyone while I
was outside.

I shake my head.

Grandmother nods, motions for me to put the basin on the
table, pours cold water onto the pine needles; it makes splashing
sounds as she mixes it, the needles dance topsy-turvy in the
water. Then she puts a steaming mug into my hand, saying that
it's hot punch and I should drink it, it was one of Grandfather's
favorite drinks. It has such a lovely fragrance that I can't bear
it, I must taste it. It's sweet, with a rum taste, smooth like silk.
I drink it in large gulps; it warms me up.

Grandmother opens the wooden box; it's filled with painted
lead soldiers. At first I think they're all the same, but then I
see that I'm wrong, no two are the same, each one is standing
differently, each one holds his arms differently, some of them
are holding weapons, others just stand there, and their faces are
different too; some of them are young and some are old.

Grandmother says, They're beautiful, aren't they?

I nod. I'm looking at one figure with his sword drawn; he's
smiling defiantly, he's very young, almost a child still, his lips
are very red.

Grandmother tells me that Grandfather made the soldiers,

and he could reenact the entire revolutionary war of 1848 with them, that was one of his favorite pastimes, he used to play with Mr. Pali, and they always ended up fighting over it.

She picks up a beaked ladle and dips it into the box, and I see that three soldiers have already ended up in the ladle. I ask her what she's doing, and Grandmother says, You'll see in just a moment. She screws the wick on the kerosene lamp higher, then holds the ladle into the flame.

I cry out for her not to do that, but Grandmother says, Too late. Smoke is rising from the spoon, the paint is sizzling, burning off the soldiers, then they begin to melt; they slowly run together; at first their legs melt, then their arms, then their faces lose their contours, and their heads also become deformed. Their bodies retain their shape longer, then they too start to melt; the three soldiers are now nothing more than three black pebbles, then the pebbles run together, they melt together, and the spoon is half filled with gray molten lead. Grandmother moves it in a circle above the flame; the burning lead, like a whirlpool, climbs up the inner wall of the spoon.

Grandmother says now we can know what the future will bring. Or if it will bring anything at all. She leans above the spoon, deeply inhales the lead vapors, then raises the spoon above the washbasin.

She tips the lead into the washbasin, pouring it out slowly; as it drips down, it looks much clearer than it was in the spoon, something like molten silver. Hissing, it spills into the water; a pine-scented vapor arises from the washbasin. Grandmother leans over the basin; I see that she wants to reach into it, but her hand stops above the water. She clutches the table as if she's suddenly grown dizzy; fear flashes across her face, then anger; with two hands she grabs the washbasin, lifts it up, and dashes it to the ground. The basin shatters into fragments; the old rug and the floor are covered with water. I look down; between the pieces of porcelain there are the hardened pieces of lead, they create the image of a grinning cat's face, with a couple of pine needles adhering to them like whiskers.

Grandmother steps over, bends down, picks up some of the porcelain fragments, puts them into her palm, presses them together, and says, Damn your wildcat stubbornness, why didn't you tell me what you saw?

I shrug my shoulders, and I say, Just because.

Grandmother asks, What color was it?

It was white, I say.

Grandmother says the winter will be hard and long.

We wipe the floor; we gather up the pine needles and the pieces of the washbasin. Of the three roosters, only one has remained whole, on a long diamond-shaped porcelain shard; just as I'm about to throw the pieces of the washbasin into the dustbin, Grandmother takes it from the dustpan, draws her nail along the shard's edge. I know what she's thinking; I grab it out of her hand, and I say, Happy birthday, then I throw it into the garbage.

Grandmother winces, and she sighs once.

NOT EVEN A WEEK HAS gone by, and we wake up to snowfall. As we're eating breakfast, Grandmother puts a pair of Norwegian-patterned knit gloves next to my plate, saying that I'll need them.

After breakfast I go out into the yard to try out my new gloves. They are a different kind of gloves; I've never had a pair like this before. They look like mittens, but you can pull the front part back, and they become regular five-fingered gloves, but without the tips covered.

A lot of snow fell during the night; the entire courtyard is covered in snow, the trees, the hedge, the woodshed. Nothing is moving in the garden; only the chickadees are rummaging in the lower branches of the walnut tree. They weren't here yesterday; the snow brought them as well, I think.

Beneath the four pine trees there is much less snow than elsewhere, just a few centimeters, probably blown there by the wind. The lower branches of the pine trees are missing, you can easily stroll under them. The branches were sawed off by Grandfather; they've never dried out properly, often resin drips from the end of their stumps.

I'm standing beneath the pine trees, I don't want to walk all over the freshly fallen snow. I bend down and try to make a snowball, but the snow is still too powdery, it doesn't stick together. I press the snow in my two gloved hands, compacting it, pressing hard so it will stick together, then I turn and throw the snowball at the woodshed —it falls apart, as if I had sprinkled snow into the air.

I crouch down, but I don't try to make a new snowball; instead, I press my two fists into the snow, leaving two round marks. I pull back the top part of my mittens, turning them into gloves; I place the tips of my bare fingers next to the circles I made, forming bear paws. I pull my fingers out of the snow so that the tips of the bear claws will be clearly visible. Fresh bear prints; the bear might have passed by here just a few minutes ago. I turn my gloves back into mittens, and I draw the bear's back paws in the snow as well. They're bigger than the front paws; this could be a big old bear. I'm thinking about why it came out of its cave when suddenly I realize that I'm being watched.

Somehow the silence became heavier. I look in the direction of the walnut tree; the branches are unmoving, all the chickadees hidden away somewhere.

As I turn my back to the pine trees, I see something out of the corner of my eye, someone standing behind the trunk of the third tree—but no, no one's there. I walk right up to the tree, stand next to the trunk; on one of the sawed-off branch stumps a large drop of resin is shining. I don't remember it being there when I came out today. I lean in closer, I inhale the fragrance of the resin, I notice the delicate whirlpool-like creases on its surface, and I know what this is, it's a fingerprint. It looks like somebody has just pressed his thumb into the fresh drop of resin.

I take my hand out of the glove to press my thumb onto the drop of resin. Not the thumb that had the scar on it, the other one. The resin is cold and smooth and very hard; the tip of my nail hardly leaves a trace on it.

Once again, out of the corner of my eye, I see movement, but now I don't turn in that direction with my entire body, I only glance over, and then very slowly I move my head. Behind the fourth pine tree, Grandfather is standing, I can just make out his outline, he's as transparent as the vapor of my own breath.

I turn to him very slowly, I don't want him to disappear. I don't even look directly at him; instead, I look at the trunk of the tree, at the end of one of the sawed-off branches there is also a large drop of resin.

Now I see him clearly—the faint glow of a white human shape—and I sense him looking at me.

My mouth goes dry, but still I speak, and I ask, Well, Grandfather, you haven't left after all?

In that moment the faint glow disappears, the pine tree makes a loud cracking sound, the snow heavily breaks off from one of the branches, and in the whirling snow, his form is clearly delineated: he's wearing a long winter coat and his fur cap with the earflaps pulled down. I see his profile, his glasses too, as he raises his hand and motions for me to follow him, and I see as he turns and starts off toward the end of the garden.

He walks quickly, leaving no footprints, but from the crunching of the snow I can tell where he's going; I follow him. We go to the back of the garden, out beside the flower bed, all the way up to the wire fence, to the yew trees flattened out by the snow.

As I get over there, I see that one branch is bent down in such a way that it has pushed the reed-woven fence all the way to the ground; now you can cross over it.

Beyond the fence, there is the cemetery.

I stand still.

The crunching of the snow grows fainter and fainter; I call after Grandfather, tell him to wait; I pull up the bottom of my coat, I step across the fence, and at one point the reed trellis caves in beneath my heel as I step over it, but the wire netting holds up, and I'm in the cemetery.

I don't even look around; I quickly follow the sounds of the crunching snow. Grandfather leads me among the gravestones covered in snow; on the statues of the saints and angels there are thick snow collars and hats, and as I follow Grandfather, the sun suddenly begins to shine.

In that moment there is complete silence; I no longer hear his steps coming from anywhere. I stop, looking at the glimmering snow, sparkling so much in the light that I have to squint.

Something moves between the gravestones, shining crimson — it's a fox. It's very close, crouching down as if it is watching something, then it jumps once, sinks deep into the snow, rolls around in the snow to get out, then shakes the snow off, stretches out long, crouches down, then jumps into the snow again; it's playing at hunting.

Slowly, I crouch down, I look at it; I've grown completely warm, my face is burning.

The fox suddenly turns toward me, it watches me with its head tilted, looking at me from the side; it seems to be smiling, its eyes glitter like resin.

I look at the fox, and I smile; I speak to it, I say, Hello. I see clearly as the fox nods once, then turns away, and like a crimson streak it disappears among the gravestones.

I stand up, looking at its paw prints. I think of how it jumped out of the snow; laughter bursts out of me, I bend down, I place my hands between its paw prints, then for a moment I touch my face to the snow.

GRANDMOTHER COMES OUT OF THE larder with a large package wrapped in tissue paper and tied up with string; she puts it on the table in front of me. She brought it down from the attic, she says; if it's really going to be a hard winter, I'll end up freezing in that thin little coat of mine.

The tissue paper rustles as Grandmother pushes the package toward me on the oilcloth; it clatters as if there are many tiny beetle legs scraping from inside. It's wrapped up tightly with the twine; I can't imagine what could be in it.

Grandmother tells me to unwrap the package, what am I waiting for.

I decide that no matter what it is, I won't take it.

I reach over, place the palm of my hand on the tissue paper; it rustles softly, and now I know what's inside; I press my hand down on it, the package compresses inward, yielding; strands of fur pierce through the paper, reach the skin of my hand.

It's a nauseating sensation. I pull my hand away, the paper springs back, the knot in the string becomes undone, the tissue paper opens; with a swishing sound the package comes undone, sprawling out on the table.

In the center of the tissue paper there is a rolled-up fur coat. It's not fox fur, it's much darker and more luminous than that, and it's tied with two wide black ribbons.

I have to reach over and touch it. I untie one of the ribbons, then the other; the paper crackles as the coat slowly unfurls across the table. The fur is so luminous that it almost seems liquid; the lining is made of black silk, it rustles as I touch it. It's as if it is shaking me; I feel an electric current running through my lower arm, like I've suddenly hit my elbow on something.

I want to pull my hand away, but I can't, I have to plunge my fingers into the fur. I grasp it, then I spread my fingers apart; I caress the coat, it tickles my skin, it's cool and smooth, I can't let it go, I run my fingers along it again and yet again.

I think of Krisztina, of how she stood in front of the whole class in her brand-new fox-fur coat that she got for her birthday; I think of how she turned on her heel, and the fur coat whirled all around her, crimson like embers. I wanted to turn away so I wouldn't have to look at it, but I couldn't take my eyes off her, I had to watch as it undulated around her; I heard the other girls cry out, Oh, that's classy, oh, it's so beautiful, fantastic, amazing, like a dream, I saw how they ran over to Krisztina and surrounded her, how they grabbed her coat, how they kept touching it and caressing the fur, and the whole time they cried about how beautiful, how smooth, how warm it was.

It's as if my hand isn't my own; it caresses the coat, slowly, with long languorous movements. The coat moves under my touch, its sleeves and collar unfold; once again I run my hands all along it; the bottom hem also unfolds onto the tissue paper, it's very long, it nearly hangs off the table. Its color is like the walnut cupboard door when the sun shines on it, at once a deep brown and a dark amber.

Grandmother says that it's not fox fur, it's much rarer and more beautiful than that, much more elegant and nobler. It's mink, real mink; I should try it on, what am I waiting for, she wants to see how it looks on me.

The coat shifts as if it were moving by itself, as if it weren't me holding the shoulders, as if it weren't me lifting it up carefully from the paper. The fur rustles; it scares me, I think for a moment that moths are going to fly out, an entire cloud of moths, and as I think that, something actually moves at the roots of the fur; it rustles and swishes. I feel the cold running across my arm; I want to throw the coat down, push it away, I don't need it, I never needed it, and as I have that thought, my nose is filled with the thick scent of lavender. It's a strong wild fragrance, I feel it in my throat. I shake out the coat; the scent is even stronger, dried lavender flowers start spinning out of it; rustling, they fall onto the tissue paper, gathering beneath the coat.

Very good, says Grandmother, I should shake it out well. She is standing there next to me, with the red-handled goat's-hair brush in her hand; as she pulls it along the fur, even more lavender flowers fall out, the smell of lavender is now unbearably strong, I know it's going to give me a headache, but I don't care, I inhale it deeply, the lilac grains of lavender flowers sit in the creases of the tissue paper.

It takes a long time to brush out the coat. After a while, Grandmother puts down the brush, and she says that was necessary, look at how beautifully it shines, the coat is in perfect shape, not at all the worse for time, lavender is a thousand times better than mothballs. Now I can put it on, she says.

I take the lapels of the coat and I open it; the black silk lining shines like fresh tar, it rustles as the back of my hand slides along it and I thrust my arm into the sleeve; even through my nightgown I can feel the coolness of the silk around my arm. Grandmother takes the other shoulder of the coat and helps me with the other sleeve, the silk, rustling, surrounds me, I pull the coat around myself, the coldness of the attic emanating from it.

Grandmother says that what's good about fur is that first it cools us down when we put it on in a warm room and then, when we go into the cold, it warms us up. She takes a step back, looks me up and down, and she says it's a little long, but otherwise it's as if it was made for me, and even like this it's good, because I'll be able to wear it for years, I should take a look, she says, and see how beautiful I am in it, I won't even recognize myself. As she says this, she is already pulling me along; we go into the vestibule. Next to the coat rack there is the long mirror; she pushes me forward and turns on the light.

It's not me there, there's a real young woman, a grown woman. I look at myself; the coat falls smoothly down my chest and my stomach and my waist, it really fits me well; it also changes my face. I look more severe and mysterious. I smile at myself, and my smile is more aloof. I look down; my nightgown is hanging below the coat, and from the lace trim at the bottom and the slippers on my feet, I know that it's still me.

I put a hand on one hip and turn to the side; the fur moves on me as if it were alive, as if it were part of me. My hand slips into one of the pockets—until now I didn't even notice that it had pockets, but it does, and there's something in the pocket, something round and flat like a pebble. I take it out and look at it; it's a tiny white porcelain jar with an animal wearing a brown fur coat drawn on its lid; it has a long neck, a pointy face, two black-button eyes; its nose pokes forward as if it were sniffing my hand. I've never seen an animal like this before, but I know that it can only be a mink.

Grandmother takes my hand, clasps her hand around the jar, and says, Oh, but how good that this is here too; she reaches between my fingers and flicks open the cover. I look down, and in the jar there is a thick, greasy, pink ointment. I want to ask what it is, but Grandmother speaks before that. She says that it's mink oil mixed with rouge and rosewater and a bunch of other things. She sticks her index finger into it and takes out a bit. She says this is the best face cream in the whole world, it makes everything blossom and look more beautiful, just watch, it'll be good for me too.

I know what's going to happen. I want to tell her not to do it, but her fingers are already touching my skin, and she is already rubbing in the cream. I see Grandmother's smile in the mirror, I know that my skin will absorb the cream, and then the fur coat will squeeze around me, it will cling to my body, it will cover my hands and my legs, my face too, I will become a black-eyed mink; I will run across the vestibule, I will jump onto the door handle, opening it, then I'll run out into the garden, up the trunk of the walnut tree, along the branches, across the fence, then I'll zigzag through the graves all the way along the cemetery, go across the collapsed fence in the back, then across the meadow to the forest, then even farther away, away from here, far away, far away; my thighs are tense, I wait for it to start.

I close my eyes, I clasp my fingers around the jar. My feet are moving in the slippers, I feel the running beginning in the soles of my feet.

WE'RE UPSTAIRS IN THE TURRET room for our drawing club. We're waiting for the drawing teacher. He's not usually late. The drawing tables have been placed in a half circle, and where there'd usually be a small table with a still-life arrangement and draperies, there's just a chair. The small table has been pushed into the corner next to the coat rack; on the table there is a plate with some brown apple cores on it, a couple of geometrical forms, a pair of tailor's scissors, and crumpled drapery.

We're waiting, everyone is quiet. I turn to the side, and I look at the large latticed window, the gray sky divided into oblong pieces. In two panes, the glass is missing, in one it's been replaced by chipboard, in the other there is a piece of plastic.

The sky is empty; very far away a tiny black dot is moving, it must be a bird.

The door opens, the drawing teacher comes in, we all push our chairs back and stand up.

There is a young woman with the drawing teacher; they both come in and stand there. The woman is wearing jeans, low-heeled ankle boots, and a red-and-black-plaid shirt with the sleeves rolled up. Her hair is in a ponytail; on one of her wrists there is a large black-and-white plastic bangle.

The drawing teacher motions for us to sit down. He says

that as we can see, he has brought a guest, this young lady is a professional artist's model. She's here because she's going to model for us. The time has come for us to draw a nude.

Suddenly, there is a great silence. I look at the woman, at her almond-colored eyes, her strong bone structure; she's not looking at us but staring off somewhere above us.

One of the boys begins to snicker and chortle, then all the boys laugh, then the girls too.

The drawing teacher goes over to the chair, picks it up, and slams its four legs on the ground, making a great clattering sound. Quiet! he yells.

He says: Only those who can look behind things can draw them properly—and the best teacher for this is nudity. We are not going to be concerned here with seeing a naked person; instead, we will look at the body, the anatomy, at how the muscles cling to the bones, how they are delineated beneath the skin. But whoever doesn't have enough courage for this may certainly leave.

Iza pushes back her chair, her face is red; her head bent down, she quickly leaves the room. No one else moves, everyone is looking at the woman.

She stands there motionless, still looking somewhere above us as if she weren't even there, then she takes the hairband out of her ponytail. Her hair is good and long.

The drawing teacher says, If you please, and he places the chair next to the woman.

The woman kicks off her boots, unbuttons her shirt—she isn't wearing a bra, she has small pointy breasts—she pushes down her jeans and underwear; she's very skinny, you can see her ribs, her bottom is very bony too. She's standing next to the chair completely naked, looking somewhere above us; everyone is staring at her cunt, and I am too, she has thick, curly, black hair.

The drawing teacher asks her to pose sitting in profile.

The model goes to the chair, sits down, folds one leg beneath her bottom, rests her other foot on the ground; she leans
back in the chair, the arm with the bangle hangs down from the
back of the chair; she rests her other hand on her thigh. Her
hair falls into her face and her eyes, covers up one of her breasts.

The drawing teacher says this is a difficult position, not
easy even for a professional, but still, we should try to do something with it. He knows that we're embarrassed, but this will
pass. We should look at her and not be ashamed; a body is just a
body and nothing more.

He says that today, unusually, he's going to draw with us.
He sits down on the windowsill and rests a drawing board on
his lap.

I look at her; a body is just a body, that's what I want to
think, but I can't think that, because I've never seen the naked body of a stranger before, I never even saw Mother naked
that often, and Grandmother only one time, when she was taking a shower; I'm thinking of the boys and what they could be
feeling; I look at the woman's stomach, I see the fuzzy down,
a pale black stripe that runs all the way down from her belly
button.

I look at her, she's motionless, stiller than a statue, maybe
she isn't breathing, maybe her ribs aren't moving. I place the
piece of charcoal onto the paper; it's obvious I won't be able to
draw anything. Especially here, in front of the others.

I think about how she sits there, unbothered by people
looking at her, and wonder what she's thinking about. I look
at her foot dangling from beneath her bottom, she has a very
skinny foot, the second toe is longer than the big toe and is a
bit crooked.

I look at the contours of her breasts, at her rib cage, the hair
standing out in tufts from beneath her arms. No, I won't be able
to draw her, this is not possible to draw, I'm not even going to

try. Iza was right, she did the right thing by leaving, I should have gotten up and left as well.

SUDDENLY THE DOOR BURSTS OPEN; it's almost ripped out of the door frame—it's the librarian. She tears into the atelier, an expression of both shock and derision on her face.

When she sees the model, she stops; she starts back for a moment, sucks in her breath, unable to speak or move; she stands there as if she too were modeling for us, then she looks at the drawing teacher, and, gasping, the curses break out of her—You filthy pig, you, she screams, aren't you ashamed of yourself?

The model doesn't move, she doesn't even look at her, she holds her head the same way she has been holding it.

The drawing teacher jumps down from the windowsill, looks at us. Leave, quickly, he says.

We all stand up, but the librarian is between us and the door, and no one dares pass by her.

The drawing teacher takes a step toward the librarian. Anka, my darling, he says. Don't make a scene, he says. The two of us can discuss this later.

The librarian shakes her head. I did everything for you, she shrieks, everything that you ever asked me to, but you needed this Gypsy whore! Aren't you ashamed of yourself?

The model then moves, throwing back her head. You're the whore, and whoever made you, your whole family, she says, her hair rippling, covering her breasts.

The librarian looks at her. What did you say, you piece of trash, what? You toss your hair, you show the children your cunt for money, I'll show you who's the whore! She grabs the tailor's scissors from the table. I'll shear you bald, you stupid little cunt, she shrieks; she runs at the model, clutches at her hair; the woman jumps away from her, grabs the chair. The drawing teacher stands between them. Anka, please be so kind, I'm asking you, he says as he grabs her wrist. Anka, don't do this, he says again.

The librarian takes a step back, pulls her hand away, looks at the woman. I'm the idiot, because I believed you, she says.

She takes another step back, half turns, looks toward the door, then suddenly twists around. She holds the scissors up to her head and begins to chop off her own hair; the scissors clatter frantically, her hair flying all over the place, she's scratching the skin of her scalp everywhere, it's bleeding. The model shrieks loudly, the drawing teacher runs over to her. My God, Anka, what are you doing? he says; he grabs the drapery, presses it down onto the librarian's head, puts his arm around her, and pulls her away from the door, then he looks at us and motions toward the door with his head.

At once we all run out of the atelier, down the hallway, down the steps. I'm the fastest one, I leave everyone behind, I don't stop till I get to the girls' bathroom; I stand in front of the sink and turn on the faucet, and with two hands I splash ice-cold water onto my face.

38

WE'RE GOING TO BE TAKING an exam on equations with two unknowns; last time I did very badly, so now I must practice. I take out the book of math exercises, open my notebook, and on the last blank page I begin to work out the problems; the main thing is that I must think only of numbers, of numbers and formulas, nothing else. It's very hard to pay attention to this, very hard to concentrate. The teacher said that I ruin it by holding the pencil as if I wanted to draw, and that's also how I write out the examples, as if I didn't want to be writing out the examples but was getting ready to do something else. I should realize that there is nothing else behind the numbers—only the blank sheet of paper.

I made up an exercise for myself as a form of punishment. Every time I notice that I'm thinking of something else, not paying attention to the numbers, I will take a fresh sheet of paper and I will begin to write the formulas, one after the other. I'll write that a plus b to the second power equals a squared plus two times ab plus b squared, and then I'll write that a plus b times a minus b equals a squared minus b squared, and so on. I'll write out each formula, one after the other, and yet, it's very hard to concentrate because this is very boring. I don't want to think that this has no meaning, but I do, because I know it's the truth, that I'm never going to do anything with this rotten algebra in my life, all it's good for is making my head hurt. I start from the beginning again, turn over a new page, and write out new equations.

I feel like I've been doing this for two hours already when Grandmother comes in; she's carrying apple slices on a small plate with nuts and honey. When she sees that I'm studying hard, she brings me something sweet to eat, quince jelly or dark chocolate or roasted sugar-coated hazelnuts; she says it will give me energy.

Before she puts down the small plate, she sees the formulas written one beneath the other. The nuts clatter on the plate because it's trembling in her hand; her face changes too, I can tell she's thinking of Miklós and Bertuka. She hasn't told me the end of the story yet. Suddenly I want her not to leave, I want her to stay and tell me, to tell me right now. At the same time, it's possible I'm not really that curious about it, I just want her to stay here so that I won't have to study, and that makes me feel ashamed of myself. Grandmother puts down the plate and looks at me; I don't want her to know what I'm thinking, so I look away and quickly reach for the plate; I break half a walnut in two, dip it into the honey, put it in my mouth, and chew on it, but the walnut is stale, it has a moldy taste, the honey doesn't even cancel it out.

Grandmother asks who am I trying to fool, her or myself? That makes the taste of mold in my mouth even stronger. I shake my head; I can't speak. Grandmother dips a slice of apple into the honey, and she says there's no point in overcomplicating matters, math is boring, and the job of all stories is, eventually, to come to an end. She holds an apple slice in front of my mouth. Yum-yum! she says, as if I were a little girl. I bite the end of the apple slice; its fresh, tart taste spreads through my mouth.

Grandmother picks up the other half of the walnut, dips it into the honey, and eats it, not wincing. She motions for me to close the notebook, sits down on my bed, pulls up her legs, and leans back against the wall covering. She begins to speak.

YOU AWAKEN AT THE ROOSTERS' first crow, and your first thought is you cannot be waking up, because you never fell asleep, not on this night, you were awake the entire night, perched on the small chair beneath the window, you were waiting for something to happen because Bertuka told you this was to be their last evening here, that somebody was going to be taking them across the border in exchange for the necklace.

You embraced her, and you bade her farewell; that evening, as she'd asked you to, you didn't fully lock the big courtyard doors, but you couldn't lie down and you didn't even want to, you wanted to see them as they left, or if you didn't see them, you wanted to at least hear them, or if you couldn't hear them, you wanted to at least know.

You sat in the dark and you waited, you observed the rhythm of your own breath, you thought of the darkness in the woodshed, you imagined you were in there with them, you imagined that you were leaving with them.

You sat and you waited, and you tried not to think of anything, and you don't remember falling asleep at all, you only remember waking up, and the crowing of the roosters, which could also have been a dream.

Your back is hurting, it's hard to stand up, outside dawn is breaking, everything is gray, then suddenly the street is filled with rose-colored light, the sky, the world, it's so strong it shines through the curtains into the room; for a moment everything is nauseatingly, dizzyingly rose-colored, this can hardly be real, this is just a dream, but you didn't fall asleep, you had to stay awake until dawn because you vowed to yourself that you were going to sit up the entire night,

*and you were going to repeat the prime numbers to yourself, just as
when you sat vigil for Miklós to be healed. You want to think about the
numbers, you want to think about which number you stopped at and
what you wished for as you whispered it, but nothing comes to mind,
not a single number, not a single thought.*

*You stand in the improbable rose-colored light, and you know for
certain that you're still sleeping, this awakening is only a dream, the
crowing of the roosters is only a dream, the dawn light is only a dream,
just as the cold sweat is, and the dread inundating you, all you can
think about is that you can't fall asleep, you never should have fallen
asleep, you have to wake up, you really have to wake up now, you have
to wake up at any cost.*

*Then from outside you hear a deafening thundering; no, it's not
outside, it's inside, it's in your ears, in your head, in your throat, and
in your spine, it sends you flying from the chair, it throws you against
the wall, it slams you down on the floor, kicks you in the stomach, grabs
your arm, and yanks you off the ground, it punches your face, pulls you
by the hair, drags you along the ground, and, screaming, it asks: Where
are they, where did you hide them, where have you put them, what did
you do with them?— it hits and kicks and slaps and yanks you around,
but you can't answer, can't even yell or cry out, the air has turned into
crystallized honey, liquid glass.*

*You know it's happening, and you don't know, it's a man in a
uniform yelling, he's hitting you, pulling you, he's kicking you, you feel
no pain, you feel only that your body is becoming brittle and more frail,
you are made of black glass, in a moment you're going to shatter into
fragments, you look at yourself and you don't recognize who this is: it's
not you that's being dragged across the floor, it's not your nightgown
that's slipping up, is not your pale legs that are frantically sawing the
air, is not your foot that is getting stuck in the small carpet and pulling
it along a few steps, it's not your spine that's being forced into an arch,
it's not your head being beaten against the door frame.*

*No, the person who they are dragging along the hallway, it's not
you, this isn't happening to you, it's not even happening, you're just*

imagining it, you're just dreaming it, it's not your nose that blood is flowing from, it's not your scalp that hair is being ripped from in clumps, it's not you falling across the threshold, it's not you plunging down the three concrete steps onto the stones of the courtyard, it's not your skin that is scraping against the edges of the stones, it's not you who is shrieking, it's not you who is yelling for him to let you go, leave you alone, go away, it's not you who is being kicked in the kidneys, it's not you who is being thrown to your knees, no and no, it isn't you, this is someone else, it's not happening to you, it's all happening to someone else.

You think all of this until you see Papa and Mama. There they are, kneeling by the base of the firewall, next to the flower bed, among the trampled-down plantain lilies; when you see their faces, you know that this is no dream, this is reality, and that's making you reel more than any of the blows. The man in the uniform lets go of you, he's standing in front of Father, screaming, he's asking him something, he jerks his head toward you, Papa's face contorts, you haven't seen this expression on his face since he had the stroke, even the paralyzed left half of his face is convulsing, Papa is saying, Leave the little girl alone, she has nothing to do with this, she's still a child, the man in the uniform yells at him to answer his question, he slaps him at the same time, the blow slides down and hits Papa's neck, his head jerks to one side, the man in the uniform yells again, Where did you hide them? Papa's face is filled with rage, bloody spittle drips down from the side of his mouth; What do you take me for, you piece of filth, how many times have I told you that I haven't hidden anyone, especially not any stinking Jews, you've got the wrong address, do you realize who you're talking to. He grabs one of the trampled-down slats from the flowers, it still has the green ornamental glass ball at the end, Papa begins to beat the thigh of the man in the uniform with the slat wildly, the glass ball breaks into shards. Take that! he yells. Take that, take that! — the slat also breaks, and Papa tries to get up; he can't; all this time Mama has been crying and whimpering, but now, sobbing, she shrieks, The poor man is ill, can't you see he's ill, can't you leave us alone, can't you understand you've got the wrong address?

You try to get up, you want to say that there's no one here, there's no one here, and there never was anyone here, then you recall that you've heard Mama speaking in that whimpering voice only once before, when, during lunch one day, Papa announced that he was retiring, and Mama asked in that same whimpering voice: What will become of us now? Papa slammed his fork down on the table and said, Enough of this peasant mentality. But you don't want to think about this, you want to think about the strength of lies, about what Miklós told you once about lies, that you have to tell a lie as if it were true, because then it will be true, and you see the man in the uniform grab Papa's hair, pull him up from the ground, press the pistol to his forehead: I'm asking you for the last time, he says, his voice is tender, almost endearing.

You get up, and you scream, Please don't hurt him, please don't hurt poor Father! These aren't your words, this isn't what you wanted to say, your voice is sharp, you say again, Don't hurt them. You're asking nicely, please, don't hurt Papa or Mama, they know nothing about it, they can't do anything about it, it's not them he should be attacking but you.

The man in the uniform looks at you, he licks his mouth, then you notice how young he is, maybe not even twenty years old, he still has the face of an adolescent. I'm counting to three, he says, motioning with his head.

Papa's eyes are gray and empty, he looks at you as he never has before, as if he didn't know, as if he doesn't want to believe what he's hearing; you think of Bertuka, of Miklós, of Bátykó, you think about how they're not here anymore, they can't be here, they shouldn't be here, the mouth of the man in the uniform doesn't move, but you know that he's counting to himself—One, two—you raise your arm, you point at the woodshed, and you say they were here, yes, you were hiding them all by yourself, no one else knew about it, they were here, but now they've gone, they're no longer here, and you have no idea where they went.

The face of the man in the uniform doesn't change, there's no trace of anger in his expression, no trace of anything; he sighs once lightly and he shoots Papa in the forehead, the thundering sound is louder than anything else; on Papa's forehead there's a black splotch, then the blood begins to gush out, crimson, the man in the uniform lets go of Papa's hair, Papa falls into the flower bed, the man in the uniform steps over to you, he grips your hair, he yanks you up, he says something, you can't hear, nothing but that thundering sound rattles in your brain, it's going to make it burst, make it explode, the pistol in the man's hand swings toward you, now it's your turn, you know that now it's your turn, let it explode, let it burst, everything is swirling around you, but then you see Mama screaming, jumping up, she's trying to grab the arm of the man in the uniform, but she can't, because the man in the uniform drags you away, and simultaneously, with a bored, slow movement, he turns the pistol on Mama, you don't even hear the detonation, you only feel it in your stomach, Mama falls to the ground, but this you don't even see, because the man in the uniform pulls hard on your hair, and he pulls-pulls-pulls you toward the woodshed.

The door to the woodshed is open, it's flung wide open, the woodshed is empty, although not completely, because among the overturned piles of wood, there is the overturned grain chest, all of the walnuts have spilled out of it, next to the wooden grain chest there is a clay statue like the one that you saw at Bertuka's house in the attic. You look at the walnuts spilled on the floor, you think that they're not here, they really left, they really and truly left, the man in the uniform says there's no one here, there's no one here and there never was anyone here, don't lie to him, there's no one here, just that damn statue, and as he says this he shoots into the statue; a black hole opens up in the clay on its chest, but nothing else happens. You know that now it's really your turn, now you will be next, you see his weapon moving; move already, you want it to move, you want to wish for that, but no, that's not what you want, you want the sky, you don't want to die here inside, you want to see the sky one last time, you want to see the walnut tree as the wind blows through its branches, this can't be true, you don't want to die, you don't want to die at all, you want to live, to breathe. The barrel of the pistol is rising, you turn your head away, you look at the grain chest, at the spilled walnuts, the pistol's detonations are still echoing in your head, and then in the middle of the walnuts you see something white, it's a white pebble with a piece of red yarn tied onto it, you know what that is, it belongs to Bertuka, the whole skein of yarn had been wound around that.

You feel your arm moving, you're going to point over there, point to the stone just as you pointed to the woodshed, you're going to cry out that yes, yes, they were here, you don't want to, you can't, you wish you hadn't seen it, and yet your arm moves, it points to the pebble; the man in the uniform sees it, he lets go of your shoulder, he steps in front of you, you grab after him but can't reach, he's already standing there amid the spilled walnuts, he bends down and he grabs the pebble, and as he lifts it up, the piece of yarn tied onto it rises from the ground, a black line remaining in its place. From beneath the earth there is a murmuring sound, no, not from beneath the earth, but from the clay man, you see it moving, and with three resounding steps he's suddenly right next to the man in the uniform; he grabs him, lifts him, he wants to throw him away, but then there's a cracking sound, and the earth beneath them opens up, no, that isn't what happens, the floorboard underneath them collapses, you see how it's plastered over with branches and earth, and below that there's a large ditch, and in the ditch are all three of them— Miklós and Bertuka and Bátykó. The clay man lets go of the man in the uniform and gestures frantically at the edge of the ditch, the man in the uniform curses once, the pistol in his hand swings around, now it's trained on Bertuka, then Bátykó jumps in front of Bertuka, the pistol thunders out, the shot hits Bátykó in the stomach, and through the echo of the detonation you hear a thunderous roar bursting out of the clay man's body; with one great blow he sends the uniformed man flying into the ditch, then he breaks into two parts and falls into the ditch, he falls right onto Miklós, you see as he collapses into dust, burying Miklós, you see the man in the uniform on all fours looking for his pistol, you see as he finds it, you see as he aims the revolver at Bertuka and shoots, you see as Bertuka hurls herself at him,

*stabbing her knitting needle into his throat, but you don't care, you only
care about Miklós, you jump into the ditch, the clay that has collapsed
into dust half swallows you up, you cry out Miklós's name, you reach
into the splintery earth looking for his hand, you're going to find it
and you're going to pull him out, but you don't find it, you look and
you look but you don't find it, then once again fingers are clasping your
wrist, squeezing it, grabbing it, you too are grabbing, you pull and
you hold, it's not Miklós, it's Bátykó, he's lying on the ground in front
of you, everything around him is black and covered in blood, he holds
your hand with two hands, he speaks, gurgling, but you understand all
the same; he says, This wasn't good for anything; he looks off beside
you, his face is empty, then somehow he looks at you again, and he says,
At least you remain alive; he says that nothing of his has remained, but
whatever he has, he gives it all to you, here, take it. As he says this his
face contorts in pain, his teeth clench; you want to pull your hand away
but you can't, he's squeezing it tightly, and then you feel that there is
something in the palm of your hand, a sharp cold stone, a small burning ember, you can't decide what it is, but your hand is no longer a human hand, your body is no longer a human body, you've changed, you
are an animal, you're a mole covered with bristles, and you don't want
anything, only to hide in the earth where you truly belong, you want
to dig, deeper and deeper, and already you're digging, you're digging
yourself into the earth, you're gouging the earth blindly, deeper and
deeper, down into the moist earth-scented darkness, down there where
no one will ever be able to find you again.*

GRANDMOTHER IS SILENT; ON HER face, it's as if all her
wrinkles have broken into shards. She swallows the air as if she
were choking, and she says, Maybe it was this way, but maybe it
wasn't. Maybe everything happened differently; perhaps it was
much simpler than this, perhaps all that happened was that at
the break of dawn soldiers came, and they went straight to the

woodshed, and behind the woodpile they found Bertuka and the others, and then they grabbed everyone out of bed, and they put everyone on the train where all the last residents of the brick-factory ghetto also ended up. Yes, maybe all that happened was that she wanted to hide her best girlfriend, and they caught her, and so she ended up in the concentration camp with her. And maybe she was the one to survive and not her girlfriend or her parents, only her, and maybe she was the only one to come back home out of all of them.

Grandmother gets up from the bed with difficulty; she clutches the headboard of the bed and the edge of the bureau. She looks at me, and she says maybe it was like that, maybe it wasn't, but no matter how hard she tries to remember, she cannot say which one was the truth.

She lets go of the bed's headboard, she stands there swaying, and she says that she never should have told me any of this. She never should have even started.

She takes a deep breath, lets go of the bureau, and sets off for the armchair; she moves like a small child who is just now learning how to walk — resolutely, clumsily. I stand up and say, Wait, I'll help you. She gets to the armchair, she tries to grab the arm, but she misses it; her legs crumple below her, and she falls to the ground.

I see she's in a really bad way. She reaches up with one hand, grabs the chair arm, tries to stand up, and can't.

I'm there beside her; I'll help you, I say. Grandmother looks at me and nods. I crouch down; holding her arm, I try to lift her up. She's very heavy; I can't move her. She clutches me, but even so, she can't get up. I try to lift her with all my strength, groaning with effort, but I can't. Grandmother groans as well.

I let go of her. I say that I'll call an ambulance.

Grandmother grabs my ankle. I tell her to let go, because I want to call an ambulance. Grandmother shakes her head, opens her mouth slowly, and speaks; her voice sounds completely different. She says something I can't understand; she says it again; her tongue moves very slowly, her speech is slowed. I speed it up in my head, and I understand what she's saying: I should reach into her pocket. I reach into it, there is her wallet with the clasp, she tells me to open it, at the bottom there's a key, I should take it out.

She tells me it's the key to the woodshed, I should go and open it up, on the wall there is a shovel, I should shovel into the earth near the cradle, and I'll find it, it's not buried too deep, the medicine is in there, I should go and bring it here. Quickly, quickly.

The wallet clasp claws at my wrist until it bleeds, but I take the key out; it's an ordinary yellow padlock key. I grab it, I run out of the room, across the kitchen, into the garden.

THE CLAY MAN WHOM GRANDMOTHER named Earth Bone is standing in front of the woodshed as I pass him; I wait for him to move and stand in front of me to bar my way, but nothing happens. The fallen snow sits on his head and shoulders, covers his face.

The padlock on the woodshed door opens easily, the door doesn't even creak; I go in and stand in the dark.

There on the wall is the shovel, I take it down, for a moment I stand there. I wait to see if the air in the woodshed fills with the sound of crying, but no, there is silence. I go to the cradle, I don't look at the doll, I drag the cradle over to one side; there is a bit of a cavity in the ground. I begin to dig, putting the blade of the shovel beneath my slipper; it cuts through the sole, but I don't bother with that, I dig.

There's a clanging sound beneath the shovel; I kneel down, scrape away the earth with two hands, grab it, and pull it out.

It's a large round cookie tin. I brush the earth off it. On the lid there is a heart painted in red.

I run, bringing it back to Grandmother. As I run, I hear something rattling loudly inside the cookie tin.

Grandmother is still lying in the same place; I kneel down next to her. She motions for me to open the tin.

It's hard to pry the lid off; I have to force my fingernail under it, and then it moves. Inside, there's a tiny bottle of medicine with a black lizard wrapped around it.

Grandmother leans up on her elbows, looks at the box; slowly she reaches over, grabs the bottle; the lizard's tail hangs down between her fingers. Grandmother holds it out to me and tells me to take it with both hands. Quickly. Quickly, quickly.

I grab it, it's cold; Grandmother clasps my fingers, whispers for me to squeeze. I squeeze the bottle, it's cold. Grandmother is holding my hand, her fingers are also cold, she tells me again to squeeze. Suddenly I feel that something is moving in the palm of my hand. It stretches slippery against my skin, it wants to slide out from between my fingers. Grandmother speaks to me, tells me to hold on to it, don't let it go. She's already speaking more normally, she's already getting better.

I don't let the lizard go; its scales scratch my skin, I don't let it go. Now it's not so cold.

Grandmother says, Watch out. She pulls the medicine bottle from my fingers. I keep my fingers closed, I don't let the lizard slide out.

The lid of the bottle springs off; Grandmother reaches into it, picks out a small red tablet, and puts it into her mouth.

She sits up, wipes her forehead with the back of her hand, puts the lid on the bottle, throws it back into the tin box, picks up the tin box from the carpet, holds it in front of me, and tells me to put it back inside.

I open my hand. As the lizard slides out, I see that it's no longer black; its scales are glimmering, glittering blue and white and silver; it glides all around the bottom of the tin box, then Grandmother quickly closes the lid.

She gets up and puts the tin box under her arm. She says that she'll take it back to its place; I should go now and wash my hands well.

I look down at my hands. My skin is covered with black earth, my nails are pitch-black.

39

FROM BEYOND THE FENCE, FROM the direction of the cemetery, I've been hearing the sound of funeral music almost constantly for three days. It could be playing on a continuous loop; sometimes it sounds like it's coming from far away, sometimes from very close. I try not to pay attention to it, but the melody always finds a route to my ear, and sometimes I hear it even when it's not playing. I cover my ears, but no matter how tightly I press the palms of my hands to them, I can still hear it, faintly.

The entire city is getting ready for the burial; it will be a huge memorial service. Péter told me he heard that they're going to be opening the mass grave, ceremoniously lifting out the empty iron coffins, and replacing them with the real coffins with the real deceased in them. It will be a huge ceremony, with many flowers, speeches, and gun salutes.

It was Mr. Pali who found the corpses. Péter told me that at first no one wanted to believe him, especially when he said that they were in the valley behind the abandoned brick factory. Everyone said that he'd certainly just come across some old mass grave from the Second World War, all he'd found was where the victims from the brick-factory ghetto had been buried. No one even wanted to go over there to excavate the site until Mr. Pali, scratching away at the ground, half uncovered a corpse wrapped up in a bag of chemical fertilizer.

When Péter told me this, I immediately thought of the map and how Mr. Pali always examined the soles of our shoes after every track practice. Every single time he asked us if we had seen traces of digging anywhere.

On the day of the funeral I'm woken up by the music at dawn; it's much louder now, as if it were here in the room, as if the musicians were playing right around my bed. I pull the pillow over my head, but I still hear the sharp notes of the violin, they shriek straight into my brain and won't let me go back to sleep. I sit up, and then I hear that it's not a violin, it's not even music; it's the kettle whistling loudly and sharply in the kitchen.

I go out; Grandmother is standing next to the kettle, watching the white steaming vapor. When she sees me, she nods at me through the vapor, then she takes the kettle off the flame and pours water from up high into the teapot.

She says that she knows I'm not hungry yet, but still she's planning to make a very big breakfast this morning, sunny-side-up eggs with toast, fried bacon, and tea with rum. The kind of breakfast about which Grandfather used to say that after you ate it, you could conquer the world.

I nod; I'm really not very hungry, but once Grandmother puts the teapot onto the table and mixes in the tea leaves, the kitchen is filled with a fresh, orangey tea scent, and my stomach grumbles so loudly that I feel embarrassed.

Grandmother smiles at me for a moment. That's what I like to hear, she says; I should go to the pantry and bring onions, goose lard, and the eggs.

· · ·

I'VE NEVER REALLY LIKED FRIED bacon, but now it tastes good. I cut off the end that curls out from under the egg and eat it without bread. I'm using the crust of the toast to mop up the rest of the egg yolk when once again I hear the funeral music. For a moment it's so loud that it makes the window shudder, and even my teeth start clattering, then it quiets down, but it's still quite audible.

Grandmother makes a wry face, and she says they're making so much noise now so that tomorrow, after they've filled in the graves again, they can think long and hard about how now there's silence, there's peace.

I tell her what I heard from Péter, that the music is playing so constantly because almost everyone in the honor guard is new, and they don't know how to march to the steps properly, and it's easier for them to practice with the music, but even so it's hard, because not everyone has long enough legs and not everyone is the same height.

Grandmother blows out some air, and she says, A pox on the honor guard, a pox on the new one and the old one too, a pox on this entire burial, on this whole big ceremony. It doesn't matter at all who's lying where, if they were burned or if they were buried, because once life flies from the body, it doesn't matter if it turns into black smoke or black mud. She could care less what happens after. She shakes her head, and she says that only she thinks this way. Grandfather saw this matter differently, so we can be happy for his sake, if for no other reason, that despite everything, this day has come.

She pushes her plate over to one side, holds out her hands in front of her; with her fingers spread apart, she grasps at the air, then she crooks her fingers into claws and circles them in the air. Grandfather saw the whole thing differently, she says again, because when Mr. Pali came with the news that the people from the Interior Ministry had seized the lower floor of the hospital and that they were keeping the wounded and the dead there,

Grandfather said that they couldn't do this, it was obvious to all that this regime was living its last hours. He would go and talk to them no matter what happened to him, maybe things could be set right, this was, despite everything, a civilized country, and something like this couldn't be allowed — the dead must be buried.

Grandmother clasps her hands together; her bones crack, and she circles her hands in the air. She's silent for a moment, then she says that everyone deserves that — everyone deserves final rites. And so it will be here too, a civilized burial. I can go have a look if I want, she tells me. I can climb up to the top of the walnut tree, I'll see it from there. I know where Grandfather's binoculars are, I'll see things in more detail than if I were actually there

I go in and take the binoculars wrapped in tissue paper from the shoebox and hang them around my neck. Before I get ready to climb up the tree, I ask Grandmother if she doesn't want to see it herself. She shakes her head, and she says no, she's not interested.

I take the binoculars out into the garden. Everything is covered in snow; the trees, the bushes, the woodshed too, the clay man standing next to the woodshed is wearing a snowy hat and a snowy collar. I walk by him, but he doesn't move, he never moves, I can hardly see the contours that Grandmother scratched into his face.

It's harder to climb up the walnut tree when it's covered with snow like this. The branches are smooth, they're slippery too, but it's not dangerous; as the branches shift and move beneath me, often the snow falls off from the branches in one piece.

I climb up to the very top of the tree, and up there, where the branches bend normally beneath the soles of my feet, I place the binoculars against my eyes. I see the podium in detail; a man in work clothes is just now lighting four large oil torches on bronze pedestals. Others are carrying wreaths, piling them in front of the podium. The binoculars bring everything close, but since I'm holding them up to my eyes with one hand, I can only hold on to the tree with one hand, making the branches sway even more below me, so that everything I see through the binoculars keeps moving, and I can't fix my gaze on anything for more than a moment. The preparations are well under way now; I see musicians, a priest in black robes nervously pacing, and people slowly gathering in front of the podium. The wind blows beneath my clothes; I should have dressed more warmly; the cold is making me have to pee. I begin to climb down. There's still plenty of time, I'll come back later.

INSIDE, GRANDMOTHER IS CLEANING; I see that she's mainly dusting Grandfather's things. She looks at me, but she doesn't tell me to help her.

WHEN I CLIMB BACK UP to the top of the tree, the cemetery is already filled with people. Between the torches, on the podium, there are about ten people standing, including two or three priests. I recognize Mr. Pali and the drawing teacher.

Behind the microphone is a tall, bald man wearing glasses; he's reading a speech from a piece of paper about the cherished heroes and the sacred dead. I know who that is—it's Iván's father. Péter told me he's already bought up more than half the city for himself; pretty soon we'll have to make a list of what he doesn't own.

I look at the people, I look at the fluttering flags, each with a hole cut out in the middle to remove the Communist emblem. I look for Péter in the crowd, but I don't see him anywhere.

Iván's father finishes his speech; for a moment there is silence, then the orchestra begins to play.

The crowd moves and splits in two to clear the pathway; the musicians come up between them; behind them is the honor guard. They march flanking an enormous black truck with rusty metal sheets welded onto the sides; there's no glass in the windows, only thick-gridded wire, and there are two huge bulldozer plates mounted onto the front. This must be the armored slag carrier that the drawing teacher talked about, the one they used to break through the gates of the secret police headquarters. On the sides, on the rusty armored plates, there are large bouquets of flowers and wreaths dangling, and on the truck bed there are two rows of black coffins ornamented in gold. I'm thinking of Ilusztina, of how she must be there in the crowd, certainly she's wondering the same thing as me—which coffin is Réka lying in?

I press the binoculars very close to my eyes; I want it to hurt. I watch as they slowly lower the coffins down from the truck, one after the other, then they place them next to one another along the edge of the large ditch. Then, with the same slow ceremonious movements, they place the iron coffins, which all look the same, onto the truck bed.

I'm beginning to get really cold again, and it's boring to watch as the coffins are slowly raised, passed from one pair of hands to the other, and lifted onto the truck bed.

One of the priests steps over to the microphone, clears his throat, and says now we will pray together, our heads uncovered, for the dear departed dead; in the crowd at once the caps, hats, and the scarves disappear from the heads, and for a split second I think I see the scarred, bald head of the librarian.

Once again the sky thunders, but no, of course not, it's the sound of weapons being fired, it booms and booms and booms, then it repeats, thundering; the crowd moves, and suddenly a man dressed in work clothes runs up to the podium with a machine gun in his hand; he's shooting into the air.

He shoves the priest aside, grabs the microphone, and yells into it, This is all well and good, and it's a great thing for our dear departed dead to get the final rites they all deserve, the only problem is that there still isn't any truth. Because truth is still not victorious—because the people lying in these coffins aren't the ones who should be there.

He shoots into the air, and he yells that the question now is this: How long will everyone tolerate the innocent being buried beneath the earth, and the guilty walking above on the streets in peace and quiet, enjoying the fruits of their crimes? With every single breath they take, they offend the eternal salvation of the sacred martyrs.

The crowd begins to murmur, a rumbling emerges as if the earth were vibrating between the graves; the man once again shoots into the air, and he yells out that he and his brothers in the ironworks fought for the truth, they gave their lives, their blood for the truth, and so now he has more questions: How is it possible that they were not invited to the negotiating table? How is it possible that he himself has no place on this podium when he was the one who stood, weapon in hand, at the front of that truck?

Once again he shoots into the air, then the weapon is silent; he's run out of ammunition. The man drops the weapon, it now dangles from the shoulder strap on his side; he steps back, grabs one of the bronze cressets, and once again begins to yell: Perhaps for everyone else, filling up their stomachs and their pockets is more important, but he, Gyurka Diszkosz, vows here and now on his own life that neither he nor his brethren from the ironworks will ever permit evil to triumph over good! If the others won't do it, then they will be the ones to bring justice; until then they will not rest, they will not rest!

After he yells this, he throws down the microphone, and with both hands he holds up the bronze torch and swings it around himself; the flame stretches out and draws a circle around him; he lets out a grunt and flings it away. The torch flies, a comet trails after, it flies above the black coffins lined up by the edge of the ditch, and lands directly in the open grave; the rest of the oil spills out of it, the bottom of the ditch is now in flames, then, in a huge cloud of smoke, the fire dies out.

From the crowd, other men in work uniforms and carrying machine guns come forward; they surround Gyurka Diszkosz, they go over to the truck, and they jump onto the truck bed, between the iron coffins. The people in the crowd quickly scatter as the truck, spewing black smoke, backs up and drives off.

The priest picks up the microphone from the ground, makes the sign of the cross, and begins to pray.

I CLIMB DOWN FROM THE tree; Grandmother is standing there, at the base of the walnut tree. She's smoking one of Grandfather's menthol cigarettes. In front of her is a large ditch, exactly in the spot where we made the bonfire; next to it, two shovels are lying on the ground. Grandmother's hair is matted, clinging to her sweaty face. I don't understand how she could have dug such a big ditch by herself in such a short time and in such a way that I heard nothing. I'm so surprised that I don't even ask her.

Grandmother gestures toward the woodshed. The clay man is still standing there, but there is no snow on him anymore.

I nod; yes, of course.

Grandmother throws the cigarette into the ditch. She says that it's time for us to give Grandfather his final rites. Now I see that next to the walnut tree, laid out on a bed sheet, are all of Grandfather's things—his razor, his vocabulary notebook, his razor strap, his chest expander, his box with the photographs, his skates, his hat, his coat, all his clothes; everything is there in one great big pile.

I look at the objects; in Grandmother's hand is the taped-together letter. She speaks. She's not speaking to me but to Grandfather; she says that she knows that there's no excuse, but she never wrote anything in any report that the secret police didn't already know, and she never wrote anything bad either, and she knows that it was all useless anyway, but here, above this open ditch, she now promises that she will go and seek out everyone, one by one, and ask for forgiveness.

She falls silent; she crumples up the letter, and I think she's going to set it on fire with the lighter, but she doesn't, she just throws it into the ditch, then she throws in the lighter as well, the cigarette case, the straw hat, and everything else, one by one.

I'm still holding the binoculars; they too belong to Grandfather. I take the strap off my neck, I hold them above the ditch, I let them drop.

40

ONCE AGAIN THERE'S BEEN A big snowfall, it catches and mutes every sound, I can hear only my own breathing, as, wheezing, I inhale and exhale; I hear that and the plastic rustling in my running shoes beneath my socks.

It's cold out, but I don't feel it. I did everything the way Mr. Pali told me to: first I rubbed the soles of my feet and the top of my feet and my shins with the camphor ointment that he gave me, then I pulled on my thin cotton socks, then I wound the thin perforated plastic foil around the cotton socks, then I tucked the ends into the tops of the socks, then over that I pulled on thick woolen socks.

From my neck the little sack with the map and the compass is dangling, but I don't take either of them out, I know where I have to go. Mr. Pali today combined the big circular run with a small one; I've run both of them so many times that by now, I could find the route in my sleep.

I know the paths, I know the tree where I have to turn in among the bushes, I know where there will be a downward slope and where there'll be an upward slope, but still, the snow has changed the route, it's made the trees and the bushes look different; now and then, when I sink into the snow up to my knees, I feel as if I've never run in this direction before.

I'm possibly about halfway through the route. I have to run up the ravine; that will take me right to the top of the hill, then I have to run all along the edge of the crater, then straight down, past the locked gates, onto the old railway bed, and from there it's easy, I just have to go along the tracks.

This is the hardest part, this long rising slope. I look forward; in front of my feet, the snow is slowing me down, it whirls up around me. For a moment the wind rises, throwing snow thorns into my face, stinging my skin like salt.

I know I'm going to want to stop soon, this is the worst part, this steep upper third of the slope before I get to the crater. Here, I always tend to think about explosions, about those poor children who found an old unexploded bomb from World War II. I shouldn't think about that, though, I should think only about running, about lifting my legs out of the snow, putting them back into the snow, out of the snow, into the snow.

I don't look up, but I know I'm almost at the top. I lean forward, kicking the snow all around me; I imagine that I'm a white snow cloud whirling up the slope of the ravine. The wind grows stronger, the snow swirls all around me, I close my eyes, I run upward, I must almost be at the top now. Panting, I gasp for breath; the end of the slope must be near now, but it doesn't come to an end; my mouth is filled with snow, I still don't open my eyes, I think that I'm never going to get to the top, but I must not think that, I must not think that, and I must not think of how easy it would be to turn back; no, instead I must count my steps, but I don't even count them, the rustling plastic stuffed into my socks does the counting for me. I'm at ten, then twenty, thirty, seventy, and then I don't even know how many; I start over, one and two and again one and two, that's enough, I have to stop, I'm going to stop, that's enough, three more steps and I will stop.

Something touches my foot from the side, brushing softly against my leg, it makes the plastic rustle. I open my eyes and take a look. A fox is running next to me; I must be imagining it, but it seems as if it's really there; it stretches out, bounding next to me in the deep snow, once again it touches my leg, I sense it brushing against the nylon underneath my sock. Hello, fox, I say to it, panting; my voice sounds like a cough, the fox looks at me, then scampers off, quickly running up the gully, the snow swirling up after it.

I see that I'm only two-thirds of the way up the slope, my exhaustion is dragging me down, but I don't care, I keep running upward, after the fox. When it reaches the top of the hill, it disappears; I know there won't be any trace of it by the time I get there, still I run just as fast as I can, my shins and my thighs are burning with pain, *Wait for me, fox, don't leave.*

I finally get to the top of the hill; at first I don't see the fox, but then I do, it's running along the perimeter of the crater, snow swirling all around it.

The sun is shining, everything around me is sparkling. From here it's easy, from this point on the route is downhill almost to the end.

I look at the fox, then I begin to run after it. Along the edge of the crater the snow is deeper; at one point I trip over a root, but I don't fall down, and I keep running after the fox. The fox is running toward the burned-down forest; after the explosion the wind carried the fire that way. I know that it's dangerous to go running there because of the charred trees, I've never gone to that part of the forest, but now I don't care, I run after the fox.

I see the fox reach the charred trunks, I see it dart among them, I duck my head, and I run.

Sometimes it disappears before me, then it pops up again, as if it were waiting, as if it didn't want me to completely lose sight of it. The powdery snow whirls, vibrating between the blackened trunks, the sunlight making them throw sharp shadows; as I run, I can't always tell an actual tree trunk from a shadow.

Sometimes the fox lets me come close to it, as if it's looking back to make sure I'm still there. I don't care if it's real or not; I think of its touch as it brushed against my leg and how it was so different than a cat's.

We run for a long time among the trees; I almost overtake the fox three times, but it always disappears in front of me. It's hard to see properly in the snow, but from the movement of the running, I can sense that it's leading me down a gentle slope.

Everything is silent; only the wind gently rustles around me, and at times the charred trees crack beneath the weight of the snow, then another voice mixes in among the cracking sounds, it's a soft, metallic jangling sound, it comes from the direction the fox is headed, it's getting louder, it sounds like a chain rattling somewhere or like the grinding of cogwheels, I don't know what it could be.

The wind picks up again, and with it the sounds grow louder, the sound of metal grinding on metal; it feels as if the wind has slipped beneath my clothes, the cold runs all up and down my back. I'm beginning to get cold, and I'm thinking that it's time to turn back, but then I see the fox again, it's very close to me now, it runs forward, straight in the direction the noises are coming from.

I dash after the fox; it disappears; I come out from among the trees. I'm standing in a large snowy clearing. In the middle of the clearing there are two rows of cages, they're made of thick wires fastened onto steel tubes and standing on stakes; they seem to be floating about twenty inches or so above the snow. In the cages, foxes are running around and around in vertical circles, throwing themselves up against the wire, they run up to the tops of the cages, it's almost as if they were flying, the movement carries them up to the top of the cage, then they run down the wire wall in the back, then once again they run up the front of the cage, without stopping, their movements rapid.

It's a nauseating and dizzying sight. I stop, I look at them, I'm surrounded by the clattering of metal and the stinging scent of fox pee, it's as if the foxes don't notice me, they keep running around and around, all fifty of them, all one hundred of them.

I know what this is. It's the fox warren, it's part of the tannery, and this too belongs to Iván's father.

I sense that they've seen me; not one of them stops running, but all of them are looking at me as I stand there in my tracksuit tucked into my red knee socks between the two rows of cages.

I look through the wire netting—the foxes' paws are gray, their fur is matted, I see their claws as they scratch between the links of the wire netting, now they seem to be running more quickly, and the clattering of the metallic mesh seems louder.

I stand between the cages, and I look at the padlocks hanging from the bottoms of the doors; they are large and black. I take the first one and I pull, but it doesn't move, its coldness bites right through my glove. I don't bother with that; I pull on the lock again, then I bend down and dig in the snow, looking for something that I can knock it off with. I find a tree branch and pull it out of the snow. I hit the lock with it, the charred black branch breaks, I hit the lock with the stump of the branch, but to no avail.

I throw the stump away; the lock is undamaged, black and cold. There is silence—I don't know when the foxes stopped running, but now all of them are standing with their muzzles pressed to the wire netting; they're looking at me, not a single one is moving.

I step back, and I stand there for a moment; I sense the tears running down my face. I want to speak, I want to say something to the foxes, I want to promise that I'm going to come back, I'm going to come back and I'm going to let them out, but no sound comes out of my throat.

I turn away; the tears on my face are streaks of ice. I can't leave, I can't leave them here locked up like this.

Something moves between the trees; I look, there's nothing there, but still I walk over. I stop; a bird flutters up between the trees, just a flash of blue, and as I turn my head to see between the trees, I see something that looks like a building. I start to run in that direction.

It's not even a building; it's the armored slag carrier truck standing there in the clearing; it's covered with the frozen wreaths and the flowers from the burial, and on the truck bed there are the coffins, all blanketed in snow.

I walk over there; the door to the driver's cab is half open. There must be a toolbox in here or a wrench, or at least a large pipe or something that is used to change tires. I climb up and see that the seats in the cab are, in fact, filled with tools—there are iron pipes, pickaxes, shovels, and crowbars, all thrown together.

I pull out a crowbar and a pickax; I put the pickax on my shoulder, and I run back to the cages.

The foxes are all running around and around in circles again, but then they stop and look at me. I stand in front of one of the cages, lift the pickax, smash it down onto the lock, and miss. I've only broken through the wire mesh, but that's good too, that will also work; I hit it again, the head of the pickax goes completely through the wire fence. As I pull it out, the mesh comes out, the fox jumps out of the hole, and now I'm already at the next cage. I smash in the cages, one after the other, at one cage I do manage to hit the lock; it throws off a spark but doesn't break; I don't care, I keep smashing in the cages with the pickax.

I don't know how much time has passed when I smash apart the last cage; my hand is aching, my arm is aching, my shoulder is aching, but I don't care, it doesn't matter, none of this matters.

I'm panting. I put down the head of the pickax, let the handle go, it leans to one side and falls into the snow. Then I notice that the foxes are all standing beneath the cages, standing on the dirty, trampled snow, and they're all looking at me.

I clap my gloved hands together, and I make a yelping sound at the foxes.

At once the foxes all start running, they start running in a circle around me, they're like a huge crimson vortex; I stand and watch them, then they run all around in circles around my heels. I hold out my arms and I close my eyes, and I too spin in circles and circles, then I spin even more quickly as they run all around me in a circle; full-throated, at the top of my lungs, I yell out, Fox skirt! That makes them disperse; I hear the snow powdering beneath their paws as they run between the trees. I stand and I watch as the forest swallows them up; I allow the dizziness to sway me back and forth.

41

I'M COMBING MY HAIR IN the small mirror; I'm putting it up. Ré alights in front of the window, shrieking once. Péter is spinning around a ball of rabbit fur tied onto a long cord, inciting Ré to take flight. I knock on the window and put my finger in front of my mouth, indicating that Péter should be quiet, there's no reason to alarm the entire street.

Grandmother is sleeping when I go out to brush my teeth; I see that she hasn't woken up yet.

I'm pinning the last hair clip when the ball of rabbit fur almost knocks against the window; Ré screeches again.

I'm coming already, I say wordlessly to the mirror, if you can't stand waiting, then why did you come to get me? You don't have to accompany me, I can go to school by myself, thank you very much.

I know what Péter would say to that; he would repeat what he's been saying for a while now, that I can put up with this for a few more days, he's not going to walk with me to school forever, but he intends to at least until the elections—because as long as the ironworkers have taken it upon themselves to patrol the streets, he doesn't like me roaming around by myself. And it would be better for my grandmother not to go anywhere. In response to this I just shake my head, but still, I mention it to Grandmother; she in turn just shrugs her shoulders, and she says, Of course, after the elections everything will be magically solved, then with one swift blow this new beautiful world will be truly free.

Everyone is waiting for the elections; some of the boys in class came up with the idea during recess that we should vote as well. There was no use in Olgi reminding them that we won't be able to vote for at least five more years, and if elections will be taking place every four years, we won't be able to vote for another eight years, so what's the point of getting so excited about it? Still, Gazsi went around the classroom with a soccer ball that had a hole cut out of the top, and whoever wanted to could throw in a slip of paper. He didn't come over to me.

Ré has just landed in front of the window for the third time —All right, all right, I'm coming.

GRANDMOTHER IS IN THE KITCHEN. She's standing by the table; the flour on the kneading board in front of her is smooth, white, untouched.

Grandmother's index finger, suspended above the flour in the air, does not move; she isn't tapping the flour, she isn't drawing spirals or lines. I stand in front of the table, place my school-bag on the floor, and I say, Good morning, but Grandmother doesn't look at me, she doesn't say anything, she doesn't move at all, she's looking at the flour. Her hand begins to move very slowly; her index finger slowly lowers down onto the kneading board, presses one single dot into the middle of the flour, then moves no more.

I speak to her, I say, It's me. Grandmother looks up; her face is white, her wrinkles are so deep—gray, sharp pencil lines. Her eyes are watery gray, she doesn't blink, she just looks at me, not even at me, she's looking somewhere behind me, as if I weren't even there. I've never seen her look so old.

Suddenly she presses the palm of her hand into the flour; she turns away, her face is filled with tears. Muttering, she says something; at first I don't understand what she is saying, the words are running together, they're not separate words, just one single word, *For-nothing-for-nothing-for-nothing*, she keeps muttering this, she's not looking at me; she bends forward, she looks at the flour, she looks at her hand, her fingers spread out, they're in the middle of the kneading board.

She closes her hands, then spreads her fingers apart, rubbing the flour between them, the flour dust slowly swirls around her fingers, covering the back of her hand, making her skin look even whiter.

I stand next to her, I take her hand; her skin is cold, her hand is cold.

Everything is fine, I say. Grandmother looks at me; there is fear on her face, as if she doesn't know who I am; her hand tenses beneath my fingers, she's going to pull it away, but I don't let her, I'm stronger than she is. Slowly I move her hand; at first she tries to resist, then she lets me, together we draw a line in the flour, not one, but five at once, five parallel lines, the trace of Grandmother's five fingers, it looks like a bird's wing, the wing of a rooster; our fingers move, we draw the bird all around — its throat, its beak, its crest, its tail feathers, its legs, its spurs. Now only its eyes are left; I raise Grandmother's hand, I tap the nail of her small finger into the flour; the end of the movement is completely hers, though.

I let her hand go. Grandmother is leaning on the edge of the table, panting, the sweat pouring down her forehead. She looks at the rooster; her breathing slowly calms down.

I tell her I'm staying home today, but Grandmother shakes her head, she says that's not necessary, she already feels better.

She taps her ring onto the kneading board, a wave moves across the flour, grows smooth; the rooster is now just a pale shadow in the whiteness. Grandmother wipes her forehead with her sweater sleeve.

As I leave the kitchen, I hear as she begins to sweep the flour into a pile, I hear her mutter to herself that she tried, she really did try, but it was so very difficult.

THE LAST CLASS WILL BE history; there are only two minutes left of recess, I can hardly wait for it to be over, I can hardly wait to get home.

I lean against the wall, standing in the corridor; I'm listening as Olgi is talking to Aliz about some book that she's reading, she's saying how exciting it is, it's a book that used to be banned but now it's been published, and I know that in a moment she's going to come over to me, and she's going to tell me exactly the same thing.

I'm yawning when I suddenly hear Eraser coming; he's really rushing, the entire corridor is echoing with the clatter of his metal-tipped heavy shoes, then he's right there next to me. He tells me to come with him right away, he has something to tell me, something important.

He grabs my arm and pulls me along the corridor, right up to the staircase landing; there he comes to a stop, and he says that last night the news spread across the city that the ironworks are going to be closed this morning, and that means that all the workers are going to lose their jobs. He says that at first he thought it was just gossip, but just now he spoke to someone who said it might be true, and if it is true and not just some terrible rumor, then only the good Lord knows what's going to happen here, because what is certain is that Gyurka Diszkosz is not only going to be patrolling the city—and as he says this, the class bell rings, we're standing exactly below it, it's dreadfully loud. Eraser curses, of course I don't understand what he's saying. He stops speaking, he looks up at the clock, he chews on his lip, the bell just rings and rings like it will never end, but finally there is silence again; my ears keep ringing from the bell. Eraser says, Well, at last. If this is the case, if they end up closing down the ironworks, then there might be problems for my grandmother and me. People had finally begun to forget all that idiotic gossip about my grandfather, but now, somehow, they've remembered it again, and they're saying things like my grandmother must know where all the dossiers disappeared to, saying maybe she was even the one who hid them. His mouth twists, and he says we both know that this is crazy, and he didn't fight in the revolution so that old ladies would be lynched in the name of truth. He owes it to the memory of my parents not to let this happen. The best thing would be for me to go home right now and hide my grandmother or take her away some-where. He'll take care of my last class. Quickly, he says; he turns and clatters down the stairs.

THE DOOR TO THE CLASSROOM is closed; I've missed the be-ginning of class. As I go in, I see that Curtains is handing out the assignment books. He didn't say we'd be writing an assign-ment; we wrote one last week, usually we don't have to write assignments every single week. This comes to my mind, then I think: Good, at least I'll be missing this one. Curtains's hand stops in the middle of his movement when he sees me; he tells me to get to my seat immediately, what was I thinking.

I walk over to my desk, take out my bag; I don't know how to say that I'm leaving now. I raise my hand, I say, Reporting, sir, for family reasons I cannot remain in school, I must go home immediately; the entire class breaks out laughing. Curtains yells at me to sit down immediately. I mutter that I can't sit down; at this he begins to walk toward me. Please excuse me, I say; I turn my back, go over to the coat rack for my coat, and take it down, but Curtains is already standing between me and the door, he says I can go, but first I have to finish my assignment like everyone else.

I say that I can't, but I know it's useless, he's not going to let me pass. I bow my head, and I say, Excuse me. I turn around, I take a step toward my desk, Curtains says, Well, you see it's not so urgent after all, he moves away from the door; I squeeze my bag to myself, quickly step back, and, as fast as I can, I run. I open the door, he reaches after me but doesn't catch me, I hear as the class roars and screams with laughter, and I think that once again that lock of hair must have slipped down onto his forehead, but I don't look back, I slam the door behind me, then run all the way down the corridor.

I LEAVE THE SCHOOL AND I have hardly gotten to the end of the street when I start to hear loud buzzing sounds. At first I don't know what it is, but as I walk along, it gets louder and louder, and then I realize what it is — it's the ironworks, the sirens are sounding. I've heard this at other times, whenever there's a change of shift; in the morning, the afternoon, and at night, the sirens sound, but then it lasts for only two minutes, and now the sirens are wailing on and on, without interruption.

The quickest route would be through the main square, but I don't dare go that way; instead, I take a detour along the upper side streets. I run as if I'm at track practice, the bag rattling around on my back; I should have left it at school, but it doesn't matter now. I hear yelling from one of the intersections; I'm not going to go that way, I take a street farther down, and the entire way I see only four people, all of them hurrying somewhere, heads bent down.

As I turn onto our street, I already know that I'm too late.

I see from a distance that our gate is open, and one of the living-room windows is broken. On the whitewashed wall is written, in large oblique black letters, INFORMERS.

The first thing I see as I go through the gate is the clay man lying in front of the kitchen in the yard in the trampled snow, among the scattered quinces and the walnuts; he's lying on the ground, face-down, shattered into pieces. I call out for Grandmother—I know she's not here, and she won't be here, but still I call out for her.

Every door and window is open; the whole house is turned upside down—the furniture is flipped over, the drawers are pulled out, the books and the papers and Grandfather's newspaper cuttings are thrown all over the place, as if a whirlwind ripped through every room; even the attic door is open, the woodshed door, nothing is where it should be.

I stand in the kitchen; I don't know what to do.

There is silence—only the creaking of the windows can be heard.

A thudding noise comes from the larder.

I go in, step across the shreds of clothes spilled out everywhere from the rag bag; I see that the flour tin has fallen off the shelf, but there's something next to it on the old worn-out Persian carpet, some kind of appliance, an old fan. One of the three blades is cracked lengthwise and held together by green tape. The cable is so old that it's not made from plastic but woven from silk, like the cord to the bicycle pump; the silk is unraveling in many places, and you can see the copper wire inside. I follow the path of the cable; at its end an old yellowed plastic plug is dug into the socket, the same socket the refrigerator is plugged into.

As I look at it, I notice that the fringes on the carpet are moving.

I go over to the fan; the switch is on the side, it's an old-fashioned toggle switch. I flip it on, and the fan, rattling and clattering, begins to turn.

I pick up the flour tin from the floor, step across the pots and the boxes; the stair to the attic makes a creaking sound as I sit down on it.

I open up the flour tin. It's almost three-quarters full. I reach in, find the sifting spoon, dip it into the flour, and begin to sprinkle the flour down from the step.

The flour falls in a dust cloud; the draft made by the fan catches it, pushes it toward the door, swirls it up; the flour spins in the air, it rises, and in the white eddy, Grandfather appears clearly. He's well delineated, a white statue made of air; I see his terrycloth robe, his pajama bottoms, the slippers on his feet; I see his face behind his thick-framed eyeglasses, there in the swirling flour; he doesn't look at me, he stands with his back hunched, he slowly raises his hands and he begins to rub his scalp; placing his feet decisively, he moves along the fringe of the old carpet, exactly as he did the first time I saw him.

It's not even morning, I think there's no point to this, but I keep on sprinkling and sprinkling the flour, I want him to at least look at me, to wave at me or say something, but no, he just keeps stepping and rubbing his scalp, just walking back and forth on the edge of the carpet.

The sound of the fan changes; I look at it; the adhesive tape is beginning to come off the broken blade, it draws green circles as it hangs off the edge of the machine, the fan is rattling even louder, the strip of adhesive flies away, the cracked blade splits in two lengthwise, the broken-off piece flies directly at Grandfather's head; I want it to stop, to remain motionless in the air or fall to the ground, but no, the yellowed plastic shard hits Grandfather. It's something like a bone knife, cutting him slantwise from below, starting from his armpit, coming out by his shoulder, it cuts him in two diagonally, chopping his head and shoulder from the rest of his body. Grandfather disappears, and this time I know that I'm never going to see him ever again.

The flour tin is still about one-third filled with flour; I dig my hand in, and then I feel something gnarled and cold between my fingers. I grab onto it; the sense of repulsion runs all along my arm, but I don't let go, I pull it out and look at it.

In my hand is the secret seashell.

I shake the flour out of it, hold it up to my ear; inside the shell it sounds like fire crackling, or an old vinyl record playing, scratching, at the end of the record when there's no music left; I hear nothing else. Please, I say, I beg you, I beg you to help me, just one word, just one single word.

The scratching dies down, then from somewhere very far away, I hear the word *nademti*.

42

I'M STANDING THERE WITH THE secret shell in my hand. I know now it will be silent forever, even the roaring of the sea will never be heard in it again. There's nothing left inside —only deaf emptiness.

Nademti—that's a nonsense word, it doesn't mean anything. Or it means something in a language that I don't speak. It makes no sense at all.

I let the seashell slide between my fingers; I want it to break into pieces. I exit the larder, go out through the overturned kitchen, then head down the steps and into the yard.

The fan is still rattling in my head, making it ache; it revolves around and around with a cracking sound, deep inside my skull. That's enough, *nademti*, I don't want to hear it again.

Then my head fills with a rumbling sound, the angry squawking of an engine. I recognize the sound, it's Péter's motorcycle. I run across to the gate, I see Péter jumping off the bike; when he sees me, he runs toward me; he holds out his arms, he's yelling out my name, and then he's right in front of me, squeezing me in his arms; he lifts me up so that only the tips of my shoes are touching the ground, he lifts me up and he holds me tight. He's trembling, and that makes me start trembling too. I want to say that there's no problem, but I can't speak, and I can't even utter the words, because it isn't true.

Péter lets me go; he holds my face with two hands, as if he wants to kiss me, but that's not what he wants; he just wants to look at me and caress my face. It's like he can't believe that I'm really here, like he can't believe he's really seeing me. His teeth are chattering as he tries to say that he thought it was too late.

I don't wait for him to finish. I grab his hands, pull them from my face; the flour dust clouds away from my fingers, and I say, Grandmother isn't here, when I got home, she wasn't here anymore.

Péter says that the ironworks have been shut down, they say they've been sold, the person who bought the ironworks wants to close them down, but no one knows who this is; the workers have set off toward the city, Gyurka Diszkosz is already in the main square with his men, they've smashed apart the new supermarket, and they're distributing the goods for free; he says he's making a new revolution if the old one isn't any good— and maybe he's right.

I tell him I don't care if he's right or not, I only care about Grandmother, what's going on with her, what do they want from her.

Don't get hysterical, Péter says, he's only telling me what's happening, that Gyurka Diszkosz and his men want justice; the revolution got off track and now they want to set it right. They're arresting all the people who served the old regime, all the people who've been trying to lie low. Gyurka Diszkosz said at the burial that he wasn't going to let the criminals walk in peace and quiet on the streets.

I think of the burial, how the torch went flying above the coffins, how the crowd grumbled and shouted. I feel dizzy, it's not possible that Péter is repeating the exact same words that were shouted out by that man with the machine gun.

I step toward him, and I push him in the chest so hard that he has to take a step back, and I ask what happened to him? This morning he detested the ironworkers, now he's parroting word for word what they were yelling out with machine guns in their hands — what in the world happened to him during these past few hours?

Don't get hysterical, says Péter, nothing happened to him, but something is really happening in the city, what happened is that they closed down the ironworks, he never would have believed that anything like that could happen, and look, it's happened.

I feel so much anger that I almost begin to weep; screaming, I ask him, Because they've closed a stupid factory, our house has to be torn apart and my poor sick grandmother has to be dragged away? Where's the justice in that?

Péter says that the people who are responsible for all this have to be found.

At that, I slap his face with all my strength; I hit him as hard as I can, and he stumbles; the tears are streaming down my cheeks. I yell at him; does he really think that my poor grandmother is responsible for this? If she's guilty, then she's guilty, but if they murder her, they won't be any closer to the truth. Why did he come here, what does he even want from me?

Péter puts his hand on his face; he says he didn't mean it like that, don't be angry.

Then what did he mean exactly? The Securitate disappeared, the dossiers disappeared, the money disappeared, there's nothing left here but poor unfortunate idiots like my grandmother. Of course, if they put her under the ground, then everything will be clear as day. The best thing would be for me to go over there and stand next to her, to share her punishment, because it's obvious — the more dead people there are, the more truth there will be.

Péter shakes his head, and he tells me, don't go there! I can't go there, he loves me, he'll do anything for me, I have to go with him now, sit on his motorcycle with him, he'll take me to the train station, he'll show me the secret weapons stash, no one has seen it apart from his gang, he'll bring some weapons, he'll speak to the boys, we'll go out into the main square, and, armed, we'll get my grandmother out.

Of course, I say, of course, we'll shoot a little into the air, then into the crowd, and great, everything will be fine. Let's fill up all the coffins we can.

As I say this, once again that nonsense word flashes in me; I hear it once, twice, three times in a row, and as the words repeat, meld into each other, I suddenly understand everything.

I say to Péter, Okay, let's go, let's go right now, but don't take me there, take me to the fox warren, it's in the forest by the turnoff from the old road.

He says that he knows the old road, but not the rest, but he'll take me wherever I want; he smiles at me, and I say that's fantastic, but doesn't he want to know why we're going there? No, he says, he trusts me.

Then he's doing the right thing, I say. As he steps toward me, I suddenly think he wants to kiss me, but no, he just brushes a bit of flour off my shoulder.

I GRAB HIS WAIST; WE'RE puttering along on the motorcycle; the mountain road is snowy, I'm afraid we're going to slip on the turn, but we don't. We get to the old road, I yell to turn off now, we turn off, the motorcycle sinks into the snow, stops, and the cages are right in front of us.

We get off the motorcycle; the cages are exactly as I left them, but I'm not interested in those now. I don't see the armored slag carrier anywhere.

It's somewhere behind the trees, if it's still here, but this time I've come from a different direction, I can't seem to orient myself, I don't recall how to get to the other clearing. There are no footprints anywhere; the fresh snow has covered everything.

Slowly, I turn around; I think of the foxes, I think of how they ran, the kind of running that only a fox can truly experience, around and around, for days, for weeks, always just around and around, in the same way, in the same spot, and now, wherever my feet will take me, I let them, I let them lead me, I take just five steps, and already I see it, it's in exactly the same spot, it looks exactly the same, only now it's completely covered by snow.

I STOP, I CALL BACK to Péter to come now, if he's curious about the truth. He catches up to me, and I tell him, as if I were explaining a math problem, that this used to be the fox warren, but it's not the fox warren anymore, because I let all those poor foxes out of their cages. This is a part of the tannery, which is also owned by Iván's father.

Péter listens to me, saying, Yes, yes, yes.

We get to the slag carrier; the snow has frozen onto the wired, withered wreaths, it looks like there are enormous crumpled-up cellophane dumplings hanging from the side of the truck.

Here, I explain, is the sacred slag-carrier truck of the iron-workers — and I myself heard at least ten thousand times about how it heroically smashed through the fence of the secret police headquarters and so forth and so on.

Yes, says Péter.

I climb up to the driver's cab, take an iron crowbar from the pile of tools; it feels much colder than last time, it burns my hand even through my gloves.

And here, I say, are the empty coffins, which were buried

then so that the people from the Interior Ministry could hide away all those poor corpses.

Yes, says Péter, everyone knows this.

I hand the crowbar to Péter, and I say fine, if that's how it is, let's open up one of these empty coffins. Already in the middle of the movement, I get fed up with the whole thing; I am neither curious nor excited, I just want to get this over with. Quickly, I say, let's do it.

We climb up onto the truck bed; I brush the snow off one of the coffins; Péter begins to force it open. It's nailed down in at least four places, but it's a good crowbar, it does the job.

When the coffin opens, I don't even want to look—I know what's going to be inside.

Because I know all too well that it's *nademti-nademti-nademti—not empty.*

I can't resist, though, I still cast a glance at the coffin, and when I see the battered gray, brown, and black file folders piled on top of each other, my stomach turns, and even though it's freezing cold, I can still sense the dusty paper smell.

There you go, I say—my grandfather had to die for all of this crap, my grandmother had to tell lies for all of this crap, all of these worthless pieces of paper, and how interesting that those fierce ironworkers made sure to bring the whole thing here, right onto the territory of their most fatal enemy. The very same ironworkers who are rampaging through half the city right now hunting them down. What short memories they have.

Because now, once again, more people are going to die, once again there'll be a day of national mourning, the elections will have to be postponed, and who will benefit from that? Who has been in charge of the National Salvation Front and the city for almost a year now?

I stop speaking; my throat is scratchy, just like after I've been running; I have to spit, and I spit; that's enough, I don't say anything else, I'm even fed up with my own idiotic, clever explanations, I'm not going to explain anything else—I only said this much so that this fool Péter can understand what's going on here; what do I care who understands what and who explains what, what do I care if it's true or if they just think it's true? I spit bitter black bile onto the snow.

Péter is standing between the coffins like a spell has been cast on him with a magic wand. He digs among the folders, picking one up and then putting it back, like someone who can't believe what he's seeing, like he can't believe it's true. That what he's seeing is real. I don't want to see him as an idiot, but I do see him that way; the bullet casings on his stupid woven bracelet hang down over his glove, they knock against the iron coffins as he pages through the dossiers. I look at him and feel nothing. Too bad.

I speak to Péter, say, That's fine, darling, but it's time to go now, we must save Grandmother. If she's even still alive. I hear my voice—it's raspy and rough, it's not me, I don't speak this way.

NOW WE'RE DRIVING IN THE truck; the engine is cold, it sputtered for a long time as Péter tried to start it up; finally he was able to get the engine running. The wheels spin in the snow, and when we finally set off, the whole clearing is filled with gray smoke. In place of the windows there's only wire mesh; the wind howls in our faces, it's a thousand times worse than on the motorcycle, I feel as if the skin on my face is about to peel off.

By the time we get to the city, Péter is pressing on the gas as hard as he can, but because of all the metal sheets welded onto the truck, it can't go too quickly; the bulldozer blades on the front keep slamming into the asphalt on the gradients, sending up sparks. We clatter and rumble along, and everyone gets out of our way faster than if the truck had sirens; the cars pull over, the workers in helmets, brandishing iron pipes and axes, walking in the middle of the street—they're also headed toward the main square—all jump out of the way; they even salute us. That's right, I think—worship and honor the holy slag-transport truck.

We're coming down the hill, out by the little cemetery, and then we make a turn by the church, and from there, I can see the main square. There are waves of smoke billowing above it; from one corner of the square a black column of smoke is rising, this I already recognize, it's the same as when there was the smoke bomb, I sense the bitter taste in my mouth.

Rumbling, we thunder toward the square on the cobblestones, the siren screams, everyone in the square is yelling, the crowd is clapping, among the many voices I hear one, a single clear voice, no one else can hear it because it's speaking to me, it's addressing me, it's yelling discernibly and understandably, and as we approach the square it becomes even louder.

I'm Réka, the ringing voice cries out, I'm Réka, it's not even a year since they shot me dead here on the square; holding the hand of my younger sister, I died, I thought until the end that she was my older sister; I'm here in the square, I'm here and I will always be here, I died here—here my blood flowed between the cobblestones, here the sands beneath the stones soaked up my blood.

Suddenly she shrieks—I didn't die for people to kill in my name, she screams, I don't know why I died, but I know it wasn't for that. She screeches this out wildly, and it pierces my body like a knitting needle; the smoke disperses before my eyes, and suddenly I see everything, everything and everyone, I see what's happening, and I also see what's going to happen. I'm Emma, but I'm also Réka, I see the entire main square, I see every corner, every bit of the square.

And I see what Réka sees, and I hear what Réka hears, and I know what Réka knows.

The smoke doesn't matter—I see and I hear and I know what is going on in this square. It is packed with people, only not in the middle; the only empty space that can be found is around an empty statue plinth, and there is Gyurka Diszkosz, standing on an overturned bathtub with all his men, all bearing machine guns, aiming them at about ten people or so, and around these people's necks are signs, tied around their necks are pieces of cut-up chocolate, coffee, dishwashing detergent, and banana boxes, and on those pieces of cardboard there are words written in red: *traitor, informer, squealer, executioner, henchman.* They all stand in line, because now the moment of truth has come, they must stand before Gyurka Diszkosz, one by one. He speaks to each person who stands before him, and he tells them that they must beg forgiveness from the people and from the nation, and whoever gets down on his knees and kisses the dear sacred stones soaked with the blood of the martyrs may arise, his only punishment will be to run along a path opening up through the crowd where he will be struck from both sides with canes and iron pipes; and whoever is so disinclined will have a shredded tire placed around his neck, shredded and soaked in gasoline so it will burn nicely when they throw the burning torch upon it, because that is there as well, the same torch that was burning in the cemetery, it's burning there now next to Gyurka Diszkosz.

I know who this Gyurka Diszkosz is, he's a failed athlete who, a few months before the revolution, was given a job in the ironworks as punishment, because in his rage, he had pushed the sports doctor out the window, the sports doctor who had decided at the last minute that he couldn't risk sending Gyurka Diszkosz to the Olympics. Everyone thought that he would calm down doing the work of transporting the slag at the ironworks, but he didn't calm down, he just got crazier and crazier, and now here he is, next to the pedestal of the overturned statue of the general who was shot in the head, standing on an overturned bathtub, deciding between life and death.

I SEE AS GRANDMOTHER COMES before him; half of a cut-out banana box is hung around her neck, and I know that they wrote the word *informer* with scarlet nail polish, because it resembles blood the most; I see as Gyurka Diszkosz speaks to her, tells her to beg forgiveness from the people, and I see as Grandmother does not beg forgiveness, I know why she doesn't, because she doesn't even know where she is, again and for the last time she doesn't know anything at all, I see as she stands there holding herself up straight, and I see as Gyurka Diszkosz asks the crowd, What shall the sentence be? And I see as the people all shake their fists in the air, as if they were trying to punch holes in that gray, smoky tin-colored sky, and they all cry out, Death! And then two workers put a tire over Grandmother's head; she nicely bends her head to help them, because the only thing she senses from this is that somebody is trying to give her something, maybe she thinks she's trying on a dress; as the tire sits on her neck, an old memory comes back to her, about how her best girlfriend gave her a red-and-white-striped knit sweater to try on so she could see how tightly the neck should be knitted or to see how the blouse's delicate lace collar peeked out from it.

I see as they push her forward, and obediently, she steps forward; they pour diesel fuel onto the tire and on her clothes, I know that the smell will make her think of how the floors used to be scrubbed with kerosene, or maybe not even that, maybe only the tar between the planks of the floor.

I know everything that Grandmother knew, I know everything about everyone, or at least I can lie about that to myself.

I know that if I want to, I can pull my hairpin out of my hair, and I can pierce the palm of my hand, and then after the palm of my hand, I can thrust it into my heart, and I can wish for the heart of Gyurka Diszkosz to stop beating.

I know that if I want to, I can pierce two hairpins above my knees, all the way through the flesh to the bones, and I can wish for everyone who is here on this square to turn into dusty clay from their thighs all the way down their legs so that they will collapse onto their knees, and they will beg forgiveness for what they are doing.

Enough; I don't want to see, hear, or know anything anymore.

Enough.

THE SMOKE RISES AS WE drive onto the square; I look at Péter. Long live the revolution, I say. I reach for the hand brake. I press the button at the end, and I pull up the clutch; the slag carrier screeches and shudders; creaking, it tilts to the side and almost turns over, but then it doesn't; it backs up onto the plinth of the statue and nearly knocks it over, but then it doesn't; one after the other coffins go flying off it, one after the other they burst open onto the cobblestones, one after the other they spit out the dossiers and the documents everywhere.

This skidding motion throws my back against the door. I feel my rib cage crack, it hurts; I cut my head on the grid, which is there in place of the truck window; it hurts, the collision makes my neck crack, makes my spine, my hips, and my knees hurt; the door bursts open, I clutch it, I climb out of the slag carrier. I'm dizzy, my head is spinning, it doesn't matter—I'm here, I'm alive.

Péter also tries to climb out; his head is bloody, his eyebrows are slit, or maybe he smashed his head in. I can't leave him here; if I find Grandmother, I won't be able to carry her out of the crowd by myself. I grab Péter's shoulder, I say to him, Let's go, while I'm thinking, You're coming with me. I grab him; he climbs out of the driver's seat.

The last coffin slides off the truck, I hear the resounding clang. *Here it is, here's what you wanted, here!* I'm screaming— nobody listens, nobody cares.

The crowd is surging, moving toward the truck, we can't run against them; instead, we run in front of them. I grab Péter's wrist, I pull him with me, we're trampling on the dossiers, we're jumping across open coffins, I want Grandmother, I have to find her. Gasping, I breathe in the smoke, I sense the smell of diesel, that's where she'll be, over that way.

When we find her, she's lying on books, cardboard boxes, and rags, all doused with diesel and piled on top of each other, the tire around her neck, Quickly, I say; I grab the tire by the biggest cut and I pull, it begins to split apart. Help me, I say; Péter grabs it too. Split apart, I say, the tire relents, it splits into two pieces, I yank it off Grandmother's neck, I throw it down.

Grandmother isn't moving, she isn't opening her eyes, I don't even know if she's breathing. Péter picks her up, he lifts her, I lift her too. Let's take her already, I say; stumbling, we begin to run with her toward the edge of the square.

Everyone is running in the other direction, running toward the truck and the coffins.

It's as if Grandmother were a rag doll, she's very thin and very small, her hair, her clothes, everything is doused in diesel.

We get to the edge of the square; with the sleeve of my pullover I try to somehow wipe the diesel off her, at least from her face and her neck. Her head jerks back and forth as we carry her; we can't stop until we get her out of here.

Quicker, I say. Péter holds Grandmother to himself, he's carrying her, moving faster now, I run next to him, I cover her with my pullover.

We run along the slippery cobblestones; behind us we hear

the crowd rumbling and roaring; we pass by a broken-in shop window; Péter slips on a shard of glass, but he doesn't fall, and he doesn't drop Grandmother.

I don't know how long we've been running for; the square is still booming and rumbling like we're only a few yards away from it. I see a parked car; as we reach it, I say, Put Grand-mother on that, here will be good. Péter puts her down on the snow-covered hood; Grandmother is so small that she fits on top crosswise.

I take her hand; with all my strength, I wish for her to live.

I think of what she told me about Miklós and about that evening a long time ago when she wrote out the numbers, one after the other, but not a single number is coming to my mind, it's like there are no numbers anywhere, I can only think of the smoothness of the white flour sprinkled on the kneading board.

I want her to stay here, to not leave me, I want her to regain consciousness, to come back, to be with me.

Grandmother just lies there; her hand is so cold that I can't determine if there's a pulse.

I squeeze her hand with both of mine. I know what I need to do now: I should press her ring finger into the snow, and with it, I should draw a lightning bolt and a flower and the sun and the moon. I look at her face, and behind her wrinkles I see Mother's face—I see my own face. I should cry out to her, I should tap her ring finger onto the snow-covered car hood, I should be telling her that she must live.

I let go of her hand—I step back.

Grandmother's eyes open.